Ch 5 p 94 - 148 - 2

p 506 - 750

The Golden Hour

Margaret Wurtele

DOUBLEDAY LARGE PRINT HOME LIBRARY EDITION

 NEW AMERICAN LIBRARY

This Large Print Edition, prepared especially for Doubleday Large Print Home Library, contains the complete, unabridged text of the original Publisher's Edition.

NEW AMERICAN LIBRARY
Published by New American Library,
a division of Penguin Group (USA) Inc.,
375 Hudson Street, New York, New York 10014, USA

Penguin Books Ltd., Registered Offices:
80 Strand, London WC2R 0RL, England

 REGISTERED TRADEMARK—MARCA REGISTRADA

ISBN 978-1-61793-637-1   6/12

Printed in the United States of America

This Large Print Book carries the
Seal of Approval of N.A.V.H.

*For my mother
and in loving memory of my father,
characters different in every way
from the parents I created in these pages*

Acknowledgments

This novel would never have been conceived without an invitation from Jane and Jerry Baldwin to join them on a visit to the source of their olive trees. So thanks are due to them and most certainly to Marcello Salom for reminiscences that piqued my interest and set my pen in motion.

I am grateful as always to the Loft Literary Center: for the fiction classes; for the referral of Kathy Coskran, who helped me find my fiction legs; and for the rented writing studio that gave me distraction-free space when I needed it most.

I spent countless hours reading widely about World War II in Italy, but I want to acknowledge three books in particular that both informed and inspired me: Iris Origo's memoir, *War in Val d'Orcia*; Tullio Bruno Bertini's *Trapped in Tuscany*; and Susan Zucotti's *The Italians and the Holocaust*.

I owe so much to Lorna Owen, independent editor extraordinaire, for her warmth, her keen interest, her fresh and astute eye, and her deft (virtual) pencil.

I am indebted to Carole Williams, to Gail See, and to my mother, Joanne Von Blon, for taking the time to read and comment on the manuscript and for encouraging me, each in her own way.

I thank my agent, Marly Rusoff, and Julie Mosow, her in-house editor, for their insightful review and sound advice on the manuscript. I owe so much to Marly for her warm support and for her sage experience in the market that put me together with NAL/Penguin.

Claire Zion, editorial director of New American Library, has brought much energy, enthusiasm and openness to the publishing process and has made me feel part of it. Thanks as well to her assistant, Jhanteigh Kupihea, for her helpful support.

ACKNOWLEDGMENTS

Special appreciation goes to my step-daughter, Heidi Castelein, for reading the manuscript not once, but twice, and for her unflagging enthusiasm. I owe most, as always, to Angus, my beloved husband—reader, feeder, fan.

The
Golden Hour

Prologue

I moved home to Villa Farfalla for a few days while Father was dying. Mother hadn't asked me to, but I knew she would need me—her only daughter—to be there, to witness this momentous shift in all our lives. My two sons were busy with their own families, my husband independent enough to tolerate my absence, so I packed a small bag, drove the several kilometers from our own *fattoria*, and installed myself in my old bedroom.

The heavy tapestry of the curtains and upholstery were faded with age, the paisley throw at the foot of the four-poster bed limp and threadbare. Years of sunlight had paled the spines of my books and yellowed the framed engravings on the walls. I felt oversize, as if I were trying to squeeze into a dress made for one of my granddaughters. The doorknobs resisted the twist of my hand; the gilded faucets yielded nothing but a rusty trickle of water at first. Had Mother or Rosa begun to neglect even cleaning the bathrooms?

℘

Papa lay in my parents' bedroom across the hall, unmoving, propped on a mountain of pillows, a light blue silk comforter stretched under thin arms limp at his sides. I thought he was asleep when I approached the bed the first evening, but when I eased myself onto the edge of the mattress, he opened his eyes.

"Giovanna." His voice was hoarse, labored.

"Hello, Papa."

He didn't answer but held me in a sober, watery gaze.

"It's good to see you, Papa. The boys, all of them, send love."

He nodded, a barely perceptible gesture, and his eyes closed again. *Too late now, we're too tired—both of us—for any more than that.*

❧

"Are you scared, Mama?" I ventured at breakfast, swirling a thin splash of milk into my coffee. Mother and I sat at a small table in the conservatory, warmed by weak sun coming through the glass roof.

"I'm not sure." She stirred her own coffee in response. "I've had so many months to get used to the idea of his dying." She reached out and adjusted a small narcissus in the bouquet Rosa had placed on the table between us.

"We're all nearby. We'll do this together."

She shrugged, shook her head. I knew what she was thinking: *But your lives will go on as if nothing has changed. I'm the one who will be alone.*

❧

Later that morning, Father was more alert. I wanted to ask him if *he* was afraid, but instead I offered, "We'll all look after Mama, I promise. You have nothing to worry about."

"I know that, *piccola*." At the sound of my childhood nickname, I smiled and took his hand. It was surprisingly warm, his grip steady and firm. How long would it be?

Our dear Rosa was a godsend. Old and stooped now, her hair pulled back in a white chignon, she had had far more experience with the dying than either Mother or I. She had been in attendance at the bedside of her own grandmother, of both her parents and their siblings. Papa, his body wasted from months of an aggressive cancer, had stopped eating or drinking the week before. Rosa kept a small bottle of morphine on a table near Father's bed, and—at the slightest sign of restlessness or pain on his brow—she would ease a drop or two between his parched lips and under his tongue. "It won't be long now," she said to me. "A few days, maybe. No more."

The third morning, he had sunk into an even deeper slumber, his head tipped slightly back, his mouth open. Rosa took me aside. "I think," she said, "if you have anything to say, you should say it now. The hearing, they say, is the last thing to go."

"How much longer do you think it will be?" I asked.

She reached for my hand. "One never knows for sure, but if he doesn't wake up at all today, he will probably die tomorrow."

Tomorrow . . . one more day. Then my father will be gone forever. Mother had announced that she was taking a short walk in the garden, so I stepped quietly to the side of his bed. There was a soft armchair pulled up next to it. Had Mother spent much of the night there? Had Rosa given her the same advice? I sat down and took his hand. It was still so warm. I thought I could feel deliberate pressure, as if he knew I was there but didn't have the strength to acknowledge it any other way.

I was oddly nervous—we hardly ever talked like this, so intimately, the two of us. Especially now, when it was all up to me, when I could only imagine his response.

"Papa . . . I just want you to know that you've been a wonderful father and grandfather. I—we all—love you so much. We'll miss you when you're—" My throat tightened around the words, and I didn't finish the sentence. I started to speak again, but then thought better of it. *No, just sit here now with what I've said. Enough.*

It had been true, just the way I'd put it—for decades, anyway. He and I had reached an understanding and a kind of easy, loving back-and-forth based on family, on his grandchildren especially.

After a while, Mother came in, flushed from her walk in the early-spring air. I gave her the armchair and pulled up another. We chatted, the two of us, in a way we felt would be comforting to Papa: memories, recent ones, about the children in particular. . . .

℘

Rosa had fixed us a light lunch, a crispy panini with ham and cheese, the crusts elegantly trimmed, and glasses of chilled prosecco. So we took a break. We deliberately skirted the subject of Papa and focused instead on the garden, on some changes Mother had been contemplating on the front terrace, a couple of new roses she had heard about, single varieties with large, flat, open blossoms. *Yes, single, how perfect.*

After lunch, we returned to Papa and sat on the chairs on either side of the bed. We each took one of his hands and held it. He was still so warm, and I could have sworn I felt a squeeze.

"Look at his face, Giovanna," Mama said suddenly.

I leaned in close to see. His head was turned slightly to one side, so his face was almost in profile. The skin on his forehead was pulled tight, and the lines in his face had begun to disappear. "My God—he looks so young, doesn't he?" I said. It was uncanny, as if fifty years had evaporated, and there before us was the Papa I had known in my youth.

I studied the illusion, fascinated, and—

as I did—I could feel my stomach begin to tighten. Images, unwelcome ones, began to tumble and float in my head. I felt slightly dizzy. I looked at Mother, searching her face to see whether she too was beginning to visit that forbidden territory, but her face was inscrutable. I released Papa's hand and stood up. "I'm tired, Mother. I hope it's all right, but I'm going to lie down for a while."

I went into my room, pulled the coverlet back, and lay down on the bed, my head swirling. I stared at the ceiling, letting long-forgotten scenes play across my consciousness in a kind of waking dream. Hours passed, in which I lived inside the memories, following them like a path through the woods that was long drifted over with leaves.

Chapter One

As I lay there, the years of the war began to come together, coalescing from fragments of childhood at first: the scarcity of food, the ubiquitous men in uniform, the insistent drone of bombers overhead, the shuttered schools. It was fall, probably October of 1943. I was crossing the square on a routine errand for Mother, trying to buy staples like flour and salt for the kitchen, when I saw my favorite teacher coming out of the market. Sister Graziella was a large woman, and in her flowing habit with a basket on her arm, she nearly filled the doorway.

"Oh, my stars—darling Giovanna!" She folded her arms around me and pressed me to her ample bosom. "This is my lucky day, to cross paths with you like this. I was just thinking of you, dear, wondering how I might find you. Here, let's find a place to talk."

She ushered me out into the square and rested her basket on a bench. Then she placed her hands on both my shoulders. "I'm looking for someone to help out at the School of Santa Maria. The building has been standing empty, and I want to do something for the young children around here who are so neglected. There are refugees from the bombing in Turin living near here, and—heavens—our own local children as well, just wasting their precious time. I have talked the town council into letting us open it for several hours a day. Nothing official, you understand, just to tutor a few of them on the side."

I took a couple of steps back and looked past her across the square. I was dying to do something, but . . . "I don't know a thing about teaching," I said. "How can I possibly be of any help?"

"Oh, you wouldn't have to teach at all. Just be there in the mornings to help us keep order. Then, in the afternoons, after the children leave, you could go over their papers. You are so bright, such a free spirit. I miss your energy and your smile."

I studied Sister Graziella's moon face, her soft cheeks framed by the stiff white headdress. I had always loved and admired her. Sister Graziella was completely benign, a spirit who radiated pure love. There was no one I trusted like this woman, and true, I'd been missing her as well since I graduated in June. There were even days—what I called my life planning days, imagining my future— when I had toyed with the idea of joining the convent, just to be like her, to dedicate my own life to such a pure vision of service.

"And Sister Elena. She'll be working with me. She's all for it, Giovanna."

Oh, God. I groaned inside. Sister Elena was another matter. I couldn't stand that woman: bony and brittle, with a jutting chin and eyes that burned into you like a hawk's. I looked away. Could I bear to be with her all day? But it was tempting. I was getting bored. The war stretched out ahead with no end in sight. Real life seemed to involve finding a husband, making my place in the world, and it all felt remote, indefinitely post-poned. I had just been thinking it was time to contribute in some way to this war, to be part of it.

"Well . . ." I drew a slow line with my toe in the gravel. "Why not. Okay, why not? I'm too idle lately. And just to work alongside you would make me happy." I hugged her and smiled. "When do we start?"

❦

We began meeting quietly with twenty young children a couple of weeks later. I reveled in Sister Graziella's proximity, and I did my best to stay out of Sister Elena's way. The children were, well, children, but they were gone in the af-ternoons. Then one morning in January, I saw a lorry pull up noisily in front of the school. A dozen or so German soldiers piled out and began milling around the sidewalk, while one of them walked boldly up and hammered his fist on the school entrance.

Sister Graziella and I stood next to each other in the hall, blockading the children behind us, while Sister Elena, her stiff back held erect, slowly drew back the bolt and opened the door. There stood a sandy-haired officer who looked to be in his mid-twenties. He was slender, and—if it weren't for the Nazi uniform—he looked approachable, almost kind. Elena fixed her icy stare on him. "Yes?"

"I am Lieutenant Klaus Eisenmann, officer in charge of preparing this area for defense against the Allies," he said in surprisingly fluent Italian. "My fellow officers and I will direct the construction of tunnels and bunkers, the work on bridges, and the storage for ammunition. We claim this school as our administrative headquarters, and now we are planning to occupy this building."

Sister Elena drew herself up to her full height. "Well, I have news for you, Lieutenant." The words grated like metal on stones. "My colleagues and I are busy constructing young minds here, and we have no intention of moving."

The two of them argued, and I have to admit I admired Sister Elena's courage, her staying power. In the end, they negotiated a compromise. The officers would take over most of the school except for a classroom off the courtyard and one small office in the rear of the building, so that the tutoring program could continue. We would use the playground in back and have some access to the kitchen.

"And naturally we will expect you to keep your distance from the children," Elena stated finally.

After they left, when the three of us were alone again, Elena grabbed my wrist and hissed into my ear, "And I know I don't have to remind you, young lady, that I expect you to keep your distance from those soldiers." Where did that come from? It made me burn with shame, and I had no idea why.

The Germans were running the country, driving confiscated cars and motor scooters. I heard that they were even living in Italian homes. I wished I could understand their language, that scratchy, angry sound that had become so much a part of our lives. I was getting tired of being careful, of easing my way around my own life like a cat sneaking past a sleeping dog. I was getting impatient, too, with the politeness that was expected of me all the time, the effort it took to make room for so many brash foreigners in our midst, and it had begun to have an odd effect on me. Their presence secretly emboldened me. Instead of seeing them as a vast, uniformed mass of occupiers, I had begun to see them as equals.

All that winter and into the spring, we worked next to those soldiers, and the walls of the school began to encase me in a separate world, one that was part of the war but at the same time a kind of refuge from it. We began to get used to the comings and goings of the specific officers who worked there, *our* soldiers. There was Lieutenant Eisenmann,

Klaus, of course, the one who had first come to the door. Then there was big Otto and the German shepherd. I have always loved dogs—and Panzer became a sort of a mascot. There was Heinz, who whistled incessantly, and Willem, whose allergies acted up in the Tuscan air, making him wheeze and spit with abandon. They were rough and loud. They were angry and impatient. But within the school, our two factions had worked out a kind of peaceful routine that allowed each of us to attend to the tasks of the day. At noon every day, for example, the officers gathered in the cafeteria while the children and I walked home for the midday meal and the sisters returned to their convent for a couple of hours during the heat of the day.

One morning Hans, a stocky blond officer with wire-rimmed glasses and a pronounced limp, showed up in our office, where I was meeting with the sisters while they planned the next day's lessons. "We have extra sausage here," he offered. "If you'd like to take it home, be our guests, please."

We took the meat, knowing that it was

highly unusual, a complete turnaround from how the Germans habitually helped themselves to whatever produce or supplies they found in the stores, in the fields, even in people's homes.

℘

What began to happen then, as spring settled in, really took me by surprise. I started watching the officer Klaus all the time. I was fascinated, trying to decide why he seemed nicer than the others. The corners of his blue eyes had deep smile lines, and in his casual way of looking off to one side, there was an openness that made me want to penetrate his inner shell. I learned to recognize his voice at a distance, and when I heard him nearby, I found any excuse— "the little black-and-white cat needs a bowl of milk," or, "I must get some water to moisten the bougainvillea next to the door"—to leave my worktable.

I could feel his eyes on my back and knew he was following my every move. I noticed little things, too, like the way he lifted his jacket to put his left hand in his pocket, and the habit he had of hitching up his pants, which emphasized how slim he was compared with the others. I wanted to know more about him, whether he had a family and how he ended up assigned to the School of Santa Maria.

It was new to me, this thinking all the time about the officer Klaus. I knew boys my own age, of course, but I was self-conscious. I was short, big breasted, and a little heavy around the hips; my hair stood out in a wiry halo around my head, even when I tied it in a ponytail. I was never one of the girls the boys tended to flirt with or tease in a friendly way, and I pretended I didn't care.

One afternoon, I was sitting alone at a long table in our classroom with a pile of papers in front of me. It was warm and humid, and a hummingbird buzzed beneath the open window behind me. I could see straight through the open door into the courtyard as the soldiers crossed, going in and out of their of-fices. Klaus passed by, laughing loudly, his heavy boots clunking along the wooden porch until he reached the sand.

I bent my head to the stack of papers, but instead, I found myself moving the pencil dreamily across my own empty tablet, the one I kept to take notes. In simple cursive, imitating that of the seven- and eight-year-old students, I began to write: *My papa's name is Klaus. He is big and tall and very handsome. He has soft hands and when he puts me to bed, he sits next to me and holds my hand. . . .*

"What are you doing, signorina?" My hand jerked, and I looked up to see Klaus leaning against the frame of the door, as if he just wanted to pass the time, to relieve the tedium of his duty. He smiled. "You are writing to yourself, no?"

I panicked and moved my arm quickly over the tablet to cover up what I had written. "I am just correcting the children's papers," I said, looking past him into the bright afternoon light.

"But no, I was watching you. You write," he said. He started to move slowly toward me, his arm reaching out, his fingers beckoning in a teasing kind of way. "Show me the paper."

I didn't know what to do, so I laughed

and leaned in across the desk, conscious that my sundress strap had fallen off my shoulder in the motion. "No no, signor, really, they're just children's papers. Here, I will show you." I shifted the rumpled compositions onto the top of my own tablet and began handing them to him one at a time. He was smiling, but his blue eyes narrowed. He leaned in, so close I could smell stale cheese on his breath. He held my arm down and slid the tablet out from under the pile. He slowly picked it up and studied the carefully written lines. I stared at the table, not daring to breathe. After what seemed like forever, he looked down at me.

"How old are you?" he asked slowly.

"Seventeen."

"Old enough," he said.

"Old enough for what?" My voice quavered.

"Old enough to wish for soft hands."

The hummingbird buzzed again, and there was a scent of jasmine on the breeze. "I was pretending to be one of the children. . . . It was only a game." I looked down at the floor, rested my eyes on his heavy boots. Then he set the tablet down, turned his back, and left the room.

I sat frozen, my ears flaming. It felt like the week before in the kitchen, when I'd dropped a lit match on the hem of my skirt. There was a split second, just before I brushed it off, when I was tempted to leave it there, to see if it would burn.

Chapter Two

Everything was quiet in the courtyard. It was after five in the afternoon. Klaus and Otto had just left, calling *auf wiedersehen* to each other. I got up from the tall pile of compositions that Sister Graziella had left for me to correct to watch them leave, making myself invisible at the very edge of the window. The dust settled back onto the ground in a fine layer of rusty red, and the drone of bees in the butterfly bush took up residence in the back of my brain. I sat down and rushed through the rest of the papers, and as I headed toward the office to leave the work on Sister Graziella's desk, I found myself almost tiptoeing. The creak of the individual floorboards seemed to echo in the silence. At the door of the classroom where Klaus spent his working hours, I paused, midstep, and was looking in when Sister Elena's raspy voice made me jump. "What are you doing here at this hour?"

My heart began to pound. It took me back to when I was fourteen, when Violetta and I tried to sneak out of school early, close to the end of the term in May. We were ready to run for it, crawling out from behind the hedge to head for the gate, when we bumped straight into the folds of Sister Elena's habit.

"You little rats, you agents of the devil," she snarled as her fists closed around our uniforms at the backs of our necks. She kept us in her office for an extra hour after everyone else had gone home, and we had to sit there while she worked. One of us would make a hilarious face behind her back, then the other. We both almost wet our pants, but we managed to keep from laughing out loud.

I looked at her. "Sister Graziella gave me some of her own work to do," I lied. "It's taken me until now to finish. I'm just going to return it to the office."

"I do not want you here alone and un-supervised. See that you leave right away, and don't let this happen again."

"Yes, Sister."

I stood there, not moving, watching her figure like a leaning flagpole clip-clop away down the hall. After putting the papers on Sister Graziella's desk, I waited until I heard the courtyard gate close behind Sister Elena. I listened to be sure I was alone, and when every-thing was quiet, I made my way back to Klaus's office. His desk was covered with dusty stacks of papers and files, and on top of the typewriter sat a light blue envelope. A hot breeze cooled the back of my neck and blew a wisp of hair into my eyes. I tucked it behind my ear. Then, ever so slowly, I stepped toward the desk.

Achtung! Privat! was stamped in red on some of the papers and reports piled across the desk. There were pages of German words that had obviously been typed on the old typewriter. There was a peel from half an orange drying there, as if it had been left for several days, and a sprig of pink bougainvillea that must have been wilting for just an hour or two. I looked down at the light blue envelope, which had a folded piece of matching paper sticking halfway out. The writing on the envelope looked spidery and thin. It had to have been written by a woman. I took my index finger and slid the paper sideways out of the envelope. My heart began to pound like a drum and my breath was fast. I opened the letter. *Sonntag, am morgen* was scrawled in the upper right-hand corner. Then, *Klaus, mein leben,* below it on the left. I couldn't read the German, but the writing was careful, exact, with hardly a correction. The whole look of it was comfortable and familiar. I turned it over and skimmed down to the bottom. It closed, *Ich liebe dich, Mathilde.*

This has to be from his wife, I thought, *or a lover who's waiting back in Germany.*

My hand shook as I refolded the letter. As I parted the envelope to slip it back in, I caught sight of something else inside. It was a small photograph, a brown-toned portrait of a woman sitting on a tapestry-upholstered bench. She looked to be in her mid-twenties, with curly blond hair and round, full cheeks. She was not overweight, but she was ample, her arms comfortable- and soft-looking. In the photograph, she held a baby wrapped tightly in a blanket, looking somberly straight at the camera. The woman's gaze was fixed on the baby, and I could see she loved it with all her heart. *Maybe this is Klaus's baby,* I thought. I stared at the picture until a worm of envy started turning in my stomach.

I was just about to slip the letter back into the envelope when I heard what I thought was the click of the front gate. I tucked the photograph quickly into the pocket of my skirt. To take it home for just one night, I thought as I hurried away. What could be the harm in that? Only to be able to look at it over and over before I went to sleep.

I was relieved when I finally arrived at the thick stucco wall that surrounded Villa Farfalla. I shouldered open its heavy wooden gate and headed up the gravel path that ran alongside the orchard toward the main house. Keeping my hand on the photograph in my pocket, I veered off to walk in the shade under the olive trees. Tonino, who looked after our orchard, was perched on a ladder, carefully pruning limbs from the center of one of the trees. While the interiors of the trees were kept open, the outer limbs were allowed to arch out and down, so the workers could reach the branches. Now they were covered with tiny pale yellow flowers that were, in those exuberant long days of late spring, beginning to be replaced by countless baby olives no bigger than capers.

"Don't fall off that ladder," I called up to him. "You're too precious to lose!"

"Ah, now at last the sun is shining!" Tonino smiled and opened his arms widely as if to embrace me in midair.

A blue cotton work shirt split where it stretched tightly over his bulging girth like the skin of an overripe persimmon.

He was like my second father. As long as I could remember, he had been there, as much a part of our gardens and orchards as the rosebushes and spreading acacia trees. He and his wife, Catarina, were tenant farmers who lived in a small house on the property. They had two sons, Pietro, who was five years older than I, and—after several miscarriages—Fello, who was now sixteen, just one year behind me.

My brother, Giorgio, and I grew up with those boys, hiding and chasing one another, stealing fruit from the mulberry trees until our fingers were stained with dark purple juice. But now two of us were gone. Pietro had died in Russia a year and a half ago, and then Giorgio had disappeared last autumn, when the National Republican Army had called him up to fight. Since then Tonino and Catarina's house had become my refuge, a place where I felt comfortable, where I could express my feelings and escape the increasingly chilly atmosphere at home.

"Your papa is looking for you, *cara*," Tonino called down to me.

I hurried up the gravel walk. When I reached the villa, I could see its rough stucco walls beginning to crack and peel. I looked longingly at the front entrance with its tall arched opening. The oak of the thick wooden door was burnished, nicked, and dented with years of use, the brass knob beginning to darken from the war's neglect. Reluctantly, however, I ducked under an overhanging branch of hydrangea and moved toward the back of the house. I opened a side door and clumped up the narrow wooden staircase to the second floor. Here, in the rear, in the five small rooms that had once been servants' quarters, my parents and I had been living for nearly four months.

❦

It had been in early February, a month after Klaus appeared at the school, when my mother and I heard a hard rapping at the door. Mother opened it to find about five Nazi soldiers standing there.

"We have official papers," said a barrel-chested officer who towered over

Mother. He held the butt of a sodden cigar in one hand, a clipboard in the other. "We must now have this villa for our living quarters, for ten officers in charge of the regional communications."

"Wait a minute!" I heard myself piping up, remembering Sister Elena's negotiations with the Germans at the school. "You can't just burst in here like this. We live here. This is private property."

"Giovanna, please!" Mother motioned me back with her arm.

"*Ja, ja,* signorina." His look was perfunctory. "We know this." Turning to Mother, he added, "The property is very large, so the family will stay in residence here, in the back, upstairs. This is a big exception, by orders. We will return tomorrow."

After they left, I exploded. "How can you let them do this? They can't just come in here and live in our house. Mother, you just gave in!"

Papa, who had come in from the other room, would not even look at me. Holding himself straight and gripping the back of a chair, he said, "Our family is smaller now with Giorgio gone, so we do not need so much space as before."

"Oh, Papa, come on. They are forcing us. It is not about the space. Isn't there something you can do, someone you can appeal to?"

"Giovanna, please. We know so many people who will be forced to move away, to evacuate. We are lucky to be able to stay here. We must accommodate them now. We have no choice, and I will hear no more from you about this."

Mother held her ground, looking at me. She was tall and trim and stood so straight. She considered me steadily, with her composed, aristocratic air. Her hair was long, still sleek and dark, and held in a low bun by a simple ornament. I knew, had always known, even though she was my mother, that she was strikingly beautiful. She was dressed for that night's family dinner in an elegant navy crepe dress with white collar and cuffs. She spoke slowly, distinctly. "Your father is right. This is not a time to display your temper. It is a moment for dignity and forbearance."

I never understood how she could react like this when things were so horrible and uncertain. "Mother, how can you always be so proper, so stuffy? Don't you feel anything? Aren't you even a little mad?"

"Of course I'm angry, but expressing it is not going to change anything." Her thin lips tightened into a straight line. "This house has been in my family for four hundred years, and I want to stay here under any circumstances."

After dinner we began packing up our clothes, emptying wardrobes and drawers, clearing small decorative boxes off the tops of tables and painted bureaus. This was really going to happen.

The previous fall, when German reinforcements were first pouring in over the Brenner Pass and it was likely that there would be no escaping a prolonged occupation, my parents had us pack up our most precious belongings: the antique silver tea service, family photographs in their silver frames, Mother's jewelry, the best linen and finest china. We took the twenty or so boxes to the far end of the attic and built a new brick wall in front of them that would stay in place until the war was over.

And now we were going to be exiled within the walls of our own home.

We removed the rest of our personal belongings but left the glittery glass candelabra on the mantelpiece, the leather-bound books on the library shelves, the china tureen and platter displayed on the inlaid wooden sideboard. If we could not be in these rooms, at least our beautiful things could continue to lay claim to the spaces for us. We lugged boxes and suitcases up the stairs and installed ourselves in the tiny makeshift quarters: two small bedrooms, one for my parents, one for me; a hastily arranged parlor; and a small room just big enough for a table and four chairs, where we could take our family meals. We would have to share a bathroom, one that was far simpler and more cramped than the gleaming tiled spaces below, with their porcelain tubs and washbasins, large gilded mirrors, and faucets shaped like the heads of mythological figures.

On matters that concerned the villa, it was my mother, Natala, whose voice carried the day. Villa Farfalla and its surrounding gardens had been her family's property since the sixteenth century, a summer retreat from life in the walled city of Lucca, fifteen kilometers to the south.

Natala had no brothers. As the eldest of three daughters, she had always been in line to inherit the property. Early on, as in many families, her parents, my grandparents, had selected her ideal mate: a third cousin, whose family clustered in the south near Pisa. He was pale, wan, unathletic, and phlegmatic, but of trusted lineage and due to inherit great wealth.

Natala was always inclined to do the right thing. However, one winter evening in 1922, she attended a large holiday party in Lucca with her parents. This is the part of the story I have always loved best. I picture Mother, eighteen, tall and slim, wearing a long gray satin gown that gleamed as it caught the light. She was dancing with her father, Vittorio, when Enrico Bellini cut in. I could just see Papa doing that, young and handsome, dressed in a dinner jacket, his dark hair combed straight back from his high olive forehead. It was a waltz, and Mother had always said she could immediately feel the strength in his solidly built body, the sureness and grace of his steps as he twirled her around the floor. He was twenty-five, from Turin, bright and well-spoken, and—though his background was unquestionably middle-class—he was a rising star in the local textile industry.

Over the next weeks and months, Enrico set about conquering my grandfather. He hunted wild turkeys with him, conferred on the marketing of his olive oil and wine. Soon Enrico had made himself indispensable, and when he asked for Mother's hand, Vittorio could find no reason to refuse.

Natala and Enrico married the following summer, in June of 1923. It was a country wedding, the reception held in the gardens of Villa Farfalla. All of Lucchesi society was there, helping them-

selves to antipasti from silver trays decorated with sprigs of lavender. They
made a handsome couple, and from
that day forward, Enrico Bellini was one
of them, the fact that his father was a
shopkeeper and his mother's mother a
seamstress all but forgotten.

My parents moved into a well-ap-
pointed small stone house on one of the
piazzas in the walled city. Father worked
for the best silk manufacturer and rose
steadily, rewarded for his keen mind for
numbers and his unshakable confidence. Mother gave birth to Giorgio in
March of 1925. Even as a mother, they
say, she became a talented hostess, a
well-liked, always considerate woman of
taste and cultivated manners. She played
the piano beautifully and volunteered for
the opera house and the art museum.

On one of their visits to Villa Farfalla
the summer after Giorgio celebrated his
first birthday, Vittorio was bouncing my
brother on his knee. He paled suddenly,
they say, pulled out his handkerchief,
and began to wipe his brow. Mother,
hugely pregnant with me, had just lifted
Giorgio to her hip when she watched

her father roll off the wrought-iron settee and collapse onto the lawn in a gentle heap.

After the funeral, my parents began spending every weekend with Grandmother Celeste at Villa Farfalla. She needed the company, and soon—to relieve her of the burden of overseeing the household—Mother began to take over the planning of meals, to see to the repair and mending of upholstery, the replanting of roses in the garden. Papa phased gradually out of the textile business and focused on managing the farming of the orchards and vineyards, the marketing of the oil and wine. By the time Celeste died, in the summer of 1930, when Giorgio was five and I was still three, my mother—at twenty-six— was the uncontested mistress of Villa Farfalla. Since the late thirties, like so many Lucchesi families, they had left the city house behind and moved out here full-time to avoid the hazards of approaching war.

℘

Now—all tradition and history eclipsed by the reality of war—we were living in five small rooms on an upper floor in the back of our own house. Mother and Papa settled into this new routine with an apathy and resignation that seemed to me to be a disease affecting everyone and everything around me. They nodded politely and greeted the soldiers whenever they encountered them. They kept the radio turned low, and they avoided talking about how the Nazis were running our lives.

Living upstairs, I could hear from below the clink of silver on our dishes as the soldiers ate their meals, smell the sour odor of cabbage and sausage that Rosa was forced to prepare for them. An acrid cloud of fermented grain hung all through the house, rising from half-drained mugs of beer evaporating on side tables that we could see through the windows as we passed. With the coming of spring, smoke from their huge cigars curled up from the terrace into my open window while I tried to sleep. Below, the murmur of their voices sounded impatient, cold, and unfeeling.

Even my dreams became hemmed in and rigid, outlined in gray shadows through which I would hurry, anxious and lost, and awake most mornings feeling disoriented and lonely.

❦

I slowed down as I reached the top of the narrow stairs. I knew I was late, but I wasn't sure what Papa wanted, whether he might be angry about something. "Papa, are you here? Tonino said you wanted to see me."

Father appeared in the doorway to the parlor. He was slightly taller than I was. Nearly fifty, he was still youthful, his hair only beginning to turn silver at the temples; he had two long, creased dimples at the sides of his mouth, and just above his upper lip a prominent in-dentation, as if someone had carefully placed a finger in clay and left an im-print there, permanently molded. His brown eyes, like shots of espresso, were powerful and penetrating, and now he looked down his long, straight nose at me.

"Where have you been? It's nearly six

o'clock. I thought we were going to hit some balls this afternoon." He wore white slacks and a sweater vest with blue and gold stripes around the V-neck, the sleeves of his shirt rolled up to the elbow. It was a casual, elegant statement, as if there were no war, as if nothing had changed. Sometimes it seemed wrong to me that we should claim these moments of class-bound leisure in the midst of such upheaval, but getting Papa to play tennis seemed to restore him to his rightful stature. Living in those few rooms, he seemed stooped, weighed down by anxiety, as if his spirit and life force shrank in proportion to the walls of our confined quarters. He went about the business of overseeing the orchards and vineyards, but his heart was not in it. He showed no interest in progress or hope for the future. Tennis was also one of the ways I could fill Giorgio's absence and give my father back a measure of the normality he had lost.

I slipped my hand into the pocket of my skirt, fingering the photograph lightly, guiltily. I had completely forgotten that I had promised to play that morning when I left for the school.

"Oh, Papa, I'm so sorry!" I could feel my cheeks flush. "I had extra work to do, and I couldn't get away until now. I'll just change."

Later, after our game, he put his arm around my shoulder. "Your smile does my heart good. Where would I be without you, *piccola*?"

❦

Once dinner was over, I was finally able to shut the door of my room. At least I still had this small measure of privacy. I reached into the top drawer of my dresser and slipped the photograph out from under a pile of silk camisoles. Seeing it there both thrilled and terrified me. What if Klaus had come back and discovered it missing? But still, here in my hand, in my own room, was this fragile token of his most inner and personal life. Here was Mathilde, the woman he loved, left behind in Germany with what must be their newborn son. Did she miss him terribly? Did he miss her? He must be lonely so far away from home.

But how odd it was, I thought, to find myself attracted to one of the cruel aggressors who had plunged our lives into such chaos. I lay back, closed my eyes, and let my imagination float on the sounds of boisterous laughter, the rising verses of a German drinking song coming from the terrace just under my open window.

Chapter Three

It was May and the nights were getting shorter, but when a rooster crowed around four o'clock, it seemed as if only a couple of hours had passed. I sat up in bed, remembering the photograph. It was still dark, the sky just beginning to fade. I frantically searched among the bedclothes and found it, to my dismay, creased and slightly rumpled where I must have turned over on it during the night. *I have to get to school before Klaus does.* I dressed quickly, tiptoed down the back stairs to the kitchen, grabbed a piece of yesterday's bread, and hurried out into the chill of the early morning. An orange glow was burning on the eastern horizon. Swallows darted in and around the tops of the dark cypress trees that stood sharply outlined against the sky.

By the time I reached Santa Maria, the sun had come up. The courtyard was deserted, the morning stillness broken only by the song of a warbler trilling from the top of a horse chestnut tree that shaded the north side. I stepped onto the wooden loggia and made my way to Klaus's office. Hardly breathing, I peeked in to make sure no one was there. The envelope was still on the typewriter, just where I had left it. I took the rumpled photograph from my pocket and was just smoothing it on the desk when I heard footsteps outside the door. I was leaning over to slide it quickly into the envelope when a shadow blocked the light from the doorway. I froze.

"Giovanna? Why do you come here so early? Why are you in my office?"

I kept my eyes down, not daring to face him. The photograph was still in my hand. I broke out in a cold sweat, and the bottom of my stomach dropped. I steadied myself, then slowly looked up at Klaus. "I . . . I was just going to tidy your desk." I paused a moment. "I found this picture. Is this your wife? Your baby?"

Klaus moved slowly, his neck stiff and his face immobile, and took the photograph. He stared down at it, traced its new creases with his finger, beginning at Mathilde's head, down her back, across her lap to the tightly wrapped blanket that held the baby. "This happens to be my wife, and, yes, it is my child, my son." He looked at me without smiling.

The heat from his body began to penetrate the morning chill. I stepped to the side of the desk. "I'm sorry. I didn't mean to disturb your things. Honestly, I just . . . think they are both so beautiful."

"*Ja*, well, of course they are beautiful." He sounded sarcastic now, anger seeping out between the words. "I have never seen my son, and this is the one photograph I have. Now look at it, will you?" He thrust it out and made me look at it again. "Look at it, Giovanna. You ruined it."

"I'm so sorry. I shouldn't have touched the letter. I feel terrible; really I do."

"Well, you should." He set the photograph back on the desk and smoothed it heavily with his hand. "You have no business here at all. Just go—right now." I thought I heard a tremor in his voice, as if he wanted to cry. He sat down. Slapping both his hands hard against the top of the desk, he lifted a file, opened it, and bent over the papers inside with full concentration. I took that opportunity to turn and run out of the office.

I ducked out the back door and into the play yard, where I leaned against the wall, breathing fast, my heart beating wildly. What was I thinking of, actually stealing from a Nazi soldier? He could easily have arrested me or had me sent to a prison camp. I paced up and down the yard, sat on one of the small swing seats, held the chains loosely in my trembling hands, and began to rock gently back and forth. Only I couldn't hold on to the fear. I slipped back into my old fantasies of Klaus, and now they were even more exciting, heightened by this new intimacy and tinged with danger. He was a man, a man far from home, a husband and a father. It was at times like this that I longed for Giorgio. I could tell him any- thing, now that we had passed the point of childhood squabbles. If he were here, I could let him in on this strange new adventure, this attraction to Klaus that I knew I had no business pursuing.

❦

I hadn't seen Giorgio since November 25, the last day that the recruits born in 1925 had to turn themselves in to sign up to fight for Mussolini's Fascist army. Around noon that day German officers came to the villa and told my parents and me the news of the soldier's disap- pearance.

"We know nothing," Papa had said, genuinely mystified. "He left this morn- ing to get his assignment, and we haven't seen him since."

That night I was sitting in the living room listening to the news on the radio, when the front door swung quietly open.

Giorgio appeared in the doorway. I leaped up and ran to him.

He put a finger to his lips. "Where are Mama and Papa?" he whispered.

"They know you deserted." I threw my arms around him. His jacket was rough and cold and smelled of wood smoke. I saw fierce determination on his face despite his disheveled appearance. A shank of straight dark hair hung down his high forehead.

"I just came to say good-bye and pick up a few things," he said. "There's no changing my mind."

I knew he had almost as much to fear from our father as he did from the Germans. Papa was deeply ashamed of Giorgio's disappearance. Mother had sat silently at dinner, worried about her only son, while Father had vented his anger. Words like "yellow-bellied" and "disgrace to the family" had settled over the table. I wasn't sure exactly what I thought about it. I knew Giorgio was driven by principle, by his resentment of the Germans to be sure, but I also knew him well enough to know that he would hate open combat and the heat of battle. Italian soldiers were hiding out all over Tuscany at that point. They were finding refuge in the woods, in caves, and living off the generosity of peasants and farmers.

"I think you're doing the right thing. But where will you go?"

"I'll be all right. Just don't worry about me. Where's Papa?" he said again.

"I'm right here." Father was standing in the doorway, his face clouded with anger. "Where in the hell have you been? Do you know you are putting every one of us in danger by running away?"

"Father, I'm not going to do the Nazis' bidding. I'm going to disappear, and you can't stop me."

"I don't care who's in command. You're in the Italian army, and you're trained to fight. Damn it, you're going to fight like a man. And I can tell you, when this war is over, you'll be rewarded for it."

He grabbed Giorgio's wool army jacket and yanked it downward, ripping it off his shoulder. "And if you're going to be so damn gutless, you don't deserve to wear this uniform. You can freeze to death, for all I care." He threw the jacket on the floor.

Giorgio stood there, struck dumb. His shoulders were rigid, his fists clenched, but he turned his back and stared at the floor.

Come on, say something. Defend yourself.

Father stalked out of the room.

"He's wrong," I told my brother. "He's living in the past. You've got to go, do what you can to help the partisans."

"Giorgio." Mother appeared in Papa's place. "I'm just so worried about your safety. Why don't you let us hide you somewhere here, at Tonino's, or in one of the sheds? Your father wouldn't have to know."

"Mother, my safety is not the point. There is work to be done. There's a war going on, and I have to take part in it. I'm not running away from my duty. I'm not! It's just that I don't want to work for the Germans."

Mother and I left him there alone, pacing back and forth like a caged animal. We searched the house and put together a bundle of warm clothes, some fresh bread and cheese. As we worked, I saw myself falling into Mother's pattern of acceptance and quiet support. I didn't want to be like her. I wanted to resist, to carve out a role for myself, to use my own energy and ingenuity to push back against this foreign encroachment.

Mother kissed him gently. "Be safe, darling. Please don't take any unnecessary chances."

I followed Giorgio to the door and leaned out after him. "I want to help you. I envy you out there, where you can make a difference. You've got to keep in touch." He nodded then, as if he meant it. That was more than six months ago.

❦

All that day, I agonized about my early-morning encounter with Klaus. I caught sight of him a couple of times; once, our eyes met quickly but he looked away. At lunchtime, I stayed in town, wandered into the general store, and saw a pair of tiny blue socks. I bought them and left them on his desk with a note: *To send to your son.*

A few days later, while I was working,

Panzer the German shepherd wandered into the classroom and dropped to the floor at my feet with a grunt—just in time for Klaus to pass by the door.

"Panzer, come!" He glanced at me. "Sorry, fraulein."

"No, I love dogs; really I do." I tried to smile. "Did you and Otto bring him from Germany with you?"

"*Ja*. He crossed the Alps with us. Otto is also from Frankfurt. Where I live with Mathilde—"

"Was he your dog? Yours and Mathilde's?"

"*Ja*, he is ours."

An awkward silence hung over us. "Tell me, when was your son born?"

"He was born the same month we moved into this school." He sat down in front of me, his blue eyes looking directly into mine. "This is why I am fighting here, for his future."

I reached out quickly to touch his shoulder. Then, as if it were a hot stove, I pulled my hand back.

Over time I learned that he had graduated from engineering school in Frankfurt, married Mathilde shortly thereafter, and then was sent to fight in Russia.

"My neighbor died there, in the Russian campaign," I offered one day. "Italy and Germany were fighting together then."

He shook his head, looked away, then back at me. "There is too much death, everywhere," he said. Klaus told me what he had endured, fighting on the Russian front: the cold, the snow, the hunger. "Every time I saw a body, I thought of the man's poor mother," he said slowly.

I thought immediately of Giorgio, but I knew better than to tell him about my absent brother. Klaus was a construction officer, so I knew he wasn't directly involved in searching for runaway soldiers, but I didn't want to take any chances. Would he turn someone in? Were all the Nazis on the lookout all the time?

❦

One afternoon, I had begged Rosa to make a blackberry pie. "Only if you pick them," she had retorted. Coming back with a full basket, I pushed my bicycle through the thick gravel on the walk when I heard male voices coming from the villa's side terrace. Leaning my bicycle against a hedge, I peered around the corner and saw, with his back to me, Klaus gesturing to another officer. Klaus in our very own garden. I ran to the downstairs pantry for a basket and a pair of pruning shears.

"Giovanna!"

I lifted my head from the yellow rosebushes bordering the terrace, trying to look casual. "Good evening, Klaus." I shot a glance at the other officer.

"What are you doing here?"

"This is our villa. I live with my family upstairs, in the back."

He left his friend and walked across the grass to his side of the hedge. "It is beautiful, this garden, this place, even in war to have so many flowers. I am here to dine with some of my fellow officers." He stood awkwardly for a moment, glanced back at his friend, shifted his weight from one boot to the other. "I wonder," he said, his voice lowered a notch, "maybe we could take a short walk after dinner? You could show me the property." He added quickly, "It will still be light."

"Yes . . . I think I could do that." I looked up toward the window of my parents' quarters. "Okay, I'll meet you, right here, at nine o'clock."

I plucked the last rose for a bouquet. As I turned to walk back, I could hear the other officer say something that I couldn't make out; then he laughed, a kind of rough, mocking guffaw. There was no answer from Klaus.

℩

Rosa set down a steaming platter of *rosticciana*, grilled pork ribs, with garlic and rosemary. We ate more pork than we used to. Meat was scarce, almost unavailable, but our family could occasionally get leftover supplies by trading our produce with the German soldiers. Our own garden still provided herbs and some vegetables.

The radio had been on all afternoon, so I braced myself for another political argument.

Mother drew herself up in her chair

and put down her fork. "They say the Allies are poised to liberate Rome any day now. It's about time."

I looked at Father. Mother had been rooting for the Allies since the Italian campaign had begun. She was afraid the Germans would ruin Italy's treasures, cause too much death and destruction, and she wanted them stopped as soon as possible.

"Well, the Germans have just concentrated their defense farther up this way, that's all," he said.

Mother blanched. "Whose side are you on, anyway?"

I jumped as Papa slapped his hand sharply on the table. "Natala, damn it, I don't like the Nazis any more than you do. But they are in power here. Like it or not, we have to play by the rules."

I knew where this was going, where it always went. I agreed with Mother, and so did most of the people I knew and liked. But Papa had a point. The Nazis were in charge.

"What, their rules? Enemy rules?" She held her ground.

"Yes. We had no right to turn against

our Axis partner in this war," he went on, "no right to make a separate peace with the Allies. What if the Germans win? Where will we be then?"

"They won't win; they can't," she said, and she pressed her lips tightly together.

"Natala, be realistic. You have no idea how strong the Nazis are. And if they do prevail, what will happen to Giorgio, to the other deserters? We have to think of our own future in this thing."

"I just can't wait for it all to be over. I want the Allies to liberate us too, the sooner the better."

Suddenly I had a hard time swallowing my bite of meat. I hated this conflict night after night. I didn't blame Giorgio for deserting, for refusing to fight with the Germans, but I also knew Father had our family's best interests at heart. We all wanted Italy's traditions to endure, to triumph. Perhaps Klaus was not so foreign, so strange. He was fighting for his own country, wasn't he? At least he wasn't a deserter. I toyed with the radicchio on my plate, my appetite dulled by the knot of anticipation growing in my stomach.

At nine o'clock sharp, I stepped tentatively into the shadows at the edge of
the terrace. The cicadas vibrating in the
air seemed to whip my heart into a faster
beat. I took a deep breath and looked
around. Klaus was sitting alone on a
wrought-iron chair, a cigar poised lightly
between his right thumb and forefinger.
He saw me and stood up, ground the
cigar neatly under his boot, and walked
toward me. His voice was gentle.

"So. You came, signorina."

"I told you I would." I turned and began walking down the garden path that
led away from the house. Klaus kept up
with me, his boots grinding noisily in the
gravel. I felt self-conscious next to this
near stranger, this alien figure in green
khakis. I glanced over at him and was
moved by his soft, clean-shaven cheek.
He was young. I wasn't used to pale
eyelashes like his, the way they glowed
in the low light.

We kept walking in silence, our arms
bumping against each other now and
then, through the rose beds, around the

fountain. I fought down an urge to hook my fingers into his brown leather belt, to rest my hand at the small of his back. We headed down a path that led to the tennis court.

"These pink roses are my favorites," I said, and as I did, he stopped.

He put a hand on my arm and then suddenly took me by the shoulders. "How did you crush my photograph?" It was not so much a question as a demand. His hands were strong, pressing my arms to my sides so hard it felt as if he might shake me. I drew a sharp breath. I looked into his face. "The truth is, I took it home the night before. It was so lovely that I just wanted to look at it. Then I fell asleep. I guess it . . ." My voice trailed off, and I began to tremble. I drew back, but a hot curl of desire cut through my abdomen. I looked away.

His voice changed, softened. "You are bothering my dreams," he said. "I want to know the smell of your hair." He pulled me hard to his chest and leaned his head down next to mine. His breath was labored in my ear. My arms pushed against him, but the sound of his breathing relaxed the fear inside of me. I held still. We stood there for a long time as the darkness thickened, breathing in rhythm, listening to the pulsing of the cicadas, then to a tawny owl hooting in the nearby wood. Neither of us dared to move.

"Giovanna, is that you?" Footsteps crunched the gravel from the direction of the tennis court, and we quickly pulled apart. "What are you doing out here— who . . . ?"

"Papa!" My hand flew to my face.

Father stood on the path, a cigarette glowing in his hand.

Klaus stepped forward. "Good evening. You are Signor Bellini?" He made a quick bow of his head. "I am Lieutenant Klaus Eisenmann. I am dining with some officers here tonight. Your daughter offered me to take a short tour. It is lovely. Indeed."

Father looked at Klaus, then at me. He drew himself up to his full height and looked squarely back at the soldier. "Yes, very well. But my daughter did not have my permission to give tours of the gardens this evening." He fixed Klaus in a stare. "Giovanna, return to your room. Now."

My heart pounding, I drew my shawl tightly around my shoulders and turned on my heels. Not daring to look back, I walked quickly toward the house.

Back in my room, I studied myself in the mirror. My long dark hair had become loose from its ribbon at the back of my neck; my cheeks were flushed. I looked different, like someone I didn't quite recognize. My body buzzed as I thought about what had just happened. But I braced myself for what I knew was coming next. There was a knock at the door. "Open up, Giovanna." Father came in wearily and closed it behind him.

I took in Father's face, but I couldn't tell whether or not he had seen Klaus and me embracing.

"Do you know this man?"

"Yes, he works at Santa Maria during the day. I see him there often. I was surprised to find him in our garden, so I offered to show him around."

"I tell you, *piccola,* these are dangerous men. They are no longer our partners. They are in command here. They were very angry about our making peace with the Allies and declaring war on Germany. They are the *enemy,* Giovanna."

"Well, you just said at dinner that we have to play by the rules. If you think Giorgio should be fighting for them, maybe I should be nice to them." I turned my back defiantly, pulled off the loose ribbon, and began brushing my hair.

"Giovanna, look at me."

I turned to face him. His jaw was tense and his eyes darkened.

"They are strong. They will take advantage of a pretty young girl like you. Stay away from the German soldiers from now on; do you hear? Both at the school and here at home."

I turned back to the mirror. "If you like, Papa. I will." Saying what I knew not to be true made me feel lonely—and made Father seem smaller than he was.

℘

I lay in bed, a light sheet over me, listening to the sounds of the night. *They are strong; they will take advantage. . . .* When would he begin to see that *I* could be strong? He could see me only as a weak little daughter, his "*piccola*." He could see strength only in my brother. I closed my eyes. I remembered a late-summer day, walking with Giorgio, when I was eleven, he thirteen. We had run into each other on the way home late one morning. I had been out gathering blackberries, a basket on my arm and a pair of gloves in my pocket to protect my hands against the thorns. Giorgio had been playing soccer with his friends. We fell into step beside each other and turned to cut through a neighbor's vineyard. Looking down the straight row, the long tendrils with their green leaves weighed down with ripening fruit, we could see something just ahead in the grass between the rows. It was a heap of something brown or gray—a large bird. As we approached, the bird reared its head and stared at us wide-eyed.

"It's a hawk," I shouted, beginning to run toward it, "an injured hawk. I think it's got a broken wing." The bird limped away from me, dragging one large mottled brown wing through the stony earth, the other flapping futilely.

Giorgio caught up with me, and we stood there, staring down at the bird. It stared back with an unblinking yellow eye. "Let's go. We're going to be late for lunch," he said.

"We can't leave it like this. It's in pain. It's tired."

"What do you think you're going to do? You can't touch it."

"Yes, I can," I said. "Help me. Here. I'll hold down the good wing, and you pick up the bird."

Giorgio flinched and backed away. "Are you crazy? That thing looks fierce."

"Please, Giorgio. I know someone who can heal it: old Maurizio the taxidermist. I know he has fixed birds' wings before. We'll take it there. He doesn't live far." I put on my gardening gloves and approached the bird carefully from behind.

"I can't believe you're going to touch it," my brother said.

I bent down and inserted my hand under its wing. The bird began to flap wildly, sending feathers and dust in every direction. It scared me.

"Come on, Giovanna. Let's get out of here."

"Just a minute. Let me try again." This time I grabbed the body fast with both hands and lifted the bird, pinning its wings to my sides with my elbows. The hawk arched its neck, biting at me with its sharp beak, but I moved a gloved index finger into its beak, calming and focusing the bird. "Just carry my basket," I said. "I know the way to Maurizio's house."

We walked slowly down the vineyard row to the end. The bird was strangely subdued, its eyes staring straight ahead. After ten minutes or so of walking, we emerged from a grove of walnut trees and saw the taxidermist's house in front of us. The yard was strewn with old pieces of wood, scattered with feathers and bones. The carcass of a long-eared rabbit was thrown up against the stucco wall.

"Maurizio! Are you here?"

We heard rustling inside; the door opened. The taxidermist was unshaven, his gray hair nearly shoulder-length. His clothes were stained and ill fitting. "What have we here?" he asked slowly. His voice was warm. He gingerly took the hawk from my arms, holding it much as I had, examining its wings. "Well, I guess you've lost half your wind power, old fella," he said.

"Can you fix his wing?" I asked him.

"I expect so," he said. "Seen this before. Couple of months, he'll be good as new."

Later that night, over dinner, I told the story eagerly to our parents.

Mother shook her head, clearly mystified by such a strange encounter. "You must be careful," she said to me. "They could be carrying parasites or foreign germs."

"Good for you, Giorgio," Father had said absentmindedly. "It's not easy to handle a wild creature like that." Giorgio said nothing.

"But, Papa, I'm the one who picked it up. I'm the one who wanted to save it."

He smiled. "Yes, *piccola.* I'm sure you were important. You probably helped give Giorgio enough courage to act."

"But no!" I was bursting with desperation and righteousness. "It was *me,*

Papa. Giorgio was too scared to touch the bird." I shot my brother a defiant look.

"Well, I expect we'll hear from Maurizio when it's ready to fly, won't we? Now, Giorgio, I'm thinking you're ready to go for a turkey shoot with me this fall. Would you like that?"

My eyes filled with tears. I looked at Giorgio, who would not look back at me. My parents went on eating, mopping up their pasta sauce with slices of bread. It was clear to me that, as a girl, I simply couldn't measure up to my brother in Papa's eyes. Mother said nothing, seemed to notice nothing. This was a battle I would have to take on myself.

I didn't blame Giorgio, not really. I knew he needed Father's respect as much as I did. I drifted back to the rough feel of Klaus's jacket against my cheek, the scent of roses, the ominous sound of the owl that hooted overhead. *They are the enemy,* I thought, as a vision of Mathilde rocking her baby pulled me gently into sleep.

Chapter Four

I was in the back of the cafeteria, washing the cotton smocks the children wore over their clothes at school, when Klaus passed through the kitchen and came up behind me. I was fully aware he was there, but I said nothing. When I finally turned around to look, he smiled, giving me a conspiratorial wink. Meeting his eyes made my face go hot, so I looked down at his belt, to the holster that hung from it. I had never seen a gun so close. I reached out and lightly fingered its handle. He covered my finger with his hand and held it there. I shuddered, a little afraid.

"I haven't seen you since our walk in the garden," he said in a low voice.

"Why do you wear a gun inside, in the school?" I asked.

He looked surprised, as if he'd never thought about it. "Well, I guess I just need to be ready for anything."

"But nothing in here ever calls for guns, does it?"

"You are right about that." He looked down at me steadily. A chill flashed down my back, and I felt my face flush.

"Have you ever killed someone?"

"What kind of question is this?" He squinted at me skeptically. "You do not really want to know."

"Yes, I do, Klaus. I want to know what it's like."

"Well, I did, yes, in Russia. More than once."

"You told me the other day that the German army was much superior to the Italians. Why is that?"

"Come, Giovanna. Please do not talk of these things."

"No, tell me. What was wrong with the Italians?"

He bent down and whispered in my ear, "I like Italians. You most of all."

I shivered and raised my face to look at him. "I'm not supposed to like Germans."

"But you do?" He cradled my face in both his hands.

"No, I . . ."

He turned to look quickly behind him, then kissed me full on the mouth. I was surprised, but then . . . his lips were so soft. I reached up to clasp my hands behind his neck, when suddenly he pulled back, breaking my grasp, and walked away.

The truth is, I didn't really like working with children. I liked going to the school every day, because it made me feel useful and gave structure to my life. But in the mornings, dealing with screaming six-, seven-, and eight-year-olds made me want to scream myself. I marveled at Sister Graziella's patience, at Sister Elena's ability to maintain discipline, but

I just couldn't emulate them. I got bored within minutes of each day's beginning.

Ironically it was my job to entertain the children who weren't working on reading or writing with the sisters. I had to oversee their games and mediate their squabbles. They annoyed me with dull questions: "Why is dust brown?" or "What is war?" or "Can I hold one of the soldiers' guns?" I got so sick of chasing after them on the playground, tired of having to listen to them all the time, of keeping them amused, and, most of all, of having to be an example of dignity and restraint.

While the children made me feel bored and juvenile, the lieutenant made me feel like an adult. He showed me an empty, windowless office down the hall from his, one whose door was normally kept shut. He took me in there once, and gradually we began to steal off for longer and longer sessions in each other's company, especially in the after-noons, when the children were gone. No one was the wiser when the two of us occasionally stole inside that office and closed the door behind us.

I was enthralled by his stories—of his school days in Germany, of his best friends who joined him at engineering school, of training for the army. I was flattered that he took the time to tell me so much. We spoke in low voices so no one would hear, and now and then—at the sound of footsteps outside in the hall—we would hold our breath and look away from each other, at the floor. Sometimes, in the interludes between stories, we would kiss, gently—long, soft kisses, holding hands and sometimes embracing. At times, I was filled with such warm feelings of closeness and intimacy that I could forget he was a German soldier.

"I think I'm falling a little in love with you," he said one day between kisses.

"Why?" I asked. "You're married to Mathilde. You're so much older than I am."

He thought for a moment. "I love your dark hair and dark eyes. They are warm and exotic to me," he said. "You are so young, so innocent, so undiscovered, like buried treasure. I know you have a fire inside of you, and I want to see it come out."

I began to feel I could trust him, so I started to tell him how I was dreaming of a better role for myself in the war. I described my best friend, Violetta, who had been receiving training as a nurse. I added that I thought work dealing with injured and dying soldiers seemed more important than correcting children's papers. But he suddenly turned to me with the flash of a new, rough, frightening look. "Where exactly is she working with these soldiers? A clinic? Tell me, Giovanna. Is it near to here?"

I looked away. "I have no idea where she is going to work." Luckily, he let it drop.

❦

The nearby farmhouse where Tonino and his wife, Catarina, lived provided a welcome escape from our family's cramped quarters. The scent of fresh bread filled the air when I stopped by one morning in early June to visit Catarina. She was doing her weekly baking and had just pulled back the flat iron cover of the deep wood oven. "I was hoping you'd stop by today. I have something for you." She placed four loaves on the table to cool and then felt behind the rusty tin of salt on a high shelf and took out a tightly folded piece of paper. I slowly unfolded a lined sheet that looked like it had been torn from a school tablet. Scrawled across it was a message—in Giorgio's handwriting: *Giovanna—come after church on Sunday to the old gazebo.*

I stared at the words. "Where did you get this, Catarina? We haven't heard from my brother in months. I can't believe what I'm seeing."

"The wheat farmer's son gave it to me earlier this week. He said he had seen Giorgio," Catarina said.

"Did he say where he saw him? Is he nearby? Were there others with him?"

Catarina looked away, embarrassed. "I . . . guess I never asked." She turned her back to me. "He was such a good friend of Pietro's. Ever since my son died, it's been so hard for me to be with his friends. I guess I just wanted to get away. I'm so sorry."

"Oh, Catarina, I understand. I really do. It doesn't matter. I can ask him myself now." I smiled and gave her a hug. "Thank you so much for this."

"You can trust me not to say a word."

℘

All I could think about was seeing Giorgio the next day, but Saturday-afternoon confession intruded. Visiting Don Federico was getting complicated. I had made my confession to him for years, reciting my sins of the week. He was an old friend of our family—a gentle, kind man whose hair had turned all white and who had to wear thick glasses to see the scripture and words of the mass on Sunday mornings. I knew he couldn't hear too well either, but still, I had to be careful of what I said.

As I entered the narrow booth, I remembered a previous Saturday. I had mentioned taking a walk with "someone Papa didn't approve of," but I hadn't added that he was a German soldier.

"Forgive me, Father, for I have sinned." I kept my eyes on the floor, avoiding the grille behind which I could picture the piercing, inquisitive eyes of Don Federico. "I was impatient with the children

at the School of Santa Maria, where I
work." I paused, took a full breath to
lend conviction to my voice. "I . . . felt
almost like kissing someone—a man—
at the school." I rushed to add, "But he
is a German soldier, so I know I must
not think of such things."

Don Federico's absolution had been
unusually fervent, my penance unusually stiff.

These little transgressions seemed to
me back then to be tiny things, insig-
nificant in the face of the havoc that surrounded us all. There was the nearly
constant sound of Allied planes overhead en route to their bombing raids;
canvas-covered jeeps and lorries carving deep ruts in the country roads; uniformed soldiers in khaki or camouflage
with rifles slung over their shoulders
standing in every crowd, on every corner. People were dying every day, and
the nearby forests teemed with partisans who sabotaged the German occupiers. Surely these, the killers and pil-
lagers, were the ones who should be
whispering in Don Federico's ear on
Saturday afternoons. Why waste his

time with the minor attentions that passed between Lieutenant Klaus Eisenmann and me?

How naive I was, and how easily I rationalized a schoolgirl crush that put everyone around me at risk.

The next day was Sunday, the day I was to meet Giorgio. I sat through our noon meal on the edge of my chair, cutting my meat extra slowly and setting my knife on the rim of the plate so it wouldn't make a sound. Papa was going on about how the olive crop looked like it might be large, so he didn't notice anything unusual, but Mother glanced over at me now and then and smiled. *That's more like it,* I knew she was thinking.

Before mass, I had put on a full skirt and a pair of comfortable sandals in anticipation of the long walk to the gazebo. Mother had taken one look at me and shaken her head. "No. You will not go to church looking like one of the farmer's daughters. Now go back to your room and come back out as a member of the Bellini family."

"Mother," I said, "I'm too old for you to be telling me what to wear."

"I don't understand why *you* don't care, Giovanna. How can I get you to see yourself as others see you?"

I did as I was told, because I couldn't risk a big confrontation. Not today.

Now I was seated in a shirtwaist that Rosa had ironed stiff, buttoned all the way up the front. Perfect for Mother's picture of the Bellini family.

When we finished I took my napkin and pressed it to my lips. "May I be excused?" I asked. "Violetta is meeting me for a walk in just a few minutes."

Back in my comfortable clothes, I set out down the front path as if I were going to meet Violetta on the road. Then I cut through the lower gardens and around the back of the tennis court. I increased my pace, tapping the trunks of the linden, then the horse chestnut as I passed. At the back of our property, I hopped over the low wooden fence and pushed into the thick underbrush. I found the old path without too much trouble—it had been sifted over with leaves. Long, thorny branches reached out to touch one another at eye level, but I continued to push my way through until I came out at the border of the Santinis' vineyard. I followed one of the rows out to the end. Then I stopped to see whether the coast was clear.

A jeep full of German soldiers rumbled up the road from the left. I wanted them to think I was just a young woman out for a stroll, so I walked extra slowly. One of them whistled as they drove by, but I just kept my eyes on the ground straight ahead. Luckily they drove on.

Bees buzzed around my ankles, but otherwise the Sunday afternoon was quiet, with not a single farmer in sight. I came to the old stone wall bordered by purple irises, turned, and followed it deep into the woods. The brambles were thick and scratchy, but at last I saw the clearing up ahead and the old gazebo. The white of its marble pillars glowed where it peeked through the dark moss and lichen, like camouflage. The old statue of Prometheus, holding a torch missing its flame, stood in the middle of the structure. The round roof was half destroyed. I could see someone sitting there, leaning against one of the columns. At the sound of my footsteps, he got up. "Giovanna? Is that you?"

Oh, that voice! I ran to Giorgio and hugged him tight. He smelled like he hadn't had a bath in months, but I didn't mind. He felt so good I didn't want to let him go.

"God, it's good to see you. Did anyone notice you?"

"I don't think so," I said. "Catarina gave me the note. She probably read it, so she might know I'm here. But no one else."

We sat down on the platform and dangled our feet the way we used to do down by the bridge over the river. Giorgio's pants were torn, and one of his boots was missing its laces. I leaned against him hard. "I've been so worried about you, Giorgio. Six *months*—why have you waited so long to contact us? It's been torture."

"I just couldn't risk it before now. I needed to learn the ropes, meet people and get them to trust me. I've been all over Tuscany—too far even to send a message."

"Trust you for what?"

"Enough to give me assignments—I'll tell you more later—but now, you've got to help us. We need food, boots, and more clothes. You said you wanted to help. Did you mean it?"

Did I? Was he kidding? But I wanted him to take me seriously, so I didn't show too much excitement.

"I think I can find some things for you," I said. "But Mother put all your clothes away in boxes somewhere." I told him then about the German soldiers living in the villa, about the boxes walled up in the attic, the three of us living up-stairs in the five small rooms. "It's so lonely without you. I just wish I could tell Mama you're safe."

"You know better than that. She'd tell Papa for sure. And then he wouldn't rest until he got you to tell him where we are. You just can't—promise me you won't."

I told him he looked thin and I listened to his stories: how he and the other par-tisans were relying on certain trusted farmers to give them food; how little there was to share among all the Italian runaway soldiers as well as the escaped prisoners of war—Canadians, English, some French; how he and some others were sleeping now in a well-hidden cave not far away.

I took a deep breath. "There is something that might help. I'm just not sure whether to tell you about it."

"What's that?"

"Well, there's this German soldier who works at Santa Maria, where I am helping with the children. He and I are sort of friends. He's nicer than the others, softer, in a way. I was thinking maybe there was some way he could—"

He grabbed me by the shoulders, so hard it hurt. "No. No. No. You don't get it. You are talking about a bastard who would send me to a labor camp in Germany without batting an eye. If you so much as mention me to him . . . Have you?"

I stared at Giorgio. He was right. I had become so used to seeing Klaus every day that I had somehow lost touch with who he was. "No, honestly, he doesn't even know I have a brother."

"Well, don't. And stay as far away from him as you can. I am serious, Giovanna."

I turned my back. "I promise I won't mention you to him, not ever." I turned to face him. "And I really, really want to help. I'll come back, right here, at the same time next week. I'll bring as much as I can carry."

Then he looked at me, raising his eyebrow the way he always did when he thought he'd won a fight. It made me mad. I was the one helping, wasn't I?

❧

Now my days were too short. I spent all my time thinking about whom I could trust, where I could find clothes and food without endangering Giorgio or me. At the school I went through the motions, but I couldn't concentrate on playing with the children or on reading their compositions. I even forgot now and then to think about the officer Klaus.

I went back to Catarina's on Monday afternoon. I had expected to find her out in the garden, but instead she was sitting in a wooden rocker in the kitchen, staring dully at the floor. Ever since Pietro's death, she had had moments like this. She seemed to close up, to curl in upon herself like a bulb in winter. There was a sheen on her cheeks where tears had recently dried. She looked up slowly and nodded a greeting.

I pulled up another chair, sat knee to knee with her. "Catarina, I'm so sorry." I offered my hand, and she took it with what looked like gratitude. "What can I do?"

"Nothing, dear. I'll be fine. I was just remembering that Pietro's birthday is coming up next month. He would have been twenty-two, a true adult."

"Catarina, listen to me." I leaned in close and lowered my voice. "Have you saved any of his clothes?"

She sat there, rocked a few times slowly. "Of course I have. They're so precious to me. I get them out sometimes and smell them, hoping just to catch a little of his scent. The soft shirts I think are especially good that way, but everything reminds me of him."

"Do you have any of his old uniforms?"

"Well, I could look. I did keep a whole

duffel bag of lighter-weight clothes he left here when he went to the Russian front."

I hesitated. I hated to risk letting anyone in on Giorgio's and my secret, but Catarina could be an important ally, not to mention a source of critical supplies.

I took a deep breath and then told her about my meeting with Giorgio. I spared no details, filling her in on the state of his clothes, his missing bootlace, his hollow cheeks. As I talked, I could see Catarina perk up. Her eyes sharpened, snapped back to the present. The old Catarina—bustling, practical, nurturing—was reemerging. She promised to go through Pietro's things over the next few days, even to give me the duffel bag itself. She agreed to bake some extra loaves of bread on Saturday.

"I think it's better that we keep this from Tonino, don't you?" Catarina asked. "I don't want to widen the risk of Giorgio being discovered."

"Well, maybe . . . but I trust him totally."

℘

On Tuesday, Violetta and I were on our way into town to buy some bread and cheese for a picnic lunch. When we stopped to admire the wildflowers, poppies, and blue flax that grew along the road, I asked her, trying to sound casual, "If one of the patients at the clinic dies, what happens to his clothes?"

She looked at me oddly. "Where did that come from?"

"Oh, I've just been thinking about things. I . . . I don't know. I've been looking for something more to do, something for the war effort, and I thought maybe I could take the old clothes and make things for the children out of the fabric."

She laughed. "But you don't even know how to sew."

"I'm sure Catarina would be willing to teach me."

"Well, if the soldier is Italian, maybe lives near here, and if the clothes are in one piece, usually we send them to his family. They like to have them as a souvenir, you know, something to keep."

"And if they're not? If they're British, Canadian, or French?"

"Well, then, I'm not sure. I can find

out, though. Giovanna, I think it's too funny you want to sew. You! It just doesn't sound like you at all."

"I guess war is unpredictable that way," I said. "It can change a person."

❧

I was churning with the thrill of the hunt. I took longer and longer routes home in the late afternoons, darting in between the stone houses to see which ones had tiny vegetable gardens tucked into the backyards. I went out of my way through the countryside, scouting the fields, checking to see which kitchen gardens were surrounded by walls, which ones were guarded by dogs, which ones had unlocked gates.

I made a beeline for the wheat farmer's fenced-in garden, where—a few days before—I'd seen a row of large heads of lettuce and a parade of healthy carrot tops. I approached slowly, looking behind me and quickly to the left and right. I had my hand on the gate and was just working the rusty latch when I heard a high-pitched yell.

"Giovanna, is that you?" I looked up

and saw the lumpy silhouette of Teresa, the wheat farmer's wife, hoe in hand, calling to me from the adjacent field. I drew back my hand and waved at her.

"Your vegetables look so healthy!" I called, my hand cupping my mouth. "I was just admiring your crop!" I remembered then that it had been Teresa's son who had delivered the note to Catarina last week, the one who had first reported seeing Giorgio. Could Teresa guess what I was doing? Had he told his mother about it?

Teresa made her way slowly toward me, her long skirt dragging over the rows of low sprouted wheat, her laced leather brogues stepping awkwardly into the rutted furrows as she leaned on the hoe for support. I hurried in her direction, intending to put as large a distance as possible between me and the vegetable garden.

"Off to the market, dear?" she asked, eyeing the basket.

"Oh, you know supplies are short everywhere . . ." I answered, leaning into the sentence, trailing my unspoken need before this woman's abundance.

"I'm sure your garden at the villa is overflowing." There was no sign of comprehension.

"How is Andrea?" I thought maybe this reference to her son might jog her memory if she knew about Giorgio.

"His wounded arm is healing well, thank you," she said. Then she moved closer. "Not too fast, we hope, because you know what that would mean. They'd be after him again." She adjusted her dark head scarf and rolled her eyes. "Such a nasty business, this war."

The conversation petered out with no mention of Giorgio, no sign that she knew what I was after. "I'll see you soon," I called to her, and hurried off, my mind churning. I wished I knew more about everyone's politics, that I had a better feel for our neighbors. But in the face of my ignorance, I had to opt for silence and utter discretion.

I stopped by two other gardens, but at each, I lost heart. I stood looking over the stone walls, eyeing the profusion of snap peas dangling from their trellises made of orchard prunings, the fava beans with their long, lumpy pods, deli-

cate yellow zucchini blossoms, and arti-
chokes bristling on strong stems. But
the day was too bright, the land too
open. At another, a brown-and-white
shepherd dog prowled the perimeter.
What if I were caught stealing? Some
people might forgive me without another
thought, but there were others who
might force me to explain and threaten
the whole venture.

ℰ

At Saturday breakfast, Father was unusually cheerful. "How about some tennis this afternoon, *piccola*? It's going to
be a beautiful day."

"Sure, Papa." I waited, took another
sip of coffee. "I promised Catarina I'd
stop by this afternoon. So maybe we
could play this morning instead."

He frowned at me, setting down his
crust of bread. "Sometimes I think you
spend more time with the farmers than
you do with your own family." He finished chewing, then swallowed. "What
is the purpose of all your education if
the only people you associate with are
the peasants?"

"Enrico," Mother interrupted. "Personally, I think it's a sign of good breeding that she's kind to the people who work our land. That's a quality I've always hoped she would have. Besides, she's been such a source of comfort to Catarina since Pietro died. You know that."

"Well, just see that you remember your place in the scheme of things, young lady," he growled, not looking at Mother. "Now change your clothes." He shoved back from the table. "I'll meet you on the court."

ℓ

I left the house after lunch, bound for Catarina's with a large market basket over my arm. Violetta had given me two pairs of pants—from an English soldier—and a French jacket that was much too warm for this time of year. I'd kept these hidden for a couple of days in the drawer of my dresser, and now they were flattened in the bottom of the basket, covered by a dish towel.

"I'm a complete failure," I moaned, setting the basket on the table with a thud and collapsing into a chair. "Now what will Giorgio do? What will he think of me? I'll probably lose my chance to help."

Catarina, with a little smile, raised her eyebrows. She beckoned me over to a corner of the kitchen. There on the floor was a lump hidden by a colorful tablecloth. "Tonino's in the orchard," she said, "but keep an eye out in case he comes back. I just haven't wanted to tell him yet." She pulled back the tablecloth. There was the army green duffel bag, unzipped, with some of its contents spilling out. Catarina began pulling, moving the things from the bag to a pile next to it. There were two men's shirts, several sets of underwear, a pair of boots, and some extra laces. There were two loaves of bread, a tied handkerchief full of dried beans, and—best of all—a gunnysack with three heads of lettuce, some tiny new potatoes, baby carrots, and fistfuls of peas and fresh beans. "I raided my own garden," she said. "Thank God it's growing well this year."

"Oh, Catarina. I love you!" I hugged her tight. "This is perfect. Can you keep it hidden until tomorrow?" I added Violetta's clothes to the bag.

"Whose are these?" Catarina asked.

I sobered, wondering how much to tell. "They belong to two young men who no longer need them. And their mothers are far away." I held Catarina close again. "I'll be back tomorrow, right after lunch."

Chapter Five

War hung over us like an insistent fog. It was always there, clouding everything, separating us from one another under a blanket of secrecy and fear. Sometimes I felt as if I couldn't breathe, as if I were fighting for air in the atmosphere that infected my relationship with my parents, with Violetta, with the sisters at school. As for the partisans, everyone knew they were hiding out in the woods and hills that surrounded us, but no one talked about it. Most people were on their side, hoping they would be able to slow the Germans down and do what they could to help the Allies' progress. People like me, or like the wheat farmer's wife, had family members who were among them, but they were silent on the subject.

Occasionally we would hear about a night raid on someone's garden, root cellar, or barn, in which some rifles or a radio were stolen. Even though it was for a good cause, it annoyed those particular landowners and frightened them, since they knew that the Germans might learn of it and punish them for aiding the rebels. I felt as if we were all in some sort of play, acting out our roles in daily life, but our real selves were hidden away. What burned inside and kept me going was a sense that in deciding to help Giorgio I was doing the right thing, working toward a higher purpose despite the impostor I had become.

On Sunday morning, I went to church with my parents. I wasn't sure where God was in all this, but I was pretty sure He wasn't cheering the Nazis on. I prayed hard that God would forgive me for all the sneaking around and the lying, and that He would keep both me and Giorgio safe until I could deliver the duffel bag later that afternoon. As for Klaus, I thought that he had a good soul locked inside. I believed he was a decent man, simply playing the role expected of him as a German soldier. Was there a difference between his mining bridges and my keeping Giorgio's activities from my parents? I kept the communion wafer on my tongue without chewing it at all. *If it dissolves of its own accord,* I thought, *I'm doing the right thing.* By the time we heard the dismissal blessing, the last bit slipped down like a spoonful of oatmeal.

℘

Catarina had stowed everything in the bag and hidden it in a remote corner of her garden under a hedge. That allowed me to give Tonino a quick hug when I arrived and for Catarina and me to head casually for the garden without attracting attention.

I gave the duffel a trial lift. Not too much weight at all, but the bag looked suspicious. We decided to take out the long gunnysack that held the vegetables in the bottom and stuff the clothes and loaves of bread in on top of them in layers. The result was a lumpy hemp bag that looked as though it held an afternoon's worth of garden harvest. I hoisted the heavy load over my shoulder and trudged through the woods to the gazebo. Another Sunday afternoon. No farmers in view, no soldiers at all.

When I arrived in the clearing, there was no one there either. I heaved the bag onto the marble base and sat down heavily, leaning against a column, the moss underneath it seeping moisture slowly up through the layers of my full skirt. It was quiet except for the occasional *rat-a-tat-tatting* of a woodpecker on a dead tree and the breeze stirring the branches over my head. It smelled sharp, like mildew.

As I waited, I began to worry. I had no idea how many people Giorgio was living with, but when I pictured the small fistfuls of peas and beans I had brought lying on tin plates, I realized they wouldn't go far. He could probably finish off those two loaves of bread in one sitting. Could they cook? Did they need pots and pans or dishes? Two things I'd figured out by then: I'd have to work a lot harder to find enough clothes and food, and I wouldn't ever be able to carry enough to make Giorgio happy.

As I was mulling these things over, I heard the crackling of twigs and low male voices. "Giovanna. You made it." Giorgio and another man, one whom I did not recognize, came out of the woods. The man was taller and older than my brother, maybe forty or so, and—like Giorgio—he had a growth of beard shadowing his lower face.

"Giorgio!" I cried, running up to him and slipping my arms around his waist.

"No." He put his hand over my mouth. "Forget that name, okay? I'm Hermes, and this here's the Fox. We've left our old lives behind us now. You have to re-member that."

I studied the man's reddish hair, his close-set, beady eyes, and his long pointed nose. Yes, clearly the Fox. I thought I could remember that one. "Why Hermes?"

"Well, he was the messenger, was he not? That seems to be my role, time and again. I like to keep moving, and I'm kind of a go-between. I convinced you to get involved, didn't I?" He opened the top of the bag that was lying on its side. "Let's see what you've got in here."

Giorgio began rummaging around inside and pulling out the items one by one, setting the clothes on one side, the food on the other. "These look like English army pants!" said the Fox in an odd, lilting Italian.

"Two pairs," said Giorgio, holding up the others. "The Fox is English. He was shot down a year ago, and after he recovered, he was unable to reconnect with his regiment or penetrate the German lines. So he's joined up with us, working with the guys up here."

When he got to the bread, he handed one loaf to the Fox. They tore into them with gusto, tearing off piece after piece, stuffing them in their mouths and swallowing them without chewing.

"Okay." Halfway through his loaf, Giorgio stood back and surveyed the meager piles. "Giovanna, this is a great start, but we've got to help you understand what we're dealing with here. Sit down."

I perched on the base of one of the

columns and leaned back against it, looking up at the two of them. They continued standing, pacing back and forth. Giorgio did most of the talking. Now and then the Fox, who I noticed had a slight limp, would add a few words of emphasis or correction.

There were fifteen men in their loosely affiliated band. Most of them were local, men from western Tuscany, from villages not too far from Lucca, who were known to one another vaguely or were friends of friends. Some were soldiers who, like Giorgio, had deserted from the Italian army. Some were recent recruits; others were older, veterans of battles in Northern Africa, Sicily, or even Russia, who had refused to continue fighting under German occupation. There were civilians, anti-Fascists, who were too old or too young to serve, who had joined with this group to do what they could to fight the Blackshirts, harass the Germans, and pave the way for Allied victory.

"There are groups all over northern Italy," he went on. "Some are really organized, almost like military units, according to the ranks they held in the army. They've got good guns and regular supplies. Others are looser, like ours."

"How do the organized ones get their supplies?" I wondered whether I could learn from their techniques.

"They've got good walkie-talkies and radios, and so they get regular signaled parachute drops from Allied planes." *That explains some of those low-flying planes,* I thought, *the ones that don't seem to be bombers.*

"Where are you living?" I asked.

Giorgio looked at the Fox. "We can't tell you exactly where, but we're based in one of the old *carbonari* camps. Remember how Tonino and his cronies would go off for a few weeks every year?"

A couple of years earlier I was in the village one afternoon and saw Tonino return from one of these outings. He was helping to pull a two-wheeled wagon piled high with gunnysacks of charcoal. He and the other guys had been wearing the same clothes for two or three weeks, and their shirts and pants, their hands and faces, were covered in a thick layer of black charcoal dust.

Charcoal making—before modern briquettes came along—was one of our local traditions. A group of villagers would leave their families and hike up into the thickly wooded hills. They cut sticks and small branches with a razor-sharp cutting tool, stacking them high in a tepee-shaped pile. Then they covered the whole thing with a layer of dirt to keep out the air and set the wood on fire. It smoldered, maybe for a week or more, while they worked on building new piles. Eventually, they would remove the layers of dirt and find the sticks underneath transformed into charcoal. We used it for cooking and exported it too.

"Those guys left campsites like the one we're using. It's near a stream and flat. And the good news for us is that it's completely inaccessible to motor vehicles."

"So do you cook?" I asked.

"We can," he answered. "And that's what I was coming to. We don't have any way to chill fresh food, so what we really need is more dried beans and pasta, hard cheese, onions, salami—even eggs—things that keep for a while. And the bread is great if you can get it." He popped the last of his crust in his mouth and grinned.

"The problem is this." I turned my back to them, because I didn't want to disappoint them in any way. "I can't carry very much, Giorgio. And I can't really get away during the week. What I need is a place closer to home where I can add the supplies little by little, some-place you can get to without my help, maybe during the night."

We suggested various barns and sheds, buildings at the edges of nearby properties. Every place we thought of had animals nearby or people who couldn't be trusted. Then Giorgio had a brainstorm. "Remember the old cellar behind the Santinis'? It's dug into the ground, and there's a trapdoor. They used to store wine in there, but then they dug the bigger caves. Someone told me he had spent the night there safely a couple of weeks ago."

"I remember it," I said. "Where we

used to play hide-and-seek with Luigi, right?"

"That's the one. You could get there easily during the week, load the supplies into it, and then we could come whenever it worked for us without disturbing anyone."

"And since Saturday is bread-baking day, I could bring the loaves when I come here on Sundays." Giorgio looked at me kind of quizzically. He went over close to the Fox. They turned their backs to me and talked in low voices so I couldn't hear them.

"Okay, Giovanna. We really might need you for messages and special requests, so I'll keep coming Sundays like this whenever I can, just as long as you know that now and then I might not show up." He was distracted now, kind of nervous, looking around like they'd stayed too long. "One other thing. You are going to need a special name too. Just in case I need to leave a note or something. What'll it be?"

That was something I hadn't thought about. Maybe a flower, or a famous writer? Maybe an animal or someone in history. I thought about hunting for supplies and remembered the raptor we had rescued together all those years ago. "The Hawk?"

Giorgio looked at me, frowned, and shook his head. "I don't think so, little sister. But you will have to carry messages and cover a lot of ground. We'll hope this brings peace and call you Columba, the dove." He kissed me lightly on the forehead, and they took off, the hemp bag slung over the Fox's shoulder.

I thumbed my teeth at his retreating figure. *It should have been the Hawk,* I thought. *You'll see what a hunter I can be.*

On my way home, a shot rang out north of me, echoing in the hills. Maybe it was a cannon or maybe dynamite from one of the bridge mining operations by the river. *Klaus?* When I neared the open fields, I saw a jeep pulled over to the side of the road and German soldiers digging in the potato field. Potatoes weren't something we ate all that often, but the Germans seemed to love them and raided those crops before anything else. *Rosa,* I suddenly thought. *I'm going to have to take Rosa into my confidence. She'll have all those basics tucked away, maybe enough to share.*

Rosa had been our kitchen maid for many years. She and her husband, Geppe, raised four children on our land, living in a small apartment in the lower part of the villa. In the years we lived in the city all winter, they would look after the main house. Three of their children were still at home. But the Germans had captured their oldest son, Gigi, only fourteen, in one of their roundups after our surrender to the Allies last September. In fact, German soldiers were still frequently driving through the villages, combing the area for able-bodied boys to send to Germany or northern Italy to work; boys were constantly on the lookout, living in fear of being snatched up. It had been almost ten months since Gigi had disappeared. Rosa was worried sick about him, but she and Geppe stayed on, working faithfully, now forced to wait on the officers living downstairs. She loved Giorgio, and I hoped that, like

Catarina, this might give her something positive to focus on.

Rosa was a tender soul, discreet and unobtrusive, who moved about with the stealth of a furtive rat. A smile rarely graced her lips, and she carried herself like a court aristocrat, her posture proud and correct. Her face was chiseled, its sharp features casting deep shadows that gave her a hollow, somewhat wasted air. As if to spite her name, her complexion was a sickly olive drab. Her waved, glossy coiffure might have been carved in marble, so consistent was its outline, so rarely a hair out of place. She wore a blue-and-white uniform starched to stiff perfection, and rubber-soled shoes that allowed her to approach without a sound, to come and go without interrupting whatever discussion or activity was happening around her.

Her kitchen, larder, and cellars were immaculate, everything in its place—piled, stacked, stashed, and labeled so that not a square inch of space was wasted. Rosa knew to the ounce or teaspoon how much of anything she had; she anticipated the shelf life of every ingredient to the day, and she ensured their use well before they spoiled by rotating recipes. That was why I had avoided raiding our own kitchen for the first week's supplies. Rosa would have noticed something missing the minute it disappeared. No, there was only one option now: I had to bring Rosa into my confidence, make her a partner in the enterprise.

I tentatively poked my head around the corner of the first-floor kitchen when I arrived home. Rosa stood at the counter, her back to me, kneading a pile of flour and eggs into pasta dough for supper.

"Rosa?" I was keenly aware of the value of her time. As children, we had learned to keep our distance, to respect her territory. She turned her head briskly, her white-powdered hands still hovering over the emerging dough. No answer. She turned back to her task.

"Rosa, may I speak with you a moment?" I waited a beat. "It's important."

"Not now, Giovanna."

I came up next to her, as if to examine the pasta dough, and stood there for a few minutes. I took a deep breath. "I'm in touch with Giorgio."

Her hands froze. I knew what was going on inside her. If Giorgio was alive, if he was safe, then maybe there was hope for Gigi as well. "Tell me." She took up the kneading again, leaning her weight into it, turning and pressing the elastic mass.

So I stood there next to her as she worked. In a low voice, barely looking at her, I brought her up-to-date. She took it all in, asking no questions, her face unmoving, her eyes trained on her task. Once she looked up. "Does your mother know?"

"Oh, no, she mustn't. She would tell Papa, and he might force me to reveal their location. No, this must be kept a secret between us. I just know I can trust you." I didn't tell her about Catarina being in on the secret.

She mulled it over as she slowly turned the crank of the roller, feeding the long strip of flat dough carefully into the mouth of the hand-cranked machine. Minutes passed. I helped her catch the soft, pliable strips of dough, draping them over my arms, setting them aside to be cut into long noodles.

At last she stopped working and turned toward me. Her face showed no emotion; her eyes seemed not to blink at all. "There are two rules."

I smiled. I couldn't help it. I wanted to jump for joy.

"You will never—ever—take anything I have not prepared for you."

"Of course not, Rosa."

"And you will not tell Giorgio or anyone else I am involved."

"If you like. I promise." I knew better than to hug her or even take her hand. "You won't regret it, Rosa. That much I know."

Chapter Six

Rosa—dear, trusted, dour Rosa—became my touchstone, the axis around which my new world revolved. Every afternoon after working at the school, I would stop by and check in with her. I was never sure how she managed to spare such quantities of food, but one day she handed me a whole sack of dried beans, the next a dozen potatoes and a kilo or two of rice. There were onions from the garden, some garlic and shallots, and dried pasta in various shapes and sizes. We exchanged few words. I simply took the food, loaded it into the bag I carried daily, and then—either on the way to school the next morning or over the lunch hour—traced the well-worn path to the Santinis'.

Life there had changed in recent months, and—I'm sorry to say—it worked to my advantage. Luigi's mother was very ill, spending more and more time in her second-floor rooms with their heavy velvet curtains pulled tight against the light. It was perhaps because of her illness that, at least until now, they had been spared from German occupation. Signor Santini was in residence, overseeing his vineyards and wine-making operations, but he kept regular hours focused on the winery and the new caves, far from the old cellar.

I could approach from the rear adjoining property, skirt the potting shed, and approach the trapdoor virtually unseen. There was a rusted iron ring attached to the door that lay barely visible in the long grass. I always held my breath, anticipating the loud creak of the loose hinges as the door swung up and back. Down a few earthen steps was a hollowed-out room lined with rotting wooden shelves that once held small barrels of aging wine. They stood empty now, laced with cobwebs. The dirt floor was littered with droppings, small bones, and tufts of rodent hair. I had taken over a couple of the cleaner shelves and quickly learned to be in and out, depositing the new supplies in less than a minute. I worried about Luigi and his brother and sister, but they never seemed to be about, so I soon forgot about them as I gained rhythm and confidence in the routine.

I would watch the pile grow to a satisfying stash, and then, a few days later, I would find the cellar empty. I presumed that Giorgio or one of his comrades had come and retrieved it all during the night. I left that day's offering with a full heart. But one Friday, everything changed.

℘

I was feeling useful in my new venture and right as rain, as if I were a legitimate soldier in a patriotic movement. That wholeness and sense of purpose carried over into my life at school. Working with the children was no longer my only role in the war. In fact, when I thought of them and their silly games, I couldn't help but feel that they were keeping me from a higher calling, that I was superior to the work. The fact that I was risking myself to deliver crucial supplies to the partisans gave me a margin of moral capital that I felt I could spend as I wished. In retrospect, it explained why I decided to take the initiative with Klaus, to tempt both myself and him in a way that I knew was dangerous.

Wednesday morning I had left home very early to drop off a delivery. When I arrived at school, no one was around. So I scribbled a note—*I'll be in the kitchen after lunch today. See you at two p.m.?*—folded it several times, and left it on Klaus's desk with a sprig of pink bougainvillea. After it was done, I agonized, but there was no getting the note back. I had the option not to show up, but that felt even more dangerous. I didn't want to anger him in any way.

At two o'clock there I was, self-consciously wiping the counters and appliances as if to be simply tidying the place. He came in quietly, having left his jacket behind. We were alone. This time he put an arm around my waist right away, led me into the corner, and kissed me before either one of us could change our minds. I felt molten metal oozing into the far reaches of my lower body. I ran my hands down the thin shirt over his back, lodging them into the tight place under his belt at the back of his waist.

"Giovanna." His breath was uneven. "I have an idea."

"You do?" I smiled up at him. "What kind of an idea?"

"Of how we can have some real time together." He kissed me again, on top of my head, then on my ear. "You would like that?"

I nodded, not sure whether to give in to the excitement I felt or listen to the fear that gnawed at my stomach.

"We'll have a picnic here at the school on Friday—in the evening after work, when everyone has gone. I'll arrange it all. You need only to find a reason to stay late and not to go home for supper." He smoothed my hair back down around my ears and rested his hands on my shoulders. "I promise it will be safe. You will come?"

❦

Over the next couple of days, I avoided Klaus as best I could. I either pretended it hadn't happened at all, that we didn't have a plan, or that I was planning when and how to call it off. Yet I was afraid he would change his mind. It was insanely dangerous; I knew that. Nevertheless, in my mind I had managed to separate Klaus from his compatriots, the rough-talking occupiers who lived in our house, who I knew were threatening the lives of our friends and acquaintances, who were making life miserable for us in every way.

With great excitement Violetta agreed to let me sleep over on Friday. I didn't tell her about Klaus, only that my family expected me to stay home for supper and that I would come after that. To complete my cover, I needed now only to work on my parents.

I came into the tiny parlor. Papa was sitting hunched over the radio, which was turned down very low. He put his finger to his lips and gave me a little wave of his hand, so I stood there waiting and listening with him. The announcer was broadcasting from newly liberated Rome, detailing the progress of the Allies, now working their way into eastern Tuscany.

That was all far to the south of us and all the way across Italy, but my heart leaped with excitement and hope. There had been steady progress reported each day, but it never seemed to change the heavy blanket of occupation that lay suffocating our own beleaguered region. At last Father looked up. He was distracted, his face creased with worry and confusion.

"They are coming, aren't they?" I offered tentatively.

"Who knows, *piccola,* who knows?" He pinched the top of his nose between his fingers. "The Germans have doubled their defenses south of us. They are strong and determined. We must never let them see that we are looking toward Allied victory. You know that."

I looked away from him at the floor.

"Did you want to ask me something?"

"Yes, Father, I . . ." He looked suddenly so vulnerable, so *reduced,* perched on his chair, hemmed in by war. Love and concern flooded over me, and I felt a stab of shame that there was so much about my life at that moment that he didn't know or have any part of. But I pressed on. I heard my own voice, coming from some source beyond me, casual and upbeat. "I wanted to let you know that Violetta and I want to spend tomorrow night at her house in the village. It's been so long, and I need a little change of scenery." I looked him straight in the eye, and I even felt a little smile lift the corners of my mouth.

He looked at me. "Well, I don't know why not." He stood up, leaned toward the radio, and turned it off. "There's a curfew on the streets, of course."

"Oh, I know that, Father. We'll be inside."

He nodded. "I'll let your mother know. She's gone to bed early."

I rushed to him and threw my arms around his shoulders. "Thank you, Papa." As I held him, my own duplicity pressed up in my throat and made me step back and turn away. "I'll see you in the morning."

❦

After Friday's lunch, I set off from home, lugging an overnight satchel that was heavier than usual. It concealed, in addition to my change of clothes, at least a dozen potatoes and a kilo of rice, which I dropped through the trapdoor on my way back to school. As I reached the school's gate, I ran into the two sisters coming the other way.

"Going somewhere?" Sister Graziella looked down at my bag with a curious smile.

"Oh, Violetta and I are planning a night together at her house," I said lightly, avoiding her eyes.

"How nice, dear. Give her my best, won't you?" She patted me affectionately on the back. I stole a look at Sister Elena, who paid no attention to the exchange.

Then everything fell into place as easily as a perfect game of solitaire. We had an extra-large number of compositions left at the end of the day, so I volunteered to stay late and finish correcting them.

"Are you sure Violetta isn't expecting you?" asked Sister Graziella.

"No, Sister. She lives close to the school, so I'll have some extra time. It's no problem." I watched both her and Sister Elena leave by the front gate.

Shortly after that, as the soldiers began quitting too, the air was alive with loud laughter, slamming doors, jeep engines starting up. Otto was the second-to-last to leave. He clipped the leash onto Panzer, calling a bit of something in German to Klaus. Had Klaus asked him to take the dog home that day? Then he was gone as well, and I knew it was just the two of us.

❦

When I look back on this moment, I am still astounded at my own hubris. There I was, on course for a rendezvous with a Nazi soldier. He was older than I was by ten years, and that's a lot at that age. Not only that, he was married and a father. Worst of all, he was the *enemy*. But my fears stemmed more from my own inadequacies than from anything related to war. It occurred to me that Klaus might have expectations far beyond my own limited experience with boys.

All sound died away. I sat there as unmoving as a small rodent in the shadow of a hawk. The papers weren't finished, because I'd been too distracted to work. I folded my hands and froze in place. Minutes went by; then footsteps approached along the wooden loggia. I stared straight ahead.

"Giovanna?" I looked up, and Klaus was leaning in through the open window. He looked young and eager and, well, kind. "Everyone is gone now."

I nodded slowly. Then he smiled broadly at me, and my fears dried up like beads of water on a hot skillet.

"Are you ready for a picnic?"

I got up, leaving the pile of unfinished papers on the table, and headed for the door. He offered me his arm in an exaggerated gentlemanly fashion and walked me back to the school's kitchen. The table was spread with an army blanket in lieu of a tablecloth, and two places were set with the school's cracked, mismatched plates. There were forks and knives by the plates, and two of the children's milk glasses standing empty. On the table were scattered a loaf of bread, a length of sausage, a hunk of cheese, a small jar of olives, and—placed in the middle of it all—a wicker-basketed bottle of Chianti. He grinned and looked at me like a proud child. "Shall we dine, signorina?" He pulled out one of the chairs and made a sweeping gesture, as if I were a princess.

"You must have just done this—so fast!" I sat down carefully, pulling my chair up to the table.

"I've had two days to plan, and it's been much easier than mining a bridge." He winked at me. "Now, *buon appetito*." He poured me a half glass of wine and began to slice the salami and cheese.

It was delicious, and I was suddenly ravenously hungry. No one was about, and being alone with him was so new and so freeing. We both ate greedily, and, lulled by the wine, we let ourselves relax.

I wanted to know more about Mathilde and the baby, but instead I asked him about how he decided to be an engineer. He told me his father had been an engineer, and his grandfather before that. He had a sister, who was also married, and whose three small children were keeping his parents busy in Germany.

"They love to have the grandchildren, so they don't miss me so much," he said, and the other grandchild—his own son—dangled there in the air like a ripe peach. But I didn't pluck it.

I was afraid he might move on to my own siblings, so I quickly said, "Tell me how the work around Lucca is going." Now, this was odd, even insane, asking the enemy for details of his defense work, but the intimate setting made it almost feel that we were on the same side.

He told me more about the Todt unit (named for a Nazi soldier) that he and his fellow officers commanded, how they had taken over the railroad, and how important the bridges were to moving about the Serchio River valley. Apparently our whole area was a key part of the line of defense for the retreat of the German troops. Areas of our valley made up part of the Gothic Line of defense that stretched all the way across Italy from Pisa in the west to the eastern Adriatic coast. "So, for us to retreat, it will be important to destroy the bridges behind us as we go, you see?"

We had almost finished the bottle of wine. I was feeling tipsy and quite comfortable now. "You know what I think?"

"What do you think, my beauty?" There was something so attractive about him, so vulnerable and sweet when he was in a mood like this. He leaned toward me over the corner of the table and rested his chin on his fist. "I'm listening."

"I think . . ." I started to giggle. "I think if you want to defeat the Italians, you should mine their wine cellars, not their bridges."

"Oh, you do, do you?" He frowned in a mock serious way. "Mine their wine cellars! That is a brilliant strategy. I will pass it on to my superior officers." He leaned over and kissed me lightly on the cheek. "And now for dessert." He carried the dishes to the sink, rinsed them quickly, and cleared the table, putting the scraps into a small canvas army sack. "Bottoms up!" He poured the very last of the wine into my glass and added the bottle to the sack. I was waiting for him to bring out the dessert, but instead he whisked the blanket off the table and took me by the hand. "Come with me." Where were we going?

He led me into the front part of the kitchen, into a cloakroom, open on one end, where in winter the children's jackets and coats were hung. A few large duffel bags were scattered there, and he laid the blanket ceremoniously over them. "Now Bacchus will feed you grapes on a silver platter."

I was light-headed and I could think of only one thing: kissing this man. We were all alone and warmed by the wine, our stomachs full of good food. He pulled me down onto the duffel bags, draping me across his lap. His hands began stroking me from my neck out across my body. Shivers traveled up my spine, and that molten metal began oozing again in my stomach and into my groin. I shut my eyes and felt his lips close over mine.

My head swirled. I had never felt quite like this before: greedy, impatient, like I couldn't get enough of his mouth, his tongue. There was now a tight knot of tension that burned in my stomach, then between my legs, that made me press my hips up, up, and pull him hard against me. I felt one of his hands reach up and begin to unbutton my blouse. He was actually doing that—unbuttoning my blouse! I drew in my breath and held it, waiting to see what it would feel like to have him touching my bare breast, when I felt the shock of his other hand going up my skirt between my legs. *Both at once.* What was happening? I pulled away a little, pushing him back at the chest. "Klaus, I'm not sure I should be doing this. I—"

He covered my mouth with tiny kisses to silence me. "It feels good, doesn't it, my beauty?"

"It does; of course it does." He opened the hand under my skirt and began to stroke the inside of my thigh. It felt soft and warm, and oh . . . that funny knot was tighter and tighter. I was so torn between the hot waves of desire shooting through me and the uneasiness I felt at the speed of it all. I was just closing my eyes again when he propped himself up on his elbow, drew the hand out from under my skirt, and began to unbuckle his belt. "I will show you now what feels best of all." What did that mean? Was he planning to take his pants off?

No, no, the thought of that was too much. I pushed my skirt down again and rolled over with my back to him. "Klaus, I'm just not ready for this. I've never—"

He stopped me by reaching over me from behind and putting his hand over my mouth. "Now, now, fraulein, now, now." He gently rocked against my hips from behind. "I'm not going to hurt you; I promise."

By now the heat had left me altogether, and I was myself again, thinking of only one thing: leaving. I pulled away—hard—and sat up. Suddenly I was aware of a rustling noise behind us. I got to my hands and knees and looked up. The long black folds of a nun's habit were blocking the open doorway to the kitchen.

I clutched at my open blouse in horror and stood up. "Sister Graziella!" Without another glance at Klaus, I pushed past her, down the hall, and out the door of the school.

Chapter Seven

"What's the matter with you?" With one look, Violetta knew there was trouble. "Is there a plane down near here? Has something happened to Giorgio?" Violetta pulled me quickly into her room.

I sat down on one of her twin beds and leaned forward, arms folded over my stomach. "No, no, nothing like that." I shook my head. "I just had a picnic with one of the Nazi soldiers at the school, and . . . and Sister Graziella . . ." I leaned over my lap and began to cry.

"You what? I thought you were having dinner with your parents."

"No, my parents think I had dinner here. We wanted to have some time together."

"We? What do you mean, *we?* Giovanna, what's going on?"

"It's been sort of going on for a while. I just haven't wanted to tell you about it. It's so crazy. Until now it's just been a kiss here or there, but tonight . . ."

"Oh, my God, Giovanna. What have you done?"

"No, no—I ran out when Graziella saw us. Nothing really happened, but I just . . . Violetta, he could have . . ." I took her hand and squeezed it tight. "I almost . . . what if I had let him make love to me? Can you imagine? The first time with a *Nazi soldier?*"

She looked at me with a face that registered not only horror but a kind of awe. "You really might have? Is he married? How did you get this far?"

So I recounted the whole thing from the beginning, how we had met. As I heard myself talking, I realized how crazy it must sound to her, how it made no sense at all. "I'm sorry I haven't told you until now. But you have to believe

me. He can be a thoughtful, kind, attractive man."

"Listen to yourself! He's a German
occupier. They are the ones who *kill* us,
who *wound* us, Giovanna. I see it every
day at the clinic."

"I know. But not Klaus. He's so gentle, almost gallant."

"Gallant! Why, because he removed
his gun at dinner?"

"No, you should have seen the table
he set up for our picnic. It was so sweet!
We drank a whole bottle of wine together, and we got so tipsy I told him
that the best way to defeat the Italians
was to mine our wine cellars. Don't you
love it?" At the memory of my clever remark, I started to giggle.

Violetta did not laugh. "Giovanna,
what are you talking about? You are giving them ideas like that? What's happened to you? Listen to me: He's a lonely
married man. He wants some romance,
sure, and then it will lead to *sex,* Giovanna. This is going on all over town,
and I can't bear to see you used like a
common serving girl. Just think about

yourself, your reputation, your future. And Sister Graziella *saw* you?"

"Oh, that part was horrible; I know. I don't know what I'm going to do."

Later, after we turned out the lights, I went over it all again. The dinner scene was now suffused with a kind of hazy romance: the table, the wine, the look of longing in Klaus's blue eyes, the silky feel of his hand stroking the inside of my thigh. But then I remembered my clutch of fear as he unbuckled his belt. And Graziella's face . . .

I didn't get home until midafternoon on Saturday, and the minute I reached the top of the stairs, I could feel tension in the air. Father had been sitting in the parlor reading, because at the sound of my footsteps, he came to the door, holding his place in the book with a finger. "Giovanna? Is that you?" His face was fixed in a deep frown, and he didn't look me in the eye. "Come in here."

I set down my bag and lowered myself onto the edge of the small sofa. A sudden wave of heat passed through my body, followed by a clammy dampness that settled on my neck and shoulders. I folded my hands in my lap. "What is it, Father? Is something wrong?"

He took his time, inserting a bookmark between the pages, and then placing the book quietly on the table. He left his hand on its cover for moment or two, not moving. Then he took a seat, leaned forward, and stared at me expressionlessly. "You look the same."

"What is it, Papa?"

"Sister Graziella left here about half an hour ago."

I felt a hot stab in my diaphragm. "What did she want?"

He got up and began walking around the tiny room, his eyes darting back and forth, his hands gesturing wildly. "Giovanna, I just can't believe what I heard. I don't really know how to say this. I thought you were going to Violetta's house last night."

"I did. I just came from there."

"Well, you didn't go there directly from school, did you?"

I thought about this a moment. I had, actually, gone directly from the school to Violetta's. "Yes, I did."

"But not in time for dinner."

I stared at him. "Why, what did she say?"

He resumed pacing the floor. "She said, Giovanna, that she returned to the school about six thirty last night in search of some book that she needed. She said that she noticed a light on in the kitchen. She said that she went in to turn it off, and she heard noises in the coat closet. . . ." He stopped and paused, his back to me. Then he faced me again with a look of utter bewilderment. "Giovanna, I just could not believe my ears."

I was dumbstruck. The thought that Sister Graziella would come here like that and tell my father. I couldn't look at him, couldn't move. My face burned, and I felt sick, dizzy. The silence was unbearable.

"Father, it's not what you think."

"She says she saw you with her own eyes."

"I know, I know. But it's not . . . I left, Papa. He never . . ." This was so painful. How could I be talking to my own father about these things? "It was just . . . kissing."

I put my head in my hands, hiding my eyes.

"Oh, Giovanna, please! I wasn't born yesterday. He's an adult, probably married."

"No, no! You have to believe me, Papa. I admit I was with him. We had a picnic. But nothing happened, Papa. Nothing bad. You can ask Violetta. I promise. He's a . . . a gentleman."

Father turned toward me, his eyes wild and sarcastic. "Oh, well, he may be a gentleman, but you're certainly no lady. My own daughter, writhing on the closet floor with a Nazi soldier. Now, there's a picture worth remembering."

"We weren't writhing, Papa. He's a good man. You said yourself we should be nice—" The hand shot up out of nowhere, and my cheek stung with the heat of a thousand needles.

"Giovanna!" his voice thundered. "You will never—ever—set foot in that school again or speak so much as a word to that Nazi animal. You will go to confession right now, then come home and think about what you have done. Do you hear me?"

I stood there, stroking my cheek, as tears blurred the image of my father's red, enraged face. I opened my mouth to scream back at him, to defend myself, but he was too mad, too strong.

"Oh, Papa. You just don't understand. It's not what you think; I swear!" I turned away, broke into loud sobs, and clattered down the stairs and out the door. I wanted Father to hear the loud sobs, but once I was outside in the garden, I held them back, my eyes and nose erupting like bubbling springs. Tight pain knotted in my chest so that I could hardly breathe. I found a bench and sat down, leaning over my knees, hands over my eyes, letting the tears spill into my fingers and soak the front of my skirt. Waves of self-pity followed one upon another: first righteous outrage that my father had misunderstood me, that he didn't trust me, didn't believe I had refused Klaus's advances and preserved my innocence; then humiliation, *agony* at the thought of Sister Graziella watching us; and finally, there was Klaus and my confusion about him. I was indignant and determined to keep seeing him despite everything stacked against us. I was so attracted to him, and I really did respect his gentleness and restraint. Why should he—*Nazi animal*—be punished for something he didn't do? But then—and here I cried the hardest, because the truth was so obvious—my father and Sister Graziella were right. Klaus was both an enemy soldier and a married man. Treachery had infused every aspect of this affair, and I needed to clear away the bilious green fog that had settled over me and clung like volcanic ash.

I picked up the front of my skirt and wiped my hands and face on the inside of it, then smoothed my hair as best I could. With one last swipe of my hands on my clothes, I got up and set off in the direction of the church and Don Federico.

Thinking about it as I walked, I looked forward this time to making a full confession. The reality of what I had done, after all, was so much more innocent than all the villainous accusations. In fact, I planned to weigh in heavily in telling of my own rebuff of Klaus's advances and cast both my father and Sister Graziella as unjust in their leaps to a conclusion and their condemnation of me. Did I even hope that Don Federico would prove to be less than discreet? Maybe he could help dig me out of this hole.

But Don Federico, a hazy, stooped figure on the other side of the grate, did not quite see it my way. "Your first sin, Giovanna, which you neglected to mention, was lying to your parents and to your friend Violetta."

"Oh, right, Father. That slipped my mind."

"And then your intentions were clearly to meet this man, this enemy soldier, in private, alone?"

"Yes."

"So you deliberately led him into temptation, inviting him to stray from his marriage vows?"

"No, Father. *He* is the one who invited *me*."

"We are talking about you today, Giovanna. You engaged with him in sinful behavior, leading you both dangerously close to disaster. It is you, my child, who are responsible for your own acts in the eyes of God."

"Well, but I was only—"

He interrupted me, droning on with no interest in hearing my defense. "The good Lord chose to intervene and save you from even greater sin. For this you must be eternally grateful to Him. But you are gravely at fault and must do major penance nonetheless."

I was a bubbling well of spiritual zeal in those days—open, starry-eyed, and eager to receive its wisdom. But confession always seemed to end the same way: I wanted to come out sparkling like clear glass, ready for a new start, and instead I emerged feeling guilty, duplicitous, and fundamentally unclean. Why, in Don Federico's version, was I—not Klaus—responsible for getting into this situation in the first place? Then, when it came to pulling back and drawing the boundaries, which I clearly did, *God* got all the credit?

I stayed in the sanctuary for a long time and dutifully prayed all the Hail Marys and rosaries I had been assigned. But on the way home, I felt no closer to

God or to my father. I knew reconcilia-
tion would be difficult and was entirely
up to me. It would happen on my own
timetable, not my father's. I found Mother
in the garden, taking notes on a pad of
paper. Working on the landscape was
her form of denial in this war. If she could
focus on beauty, on somehow maintaining an illusion of peace and prosperity,
maybe it would all simply disappear. The
proper care and feeding of roses, the
need for pruning rosemary bushes and
lavender . . . if she could lose herself utterly in it all, she could momentarily forget her worries about Tuscany's future,
about Giorgio, and now, I presumed,
about me. Did she know? Had Father
talked with her? I wasn't at all sure. In
spite of living crammed together in such
small spaces, they seemed to move as
two separate spheres these days, barely
touching, repelled from each other
gently, not coming together even if they
had wanted to—as two like ends of
magnets.

I knew, however, the minute I saw her
face that, in this case, an exception had
been made. Mother heard my approach

and straightened her back and shoulders, sliding the pad and pencil into the pocket of her loose, shirt-style jacket. Her hair, as always, was perfectly coiffed, her blouse pressed, her slim figure neatly attired in creased trousers—the most casual thing she ever allowed herself to wear. She looked me up and down like a schoolteacher.

"Mother, I really need to talk with you. I need to explain what happened. Can we go somewhere where we can be alone?" I felt a fluttering under my rib cage, like a trapped bird. Why was this so hard? She was my own mother, after all.

There was a formal section of the gardens at the front and to the west side of the villa: a series of enclosures lined with low, clipped hedges separated by gravel paths. We set off in that direction and began walking slowly down the central path until we came to a tall urn at the far end planted with bright coral-colored geraniums. There we turned and headed for a small grouping of wrought-iron chairs that looked over a low balustrade out to the valley below.

Not a word was said until we were seated. "Mother, I don't know what Father told you, but he does not know the whole truth." She sat still, back straight, her lips a thin line, her hands resting in her lap. Her reticence always had the same effect on me—eliciting a torrent of words like a flash flood rushing and swirling its way into the desert.

The story poured out, breathlessly, much as it had for Violetta, but I skipped over a few details. I lingered on the dinner scene. Even in my own mind it had taken on new, exquisite touches. A small vase of flowers had appeared. The silverware was carefully aligned; the cheese had been thinly sliced and artfully arranged.

Then, when I got to the closet, what? I must have told her—she was a woman too, after all. I know I mentioned the duffel bags. I think I said we were "sitting" on them with our backs to the closet opening. I told her he had kissed me several times, that I truly was attracted to him, but that I put a stop to things and told him Violetta was waiting for me.

"Enrico said Sister Graziella saw you lying on the floor." Mother's lips trembled and she looked away. "She said he wore no jacket and your skirt was up around your waist, Giovanna."

"Oh, God," I groaned. "I didn't want to mention that, but that was all! You have to believe me." I stood up and put my hands on her shoulders, shaking them gently. Tears were running down my cheeks. "I'm not lying to you, Mama."

"But you lied to us about going to Violetta's for dinner, so why should I believe you about this?"

"I know, Mother. I am sorry about that. I did go right there, but just a little later." She shook her head and gave me a look that silenced me. I thought of all the pain and anxiety she had had to endure with Giorgio's absence, not even knowing whether he was alive. My own actions— at least this story of Klaus—suddenly seemed so ridiculous and shallow.

Chapter Eight

Mother and Father were already seated at the table when I arrived for dinner that night. The room, formerly a servant's bedroom, left just enough space for us to sit at the round wooden table and for Rosa to serve. As usual, the table was covered with a simple white cotton cloth and set for three, the place nearest the door left empty.

I noticed that Mother had changed from her gardening clothes into an immaculately pressed shirtwaist, every hair slicked back into a neat bun at the back of her neck. I could feel her cool eyes sizing me up: my hair crimped with humidity, loose tendrils glued to my forehead, and my old dusty pink blouse—a size too small, with a child's puffed sleeves—clinging tightly to my breasts, its tails on one side not tucked into my skirt. Father glanced at me, then looked away as I took my place between them and whisked the napkin into my lap without unfolding it.

No one spoke. I fixed my gaze on the small terra-cotta pitcher in the middle of the table that Rosa had filled with a fistful of herbs: spiky rosemary, leafy sprigs of oregano, and three stiff swords of lavender crowned with violet tufts. Then I slowly began running my finger down the curved handle of my fork, as if I were stroking the silky spine of Valentino, my favorite cat. The walls pressed in, squeezing the tension in the room, making the space seem more confining than it already was.

Rosa broke the ice by coming in with a steaming platter of *spaghetti con pollo e pomodori.* The pungent smell of garlic and tomato sauce filled the room and forced us all to breathe a little easier.

Mama lifted a birdlike portion onto her plate. "Oh, Rosa, this smells delicious," she said. I piled a generous helping onto mine, and Papa emptied the platter. When Rosa had gone, Mother cleared her throat. She never launched into a conversation without delicately announcing herself first.

"Now, Giovanna, I know this is difficult, but let's talk about what's next for you. Your father and I do not want you to continue at the School of Santa Maria."

I stiffened but said nothing.

"I wonder, dear, if you've heard about the nursery school group that has been started at the Church of Santa Clara. I know they have a dozen or so children—just the very young ones."

I took a quick swallow of water from the thick tumbler and set it down so heavily a little sloshed on the table. "Mother, please." My jaw was tense and barely moved. "I *hate* working with children. I really do." I shook my head. "Frankly, I've been thinking anyway of not continuing at the school. They drove me crazy, if you really want to know."

Father laughed. "Well, now you tell us." He looked at Mother and added sarcastically, "We thought you were enjoying your work all this time, but I guess it wasn't the children that kept you interested, eh?"

Mother shifted in her chair and concentrated on winding spaghetti around her fork.

"So, now that you don't like children," he added, "I have just the solution. Harvest is coming up in the next few weeks, the grapes ready for crush. There's plenty to do around here. How about if I put you to work helping me? No children in sight—guaranteed."

God help me. That was the last thing I wanted to do, to be tethered to Father all day long. In desperation, I piped up. "No, Papa." I looked from him to Mother, then back again. "No. The harvest is one thing, but I really want to be part of the war in some way. If I can't fight against the Nazis, I just want to be part of it. Violetta tells me they need help at her clinic. I thought that might be a good idea, and I could pick up some medical skills that I could use for the rest of my life—"

Father broke in. "Well, damn it, who says making wine and olive oil isn't helping the cause—" But Mother cut him off, her mouth still full of food.

"Is that the one Marchesa Falconieri is operating on her property? They say there are more POWs and wounded partisans every day." She looked across the table, almost pleading. "Enrico, she does have a point. And maybe Giovanna could pick up some news of—"

I knew whom she was about to mention. I focused on my now empty plate, bracing myself for a round of tears, but none came. Only silence. I saw Rosa come in to clear the plates, and then I looked at Mother. She was pale and staring straight ahead—wide-eyed— holding her hands to her throat. I froze.

Father stood up. "Jesus! She's choking; we've got to hit her on the back." He lunged in her direction, but Rosa stepped coolly in his path and put up her hands to stop him.

"No, no, signore, please don't. I've

seen this too many times—that just makes things worse."

She walked behind Mother's chair, leaned over, and grabbed her from behind, lifting her up and shaking her out like a rag doll. A piece of chicken flew out onto the tablecloth, followed by coughing and the sound of sucking air. Then Mother put her head on her folded arms and collapsed in racking sobs. "Oh, thank you, Rosa, dear. I couldn't get my breath. I just—"

But it wasn't about the choking. The tears were about Giorgio, and the floodgates had just been reopened. I ran to her side, leaned over her, and stroked her back, hugging her to me. "It's okay, Mother; really it is. Giorgio's fine. I just know it." I looked at Rosa, but her back was turned. "I'll use my time at the clinic to find out everything I can. I'll ask everyone I see. I think this will be the right thing for me to do."

Father stood straight, observing the scene. Without a word, he went back to his chair and pushed it in slowly.

I stood tall myself, looking directly at him. "I will talk with Violetta about the possibility of volunteering at the clinic. I also plan to make a visit to Sister Graziella at the convent to apologize to her."

℘

The next morning after church, I sidled up to Violetta and linked arms with her. "Will you take a walk with me?" I hoped the pressure I was putting on her arm would convey the urgency of my need.

She broke away from her parents with a wave and led me out toward the road to town. "You're pinching me. What's going on?"

"Sister Graziella told my father." I was breathing fast, leaning into her. "They want me to stop working at the school."

"I'm not sorry, Giovanna. I want you to get away from that man too."

"But what will I do with my time?" I hoped Violetta would think right away of the clinic, but I knew it wasn't so simple. The two of us had been best friends for years, but we were competitive too. It seemed that we got along best when we kept our involvements separate.

When we were ten, there was a school festival that included footraces and other mock Olympic events. Violetta and I were both the fastest in the class, but she was taller than I was by at least a foot, giving her a natural edge. She beat me consistently in the trials and even suggested that I sign up for the long jump instead. I still cringe to think of it, but before the race, as we were changing clothes, I dropped a small pebble into the toe of her shoe. The gun went off, and Violetta shot ahead, but as we rounded the curve at the other end of the oval track, I watched her begin to limp a little and give her foot a quick shake. It was just enough of a pause to let me catch up and pass her in the home stretch.

"Nice going, Giovanna," she said, refusing to meet my eye. "I had a darn stone in my shoe, and I just couldn't run the way I usually do." She won every race after that.

I never confessed my dirty trick—either to her or to the priest—but I think I had always expected God to even the score, particularly at moments like this.

I waited silently, feeling her inner debate. The clinic was clearly her territory, the perfect outlet for her particular interests. She had a nurturing, patient temperament, just right for working with the sick and wounded. As usual, her warmth and her inclusive nature won out, reminding me what a heel I'd been all those years before. "But how about the clinic?" she said. "We need help desperately." She stopped and took me by the shoulders, beaming. "We could be together every day—it would be fun. Please say you'll come and talk with them."

§

I had kept my church clothes on, which made for rough going on the way to the gazebo. The path I'd been traveling was beginning to show evidence of use, and it occurred to me that I should vary my route from week to week to avoid giving our meeting place away. So I decided to take the long way around—partly to let the path grow over and partly to save my skirt and good shoes by walking on well-traveled roads. As I walked, a horse-drawn wagon appeared far up ahead, then slowly grew larger as it moved in my direction. I could see that it was piled high with hay and that two people were sitting on the bench. Then I recognized Serafo and Esta, the farming couple who were overseers for the large estate adjoining ours. They were friends of Tonino and Catarina's, and had known me since I was very small.

Esta was dark complexioned and grossly overweight, the navy cotton of her full skirt stretched tight over the flesh of spreading thighs. Her hair, mostly silver now with age, was parted in the middle and pulled back into a tight bun, making her round, weathered face appear all the more manly and severe. Serafo, Esta's physical opposite, sat erect with the reins in his hands, his skeletal frame occupying a mere quarter of the space on the seat.

"Giovanna, is it really you, darling?" Esta called as they pulled to a stop next to me. Their horse leaned his neck down and began loudly pulling clumps of grass out of the dry, stony earth.

"Yes, Esta." I smiled brightly. "How nice to see you both."

"What brings you to this neck of the

woods?" she asked. "I don't think I've ever seen you out walking so far from home." I looked past them, my eyes darting back and forth. I knew the turn to the convent was behind me, but I was desperate for an excuse. "I was, uh, just heading for Saint Agnes to see Sister Graziella."

"Oh, well, dear, you've missed the turn altogether. It's about a half mile behind you. Serafo, we must give Giovanna a lift. It's not too far out of our way."

"No, no—I'd really prefer to walk. It's such a beautiful day." I tried to look relaxed and in the mood for physical exercise.

"We won't hear of it; will we, Serafo? Now, Giovanna, you climb up on this wagon right this instant. We'll take you there, and we won't take no for an answer."

Serafo reached down and offered me his bony hand. What choice did I have?

"Easy does it, now. Up with you, young lady." He moved all the way to the end of the bench, and I wedged myself in between the two of them, my stomach clenched like a tight fist. I was already so late to meet Giorgio, and now surely I was going to miss him altogether. Worse, going to the convent was no longer a choice I had to make.

The cart bumped and rattled along the dirt road. I inhaled dust and the acrid smell of Esta's underarms while she fired questions at me: How was Catarina; what was it like living with Germans in the house; hadn't she heard I was working at the school; had we any word from Giorgio? I answered her inquiries as vaguely and casually as I could until at last we reached the long driveway lined with arborvitae that curved up to the convent of Saint Agnes.

I tried to look relaxed as I waved good-bye, but I was dizzy with fear. I hadn't had time to plan this moment, and now the reality of what I was about to do was all too present. I knocked timidly on the huge carved wooden door and stood shifting from one foot to the other, hoping no one would hear. After three or four minutes, the latch clicked and the door swung slowly open. A nun I had never seen before stood before me. Like Sister Graziella, she had an open, kind face, but she was thin and even shorter than I was. "Yes? May I help you?"

"Good day, Sister. I'm . . . I'm here to see Sister Graziella."

"Is she expecting you?"

"No, but . . ." I hesitated. "I have been working with her at the School of Santa Maria."

"You must be Giovanna then!" Her smile brightened. "Graziella speaks of you so often. Come in, dear, won't you?"

She took my arm and led me to a small group of stiff-backed chairs in the corner of the entry hall. I watched her face to see just how recently she might have heard anything about me, but her welcoming posture didn't waver. "I'll just go and tell Graziella you're here."

I sat there for five minutes, then ten. It was eerily quiet. With the large front door closed again, there was no open access to the outdoors, so even the birdsong was silenced. Occasionally quick steps echoed down a corridor off to the left that was barricaded by an iron gate, but no one appeared. At last, I heard the measured, intentional gait I knew so well. Sister Graziella quietly opened the iron barrier, closing it as softly as she could behind her. I stood up and instinctively bowed my head, staring at the floor. My scalp tingled at the top where I felt she must be looking at me.

"I am so glad you came," she said carefully. "Let's find a place where we can have a private talk, shall we?" I followed her down the hall to a small parlor. She invited me in, shutting the door to ensure our privacy. We sat knee to knee in two comfortable stuffed armchairs in a corner of the room. A window was open, letting a breeze gently ripple the filmy white curtain that let in the light. Unexpectedly, tears welled up and began spilling down my cheeks. I sobbed out loud and leaned over, not wanting to look at her.

"Sister Graziella, I don't know what to say." I hiccupped. "I'm just so sorry that you had to . . . to see me like that."

"The problem is not my having had to see," she said. "The problem is what you did."

"Oh, I know, I know. It was so wrong—

wrong in every way. But I want you to know that I . . . I . . . Nothing really happened, Sister. I would have ended it even if you had not been there."

She looked at me long and hard. "Lieutenant Eisenmann is really a very kind and sensitive human being, isn't he?" she said. "Do you love him, dear?"

"No," I answered quickly, and looked away. "I am so attracted to him, and I really care for him, but, Sister Graziella, I don't know if you can . . ."

"Take your time, dear. Trust me. I'm not as ethereal as you think I might be. I spent a few years living before I made my commitment here." She waited patiently while I took that in.

"No. I've been a little bit in love with Klaus, and it's become something I think about all the time. But I don't really *know* him. I can't say that I care deeply about him—not in any life-changing way."

"He is married, isn't he?" she said. I nodded, and tears welled up again. "And, I would imagine, he is lonely too."

I nodded again and added, "He even has a baby son." My face contorted, and I leaned over and put my head in my hands. "I had no right to stay that night, to be alone with him, but I . . ."

"You're young, dear, and so naturally ready for this kind of thing." She looked dreamily out the window. "There is nothing wrong with physical intimacy and the expression of love. God has surely designed us to communicate in this profound way, but it must be accompanied by deep commitment and in the context of marriage."

"I knew it was too much too soon. I think that's why I stopped him." I looked at her, wondering whether I could truly trust her as much as I was feeling I could. "And the war, that makes everything more complicated."

"Yes, the war. The war indeed." She smiled. "Giovanna, I want to say something, to be clear about something."

"What is that?"

"I admire your openness, your guilelessness. I find it a valuable asset to be able to look beyond obvious categories and barriers and extend your feelings. You sought out the individual soul in Klaus and tried to relate to that, not to his persona as a German soldier."

"Yes, yes—exactly!"

"But sometimes," she went on, shaking her head, "sometimes we must balance one value against the other and weigh them carefully. I am sure there are many, many nice people who are members of Hitler's army. But in time of war, we must—we *must*—commit ourselves to overcoming a greater collective evil. Sometimes I wish the Church were clearer on that score." She looked away.

"So the fact that he is a German soldier should take precedence over the goodness of his soul?"

"I think you should think twice about entrusting any German soldier with your very innocence, your precious innermost self—even if he is as fair and thoughtful a person as the lieutenant clearly is."

I was so relieved and so grateful, I came closer and hugged her tightly, resting my head on her shoulder.

"I want to emphasize, Giovanna, that although I understand, I am truly disappointed in you, and I will expect you to make amends for this incident in some way. I want to think about what that will be, and I think you should too. You have been to confession?"

"Yes, Papa made me go right away to Don Federico."

"And you did what was required?"

"Yes, Sister, I did."

"I wonder if it wouldn't be best for you to look for another way to spend your days, to leave the school."

"I have been thinking about that."

"I'm not sure that's a punishment at all, is it?" There was a twinkle in her eye.

I nodded, and the sudden thought of Sister Elena made me flush hotly. "Does Sister Elena"—I looked at the floor—"hate me even more?"

"I haven't told Elena a thing. Let's just say that what happened will remain a little secret between you and me."

I threw my arms around her. "How can I thank you?"

"What you learn from this will be my reward. And don't forget—I will still expect some sort of compensation. Now, is there anything you would like me to tell Lieutenant Eisenmann?"

I had been planning to go back to the

school, to talk with Klaus myself. But now it seemed clear that I wasn't welcome there. My never showing up again would surely cause him to worry and to blame himself for my having left.

"Maybe I could write him a letter and you could deliver it tomorrow."

She nodded and led me to a small desk in the parlor, where there was a stack of stationery engraved with, *Convent of Saint Agnes,* and an etching of the old stone building perched on top of a hill. Sister Graziella excused herself. "You may seal the envelope, dear, and leave it with the doorkeeper. I'll take it to him tomorrow." She crossed herself and left the room.

It took me quite a while to compose the note, and I made so many false starts that I ruined five sheets of the stationery before I finally wrote:

Dear Klaus,
Thank you so much for the delicious picnic dinner. I have decided that the medical clinic can make better use of my time and energy, so I will not be returning

**to the School of Santa Maria. I
hope that the war ends soon and
that you make it safely home to
your wife, Mathilde, and your
baby son.**
Very sincerely yours,
Giovanna Bellini

I gathered up all the scraps of the
earlier notes and folded them into my
pocket. I stood up and turned to leave
with the final note in my hand. To this
day I am stunned at what I did next.
Perhaps it was the schoolgirl rebellion
that seemed to ignite in me in this sanctified place. Perhaps it was the rush of
youthful hormones that pulled me back
to the possibilities on that closet floor.
Certainly it was an irrational and impet-
uous act. I rushed back to the small
desk, took another piece of paper and
an envelope out of the drawer. Before I
could waver, I scrawled:

**Klaus—I must see you. Meet me
in the playground Wednesday
night at five—**
Giovanna

I sealed that note as well, stuffed the other one in my pocket, and handed the new one to the trim little sister at the door, saying, "Please give this to Sister Graziella." Then I ran like the wind down the convent's long drive and headed toward home.

Chapter Nine

Violetta's clinic was hidden away on the grounds of a vast estate owned by Marchese and Marchesa Falconieri. Like our own, only much larger, this complex was a collection of twenty or so small working farms scattered over three thousand acres. The features of the *fattoria*, or central farm, were clustered around the main sixteenth-century villa and included formal gardens, the granary, the cellars, the oil presses, and the dairy.

The marchesa herself was a bundle of energy—of English and American origin—who had moved to Italy at eight years old with her mother after her father died. She grew up surrounded by the best families of Florence with names like Rucelli, Strozzi, Frescobaldi, and Niccolini, living in a community of British émigrés, but she went to Italian schools, spoke Italian like a native, and was at home with Italian history and literature. Eventually she married the wealthy Italian marchese Leonardo Falconieri, and was a popular, trusted member of the extended Lucca community. I knew her only slightly, my parents having introduced her to me on several occasions, but she was reputed to be not only generous and intelligent, but a woman of considerable courage.

Since their purchase of the property (now renamed Villa Falconieri) in the mid-twenties, and thanks to financial help from Mussolini and the Fascist party, they had significantly expanded the business and improved the lives of their peasant farmers.

So far Villa Falconieri had been spared occupation by German soldiers, but like so many of us in German-controlled northern Italy, the family walked a thin line between doing whatever it could to aid those fighting Hitler and avoiding detection, which would mean certain punishment or even death.

The word among her friends—and my mother was one—was that the marchesa had begun by offering food, shelter, and often first aid to a succession of escaped prisoners of war. Her English was a natural magnet for those lost souls, and her reputation as a warm, understanding, exceedingly generous provider became known in close circles. She used her own network of farmhouses to keep these fugitives hidden for a brief time, then sent them on their way. Soon, however, as word spread throughout the Serchio River valley, demand forced her to create a fully operating secret clinic, undiscovered by the Germans.

There was an ancient stone structure on the property that had originally been built as a chapel. Mass was still celebrated there on feast days for the farmers and their families who lived on the estate, the ancient bell in its tower tolling slowly to draw the residents throughout the vineyards and fields to gather on those now increasingly rare occasions. Connected to the sanctuary at the rear was a two-story stone annex that, over the decades, had variously served as a kindergarten, a rest house for pilgrims to Rome, a schoolhouse for local children, and now as a makeshift hospital for victims of war.

At first, the marchesa had made do with help from the farmers' wives who lived about her own estate, but the demand and the pressure on them had become too great. She found a couple of trained nurses, whom she paid, and then recruited young women from the village like Violetta to work regular shifts once the nurses had trained them.

❦

I arrived at the clinic on Monday morning and, as instructed, I camouflaged my bicycle in the thick underbrush before entering the building. Coming in from the bright summer day and climbing the dark, rough staircase, dank with mildew and hemmed in by moss-covered stone walls, to the second floor, I found it hard to see. But as my eyes adjusted, I could make out two rows of cots, one along each wall of the large open space. A central aisle divided the room in two halves. I nearly gagged from the smell—a powerful mixture of disinfectant layered over the stench of burned or rotting flesh, unwashed bodies, and full bedpans. Ammonia fumes assaulted the back of my throat, and my eyes began to water.

I could see the outlines of bodies on half the cots, and four or five women were busily moving throughout the space. On my immediate left, a curtain of army blankets had been strung from a frame of pipes, and a deep moan rose from behind the folds of rough gray fabric. On my right, a rope hung from the ceiling, cradling a man's ankle and holding up his leg encased in a plaster cast. All I could see was a tangle of greasy black hair on the pillow, his face turned away. The rest of his body lay covered by a rumpled, stained cotton sheet.

Two other men, propped up against their pillows, chattered amiably from adjoining cots, the smoke from their cigarettes curling lazily above them and merging into a single cloud.

As I stood there, taking all of this in, a slim, erect figure walked briskly in my direction. She was casually dressed, a loose kimono-style smock over her tailored shirt and slacks, her light brown curly hair tousled in an attractive bob.

"Giovanna! You're here! I was delighted when Violetta said we might expect you this morning." The marchesa flashed me a warm smile and took hold of both my upper arms in a gentle squeeze. "How is your mother, dear? It's been so long since I've seen her."

"Oh, she's fine, thank you." I tried to focus on her face, but my gaze kept wandering off to take in all that was happening around me. "She asked me to give you her best."

"Oh, thank you. You are more than welcome here." Up close, I could see her pale eyes were blue, tending to lavender, like flax blossoms. Her skin was pinkish in tone, almost translucent, and she had a sprinkling of freckles over her nose. "I believe you'll find Violetta at the last bed on this end. She can show you around and give you a sense of what we're about."

I walked slowly in the direction where she had pointed. I passed one of the nurses, holding a man's head as he vomited into a pail beside his bed. On another cot, the sheet was pulled all the way up and over the head of the body lying there. Could he be dead?

Violetta saw me and gave an excited wave. "Giovanna! You made it. Come here—I want you to meet Frederick." She grabbed me and whispered in my ear, "He's my favorite at the moment."

A blond, strikingly handsome man lay there under a sheet, his curly hair resting on a rolled army blanket. He looked up at me and smiled. "*Buon giorno.*" He pronounced it *bahn jornow,* with an English lilt. "We've been having some Italian lessons," she said, "and Frederick is doing really well. This is my friend Giovanna." And she placed me to his left side, moving back with practiced confidence to his right. As I watched, she drew the sheet down, revealing a leg wrapped with strips of linen cloth that were soaked through with blood, much of it still brilliant red. Violetta kept up a steady, cheerful banter with Frederick, who winced with pain while she began slowly unwinding the bandages. With each turn, I could see more and more of the mangled flesh that hung in strips around an exposed bone gleaming white in the dim light. Suddenly the back of my neck felt as if it were floating. I swallowed rapidly over and over as an irresistible pressure pushed up in my throat. I retched and doubled over as the floor came up to meet me.

When I opened my eyes again, Violetta was leaning over me, fanning my face with her handkerchief. "Giovanna—Giovanna—are you all right?" My field of vision came slowly back into focus; then the utter humiliation of my position descended on me. How could I—healthy, robust, and young—have fainted in the midst of all these soldiers suffering from horrific diseases and injuries? I sat up, my head throbbing where it had hit the stone floor, and looked around. A couple of women were looking at me curiously, but for the most part, they had stuck to their duties and ignored me.

Now I had let Violetta down as well. Her friend had turned out to be a weak sissy who couldn't even look at an injured leg without keeling over. I was furious at myself. I brushed my skirt off with both hands, smoothed my hair, and sought to convey a sense of both seriousness and commitment.

"I can't imagine how that happened. Silly me, I skipped breakfast this morning," I lied, "and the hunger must have overtaken me. . . ." I noticed, to my relief, that the marchesa was nowhere in sight.

"It's all right, Giovanna. It happens. Don't give it a second thought," said Violetta, thrusting a pan of warm water into my hands. "Now, hold this while I rinse out these bandages." The red blood swirled into the basin as she squeezed the strips of linen. *No worse than my own menstrual blood when I wash out my underwear,* I thought determinedly. *This is only blood, just natural. These people are healing, getting better, and it is part of the process.* I managed a weak smile at Frederick there on the pillow.

"Where are you from in England?" I asked, and had to repeat it slowly, wondering if I could manage to put together a few sentences in my schoolroom English.

The morning dragged on endlessly. I shadowed Violetta, fetching instruments or water or new bandages as she went from bed to bed, constantly cheerful, warm, and caring. I admired her with every inch of my being. I didn't faint again, but several times I had to look away as she emptied a bedpan or wiped up vomit from a freshly made bed. Try as I might, I just couldn't *feel* the kind of desire to heal and help these people that Violetta clearly had. I was shy around them, impatient with their pain and complaints, and disgusted with their bodily fluids and open wounds.

At last it was time for us to take a break. We sat outside in the warm sunlight, eating our lunch together, sprawled on the long grass. "I just don't know if I can do this," I said. "I'm just not you— not anything like you. I'm not sure I'm cut out for this kind of work. But—" I stopped. "Violetta, can I trust you? Really trust you?"

"Of course. What are you talking about? Of course you can."

I knew that widening the circle of confidantes was dangerous, but there was no way I could do this job right and keep my pledge of support to Giorgio. "I'm not really here because I want to work in the clinic," I said. "In fact, when I think about you spending day after day with these sick and dying soldiers, I just don't know how you do it."

"I really do love it," she said, looking me straight in the eyes. "I just know this is my calling."

"And it clearly is," I answered quickly. "But I don't think it's mine."

"So find something else." She was getting irritated now, as if I had somehow belittled the clinic and her role in it. "I won't be hurt if you don't come."

"Here's the problem, Violetta. I need the job as a cover."

"A cover?"

I bent over and worked a patch of long grass, stroking it, braiding it, trying to decide whether I should tell her anything at all. Then the story began spilling out: the note from Giorgio, the meetings at the gazebo, the Fox, the supplies I had taken to the Santinis' cellar. "I just feel that right now the war effort itself—stopping the Germans and driving them out of here—is the most important thing. And, of course, my brother. I want to stay in touch with him however that's possible, and make sure he's safe." My shoulders ached from the tension of it all. I worried that the very telling of it was some sort of a betrayal of Giorgio. But what choice did I have?

Violetta looked away and sat thoughtfully for a long time. "You know, it's odd," she said. "When I think about traveling around the countryside, searching for supplies right under the nose of the Germans, having meetings with partisan soldiers—that takes a kind of courage that I'm sure I don't have. I feel secure here, hidden away inside the clinic, where I don't think we're so likely to be attacked. I guess we're all made differently. I think what you're doing is brave and loving and really important. So let's figure out how we can arrange a cover for you. You go now, and I'll ask around, see what we can do."

"Without giving me or Giorgio away?"

"Do you trust me or don't you?"

℘

I knew the schedule at the School of Santa Maria so well. It would be rare for anyone to be left at five p.m., either the nuns or the German soldiers. On Wednesday evening, I strolled casually into the vicinity of the school, pausing and peeking through the rear hedge. All was quiet. I waited, watching for any sign of Klaus, listening for the sound of his footsteps inside. Nothing. It was five p.m., exactly—I knew that. I squeezed between two bushes and entered the schoolyard. No one was in sight. Maybe he was just watching from inside, I thought. I sat on the swing, where I knew he could see me, and quietly rocked back and forth, my feet gently scraping the ground.

I had no interest in a permanent relationship with Klaus. I was clear on that. And he, of course, was married. Yet I couldn't deny my feelings for him. We had forged too close a bond in the last months for me simply to disappear. I wasn't sure exactly what his expectations were, but I wanted to find out. I was just drifting off into a fantasy of his warm breath on my ear when a tap on my shoulder made me jump. I nearly fell off the swing as I wrenched around. There he was, standing behind me with the note in his hand.

"I was not sure what to expect when Sister Elena handed this to me and I saw the writing paper from the convent," he said with a smile. "I've missed you since our little picnic."

Did he say Sister Elena? I tucked a lock of unruly hair behind my ear. *He must have been mistaken. He must have meant Graziella.* I smiled back at him, and he drew me to him, holding my head against his chest and stroking my hair. "That's my beauty, my treasure," he said.

I leaned into him, feeling his heart beat beneath the rough fabric of his uniform jacket, and put my arms around his waist.

"Come inside," he said. "There is no

one here." Then he laughed, adding, "No one yet, anyway." He took his jacket off and slung it over his shoulder.

We settled in the kitchen, probably because of our memories of the picnic, and sat down together on a couple of the small chairs. He leaned forward eagerly, his elbows on his knees. "How are you, my beauty?"

"Sister Graziella told my father what she saw the other night," I began.

"And?"

"Well, my parents are very angry."

He nodded. "Yes, I can imagine that."

"I went to the convent and spoke with Graziella myself, and she doesn't want me to work at the school anymore."

He gave a quick little nod and looked away. "This is no problem. We can meet here in the evenings. You will bring sunshine into my life, just when the sun is getting low." He leaned forward, taking my hands and kissing me gently, as he always did.

"But, Klaus, you are married. I think about Mathilde, about your baby, and I just don't know. I . . ."

He stood up suddenly and began

walking back and forth as he talked. "Giovanna, who knows how long we will be here or what could happen? The Allies could come along at any time. I could be killed just setting a mine on one of the bridges. Life is so uncertain that we have to live as if we have one day only." He took my hand again. His eyes were beginning to tear up. "You are precious to me, and I—life here—would be empty if I could not see your wonderful smile. *Ja*—you are my home now, so far away from Germany."

I could see that he meant it, every word of it. But as he talked, I became more and more convinced that my situation was not the same as his. I was not far away from home. This was my life—my real one—and I needed to live it in the best way I could. Not to mention the danger he posed to my work with Giorgio and the risk of discovery. Now it was my turn to stand up. "It just doesn't feel right to me. It isn't what I want in my own life right now. I've found another place to work, and . . . I just can't come back here."

He rose to his feet and grabbed me,

pulling me tightly to him. "No, don't say these things, Giovanna. You must not . . . you must not make me sad."

I pushed him gently away with both arms. "I don't want to make you sad. I don't. But . . ."

"If you make me sad, then you will make me angry too. I don't want to be angry with you, my treasure."

I was crying now. This was hard, so hard. "I'm not angry with you, Klaus, and I don't want to hurt you, but I just can't see you anymore. I have another life to lead."

He stared at me. "Well, then, you go ahead and lead your life. I will not be part of it." He grabbed his coat, turned, and left, slamming the cafeteria door in his wake.

The sound reverberated in my ears for hours.

℃

Violetta showed up at Villa Farfalla the next evening. She greeted my parents with a big hug. "We are so thrilled that Giovanna will be working at the clinic," she said, avoiding my eyes. "The work is so important, and she will be a valuable member of the team. Of course, the hours are unpredictable, and emergencies do happen. I just wanted to be sure that you've accepted that and that you will be willing to let her come and go when she's needed."

Mother nodded. "We're just so thankful for the work the marchesa is doing," she said. "I don't know how I'd sleep at night if there weren't someplace around here for the wounded to be taken care of. And for Giovanna to be part of it . . . we're so pleased."

I thought of the marchesa, her smock spattered with blood, parsing her valuable time between nursing the wounded and finding shelter for escaped prisoners—not to mention her own family. Mother had no idea how dedicated and brave the marchesa truly was—my mother, who passed her days overseeing the garden and planning the family meals. She spent her mental energy resenting the Germans, worrying about Giorgio, and feeling sorry for herself; she had no energy left to actually do anything to help.

I looked at Father. "What do you say, Papa? Are you sure it's all right with you?"

He looked at both of us. "Well, I've never thought of Giovanna as much of a caregiver type. But I guess war makes fools of all of us. If that's what you want to try, *piccola,* I've got no objection. Just don't faint and hit your head." He looked at Mother, rolled his eyes, and laughed out loud.

I felt hot tears well up and fought them down. Without looking at him, I took Violetta by the arm. "Let's go into the garden and you can begin my schooling right now."

When we were alone, I grimaced. "I just can't please him no matter what I do." We walked to a bench and sat down. "But now, tell me: What have you arranged? It sounds perfect from what you said to my parents."

She smiled mysteriously at me. "You always were the organizing type," she said. "How would you like to be in charge of the supply closet? You know, straightening the shelves and making sure everything is in its place."

"Are you kidding? That's all?" My relief must have been obvious, because she started laughing hysterically.

"You thought I'd make you empty bedpans? Giovanna, it's no problem. It's all volunteer anyway, and I just told them you were good at that sort of thing." She sobered. "If I were you, though, I'd come upstairs now and then so the marchesa and other people get to know you. Make it known when you are there. Then, if anyone asks, they'll be ready to corroborate your cover."

"Okay. I'll try not to faint and hit my head while I'm at it."

Violetta laughed and got up to leave.

"Wait." I grabbed her. "Before you go, I have to tell you about what happened last night."

Violetta listened with full attention. At the end, I added, "The strange thing is that he said it was Sister Elena who had given him the note, not Sister Graziella. Do you think it's possible that Elena found it and opened it? There was no envelope in his hand. I was so absorbed in our conversation, I didn't think about it last night."

Violetta thought for a moment. "I'm sorry, but you know how relieved I am that Klaus is out of the picture. But what about Sister Graziella? If Elena did open it, she probably showed Graziella the note. She might even be planning to tell your parents you decided to meet Klaus. And none of them knows yet how it all turned out."

"You're right—after all the trust she put in me, I'll just have to find a way to see her again and beg her forgiveness." And my parents'. I hadn't even considered the possibility that she would show them the note. "I just can't worry about it now, Violetta. There is such important work to do."

Chapter Ten

Friday night was the eve of St. John's Day, a celebration I had always looked forward to until the war called a halt to our rituals. Named for John the Baptist, the holiday paid homage to water, fire, and plants, coming as it did nearly on the summer solstice and at the front end of the growing season. On that night, in its long, lingering dusk, we always lit bonfires in front of houses, in the court-yards, and along the lanes. People threw kindling, old furniture, bundled straw—whatever would burn—on these fires until the flames reached up, crackling hungrily with a fierce, hot heat that could purge a person's soul. The whole area was dotted with these fires, almost like earth stars twinkling as the last of the light faded into darkness.

The Germans had imposed a curfew in the village from six p.m. until six a.m. The SS soldiers, who wore black uniforms with a zigzag yellow lightning sign on their collars, patrolled the streets.

Out in the country, where we lived, there was not as much surveillance, and a few of my friends had hatched a plan to light a bonfire Friday night—just to prove that it was still our country, that we could be who we wanted to be. It was a cheeky thing to do, but we were young and heedless.

Two boys—Flavio and Luigi—were the ringleaders. They were seventeen and still too young to be recruited to fight, but they were by no means safe. Boys like those two were constantly on the lookout, living in fear of being snatched up for labor by Nazi soldiers. That made them mad enough to want to pull off a rebellious bonfire. The two of them had been working all week, secretly stashing wood and straw and other burnable items near the place in the lane where they had decided to have the fire.

Flavio, who had light, curly hair and a sweet smile, was Violetta's cousin. I loved him for his shy manner and the way he doted on animals. He would never have come up with this idea, but he would do anything his best friend, Luigi, said to do. Luigi Santini, our neighbor, was a lot taller, all gangly limbs and big feet, with a bad complexion. It was Flavio who had worked up Violetta's enthusiasm about the fire, and she had recruited me to come along. I had always loved the St. John's Eve fires, and I was ready for some excitement.

We had dinner at home as usual that night. So far there seemed to be no word from Graziella about my note to Klaus. Toward the end of the meal, I flexed my jaw until a yawn began spreading into a real one. "I guess it's been a long week for me. I can hardly keep my eyes open," I said.

"Maybe you should think about limiting your new schedule at the clinic to the mornings," my mother said.

That was the last thing I wanted to do, but I yawned again. "I'll think about it, Mother, but now, if it's all right with you, I'm just going to go to bed early." I got up and slid my chair carefully back to the table. "Good night, Mama." I kissed her. "Sleep well." I kissed Papa on the cheek and went to my room, closing the door.

Outside the open window, it was still light. I thought I smelled a whiff of smoke, but that was probably just my imagination. I picked up a book and stared blankly at the pages, listening hard.

After dinner was cleared away, my parents spent a half hour in the tiny parlor before going into their room and shutting the door. I put on my softest, most comfortable shoes, pulled on a sweater for the night chill, and cracked my door as quietly as I could. No one was about. I tiptoed silently down the stairs and out into the thickening dusk. It was about a quarter to ten.

The group was already gathered in the lane half a mile or so from Villa Farfalla's front gate, silhouetted in front of the flames that were taking hold. I came up behind Violetta and surprised her with a quick hug. "I was beginning to wonder whether you were going to get away," she said, taking my hand. Sparks were flying as Flavio and Luigi piled more and more kindling on the fire.

Then I noticed a third boy working with them. Ignazio Lazzari had not been part of the original plan, but he had heard about it somehow and, as Violetta whispered to me, had already been there when they arrived. He was in the boys' class at school and was a notorious troublemaker: loud and rough, with a perpetual sneer on his face.

"What's the matter, Giovanna, have a hard time sneaking out?" He laughed a little too loudly and gave me a quick shove toward the fire.

"Hey, watch it!" I shoved him back, folded my arms, and backed away. Then I noticed an army canteen hanging over his shoulder on a canvas strap. He took a swig.

"Want some grappa?" His lip curled into what I supposed was a smile.

"No, thanks." I retreated to Violetta's side.

A chair with a frayed rush seat went onto the fire and the flames leaped up with a vengeance; then a whole bale of bound hay sent a shower of sparks in an alarming arc over our heads. "Maybe that's enough for now," called Flavio. He was trying to keep his voice game and friendly, but I could tell he was getting worried. There was no way we could keep this fire small now. It must have been visible for miles.

Underneath the crackling and roaring of the fire, I heard the low rumble of an approaching vehicle. The boys, who were closer to the fire, didn't hear it, but Violetta's head turned at the same moment as mine. In the low light, beyond the halo of flames, we could just make out the outline of an open military jeep. We looked at each other, wide-eyed and silent, as it headed our way. Then it pulled to a stop just across the street next to a low stucco wall. Four German soldiers were outlined there in full uniform.

Ignazio, whose back was to the jeep,

took another swallow from the canteen. "Take that, you sausage swine, you Nazi vermin," he shouted, fluttering an open book onto the flames. "Let's see who really owns this town."

Doors slammed loudly, and the soldiers got out. As they came closer into the glow of the fire, their faces were clearly visible. One of them was Klaus. He looked straight at me but registered no surprise. He looked handsome and powerful, and I felt a flare of regret along with foreboding fear.

The three boys saw the soldiers now and knotted together, staring back at them like cornered game.

Two wore the SS emblem on their black shirts; Klaus and the other man wore the green khaki uniforms of the construction corps. An SS officer strode over and poked a finger straight into Ignazio's chest, knocking him back a step or two. "Just where is the sausage swine? Just who you call the vermin?" He yanked the canteen off his shoulder, took a whiff, and threw it on the fire. He grabbed Ignazio by the back of the neck, and the other SS officer grabbed both

Flavio and Luigi roughly, one on each arm.

Klaus broke from the group and came over to where Violetta and I were standing. "Are these friends of yours, Giovanna?" He said it sarcastically, loud enough for everyone to hear.

I nodded, looking at the ground. I was frozen.

"You know it is *verboten* to be out here like this."

I nodded again, not looking up.

He walked off to the side and motioned the other soldiers over to him. They all put their heads together, holding the boys off, and talked in low voices. One said, "*Jawohl,*" and slapped Klaus on the back. The others chuckled. They let Flavio and Luigi go with a shove; then they headed back to the jeep with Ignazio in tow. Klaus turned back to the group. "You will put out this fire now. We will come back in one half hour. If you are still here, you will all come with us." Before he turned to go, he stared back at me, poker-faced, mocking, and held my gaze.

I took Violetta's hand and dragged

her off, leaving the boys to put out the fire.

I was crying, inconsolable. "That was Klaus," I sobbed. "It's my fault, what's happened to Ignazio. We'll never see him again."

She put her arm around me. "*Shhh.* You don't know that it's your fault. Really, you don't. Maybe they would have taken all three of them. Maybe Klaus saved Luigi and Flavio because of you."

She might have been right, but that was not the way it felt to me. Klaus was angry and hurt; Ignazio was small recompense. I still burn with responsibility at the memory decades later, but that was only the beginning.

MARGARET WURTELE

Chapter Eleven

It seems ludicrous to me now to think that at seventeen I could envision myself affecting the war in any tangible way. Nevertheless, a raw energy and power surged through me that was naive, to be sure, but left me nearly fearless. I turned my entire focus to supporting the partisans. I was determined to impress Giorgio and to protect him in whatever way I could—and underneath it all, perhaps, to atone for my treachery.

All the next week, I hounded Rosa mercilessly. I raided two gardens after dark, telling my parents that training at the clinic was keeping me late, and I amassed quite an impressive store that I knew would make Hermes proud. A third garden that had been tempting me was the Santinis' own. A cheeky and dangerous move. The garden was between the cellar and the house, fenced in iron, and shielded by a row of arborvitaes from any direct surveillance.

After I dropped off that day's supplies, I crept slowly up the path toward the house, my empty sack over my shoulder. I could see the gate was unlocked, so, with a quick glance up ahead, and feeling secure in the deepening dusk, I gingerly lifted the latch and stepped inside. The perky green tops of the onions beckoned to me, so I wrenched one from the black earth. Its underbelly was firm, white, and rounded to the size of a golf ball. Greedily, I pulled out a whole row, stuffing them into my sack and leaving a crumbled ditch right down the garden's center. I yanked tens of handfuls of swollen, nearly dried pea pods off the huge, fading tangle of vine, and unearthed a dozen or so garlic bulbs.

Thank God I had everything in the sack and had already latched the gate when I saw the frail figure of Signora Santini, her shoulders draped elegantly in a rose-colored shawl, leaning on a cane and making her way slowly toward me down the path. Her skin looked sallow, even in the dim light of evening, and dark circles made her protruding eyes seem hollow. She stared at me quizzically, as if she were searching her memory, trying to orient herself.

"Giovanna? Is that you? What on earth are you doing here at this hour?" She eyed the sack.

Frantically I searched for an explanation, since I was facing the house, after all. "Oh, signora, I'm so surprised to see you outside! I've heard you've been quite ill. Mother suggested I pay you a visit, but here you are, up and about, catching a breath of air. Imagine that!" I shifted the canvas bag under my arm, pressing the top closed so she couldn't see inside. "I intended to get here much earlier, but my work at the clinic held me up." I was running off at the mouth now. "And I just thought I'd come back here to look to see if maybe I saw a light in your window, if maybe you were still up and I could safely announce myself."

She stood there, staring, her hand trembling on the head of the cane. "I felt slightly better this evening, thank you." She spoke slowly and deliberately, in a low, cultured voice that made me feel like a babbling idiot. Then she added, "Luigi tells me he thinks someone has been using our cellar as a supply drop. I thought I would investigate. I don't suppose you noticed any men lurking back there."

My face flushed hot. "Men? Why, no, no men at all. What do you mean, supply drop? Supplying the partisans?" I could feel my pulse racing, surely visible at the hollow in my neck where my blouse was open.

"You heard me, exactly." She glowered, as if defying me to explain myself further. "Our family is in a vicious tangle over all of this. My husband is a stubborn Fascist, and he'd report anything suspicious to the Germans; you can bet on that." She paused. "But I . . ." Her face shook slightly from side to side as she went on. "I'm terrified for Luigi, who turns eighteen next year and might be forced to fight. Rumors are that the partisans are making real inroads, interfering with German plans for this area. I'm all for it. Whatever they can do."

Relief slowly infused my blood like a river settling out after a storm. This could be important. I gently took her elbow. "Signora Santini, you're tired. Let's sit down on the bench over there and have a chat."

❦

The moss at the foot of the gazebo's columns was soaked after a badly needed rain the night before. I was forced to stand, to pace in circles, while Sunday afternoon crept by no faster than the hands on a clock. Well, why shouldn't Giorgio be late? I had stood him up completely last week. I looked nervously at the sky through the lacy canopy above me—zinc, definitely gray. Would it rain again, catch me so far from home?

I did have work to do, though, mental work. The Santini situation was complicated. Signora Santini had given me her unqualified permission to use the cellar as a depository for supplies. She had been helpful too with details of her husband's schedule and the hours of the day she felt were most advisable for pickup and delivery. Luckily, he was quite predictable, a man of routine. She warned me, though, that if he found out, it would mean serious trouble for me and for the men I was helping. She would have to deny any involvement, and I would be on my own. She had given me free rein as well in the garden, trusting me to gauge the amount I could take without its being noticed, and she promised to hold back on her own use of the basic onions and garlic, beans and potatoes that I needed most.

The question in my mind concerned Luigi. He and his mother were of one mind, and here was potentially another healthy, resourceful person who could be useful to the cause. On the other hand, he was my age, and—what could I say?—a boy. I just didn't trust him the way I could trust Violetta. And his friends . . . I cringed, thinking of poor Ignazio Lazzari. Would Luigi blame me and take revenge? No, I would have to go it alone at this point and hope to elude Luigi as I came and went on the property. It had worked so far. He slept late and never seemed to be about in the evening.

Where was Giorgio, anyway? Impatience was gnawing in my lower back. Maybe I should just leave—put a note where he could see it and call it a draw: one week for him, one for me. I was pulling my pad out of my pocket when a low murmur rose from the woods to the north. I held my breath. Yes, male voices. I smoothed my hair, redid the barrette.

There were four of them this time: Giorgio, of course, and the Fox. With them were two other men. They were strikingly similar—both of medium height with curly dark hair, both dressed in tattered camouflage, items of clothing obviously put together randomly from different national uniforms. One of them wore a patch over one eye; the other had his arm in a sling, a filthy length of gauze wrapped and knotted around it. Odd. I couldn't identify exactly the feeling I got observing them, but I sensed a tentativeness about them, that they didn't quite belong, as if Hermes and the Fox were in charge and these two were lucky to be along for the ride.

"Columba!" Giorgio gave me a quick hug. "I wasn't sure whether you'd make it this time." His eyes darted about, as if he were looking for someone lurking in the shadows. The Fox had wandered off and was peering down the path I had come on.

"I'm so sorry about last Sunday. I can explain, but it's a long story. Remember how I told you—"

He reached out and put three fingers flat over my lips. "You're forgiven, Columba. We don't have time for explanations right now. First of all, the good news. Things are really heating up around here. The Allied forces have reached Pistoia in their march up the peninsula and are positioned to penetrate the Gothic Line just south of here. If that happens, the Germans will have to abandon the front and retreat up the river valley to northern Italy. We're doing all we can to harass them, intercept their communications, and make it difficult for them to stay around here."

"I thought the Allies wanted the partisans to do only defensive work, not to attack the Germans," I ventured.

He looked irritated. "Screw that, Columba. It's evolving. Right now we just need your help with something specific." He pulled me over to the two men. "These are two brothers I knew at military school. This one we call Patch. He was a couple of classes ahead of me in school." I reached out my hand to shake his, trying to focus on his good eye and not wanting to appear to be staring. He glanced at me and then looked at the ground. "And this is Moses. He was in my class." He clamped a hand on Moses's good shoulder and gave it a squeeze. Moses, his right arm in the sling, reached out his left and gave me a warm smile.

"Hi, Giovanna. Giorgio's talked about you so often over the years." His brown eyes were overlaid with green, the color of the wet moss beneath our feet. When I looked into his eyes, I felt suddenly as if he were indeed familiar, as if I had, somehow, met him before.

"Damn it, Moses, I told you not to use her name. You've got to get used to that."

"Okay, then, *Columba*. It's nice to meet you." He winked.

"It's Moses here who's the problem. You can see his arm is hurt. He was helping us work with some explosives and got caught in an accidental flare-up. It's been bandaged for the last couple of days, but I think it's infected, and we need medicine and some new bandages. Do you want to see the wound?"

"No, no!" I backed off too quickly and was embarrassed by my own squeamishness. "I'm sure I can imagine what it looks like. As it turns out, I've been working in the clinic at Villa Falconieri for a week or so. I think I actually can be of some help here."

"I thought you were working at the school."

"That's part of the long story I was

going to tell you," I said. "I'm not going back there anymore."

Giorgio studied me, squinting, a little smile playing about his mouth. "I can't wait to hear this one. But we really don't have time right now. We've got to get back." He took me by the hand and pulled me over to the other side of the marble platform, leaving the three men talking quietly together. He draped an arm around me and rotated us so our backs were to the others. "This is a little touchy, but I think I'd better tell you." There was a new tone in his voice, serious and guarded.

"Tell me what?"

"Those two guys are Jewish. You've got to be really careful about this, little sister. They can't stay with us long—it's too much of a risk for everyone. But I told Moses I'd get help for his arm. Can you come back midweek? I don't think it can wait until Sunday."

I glanced back over my shoulder, quietly absorbing this piece of news, looking at the two brothers with new eyes. Everyone knew the Fascist party had some laws on the books about Jews, but I wasn't aware that they posed any real danger to them.

"What do you mean, too much of a risk?"

Giorgio looked at me and rolled his eyes. "Are you so naive as that?"

I stared blankly back at him.

"Since September, since the occupation, the Germans have had an all-out manhunt for Jews anywhere in Italy. If they're found, they're put on trains and sent . . . I don't know—east somewhere. I guess they're put in prison camps or forced to do hard labor."

"But why?" I knew of Jews, of course, but as far as I knew, that term had always just referred to their religion. They'd worked with Father as bankers or in the textile business.

"It's happening all over Europe, Giovanna." Giorgio was whispering now. "It's part of what Hitler is trying to do. Don't you remember hearing about the racial laws? It's all connected. The hard-core Fascists believe Jews are inferior—polluting our population—and they just want them out of here, separate."

I looked back at Patch and Moses

again. There was nothing to distinguish them in looks or manner from any of the other friends my brother had shown up with over the years.

"Giorgio, are you sure?"

"Am I sure? Do you remember the Lazzato family, the guy who worked with Father and moved to New York a couple of years ago?"

I did. We knew the Lazzatos well when we lived in Lucca most of the year. Signora Lazzato was a fine pianist who used to play duets with Mother on occasion. Her husband had a reputation as an ace salesman who Father thought was destined for big things. Then, all of a sudden, they had left the country. "I thought they went to New York to start a business there."

"That's what they told everyone, of course, but those two could see all of this coming. They were smart—and damn lucky too, let me tell you. Today it's impossible to get out. Most of the Jews in northern Italy are hidden away somewhere. They've been on the run since September, but now it's really bad.

These guys are red meat to the German wolves."

How could I have missed all this? No one talked about it; that much was certain. I wondered what Klaus would say. "Where are they all hiding?"

"How should I know?" Giorgio looked away, irritated and impatient. "We've got to go now, keep moving. Just tell me you'll get the medical stuff and be back here Wednesday about five."

I nodded, studying the two men.

"And, Jesus, don't tell a soul about this, Giovanna."

℘

I spent the next twenty-four hours mulling over what I had just learned. I just couldn't believe it was true, that a whole segment of the Italian population was being singled out and hunted down. Were Jews a threat to the Germans in some way? What were they afraid of? Were the marchesa and others like her hiding Jews along with the escaped prisoners? Mostly I was ashamed that all of these new developments were not new. They had been going on for months—years, really—while I had remained oblivious.

I resolved to try to find out what my parents knew. We were gathered around the small table as usual the following evening. After Rosa had left the room, I took a tentative sip of wine. "Do you know about what's been happening with the Jews?"

Father looked at me and laughed. "The Jews! Now instead of talking about Jews, let's talk about you, young lady. Sister Graziella stopped by again this afternoon looking for you."

I felt my hands go cold.

"I told her you were working at the clinic, but she didn't have time to go there. She said she needed to see you about an important matter, and that she would expect you to be at the convent on Friday afternoon."

"Did she"—I stared at my plate, pushed a piece of spinach with my fork—"say what it was about?"

"No, she didn't. But, Giovanna, I have to say I didn't get the feeling she was pleased. Has something happened?

Does she have some new reason to be upset with you?"

She had not told them about the substituted note. An image of her plump, warm hands with their neatly trimmed nails and single gold band flashed in my mind. How could I possibly repay her? On the other hand, I knew that Father had not yet forgiven me; nor was he likely to give me a second chance anytime soon. There was an edge of sarcasm in nearly everything he said to me since the incident with Klaus. He was seeing me with new eyes, and he wasn't sure he liked what he saw.

"No . . . but . . . Papa, what about the Jews? Do you know about what has been happening to them?"

Silence. Father looked at Mother. "What do you mean, 'happening'?"

"Well, I've heard they're all being hunted by the Germans, having to hide out to avoid being sent to prison."

"Who told you that?" Father was being deliberately casual.

"Oh, someone at the clinic mentioned something about it today."

"Someone Jewish?"

"No, just someone. People were talking about it. What exactly are the racial laws?"

He clenched his jaw. "Giovanna, what does this have to do with you? This doesn't concern us." He tore off a piece of bread.

"I just want to know. If there are laws, why can't we talk about them? You've been part of the Fascist party, Papa. What are they for?"

Father put down his fork and pushed his chair back a little as if to give himself space. "They were just something Mussolini had to do—to get along with the Germans, that's all. They've been on the books, but I don't think anyone's taken them all that seriously."

Mother shook her head. "Until now, that is. The truth is, they are cruel; that's what they are."

"But why? Just because of their religion? What have they done wrong?"

"Nothing, Giovanna. Nothing. It's just a policy, something the government decided to do." Father's fingers were turning white where he was gripping the edge of the table. "Your mother and I have no problem with those people. As you know, I worked with a couple of Jews in Lucca at the company. They went to military school with your brother. We're not part of this at all. So just forget about it. It doesn't concern you, and it doesn't have anything to do with us."

As I sat there, looking at Father and listening to him, inside I began to rise, to swell. I felt for a moment as if I were watching the scene from above, perched high like a bird on a branch. I knew he was wrong about this, and his being wrong shrank him somehow to the size of a child or even a tiny animal. But it was funny, because the wrongness, the smallness, made him suddenly—despite his unhappiness with me—easier to love. Like he couldn't hurt me in the same way anymore, like being his daughter was now, oddly, something I could accept with equanimity.

"Okay, Papa, I'm going to bed now." I kissed him tenderly on the forehead, and my lips lingered there, feeling the deep lines between his eyes.

I tossed and turned for a long time, trying to let go of the day, of Father and the meeting I would have to have with Sister Graziella. At one point, thinking about my time at the gazebo, I remembered a tiny thing. Giorgio had herded the three others away like a mother dog with her pups. Just before the forest swallowed Moses's camouflage, I saw him turn back to look at me one more time. It wasn't anything you'd notice, really, but I happened to catch him. He knew it too, and being sure of that allowed me finally to drift off to sleep.

Chapter Twelve

Father's words insinuated themselves into the base of my skull and stayed there, pricking and irritating me like a rough collar that I couldn't loosen or take off. *It doesn't have anything to do with us.* But it did; of course it did. Maybe we couldn't change the Germans' determination to rid Italy of Jews, but couldn't we at least talk about it? And couldn't we—no, shouldn't we—be actively doing whatever we could to help?

I agonized about this for the next day or so, not saying anything to anyone, but thinking about it all the time. The thought of them hiding gnawed at me. Somebody was aware of what was happening and cared. But who? Who was worrying about the Jews? Everyone in my life was so busy worrying about the partisans and their own missing sons. Of course, Giorgio and his fellow fighters were in mortal danger too. If the Germans got hold of them, they could and probably would be shipped off to prison or labor camps as well, so what was the difference?

I knew there was a difference and that it lay in the racial laws and everything they implied. But it made me boil, and the anger I felt started consuming me. I needed to get back to Patch and Moses so I could find out more.

℘

"Violetta, I need some advice." She was busily making her rounds, moving from bed to bed, intent on her tasks, and not really paying any attention to me. I padded after her like a dog. "What exactly should you do for someone who has an infected arm?"

"How big is the wound? What does it look like?" she asked absentmindedly, bending over and smoothing the sheets under a bearded old man who was snoring loudly in his sleep.

How could I have been so stupid as not to look at it? Typical me, worried more about my own stomach than helping Moses. I would have to make this up. "It's a wound that came from getting too close to an explosive," I began, pretending to be both confident and casual. "The flesh is . . . open and bloody, and now . . ." I searched, hoping for inspiration. "It's infected. It's kind of . . ." I remembered a skinned knee I had had years ago. "There's pus around it, and it's turning sort of green." That was the best I could do.

"Okay, Giovanna." She sighed impatiently, turned to face me, and wiped some sweat from her forehead with the back of her wrist. "Come with me." I could tell she just wanted to get rid of me, but at least I'd gotten her attention. "Whose arm is it?" she asked as I followed her down the narrow stone stairs and into the chapel, to the supply room. "Anyone I know?"

"Just a guy who's working with my brother," I said. "I don't know him either, but he was in Giorgio's class in school."

Violetta rummaged in the shelves, pulling out a roll of gauze, tape, and a bar of soap. "Clean it really well before you bandage it. Then, if it's seriously infected, you could give him a shot of penicillin." She added a small bottle of sterile water.

"A shot? Come on, Violetta; you know I couldn't do that."

"Well, if he has a fever, you really should. An infection like that could be dangerous. It's a new medication and there isn't really much of it available, but we have a little here. If you need it, I'll give you a dose and show you how. Here, take a thermometer for now." She bundled everything in a piece of paper and handed it over. "Good luck, and let me know what happens. If it gets worse, you could always bring him here."

I nodded, but I wondered, Could I? Were any of these patients Jewish? I didn't think so. I certainly couldn't risk it until I knew more.

Giorgio, Moses, and Patch were already there when I arrived at the gazebo on Wednesday afternoon. The medical supplies were tucked into the bottom of my bag along with some fresh bread and as much extra rice and beans as I could carry. I had been trying, on the way there, to recall Moses's face. I could remember the greenish eyes, the curly hair, and the sly, intimate grin, but I couldn't put them together into a cohesive whole, one that would tell me why he had felt so familiar, as if I'd met him before.

I put out my hands to my brother right away, but it was Moses's face I looked at: It was open, fresh, and innocent— utterly unguarded. That was the quality I had been unable to re-create. He must have been Giorgio's age, but he looked younger, so vulnerable, and utterly trusting. That didn't fit with the camouflage clothing or what I now knew him to be: a hunted Jew.

Giorgio's face lit up as I unpacked the

food and handed it over one sack at a time.

"I can't tell you what a difference this is making for us," he said, tearing off a piece of bread and handing the loaf to Patch. "I don't know how we'd survive without you."

Patch took the bread without comment. His one eye refused to look at me or make any connection at all. He turned his back and began breaking little pieces off, hungrily, almost angrily, and stuffing them in his mouth one after another. Moses stood patiently by, looking at me, a wry smile tugging at the corner of his mouth. Then he winced suddenly as Patch thrust the loaf under his bad arm from behind. "Hey, watch it, will you?" His face had a satiny sheen that erupted here and there on his upper lip and his forehead with drops of perspiration.

"Did you bring something for Moses's arm?" Giorgio was pacing nervously, impatiently.

I nodded.

"I'm going to take Patch with me and leave you here. Moses, you know how to get back, right? You'll be okay by yourself?"

He gave his assent, and the two of them were gone in a flash, making hardly a sound as they headed off through the woods in a slightly different direction from the last time.

We watched them go, standing there side by side, looking after them a little too long. Then we faced each other, suddenly shy. "I really appreciate this," Moses said. "My arm is killing me. Normally I'm not one to give a little pain too much attention."

"How did it happen?" I asked him.

"Oh, God. We had a small sample bomb, just to see how the detonation would work. I carried it way out and put it on the ground, and someone else hit the plunger. The fuse was so long they couldn't see me, and I guess they thought I had let it go. It went off so fast—the damn thing exploded before I knew it. I was wearing gloves, but it tore into my arm." He loosened one end of the filthy strip of cloth.

"Could we go sit down?" I was feeling light-headed, not at all sure I was up to this. "I need to get some stuff out of my bag."

"My name is Mario, by the way," he said. "Mario Rava. And my brother's name is Cecilio. I guess we haven't really been properly introduced." He smiled.

We perched side by side on the mossy edge of the marble platform, and I watched, mesmerized, as Mario began unwinding the makeshift bandage. It caught now and then and stuck where the blood had dried into a kind of glue. Then I had to look away as he reached the soft heart of the wound. His breath was uneven, stopping while he held it, then hissing as he let it out hard. "This really hurts," he said, and, at last, "Okay. That's it."

I made myself look. The cloth lay in a heap on the ground. There were small scrapes and scabs scattered from his wrist to just above his elbow, but the whole top of his forearm was torn away. An exposed mass of flesh lay open, wet with blood and rimmed with yellow-green pus, a faint odor of rotten meat rising in the heat. An insistent pressure at the hinge of my jaw made me start swallowing fast. An image flashed—of Father's face, laughing at the thought of me keeling over at the clinic. *No,* I thought. *You are not going to vomit or faint again. Not again.* I looked away, up at the treetops, and gathered myself. I rummaged busily in the bag, unrolled the paper bundle, and pulled out the bottle of water and the roll of gauze. *I can do this. I will do this.*

Mario fished in his pants pocket and pulled out a knife. "Do you need this, maybe? To cut the bandage?"

I hadn't even thought of that. Gratefully, I let him saw off a length of gauze. Then I doused it with water and rubbed it over the bar of soap. "Close your eyes," I said. "This is going to sting." Gently but firmly, I stroked the open wound in slow pulls toward me. When the gauze was soaked and filthy, I unwound more, formed a new pad, and began again.

"Giorgio tells me you're Jewish," I offered tentatively. I thought maybe some conversation would take his mind off the pain.

"Well, with a nickname like Moses, I guess that's pretty obvious." He laughed and squeezed his own knee hard while I went on stroking.

"I'm sorry," I said. "I don't mean I'm sorry you're Jewish, but sorry . . ." What was I sorry about? *Sorry the Germans want to get rid of you; sorry my parents think it's none of our business?* "I'm sorry. This is a horrible war."

The silence hung over us. I finished cleaning and rinsed with plain water. He began to relax, stopped clenching his fist and squeezing his knees together.

"This might sound naive," I began again, "but where are all the Jews hiding?" On second thought, that was too big a question. "Where are your parents?"

Mario took a deep breath and let it out slowly. He looked at me full in the face and shook his head. "I'm afraid I don't know."

"When did you see them last?"

"In early January." He gazed off into the distance. "I can't believe it's been almost six months. They were just gone when we got home."

"What do you mean? Who got home?"

He sighed. "Oh, God, Giovanna. This

is a long story, and it's not easy to tell." He looked down at his arm. "But I guess we still have to bandage this, so I'll tell you a little."

I said nothing, hoping he would go on.

"My papa is a military man. He was a decorated army officer in World War One, very big in the unification efforts. So in the beginning, we were exempted from the racial laws."

"Because he was a war hero?"

"Yes. At first anyone like that was eligible for a special category on a case-by-case basis. My father was even a member of the Fascist party for a while. He was a Blackshirt in the march on Rome that installed Mussolini in power in 1922. He was so patriotic—passionate about our country—and just got carried away by the Fascists' dreams for a strong and powerful Italy. Mussolini wasn't anti-Semitic at all in those days, you know. So Father definitely qualified for the exemption."

"My father was a Fascist, too." Suddenly that sounded callous, all wrong. But he ignored me and kept going.

"But then in November of 'thirty-eight,

they eliminated the 'discrimination clause,' and there were no more exceptions to the racial laws. Father was one of the top executives at the Banca Ovazza in Turin, but he had to leave his job. Jews were no longer allowed to work there."

I anchored one end of the long strip of gauze at the top of Mario's arm, where it was pretty well healed; then I began slowly winding it around and around— not too tightly—gradually covering up the cleaned wound. "So what did you do when he couldn't work anymore?"

"Well, we were lucky in that we had plenty of money. Like a lot of other Jews in that position, we moved full-time to our country house, in the hills outside Turin."

How much like our own life his sounded, I thought: the executive job in the city, the country house. I studied his angled forehead over deep-set green eyes, the fine lips that seemed always to have a slight smile playing about them. "How old are you?" I asked gently.

"I'm twenty. I was born in 1924. Cecilio's twenty-two." He looked up. "So if you're Giorgio's younger sister, you must be—"

"Seventeen, but I'll be eighteen next month." It seemed important that he not think me too young.

Mario nodded. Then he got up, suddenly edgy and distracted. "Hey, Giovanna, I can't tell you how much I appreciate this. But I've got to go now. I can't stay here."

"Wait. There's one more thing we have to do." I took out the thermometer, shook it down. "You've got to sit still long enough to do this. It's important." I held it out to him like a nurse, and he dutifully opened his mouth, let me slide the glass rod under his tongue, then closed his lips gently around it. Softly modeled lips they were, neat and symmetrical, like a woman's. A drop of sweat slowly rolled down from under his nose and hung there. I wanted to wipe it off with my thumb, but I held back.

"Mario, I . . ." This was an opportunity, and I had to take it. "I want you to know I'm really sorry all this is happening to you and your brother. It isn't right." I didn't know what I was about to say, but I pressed on. "If you need anything, not just food, but help of some kind, let me know." I looked away, feeling the breeze lift an unruly curl next to my ear, listening to the *kick, kick, kick* of a great spotted woodpecker overhead.

I reached for the thermometer, then tipped it just so in the light: 102 degrees.

"You've got a fever," I said. "A high one."

He winced. "I was afraid of that. I really don't feel very well. Do you think it's my arm?"

"I do. They told me at the clinic that means infection. And it could be serious. You're going to need a shot. Can you come back tomorrow?" I began stuffing all the old bandages and debris into my bag.

He looked nervous, shook his head.

"Mario, you've got to. You *have* to." I was surprised at the intensity in my own voice. Suddenly this mattered more than anything had in a long time. "I'll be here, right here, at noon tomorrow. Don't let me down." I shouldered the bag, turned my back, and walked away, not waiting for an answer.

I slipped quietly out of our quarters and down the stairs just after sunrise the next morning. My plan was to pass by the Santinis' garden for some vegetables to take with me that Mario could deliver to the boys, then to go to the clinic to pick up a dose of penicillin. I parked my bike on the road and circled around the back way toward the garden. As I neared their property, I saw Luigi sitting by the path. His bicycle was turned over nearby, and he was bent over, hugging his knees to his chest.

I approached warily, still not sure whether he might be blaming me personally for Ignazio's kidnapping. "Hello, Luigi," I said casually. He seemed lost in his thoughts, not in the least hostile to me. "Is something the matter?"

"I've just heard about the evacuation, and I'm worried about Flavio."

"Evacuation?"

"There's a poster hanging in his village by the fountain. It says that those people and all the villages of the Serchio River valley are to be evacuated beginning on July fifteenth—that's the day after tomorrow."

"Where will they go?"

"We talked with Flavio's parents, and they said they had heard that everyone is supposed to be loaded on trains and taken to some unknown destination in the north. They would be allowed only one suitcase and have to leave everything else behind. Everyone in the village is talking about it. I guess the parish priest has announced that there will be a meeting to discuss it tonight."

"But that would mean Violetta's family, too!" I leaped to my feet and brushed my skirt off. "Luigi, I've got to run. I'm really sorry about Ignazio, and I'm so glad you're okay." The vegetables forgotten, I picked up my bag and took off for the clinic.

Chapter Thirteen

Violetta was not at the clinic when I arrived. I feared the worst—that she wouldn't even show up—but I busied myself tidying the supply room while I waited. I sifted through piles of bandages, rolls of flat cotton enfolded in blue paper, small white laundered towels, large containers of aspirin, and bottles of evil-looking mercurochrome. I returned things to their assigned spaces and neatened the piles. No sign of penicillin anywhere. What if she never came? I was searching through a basket on the bottom shelf when the light in the room dimmed. Someone was standing in the doorway. I turned, and the marchesa leaned in.

"Giovanna, why don't you come out here? Violetta has just arrived, and as her good friend, I think you should hear what she's saying."

There were three other nurse volunteers clustered around Violetta near the entrance to the annex. She was talking animatedly, and as I came closer, I could hear that it concerned the evacuation.

"They say we will be able to take only what we can carry, and that all our houses are to be abandoned—I suppose for German troops to move in and take them over."

"Is it true everyone is to be put on trains and shipped off?" I asked.

"It is, but from what my parents say, most people are just planning to run off into remote parts of the mountains and stay with friends or family in those inaccessible areas—not to go forcibly by train."

"What will your parents do?" asked one of the other nurses.

"They are planning to climb up to Piegaio with my aunt and uncle. We have some third cousins who they think will take us in." That would mean her cousin Flavio would go as well. Poor Luigi would lose his other good friend.

There was a moment of silence while we took this in. Then the marchesa spoke up. "Violetta, I just cannot afford to lose you. We are far enough from the river in this part of the countryside that we won't be included in the evacuation—at least not yet. I want you to stay here with me and my family. We have a room for you in the villa. You can work in the clinic by day and help me with the children if need be. Do you think your parents will allow it?"

She stared at the marchesa. I could tell she was torn. I knew she wanted to be with her parents, but she would also rather stay here. She glanced at me, then seemed to make up her mind. "I'll ask them tonight. There's a meeting about all of this at the church, and we can decide together."

The group disbanded, and the other nurses climbed the stairs to the clinic, but I pulled Violetta aside. "We'll talk later. Right now I need that dose of penicillin," I said quickly, "and I can't find it in the supply room."

❧

I didn't see Mario at first when I arrived in the clearing. Thinking he wasn't there, I started to pace around the gazebo, but when I reached the back, I saw him lying curled on his side, tucked in behind the legs of Prometheus. Not sure whether he was awake or asleep, I leaned over to see his face. His eyes were closed, and he was breathing heavily. His forehead and nose were wet with perspiration. I reached out and gently shook his shoulder.

"Oh—I'm sorry." He sat up slowly, trying to get reoriented. "I must have fallen asleep." He was holding the bandaged arm protectively, even though it was in a sling. "I'm just so tired lately. It must be the fever. I can hardly keep up with the other guys." He managed a wan smile, then looked serious. "Were you able to get some penicillin?"

I pulled a wrapped paper package from my bag and held it up. "Here it is.

Now I just have to muster the courage to give you the shot." I smiled and winced. "I've never done this before."

"Trust me, Giovanna. No shot could ever equal the pain in this arm. So even if you botch it, it won't make much difference." He gave me an encouraging smile. "What have we got to lose?"

"So . . ." I loosened the packet and slowly pulled out the vial and the hypodermic needle. "I can either give this to you in your other arm, or . . ." I paused, embarrassed.

"I only have one arm to speak of, so I'd better not risk making that sore, too. I guess that settles it." He turned and unbuttoned his pants until they were loose enough for him to lower the back waistband enough to expose an area of flesh on his behind. "Will this do?"

I pulled out a small bottle of rubbing alcohol and tore off a piece of cotton. I soaked the cotton and swabbed the fleshiest place I could find. My hand shook as I filled the needle from the vial as Violetta had shown me. When it was full, I put the vial and packet down and took a deep breath. "Here goes."

I held the needle in my right hand and moved it toward the target. Why hadn't I practiced this somehow? My hand was trembling violently, and my wrist seemed suddenly weak. I grasped the instrument like a pen between my first and second fingers, but when I stretched my thumb back to reach the plunger, my whole hand shook so hard the needle dropped to the dust at my feet.

"Oh, Mario," I cried out. "I've dropped it! I was afraid of hurting you." I picked up the needle, now caked with dirt all the way to the tip. *Should I wipe it with alcohol? Try to sterilize it again?* I had no idea whether that would work. I might do more harm than good. "I'm afraid this just isn't going to work. The needle's too dirty now. I'm so sorry. I've just let you down horribly."

Mario, still facing the other way, pulled his pants up and buttoned them. He lowered himself slowly onto the marble platform. "That's all right, Giovanna. I don't blame you. I couldn't have done it any better myself." He sighed deeply. "You have no idea how little energy I have."

He began to describe how much work the group of partisans had to do each day: the cooking and the cleanup for three meals a day; the foraging for food and fuel for the fire; the sending and receiving of messages with other clusters of rebels in the area; the building of explosive devices, the testing and the eventual and very dangerous planting of the bombs. "They obviously don't send me or my brother on those missions into the German camps," he said. "I'm committed to this work, but I just find it hard to keep up."

I could hear deep fatigue in his voice, and fear—not only for his and his brother's safety but also for his own health. A rush of feeling came over me. I wanted fiercely to protect this man I hardly knew, and more than that, to set about it right away. "Mario, I don't think you should stay with Giorgio and his band anymore. You're so sick, and it's just too risky— for you and for them. I have to think of my own brother too."

He stared at the ground, saying nothing for a while. Then he looked at me.

"But where would I go? I couldn't leave my brother behind. I just couldn't."

Where *could* they go? The enormity of that question hung in the air like a huge soap bubble that was about to burst. "I have no idea, but I promise I'll think about it and come up with an answer. I have some ideas, but I'll have to see. It's Thursday, and we usually meet on Sunday. Will you be there?"

He nodded.

"Your brother too. And bring your stuff—be prepared to come with me."

Chapter Fourteen

I had been watching the marchesa closely ever since I had begun working at the clinic. For someone in her position, she seemed not to care about what she wore or how she presented herself; she was utterly absorbed by the demands of the work she had to do. Yet she was also the kindest, most generous person I had ever met. She always took the time to stop at each bedside and chat with the patients. And I knew from Violetta that she also welcomed meetings with the volunteers one on one, to encourage them and give them any help they needed.

So I was not surprised when she approached me as I wheeled my bicycle into the thicket later that afternoon. Beaming, she threw her arms out wide. "Isn't it a beautiful day? It's so good to see you here, Giovanna. I can't tell you how appreciative I am." Her face darkened, took on a more serious air. "How is it going for you, my young friend? Is there anything you need? These are hard times, and we all need to support one another."

"Oh, no . . . everything is just fine, thank you." I smiled politely. "I'm just glad to be able to help." I wanted to trust her. In fact, I admired her so much, something made me want to show her I was a person who took herself seriously, who had a role in this war just like she did.

"You can't fool me, you know." She moved closer to me. "I pride myself on having better than average intuition. Do I detect a tiny hesitation in your response?"

I tucked the bike under a big branch.

Dared I prod her a bit? She knew so much about the area, and, no doubt, she understood all aspects of the war. I turned to walk beside her. "Well, actually, there is something I've been wondering about."

"What is that, dear?"

"I know you have been so generous with all the escaped prisoners of war who have come through here—the English and the Americans especially."

"You know my mother was American and my father English. It seems right for me to help them."

I hesitated. "Have you ever had any . . ." I forced myself to say the words. "Have you had any Jewish people ask for your help?"

She took my arm and turned so that we were walking away from the clinic toward a bench that sat next to the entrance of the chapel. She said nothing until we were sitting down. "Giovanna." She spoke in a low voice, almost a whisper. "You know that we are in great danger here, taking in these prisoners and wounded soldiers."

"Of course I do."

"And I am dedicated to the work we are doing."

"I know. I have so much respect for you."

"But the Jews. That is a risk of a different order. There is something so sinister, so *beyond* war, in the threats to them. I just don't know what to make of it."

"But have you had any come here?"

"I will tell you that yes, I have."

"Are they here?"

She looked away from me. "No." She shook her head a little, as if reassuring herself. "They are not. I just didn't feel—how should I say this?—that I was the right person to deal with their situation." She combed her curly hair back from her forehead with her fingers. "I was in enough danger with the work we were already doing."

"But what did you do?" I said. "Where did you send them?"

There was a pause before the marchesa looked directly into my eyes.

"Giovanna, where are your sympathies in all of this? How do you feel?"

"Oh," I said quickly, "I believe they should be helped in any way possible."

"In that case, I'll tell you." The marchesa took a deep breath, then continued. "I referred them to the Church. Believe it or not, it is the Church that is doing the most work in this area."

I nearly fell off the bench. "What do you mean exactly by 'the Church'?"

"There are several priests in the region, both in the countryside and in Lucca, who are involved—who refer people to citizens who will hide them, who even hide them themselves on church property. I've heard there are convents too, that many nuns are proving to be heroines in this thing."

Nuns? Could it be that Sister Graziella and her compatriots were housing any Jews at the convent of Saint Agnes? How could I have managed to damage the one relationship that could possibly help me?

I stood up. I had to talk to Sister Graziella right away. "Thank you, Marchesa. I appreciate your trusting me with this information. I need to get back to the supply room."

She reached out her hand. "Is there a specific reason you wanted to know?"

"Oh, well, no, I . . ." I started to lie to her, but I knew I owed her more than that. I owed her at least the same dignity and openness with which she had treated me. "Let's just say that I know of a situation in which some shelter might be necessary, but"—I started walking back toward the hospital—"this is something I can handle on my own."

"Good for you, Giovanna. You're a woman of heart and courage." She put her arm around my shoulders and pulled me to her. "Just know that you can come to me anytime if you need advice—or even just encouragement."

❦

I didn't want to appear at the convent empty-handed, so I persuaded Rosa to sacrifice a jar of her lavender honey. I took a small cracked pitcher from the larder as well, gathered a bouquet of roses, cornflowers, and dahlias from the garden, and laid them in my bag.

On my bicycle the tree-lined driveway seemed longer and much steeper than it had in the horse-drawn cart. I could feel my anxiety mounting. At the top of the hill, next to the gravel courtyard, I spied a rusted pump in the corner of the garden. I filled the small pitcher with water and arranged the flowers as artfully as I could. All the while, I rehearsed lines of contrition, of gratitude, of devotion, as I fought down the fear that Sister Elena would be there and somehow haunt and spoil the upcoming reunion.

At last, I rapped three times, my knuckles making only a faint sound on the great door. After a moment or two, the same compact little nun raised the latch on the inside and swung it open.

"Oh, yes, Giovanna. Graziella is expecting you. What lovely flowers!"

There was no one else around. The air was stale, and the walls gave off a faint odor of mildew. Our footsteps echoed as I followed the little nun down the corridor to the same parlor where Sister Graziella and I had met before. She ushered me in, then closed the door, leaving me alone to wait. I set the bouquet of flowers and the honey on a low table and perched on the arm of one of the soft chairs. My hands were cold. I folded them in my lap, then crossed my legs and pressed my fingers between my thighs to warm them. The small desk with its drawer of stationery loomed in the corner. Filmy drapery billowed at the open window, and a rooster crowed somewhere nearby.

This room was so formal and elegant. The whole place reeked of *righteousness*. It was impossible that the nuns were hiding Jews anywhere within its cloistered walls. What a silly notion, a preposterous idea. The marchesa must be mistaken, I thought.

There was a firm double rap, and the doorknob clicked. "Come in!" I said, more brightly than the occasion warranted. I stood up quickly.

Sister Graziella did not smile. Her habit swished as she walked purposefully over to the armchair beside mine. "Sit down, Giovanna. Please." No mention of the honey or the flowers.

She sat there without speaking, her hands in her lap and her eyes closed. Was she praying? The rooster crowed again. More silence. Her face, her mouth and cheeks, sagged in utter relaxation; her breath became even and slow.

Slowly my own eyes closed, and I too began to resign myself to this shared silence. My head was full of questions, and my brain bounced like a tennis ball from one to another: Was she angry with me? Did she even know about the note? What had Sister Elena told her? Why had she not acknowledged the gifts I had so carefully brought along? A beam of sunlight from the window behind us moved slowly, creeping gradually across my shoulder, warming my back. My own breath calmed, dulling my nerves. Soon my questions faded; there was only the warmth of the sun, the breathing, and silence.

At last—after maybe fifteen or twenty minutes—Graziella's arm lifted, made the sign of the cross. "In the name of the Father, the Son, and the Holy Ghost," she murmured. "Amen." We opened our eyes together. She studied me for a moment or two.

"Tell me who you are, Giovanna."

"Who I am?" What was I to make of this question?

"Yes." She was serious, patient.

"Well, let's see." I giggled a little. "I am the seventeen-year-old daughter of Natala and Enrico Bellini. . . . I am the younger sister of Giorgio. . . . I am a friend of Violetta . . . a keeper of the supply closet at the marchesa's clinic. I am—" I stopped, not sure how to go on. None of that seemed to matter right now—to me or to her. I tried again.

"I am a person who . . . hates this war."

"Go on."

"I am someone who sees the huge injustices of it—the Germans' tactics, their evil goals. I want to make a differ-ence, to do what I can to stop them."

"And?"

"My brother is fighting for a just cause, and I want to support him. And I have just learned what they are doing to the Jews, and I want—"

She held up her hand to stop me. "All right. So you, Giovanna, are a child of God. You are here to do God's work in the world. You know that."

I nodded.

"You need to listen carefully to what

comes from deep within your heart. And you must act from that source and no other. Do you understand?"

I nodded again.

She stood up and began pacing back and forth. "Sister Elena showed me the note you wrote to Lieutenant Eisenmann. I would guess that you regret doing that, but I am afraid, Giovanna, that you must nonetheless make restitution for it. You deceived me and your parents; you used our convent stationery for your own devious ends. Is that correct?"

I nodded, staring at the floor. "I'm so sorry."

"I know you are. I truly do. But that does not change the need to make amends. Do you know how to use a broom?"

And so it was I learned that each morning for the next three weeks I was to show up at the convent and sweep the floors. I was to do it prayerfully, Sister Graziella explained. I was to focus on only the task at hand, the rhythmic back-and-forth of the broom, the growing pile of dust, the gradually gleaming stone or shining tiles. Worse, I was to

tell my parents exactly where I was going and why. "Tell them about the letter," she instructed.

My encounter with Sister Graziella
stayed with me. I felt as if I had taken
on a kind of internal ballast. I thought
often of the interval of shared silence
until it became a refuge of sorts. If I began to worry or become anxious, I would
try to recapture the calm and centered-
ness of our time together, breathe
deeply, and let her words echo in my
head: *Listen carefully to what comes
from deep within your heart. You must
act from that source and no other. . . .*

❦

"I have a confession to make."

My parents and I were elbow to elbow around the table as usual. "I met
with Sister Graziella this afternoon, and
I want to tell you exactly why she asked
me to come to the convent and what
we spoke about."

Mother's hands began fiddling with
her silverware, her napkin, her glass.
She glanced quickly over at Father, then
down to her plate, not at me. He sat up

taller in his chair, put down his fork, and said, "This is a story I'm not sure I want to hear."

"No, Papa. It's okay."

I began recounting what had happened since our last discussion about Klaus: how I had met with Sister Graziella the first time to apologize, how I had decided, with her blessing, to send a note to Lieutenant Eisenmann to explain my disappearance. Then I added how, on a strange impulse, I had written, instead, to ask for a rendezvous.

At that, Father banged the table with both hands so hard the forks jumped on the plates. "My God, Giovanna, I can't believe you would do a thing like that—"

"Wait. Papa, hear me out. Please."

Mother put a hand on his forearm. "Let's just listen, Enrico."

So I went on to disclose our encounter at the school. "I told the lieutenant that I have my own life to lead and that I do not want to see him again, that I will not be returning to the School of Santa Maria." I looked at Mother, who nodded reassurance.

Father pressed on. "So that's why

Sister Graziella asked you to come to Saint Agnes today. Sister Elena had opened and then shown her the note?"

"Yes. And she felt that I needed to make amends for it, for deceiving her and the two of you."

He nodded. "And?"

"And now I have to go to the convent every morning first thing for the next three weeks. I have to . . ." I hesitated a moment, because it sounded so ludicrous somehow, so embarrassing. "I have to sweep the floor."

Father let out a loud guffaw. "You? Sweep the convent floor?" He looked at Mother. "Well, that's a skill we can probably put to good use around here. How about the winery after that?"

Mother cleared her throat. "I trust Sister Graziella to know what's right. And I'm sure both your father and I feel good about your spending time up there. Will you keep working at the clinic?"

"Oh, yes—I'll still go there every day after I'm finished at Saint Agnes."

Mother took her napkin and pressed her mouth with the corner. "Thank you, dear, for telling us all of this. It can't have been easy."

Father pushed back his chair. "And that damned Nazi is out of the picture. That's the good news."

The meal was over. I had done exactly what Graziella had asked me to do. I wondered whether she'd had any idea how this would help me prepare the ground for what lay ahead.

Chapter Fifteen

News of the impending evacuation swept the valley. It preoccupied everyone living in the countryside as well, beyond the immediate reach of the orders. My parents felt sure that they could remain at home, and in fact, they congratulated themselves that Germans were already ensconced on their property, making their own departure unnecessary.

As the villagers prepared to escape into the hills, they knew that they could take only as much as they could carry. Rumors were flying that jewelry, photographs, bicycles, sacks of grain, wine, china, and crystal were being bricked up in back rooms, stuccoed over, smeared with ash, and marred to look old. There was no time to waste and no guarantee that even their houses would still be there when they returned.

℃

Saturday, the day of the planned evacuation, I showed up on time for the first day of my floor-sweeping duties. Sister Graziella was nowhere in sight when I arrived, but a tall, slender, pale-faced novice named Sylvia, no older than I was, had been assigned to take me under her wing. I was to begin indoors, she explained, sweeping the long tiled corridors in the noncloistered section of the convent, then move on to three exterior courtyards paved in cobblestones of rough local marble.

I was clumsy at first. The crude, uneven sticks made it hard to cover the ground smoothly. I kept missing places and having to go back and redo them, especially inside. The broom's bristles had been bound into a round shape that made it nearly impossible to get into corners or close to the walls. I kept breaking the straws in my attempts to do so, leaving broken pieces strewn all about that had to be cleaned up as well.

Sister Graziella's admonition to do this work "prayerfully" made me laugh to myself. How could anything so awkward, so frustrating, so poorly executed be considered a prayer? She was right about one thing, though: My mind didn't have a chance to wander, so hard did I have to concentrate on making the broom do its job.

I had been working for at least two hours and was just finishing up the third of the courtyards when a voice called from the columned galleria along one side. "I never thanked you for your gifts yesterday, Giovanna." Sister Graziella was standing there, her hands on her hips, grinning at me. "It's a lovely little bouquet, and the honey is delicious."

This was my chance, and I had to seize it. There was a semicircular bench in the corner of the courtyard, backed by a clipped hedge. "Could you sit with me for just a minute?" I asked, sweeping the last of the leaves and clippings into a small pile. "I want to bring you up-to-date on my parents."

We were all alone. I quickly told her about dinner the night before, how I had told Mother and Father all about the letter and my restitution program.

"Good for you, dear. I'm proud of you. Now I'll let you get back to work." She stood up to leave, but I pulled on her habit.

"Wait, Sister. I . . ." How could I possibly do this? "I have to talk with you about something else. It's important." This was too much, too soon, but I had no choice, no choice at all.

She sat back down, wrinkling her brow in concern, and I took both her hands in mine. "Remember how you said that I must act only from a source deep in my heart?"

"Yes." She smiled. "What is it, dear?"

"Oh, this is so hard." I dropped her hands, stood up, and began pacing. "I might be making a big mistake, Sister Graziella." She was listening attentively; I could see that. She understood the importance of what I was about to tell her. "First of all, my brother. You remember Giorgio?"

"Of course."

So I filled her in. "It's so dangerous out there. I worry terribly about him—all of them. And it's risky for me as well."

"Do your parents know you are in touch with him?"

"No. Mother is so anxious—she doesn't even know whether he is alive. But if I told them, I'm afraid Father would force me to betray them. He's furious that Giorgio deserted, and he might want to make him turn himself in."

"Oh, I doubt that he would do that. Not with the Germans as vicious as they are. I really don't think he would." She shook her head and shrugged. "So how can I be of help?"

"I'm not asking you for help with my brother. I'm afraid there's more to tell." I took a deep breath and sat down next to her again.

"The other day, he showed up with two friends from military school, two brothers. One of them was badly wounded. I've been tending to his wound with supplies from the marchesa's clinic, but it's serious. He's very sick, and I don't think he should stay with the partisans anymore." I stopped talking, and my lips began to tremble.

"Can you take him to the clinic?"

"I could. Maybe I . . . Well, the truth is, the marchesa would rather that I not do that." There was a long moment of silence.

"What is it, dear? You're shaking." Sister Graziella put her arm around me and pulled me to her. "What is it, Giovanna? You can tell me."

I bent over my lap, facing away from her. "Until almost a week ago, I didn't even know about all of this, but now . . ." I put my fingers over my eyes, my head still in my lap. "Now it's the only thing that matters."

"What is, dear? What is the only thing?" Her hand was heavy on my back.

"Mario and his brother are Jewish." I stayed there, bent over my knees, holding my breath.

The hand slid slowly down from my shoulder blade along my spine. Then it lifted. She got up, walked a few feet away. I let out my breath slowly, inaudibly, and waited.

"What do you want from me?" Her voice had found a new low register, and it was guarded, dark. I thought I heard anger threaded through it. Was the anger at me?

"The marchesa told me that there are people in the Church . . . some priests and nuns. She did say nuns; I know she did. People who might help. I just thought maybe, Sister Graziella . . . I had no idea, but I have nowhere else to turn. I need someplace by tomorrow, and I thought . . ." I sat up and looked her straight in the eye. "I thought maybe Mario and Cecilio could come here."

She pulled herself up to her full height and looked at me. In a loud, sure voice, her jaw tight, she said, "I'm sorry, Giovanna. This is a cloistered convent. You are gravely mistaken. That is not even within the realm of possibility."

I stared at her face, a looming carved marble sphinx. "It's not?"

"No, it's not."

"But what am I to do?"

Just then, another nun strode rapidly

through the galleria. Sister Graziella glanced at her, then back at me. "That, my dear, is something you will have to pray about. I cannot help you. I'm sorry."

She reached out her arm in a gesture that said we were finished with our tête-à-tête. We left the courtyard together and entered the convent, heading down the hall toward the front door. "We'll see you tomorrow, I presume? You will have to do your sweeping later on Sundays in order to have time to go to mass."

We reached the door to the parlor halfway down the hall. "Wait just a minute, Giovanna. I want to send a note to your parents—to let them know how pleased I am with your progress here."

She stepped into the room, leaving me in the hall to wait. After a couple of minutes, she returned, pressing a sealed envelope into my hand. "Now. You've made a good beginning. We'll see you tomorrow." And she led me the rest of the way down the hall.

I swallowed hard, fighting back the urge to cry. "Yes, I guess you will. I'll see you tomorrow." The huge wooden door creaked on its hinges and closed behind me. The latch dropped into its slot with a loud clank that echoed in my head as I coasted on my bicycle down the long drive.

As I rode along the lane, back toward home, the stiff envelope poked into my leg with each turn of the pedals. What could she have told my parents? Was it really a progress report, or had she said more? She had voiced doubts that my father would make Giorgio turn himself in to the Fascist police—was it possible she was alerting my parents to his activities with the partisans? It would be wrong to open it, but I couldn't be too careful. I stopped my bike, straddling it there on the road, and pulled the envelope out of my pocket. To my surprise, it was addressed to me—*Giovanna*—not to my parents. I slid my finger under the seal and pulled out the now familiar card etched with a drawing of the convent of Saint Agnes. It read: *Bring the young men with you tomorrow afternoon. Come the back way and meet me in the entrance to the wine caves at exactly two p.m.* There was no signature. A hundred roses bloomed in my heart.

When I reached home, Violetta's bicycle was leaning on the wall next to
the entrance to our quarters. I found
her in the parlor, talking excitedly with
Mother.

"They each had a small suitcase in
one hand and a satchel in the other, and
they just took off—to go the whole way
on foot."

"What about the train the Germans
promised?"

"No one wanted to take that. They
were afraid it would go too far away,
and—with all the rumors about the J—
Well, let's just say no one wanted to do
that."

"So where are they headed?"

"People are streaming into the forest,
into the hills. Germans are now crawling
all over town."

Mother knitted her brows together.
"And your family?" She knew Violetta's
parents well.

"We have some relatives in Piegaio.
They couldn't get in touch with them
ahead of time, but we're assuming they'll
take them in. I hope we're right."

"Your parents and . . ."

". . . my aunt and uncle and Flavio. I'm counting on Flavio to help my parents."

"So you decided to stay?" I broke in.

She turned to look at me, and her eyes filled with tears. "Oh, Giovanna. I'm still not sure I did the right thing, but— yes, I decided to move in with the marchesa. I took a small suitcase over there before I came here. I just had to talk with you." She suddenly lifted her head, as if remembering something important. "How's your friend's arm? Did you ever give him the injection?"

"What friend?" said Mother. "What injection?"

"Oh, just a man at the clinic. No one you know." I shot Violetta a warning look. "Let's go take a walk, okay? I want to hear more about the village.

"Are you crazy?" I seethed, when we were a good distance from the villa. "Mother doesn't know anything about Giorgio, and it's one of his partisan friends who's wounded. You've got to be more careful, or you'll ruin everything." My fists were clenched. Then I turned and looked her square in the

face, blinking back tears. "And to answer your question, no. I dropped the
needle and couldn't give him the shot.
I'm going to have to find some more."

❦

On the way to the gazebo late Sunday
morning, it suddenly occurred to me
that with everything going on—the evacuation, Friday's visit to the convent, and
the beginning of my restitution program—I hadn't left a single thing in the
supply drop since I had handed them
the supplies a few days ago. Was my
food the only food they were getting? It
couldn't be, could it?

Before I started helping Giorgio and
the partisans, they were scrounging
supplies somehow and just barely managing to survive. I felt a nagging irritation with Giorgio, as if he and his needs
were beginning to interfere with my *real*
work in the war, the work that had to do
with the Jews, not the partisan efforts.
But that's ridiculous, I told myself. *He's
my brother, and that's where my loyalties lie.*

It was already noon when I arrived at

the usual spot. Cecilio and Mario were there, and so were Giorgio and the Fox.

"So, what have you brought us?" Giorgio could barely contain his annoyance. "I'm assuming you saved the rest of this week's supplies to deliver personally." He stood there, his hands on his hips. "Come on, hand it over."

I was empty-handed. "Giorgio, I . . . I just didn't have time in the last few days. I'm sorry—I've been busy."

"Busy!" He looked over at the Fox with a sarcastic sneer. "Did you hear that? She's been too *busy*." He stood over me, close, so I could smell his breath. "Well, little sister, I don't really think you know what busy is. We are *hungry,* God damn it, while you are back there living in your cozy villa in the lap of luxury. I'll bet Rosa's still waiting on you hand and foot, isn't she?"

I wanted to tell him what it was like at home, eating in that cramped cage of a tiny room, the three of us, but I held my tongue. "Come over here a minute. I need to talk with you alone." He followed me to the other side of the clearing.

"I came to take Mario and Cecilio to a safer place."

He sobered. "Did you really find one?"

"I did. I can't tell you where right now, but I just didn't think that with Mario's arm and all, you needed to have to worry about them. It'll be safer for all of you this way."

He nodded. A boom echoed overhead, and we stopped talking. "They're close, Columba. They're penetrating the river valley right now, settling in, preparing to make a stand there. We've got plans for them, though. You can count on that." He turned and led me back to the group.

"Okay, Patch and Moses, stay here. You're going with Columba. The Fox and I are heading back to camp." He started to leave, then stopped and came back. He shook hands with Cecilio, his other arm on his shoulder. "Hey, thanks for everything, Patch. And Moses." He hugged Mario. "Be careful, okay? You're in good hands." I watched them cross and duck into the woods. "And Columba," he shouted back, "I'm counting on you to fill that cellar."

After Giorgio and the Fox disappeared, the three of us stood there awkwardly for a few minutes in silence. "Did you bring your things?" I asked.

"What *things*?" Cecilio growled. "We really don't have any *things*. We're not tourists, you know."

I winced. Cecilio was a guarded fortress with guns pointed my way. Mario jumped in. "We ended up sharing our few extra pieces of clothing with some of the guys who needed them more than we did," he said. "We'll be fine. We're used to this. Don't worry."

"Where are you taking us, anyway?" Cecilio looked at the ground, as if it weren't a big deal, as if he didn't really care.

"I'm taking you to a safe place." I looked at Mario. "You'll just have to trust me on this one. It's not what you might expect, but it's the only option we have right now."

"Giovanna, we . . ." He glanced at his brother. "We just can't thank you enough for this. It's a big risk for you. I know that."

"Well, we aren't there yet," I said.

"Let's wait until you're safe before you thank me." I motioned for them to follow me.

"Let me take that," said Mario, as he slung the bag I had been carrying over his good shoulder. "It's the least I can do." *At least there's almost nothing in it,* I thought.

We set off into the thick of the forest that surrounded the old gazebo, picking our way through brambles, stepping gingerly over mossy fallen logs, snaking our way in the general direction of the convent, avoiding any path I had ever taken before. I led the way, with Mario right behind me and Cecilio trailing him by several paces. In the distance, the bell tower tolled once. Two o'clock was only one hour away.

The going was difficult, so our pace was slow. Instead of following open roads, we had to cross them quickly and make our way along fences or stone walls between fields, where trees and underbrush could offer us some shelter. Once, a jeep full of German soldiers approached in a cloud of dust. We crouched low, holding our breath until the dust dissipated and we could no longer hear them. We didn't talk much. The tension between the two brothers stretched like a membrane over the silence, and I was afraid even a word from me would puncture it. At this point, getting there was all that mattered.

Mario's breath was labored. It was clear he was in pain, and I consciously slowed my pace even more than the terrain warranted. His rasping and an occasional low groan were the only efforts at human interchange. They had to be hungry too. How could I not have thought to bring some food along?

At one point, I left Mario and Cecilio sitting against a low stone wall. I ventured close to a farmhouse, thinking I might find a vegetable garden to raid. As I inched my way toward the high fenced area that looked promising, a deep, throaty growl startled me from the right. A large brown ridgeback lay chained to a stake. He stood up, pulled his tether tight, and curled back his lip, daring me to take another step his way. I had to go back to the brothers empty-handed.

"How much farther is it?" asked Cecilio when I got back. His brow was furrowed in irritation. "My brother's not doing so well."

"Do you see that hill above the patch of forest just ahead of us?" He nodded. "That's where we're headed. It shouldn't take us more than another twenty minutes, assuming we make steady progress." I looked at Mario, whose face had taken on the satiny sheen of perspiration I had seen before. "Can you make it?"

"I hope so," he said. "I'm not feeling well at all, Giovanna. But let's keep going."

Mario was stumbling now, his gait off balance and uneven. Now and then, he reached out his good arm and steadied himself on my shoulder. We made only twenty or so steps before we had to rest again. Each time we stopped, I tried to be patient and sit peacefully with them, but I knew our progress wasn't fast enough.

"Look, Cecilio," I finally said. "We just aren't moving as quickly as we should be, and we have to be there by two o'clock. Is there something you can do to support your brother or help him along?"

He stared back at me, and I swear I saw a mocking look in his one good eye. "Well, Columba"—his sarcasm was clear—"if we don't get to your 'safe place' by two o'clock, then I guess that means we won't be able to stay there, doesn't it?"

He really didn't care, did he? Hot tears welled up. "Maybe not, I don't know. I only know I was told to be there at exactly two. Someone is doing me a special favor, and I want to honor her and be there on time." I had a lump in my throat, and I was afraid I would start to cry.

I looked at Mario for support, but he was slumped over on the ground, his eyes closed. "If we move fast now, we can still make it. Can't you please just let him lean on you, or can we support him together?"

Mario stirred. "Just go," he said. His lips barely moved. "The two of you. I'll be all right here, and you can come back for me later."

"Sorry, brother," said Cecilio. "We made a pact, remember? Whatever happens, we don't separate. We're in this together." He looked at me with a triumphant glint in his eye.

"But we've got to move," I cried. "*Now.* Your lives depend on this."

Mario took shallow breaths. He didn't stir. Cecilio stared at me, defiant, mute.

I spun on my heels and pushed my way through the underbrush, headed for the convent, alone.

MARGARET WURTELE

Chapter Sixteen

The old wooden door to the wine cave vibrated against my spine as the tower bell tolled once, then again. Two o'clock. I sat leaning hard against the rough, grooved wood, knees drawn up to my chest, my chin resting there. Anger at Cecilio smoldered like flaring coal in my stomach. How dared he defy me after I had put both myself and the nuns at risk to try to save him? He was thinking only of himself and not his brother, who so desperately needed attention and shelter. I hated him, his mocking eye, his curled lip. But Mario. He was so gentle and kind, so vulnerable. In spite of it all, I admired their commitment to stay together as brothers no matter what happened.

A clank, then a scrape like a heavy metal bolt sliding on the inside of the door. The thick slab gave way behind me. I jumped to my feet as the door creaked open on its hinges. A musty smell of damp earth emanated from the blackness. I pushed the door open a little wider and stepped in. The air was thick with traces of old oak, of fermented fruit. I opened my eyes wide to try to penetrate the darkness, but I saw only the stripe of sunlight that fell across the earthen floor from the open door.

"Sister Graziella?" My voice was low, tentative. "Are you there?"

"Where are the two young men?" The voice coming from the blackness was dry and rasping, not Graziella's at all, but familiar nonetheless. A towering form materialized in the shaft of light: Sister Elena.

I shrank, my pulse racing, cowering against the door. "Sister Elena—I was to meet Sister Graziella here today."

"Yes, well, but this is my territory, I'm afraid."

"Your territory? The wine cellar?"

She ignored the question. "Where are the two men?" she repeated, not smiling.

Could she know? Could this mean that *she* was somehow the one who would help us? And now here I was, without them, disappointing her again. I explained that I had tried to make the two-o'clock deadline but that Mario was too ill to move and Cecilio refused to leave him. I was flushed with heat, and my voice felt thin and tight in the back of my throat. "I'm so worried about Mario, about both of them alone out there, and . . . Sister Elena, he's so sick."

I stared at her face—her jutting chin, the dry, sallow skin, the thin lips drawn down into the ever-present frown. She was a long-necked tortoise, her draped habit a thick, impenetrable shell on her back. But for the first time, as I stared into those closely set, hooded eyes, I saw something else there. They flashed as they always had, but this time I read it not as anger, but as determination and fierce resolve.

She wasted not one minute on sympathy or concern but was all business. "Wait right here, Giovanna. I will fetch Guido the winemaker. You will take him with you to find the men. He and the brother can carry the wounded one back on a blanket." She turned and disappeared back into the dark cellar.

❦

Guido was shaped like a wine barrel. He wore a soiled kerchief knotted loosely around his thick neck and a stained leather vest that had no hope of coming together across his massive girth. Pantaloons draping much thinner legs were loosely gathered into his rough laced boots. He walked more like a duck than a man, each side of his trunk heaving forward in turn, propelled by an awkward, shuffling gait. He wheezed with every step, expelling clouds reminiscent of the wine cellar's damp, fetid air.

I felt instantly at home with this bear of a man and knew that I could trust him. There was no holding back on his part, only warmth, interest, and concern.

"These two brothers?" he asked, huffing and puffing behind me as we made our way down the back of the forested hill.

"Yes, that's why they want to stay together," I answered.

"One wounded, you say—how bad?"

He shook his head from side to side and made a clucking noise with his tongue as I described Mario's arm and what I was sure was a serious infection. "Can't keep 'em at the convent, you know. Women only there."

I turned to look back at him. "But I thought . . . I thought maybe Graziella had arranged—"

"Nope." Heavy footsteps echoed my own. "Not there. Elena, she's taken in a few women, but no men."

So it *was* Sister Elena after all. "But then why would she tell me to—"

"The wife and I, we'll keep 'em for a little while in our place. We got a storeroom that'll work for now. Done it before."

We walked on, picking our way through the landscape in silence.

"They friends of yours?" The question was simple, but I wasn't sure how to answer. I thought of Cecilio's wary, hostile eye and shivered. But whenever my thoughts drifted toward Mario, there was a soft, teasing ripple, like a downy feather lifting in a slight breeze. "Yes, they are." I said it before I really planned to. "That is to say the wounded one more than the other."

I looked back at Guido and saw him nod to himself.

Mario was lying on his back, unconscious, when we found the two brothers right where I had left them. We burst into the small clearing, and Cecilio, seeing Guido, leaped to his feet. His upper lip was fixed in a sneer that spoke volumes. Guido, on his part, wasted no time.

He unrolled the blanket, lifted one side of Mario's body, and stuffed half of the blanket underneath. "Pull it out the other side," he barked to Cecilio, motioning with his hand. "Now you take the two corners at the feet, and I'll take the head—and don't give me any guff, sonny, you hear? You're gonna have to spend a little of your precious energy, but we'll get your brother into bed, by God."

℘

Guido's wife, Serena, was as round as he was. Her dark hair was plaited in a long braid that wrapped around her head like a halo. She moved smoothly, deliberately, and was surprisingly grace-ful for such a large woman. She had been expecting us; that much was clear, and if she resented this intrusion into their private lives, she made no sign of it. We followed her back to a small stor-age room behind the kitchen where a stained canvas army cot had been set up. There, with relief, Guido and Cecilio set down their burden.

Mario's face was ashen, his jaw slack. Serena felt his forehead with the back of her plump hand and slowly shook her head. She stroked the bandaged arm, then laid it gingerly across his stomach. "He's very sick. You know that." She looked at me. "I will do what I can, but I . . ." She shook her head.

Shame at my own ineptitude washed over me in the presence of such solidity and generosity. "There is a new medicine," I said, "one that can help fight an infection like this. I . . . I tried to give him a shot, but I dropped the needle and couldn't do it. I'll come back tomorrow. I'll bring another shot—and fresh bandages too." The enormity of what this couple was doing was suddenly clear. "I don't know how I can thank you for this."

"It won't be for long. I told you that."

Guido shot a glance at Cecilio. "You've got to lie low here, fella. Stay quiet. And my wife's going to put you to work; you can bet on that."

℃

When I got home, I found Rosa chopping garlic and onions for Sunday evening's dinner. She looked up, her eyes watering. "It's about time, young lady." She clucked. "I was beginning to wonder whether our boys would starve to death." She wiped her eyes with her apron, then settled her hands on her hips, her back stiff and erect, waiting to hear what I would say.

"I'm sorry. I've had other things to do, and now Giorgio's so angry that I've been neglecting the Santinis' cellar."

"Did you say the Santinis?"

"Signora Santini gave me permission to leave the supplies there and even to help myself to some vegetables from their garden. That's where I've been taking most of the food."

"But Pia, their kitchen maid, is a good friend of mine." Rosa pursed her thin lips, furrowed her brow. "I wonder if she knows. She's never mentioned it. Maybe she could help us."

I thought of what it would mean to add the accumulations of another family's supplies to our own. "That would be perfect, if she can be trusted. Could you ask her?" I let myself down heavily on a wooden chair. "I'm just so overwhelmed. I have some duties to perform at the convent every morning, all my work at the clinic, and now"—I looked away from her, out the window—"there's something else. A whole new thing I just can't talk about."

She raised her eyebrows quizzically.

"You've got to trust me. This one's just too big. But what it means is . . ." I swallowed hard and gripped both sides of the chair seat. "I don't know how long I can go on supplying Giorgio's men." I stood up and took hold of her hands. "Is there any way you and Pia could take that over? You'd be much better at it than I am, and maybe you'd even have fun doing it together. I just can't be in four places at once."

She turned back to the butcher block and began peeling and mincing cloves of garlic, one after another, without saying a word. It smelled delicious, and my mind wandered back to the winemaker's house. How, I wondered, would Serena and Guido do with two extra mouths to feed?

At last she stopped, looking down, knife frozen in the air. "I will talk with Pia. I will take what I have now over there tomorrow."

"Oh, Rosa, you have no idea how much this would help." I reached my arms around her sinewy frame from behind and hugged her.

"Just go," she said. "Just go."

❧

I was so exhausted at supper I could barely lift my fork. Rosa came and went without giving me so much as a single glance. I sat up straight, not wanting to call attention to myself.

"Does it seem to you that Rosa's cooking less food these days?" Father scraped the last of the *fagioli* from a platter onto his plate when she had left the room.

"Easy, easy," Mother said. "She does the best she can. I'm sure supplies are hard to come by."

I kept quiet, vowing to cut down on my own portions. Below us a couple of German vehicles pulled to a stop. Hearty shouts rose as some of our housemates greeted the new arrivals. There was rough, bold laughter, then the slamming of doors.

Father seemed to be working himself up to something. He mopped his entire plate with bread, picked up his wineglass, then his water, moved his fork from one side of the plate to the other. "I don't know much more than this, but apparently there was some action in the river valley today."

Mother looked up. "What's that, dear?"

"In Diecimo. Apparently since dawn yesterday, when the evacuation began, the Germans have been taking over the town building by building. They've moved into the vacant houses, set themselves up in the restaurants—"

"Well, we know what that feels like." She rolled her eyes. "At least they don't have to live in the same house with them."

Father ignored her and went on. "So last night—it was Saturday night, you know." He paused. "A lot of them were gathered in the cinema watching some German movie when a partisan bomb went off."

Mother and I both set down our forks at once.

"It blew the place up, killed a bunch of them too."

"Germans or partisans?" Mother's face drained to the color of the tablecloth.

"I don't know." He avoided looking at her. "The radio only mentioned Germans, but who knows?"

Tears welled up in Mother's eyes. She folded her arms across her chest. "Enrico, I'm not sure I can take much more of this. What if Giorgio was part of it?"

"Oh, come on. There are hundreds of those guys all over Tuscany. I doubt that Giorgio would be working quite so close to home. But war is a dangerous business. You know that."

I stared fixedly at my plate. What if it *was* Giorgio's band? My stomach twisted into a knot as I imagined the possibilities. An image of Mario's oozing arm floated into my consciousness, and I was surprised to note that my first thought had been not of my own brother, but relief that I knew exactly where Mario was. "Don't worry, Mama." I kept my voice calm to hide the feelings behind it and reached out and stroked her arm. "I'll see if there's any news tomorrow at the clinic."

"Hell, it's progress, isn't it?" Father broke in. "Maybe they're doing some good after all."

Was it possible I caught a note of pride in his voice?

❦

I could not sleep that night. My mind was ablaze with images of exploding stone and splinters of wood, of torn up-holstery seats and, worse, bodies tossed and thrown in every direction. I dared not imagine that Giorgio had been there, but this was his territory in a way. Di-ecimo was not far, nestled in the river valley not ten kilometers away.

I imagined the German soldiers, re-laxed, their arms about the seats beside them, laughing, enjoying a film. What if Klaus had been among them? In spite of myself, I worried about him as well. I turned over and over, on the one hand thinking anxious thoughts of Giorgio and his band, on the other focusing on the soldiers I had come to know at the School of Santa Maria. Underlying it all was a steady dread about Mario's arm and the infection that was slowly rob-bing him of strength and maybe life.

I must have fallen asleep at some point, because the next thing I knew,

daylight rimmed the shutters. My eyelids were swollen and dry, pulled apart,
and my head was thick with fear and
exhaustion.

℘

I found Violetta outside the clinic supply
room, deep in discussion with the
marchesa. They were clearly arguing
about something, so I parked my bicycle and approached slowly, trying to appear distracted.

"But why wouldn't you give priority to
one of the partisans?" Violetta was
pleading. "You may be English, but he's
going to die today unless we at least try
to fight the infection."

"I'm sorry, dear." The marchesa put
an arm gently on Violetta's shoulder. "I
love and admire your compassion. I
really do. This is so hard. But ultimately
this is my clinic, my property, and I alone
am the one who has to make these difficult decisions. Captain Ashbery has
turned the corner. Unless we finish the
series, all of our progress will be lost.
There is no guarantee that this new sol-

dier will last the day—no matter what we do."

Violetta turned and stalked away, her mouth tight. She saw me, grabbed my hand, and pulled me away behind the building. Tears were streaming down her cheeks. "She's"—her breathing was so fast she couldn't get the words out— "going . . . to kill him."

"Who? Who, Violetta?" I held her by the shoulders and shook her. "Stop it. Just breathe. Tell me what happened."

She nodded, then found the rhythm in her breath again. "I was walking in the nearby field yesterday evening. There was a man lying there. Oh, Giovanna. It was awful." She shook her head, tears brimming again. "He was dressed in rags, old military clothes of various kinds. I guessed he was a partisan, but he was in such bad shape, I couldn't . . ." She began to cry again, her hands covering her face. "Oh, God. His hair and whole forehead were burned off; his shoulder was blown away—he was losing blood fast, but I got him to stand up and lean against me. 'There's a clinic nearby,' I told him. 'If you can walk, just come with me. I'll find you a bed.' I guess his legs were okay, because we finally made it back here. He has some kind of accent, but he speaks Italian. He told me he had been part of the bombing in Diecimo last night. I have no idea how he made it this far."

"But why won't the marchesa help him?"

"We have only two more vials of the penicillin left. She hasn't even seen him. She just insists that it is reserved for this English parachutist who's already so much better. He's going to make it, but she says the infection can flare again if we don't give him another round."

"The partisan—is he still conscious? Can you take me to him?"

We raced up the stone staircase and down the aisle between the lines of cots to where a stained, wrinkled sheet hung on a wire, separating one bed at the very end. A man with a long, bony frame lay covered with an army blanket. His head was wrapped in bandages to the eyebrows; his shoulder was bleeding so profusely that the bandages were already soaked through. His breathing was barely perceptible.

I knelt by the bed and took the hand of his good arm. He stirred a little, mumbling. I leaned over him and, when I looked closely at his face, saw the cut of his jaw and the freckled, translucent skin, my own breath stopped. It was the Fox. I brought my lips close to his ear. "Fox. It's Giovanna; it's Giorgio's sister, Columba."

His eyes opened a slit, and he moaned. His lips were parched and cracked. "Do you want some water?" I asked, stroking his cheek gently.

He shook his head slowly. "There were twenty of them in there, maybe more."

"Germans?"

He nodded once.

"What happened to you?" I whispered in his ear.

"I placed the bomb. It . . . went off . . . too soon . . . caught me on the way out." His breathing seemed to stop altogether.

"And my brother?" I shook him rudely, insistently. "Giorgio—is he okay?"

I waited while he took another slow

breath. He opened his eyes and looked at me. "He was the one manning the plunger—two houses away. . . . So hard to time those things." His eyelids closed. "He's okay. . . . I'm sure. But they had all run away when I came out. I . . . I got disoriented and just ended up here."

I rose and saw that Violetta was still standing next to the bed. She spoke in a low voice, staring at the cot. "You know this man?"

"He works with my brother." I turned to walk away. "Not only that," I added. "Tell the marchesa he's English."

I marched down the aisle between the rows of beds, looking neither right nor left. I slowly descended the stone staircase, wincing at the bottom as the bright morning light assaulted my eyes. The door to the supply room gave as I leaned gently into it. There was no sound as I closed it carefully behind me. I squeaked open the cupboard where the penicillin was kept, and sure enough, there they were: two vials. My heart was loud in my ears, and sweat beaded on my nose and forehead. With trembling hands, I wrapped the medicine carefully in a piece of cloth and took three new syringes from the box, along with cotton pads and a bottle of alcohol. I stuffed them all into my shoulder bag.

Then I walked slowly, nonchalantly to my bicycle and pedaled away.

Chapter Seventeen

I was aware, the closer I drew to the winemaker's cottage, of being anchored by a pervasive dread. Each revolution of the bicycle's pedals seemed to take more and more effort. The drag was not, I knew, due to the terrain. I was weighed down first by terror that Mario had not survived even the night, and then by anxiety that if I did find him alive, I would once again be unable to accomplish the simple deed.

As I negotiated the ruts in the road, I began slowly to accept the fear. I knew it was there; I knew there was good reason for it, so a new determination took hold. It came over me like an advancing bank of thunderclouds—fierce resolve, charged by anxiety. If I found Mario alive, I would not fail him this time. I imagined my own confidence in front of Serena's watchful gaze; I visualized my hand, steady on the syringe; I pictured the life-giving serum entering Mario's bloodstream and restoring him slowly to health.

Serena took a long time to answer my knock on the door. It was too loud, perhaps, too resolute for it to be me, to be anyone but a German soldier. When she did crack the door and peer out, her face brightened instantly.

"Giovanna! Thank God you are here. Come in, come in."

"How is Mario?"

"Do you have the medicine?" she asked, ignoring my question.

I nodded, holding up the bag.

She took hold of my arm and guided me back through the tiny kitchen. On the rough wooden table, a fat loaf of new bread, crusty and round, nested on branches of fresh-cut rosemary that would infuse it as it cooled. A pot of soup bubbled on the woodstove, filling the kitchen with its moist steam, its scent of onion and old bones. At the door to the storeroom, she paused. "Prepare yourself. He will not last much longer, I'm afraid."

The afternoon light was beginning to fade, making it hard to see in the tiny storeroom. Mario lay on the folded army cot, wasted, waxen. His jaw was slack, his hollowed eyes closed, his skin stretched like yellowed parchment over the bones of his cheeks. His breathing was shallow, labored. Out of the corner of my eye, I took in the figure of Cecilio, arms folded, leaning against the corner of the room. I did not acknowledge him but went right to work.

It was just as I had rehearsed in my imagination—I felt calm and confident, and I rode the fear like a boat floating on waves. I turned him on his side, and as before, I swabbed a spot with alcohol, filled the syringe from the vial. But this time, I positioned the needle at an angle with a rock-steady hand and slowly, without a tremor, pushed the plunger all the way in. As I held another cotton swab over the site and gradually removed the needle, I exhaled a silent prayer. It was for the Fox, for the repose of his soul, and for my own absolution.

℃

I sat still for a long time, watching Mario breathe. Who was this man for whom I had possibly just sacrificed a life, maybe two? I couldn't explain the urgency I had felt, the compulsion to rush to his aid, the magnetism that drew me then and that kept me now at his side, hanging on his every breath as if my own depended on it.

I looked up at Serena. "That's it. I don't know what else we can do except wait for a change. He'll need another shot in a few days." I took the extra vial and handed it to her. "Here—hide this where it will be safe."

"How long do you think it will be before we can move on?" The voice came from the corner. Cecilio, arms still folded, his fingers white as they gripped his upper arms, was tapping his foot nervously on the floor.

Serena put her hands on her hips. "You're not going anywhere for a while," she said. "Your brother's a sick man, and your short fuse isn't going to help him heal any faster." She looked at me. "Cecilio here is like a fly caught under a jar. He's got to learn to relax, to settle in with some patience."

"Patience? You want me to have *patience?* It's been three years since these Nazi vermin have been crawling all over our country. Three years! Who knows what's happened to my parents? I haven't seen anyone I know for months and months. I just want to get the hell out of here."

"But the Allies are close," I said. "They're working their way in this direction. You just need to hold on until they liberate us, until the Germans are forced to leave."

Cecilio leaned over the cot, his head directly over Mario's, and stared. There was no visible change in his brother, who lay inert, pale, his chest rising and falling almost imperceptibly with each shallow breath. "Well, I just don't want to wait here anymore, okay?" I thought he looked as if he might cry. "How do I know that this medicine will do any good? I feel like a sitting duck in your cottage here." He began pacing, filling the tiny room with his frustration, forcing Serena and me to flatten ourselves against the wall to give him space. "At least the partisans are *doing* something. I'm going to go find them again."

"You can't." I gasped. "Cecilio, please think about it. Don't do that. They're in enough trouble without having to hide you as well. Just stay here. As soon as he's well enough, I'll find you both another place to stay. I swear I will."

He turned to face me. "I don't want to leave Mario, but I just can't stay here biding my time another minute. I'll stay in touch somehow." He turned back to the cot and paused for a moment, looking down at his brother. *What about your pledge to stay together?* I thought, willing him to honor it, but he lifted his jacket from the end of the cot and left the room. I watched him as he crossed the tiny kitchen, grabbed the fresh loaf of bread off the table, and took off out the door into the gathering dusk.

℈

There was nothing more to do except wait—and hope. I avoided the clinic for the next couple of days. It was fear, of course, that kept me away, and anxiety about Mario. I wanted to stay close to Guido and Serena's cottage. I showed up bright and early in the mornings to carry out my sweeping penance at the convent. I looked in vain for either Sister Graziella or Sister Elena. Only a few young novitiates seemed to be about. I wondered, as I made my rounds, where in the vast reaches of the old stone complex could the women and maybe even children be hidden? Once, when I had finished sweeping a corner stair-case, I was drawn down a long hall by what I thought were female voices. I passed a row of tightly closed wooden doors, their imposing metal keyholes staring at me like so many watchful eyes, but as I stole up and down the length of the corridor, I heard nothing but the squeak of my own shoes on the stone.

Sister Graziella was right: I began to find the sweeping a meditation of sorts.

As I focused on the thick, stiff straws and followed their determined motion back and forth, up and around, my mind began to quiet and settle in the present moment. It was the only time during the day when I could set aside all my worries—about the marchesa, Giorgio, and even Mario. I seemed just to breathe and sweep, sweep and breathe until time melted away. Afterward, I felt refreshed, as I had that afternoon when Sister Graziella and I sat in silence together in the parlor. Each day I felt good about completing the penance, but more than that, I appreciated the respite from my worries. I had found a deep well of peace that I began to associate with Saint Agnes, and it became the highlight of my days.

Nevertheless, these past two days when I closed the big entrance door behind me, I felt the marchesa weighing heavily on my conscience. I had betrayed her—deliberately stolen from her, no doubt at the cost of one or two men's lives. By Thursday morning guilt plagued me so during my sweeping that when I was finished I went straight to the clinic, not even stopping to check on Mario's progress.

I parked my bike and stood there for a few minutes, trying to decide what I should do next. I heard agitated voices coming from the tower calling, "Careful now," and, "Easy does it." Violetta and another young nurse emerged, followed by two men struggling to balance a stretcher between them. I hung back, but I could see a figure lying on it wrapped head to toe in gray army blankets. I was about to step toward them when the marchesa emerged, bringing up the rear. She looked terrible. Her clothes were disheveled and stained. She ran her fingers through her unkempt hair, pulling it back off her face. I could see she had been crying. "Just lay him down in the shade over there for now," she said wearily. "I'll ask my husband to bring the jeep around."

"Giovanna!" Violetta's voice was sharp. "There you are." They all turned their heads to look at me.

I stood there mute, my heart beating so hard I was sure all of them could hear it. I looked at the ground, then took a tentative step forward. "Who's . . ." I waved a hand toward the stretcher.

Violetta was frozen, staring at me. I could see her blink back tears and shake her head the tiniest millimeter back and forth. No one else noticed, but I knew her so well, I knew exactly what she meant. She was warning me not to say anything; she knew I had taken the penicillin.

"He's the son of an old family friend, I'm afraid," said the marchesa, wiping a tear from her cheek with the back of her hand. "He parachuted into this area about three weeks ago when his plane was hit by German artillery. He was doing so well at the end of last week, but . . ." She hesitated. "We ran out of penicillin, and"—she took a deep breath—"the infection got away from us last night. Now I'm going to have to wire his family. He's their only child." Her face twisted in a fresh wave of grief, and she turned away, walking off in the direction of their villa.

We watched her go without speaking. The men continued on, carrying the stretcher and laying it down gently under a spreading linden tree. Then they sat down next to the body to rest.

I approached Violetta. "And my brother's friend?"

"The redhead? Oh, he died that same night." She looked at me straight on, defiantly, speaking under her breath. "How could you, Giovanna? How could you do that, just take it like that? I can't believe it."

"What does the marchesa think?"

"Oh, I just told her it was missing. I never told her that you were there that day. In fact, I told her the redhead said he was a friend of your brother—so she would think you'd want him to get the shot, at least. But why? Why would you do that? You knew how much we needed it."

I looked around. The marchesa was out of sight; the men were talking quietly under the tree. "Walk with me," I said. "We need to talk." I took Violetta's arm in mine and led her off toward the other side of the tower.

"It's that same man, isn't it?" she asked. "The one I gave you the other penicillin for."

I nodded.

"Who is he?"

"Can I trust you to keep a secret?"

"I haven't said a word about Giorgio to anyone."

I took her hand. "He's Jewish."

She looked at me soberly, then nodded. "And?"

"And I can't explain it, but I'm so drawn to him. I don't know why, even though I hardly know him, this really matters to me."

"He must be very sick."

"He would have died without that penicillin. I'm sure of that. I feel so terrible about the marchesa's friend, but I . . ." Hot tears blurred my vision, and I started to sob. "I should never have taken it, but there was no question. I had to do it. I just lost all sense of right and wrong. What should I do?"

Violetta straightened, and her face hardened. "I know you. I know how much you want to confess, but take my advice: Don't do it."

I gave her a questioning look.

"Those two men—your brother's friend and the parachutist—are already dead. Nothing's going to bring them back now. This is war, and I've seen a lot of death in this clinic. That's just the way it is."

"But I owe her an apology. I feel so terrible."

"I know, but just give her time. You also need her as an ally and friend. We both do, and I . . . I've been covering for you. If she finds out, it will implicate me as well. Let's just wait. You never know how it's going to go." She looked away, then back at me. "Where is he—your friend?"

"I can't tell you that. But, Violetta . . ." I giggled in spite of myself. "You'll never guess who's really saved the day."

She shrugged.

"Who's the last person you would ever turn to if you were in trouble?"

A little smile tugged at the corner of her mouth. "A nun?" I nodded. Violetta's eyes popped wide. She shook her head in disbelief. "No. But how . . ."

The sound of an approaching jeep sobered us both. We linked arms and headed back to pay our respects to the marchesa's family friend.

ℒ

"Do you ever hear from your friend Signora Lazzato?" I came upon Mother later that afternoon, bent over a potted cone-shaped topiary, her most delicate pruning shears *snip-snip*ping microscopic portions of leaf away as if she were painting a tiny landscape on a piece of porcelain. Her hand paused in its work. She lifted the tool slightly and murmured, without looking at me, "Why ever do you ask that, dear?"

"I remember you used to play the piano with her. Then she left for New York, and I just wondered. They're Jewish, right?"

She straightened and assumed her usual posture, holding herself as elegantly as a dancer on point. She removed her gardening gloves slowly; then with one finger she smoothed off the sheen of perspiration that had formed along each side of her nose. "They left for New York because Signor Lazzato felt the business opportunities were greater there." It had a rote feel, like a line of poetry that had been committed to memory but never fully absorbed.

"But wasn't he one of the best silk salesmen? I even remember Papa saying once that Signor Lazzato was his chief rival for vice president of the company."

"Mmm. He was very talented in that way, very good with people." She squinted at the topiary, studying it closely for flaws.

"So why would they leave for New York? If he was so successful here, why wouldn't he want to stay on and move up, take on more responsibility in a company he knew so well?"

She snipped an errant twig, gloves still off, then straightened again, sighing. "It was more complicated than that, Giovanna. Your father . . ." She looked up at the sky and fanned herself lightly with the loose gloves. "There was a lot of talk in the party then about changing the rules for people of Jewish background."

"And Papa went along with that?"

"Well, dear, as I remember it, he wasn't sure, but there were pressures on Mussolini in those days. Our allies had certain expectations."

"I know, Mama, but it wasn't right. Those rules were absurd. You said so yourself. Look now what Hitler's done. Father must have known they were bad."

"Your father wasn't *for* it, you understand, but he had his own reputation to think about, his own standing in the company."

"But if Signor Lazzato left, it would clear a path for him, right? No more competition. He'd be the obvious heir apparent. How convenient." When I pushed Mother like this, I always became acutely aware of the physical differences between us: her height, her elegance, my own sloppy dress and lumpy lines. It made me doubt my own feelings. "Wasn't he ashamed of the party? The Lazzatos were good friends of yours, right?"

"Olivia was a dear, dear friend of mine. We had the music, and . . ." She smiled at the memory, a wave of animation sweeping her face. "She had such a great sense of humor; we used to—" She broke off suddenly, sobering. "But your father didn't feel the same way about them, so even though we were neighbors, we rarely got together as a—"

She pushed that away and added quickly, "Enrico used his own contacts to get them safe passage. They were so grateful, but—as you say—maybe he had some of his own self-interest at heart."

"He wanted to take over the company."

"Yes, but now, in retrospect, Giovanna, he may have saved their lives by helping them leave." Mother picked up her gardening basket and handed it to me to carry. She put an arm around my shoulder and gently led me across the gravel terrace toward the villa. "As you know, your father's family background just isn't the same as mine. I think he's tried to learn to be more tolerant, especially now, with all that's been happening, but he doesn't . . . he's never—"

"He just thinks they're *different,* right?" My voice was tight in my throat, and tears sprang to my eyes. "I see where you are going, Mother. And I don't like it at all." I broke away from her and ran toward the house, letting the basket slip from my hand. I heard a loud clatter as the tools, one by one, hit the gravel behind me.

⟨ℭ⟩

Saturday morning, after my time at the convent, I was surprised, as I approached the cottage, to hear a male voice. I knew Guido would be at the winery at that hour, so it could only be Mario's. Every cell in my body quickened as a wave of anxiety swept over me and settled in my gut. The door was unlocked, so I tapped lightly and entered. I could hear Serena back in the storeroom. "No. I'm sorry. He's not here. I'm sure of it."

"He must be nearby." That was Mario. "My brother would never leave me. We had a pact to stay together no matter what happened."

I opened the storeroom door slowly. Mario was trying to sit up on one elbow, and Serena was pushing him back down. "No, no. You just rest. There's nothing to be done."

"I hear him! He's back! I just heard the door," said Mario. Then he saw me. He looked confused—as if he were searching his memory, trying to connect my face with something.

"You remember Giovanna," said Serena. "She's the one who brought you and your brother here."

His face was gaunt, shadowed by a week's growth of beard, but for all that his hazel eyes burned more intensely. "Giovanna . . . Giorgio's sister."

"That's right." I smiled. "It's good to hear your voice again." I wanted to reach out my hand to him, but I kept my arms folded instead.

"Where's my brother? Where's Cecilio?"

I glanced at Serena. "We don't know. He said he was going to find Giorgio again . . . but it's been five days since he left. We haven't heard a word, I'm afraid."

He rose again with great effort, trying to sit up. "I need to go after him. He's my big brother, and we promised to stay together."

"You can't, Mario," Serena said.

"You're not strong enough, and it's much too dangerous. Just rest now. We promise we'll ask about him and let you know if we hear any news at all." She put her hand on the small of my back, gently pressing me into her place. "I'll get some soup. I've just got it warming on the stove."

Mario lay back, exhausted. He was quiet for a few long minutes, his eyes closed. Then he looked up at me. "How could he do that? Leave me here? We promised." He looked away, toward the wall, and a tear eased out of the corner of his eye and slid slowly down his cheek. I watched it meet the roots of his sprouting beard and dissipate.

"He was angry," I said, "and probably scared."

Mario remained quiet.

"I guess he just ran out of patience," I added.

"He's like that."

"He'll be fine, I'm sure," I said quickly. Then, because I was afraid I had not been convincing enough: "He'll find someone to help him. Don't worry."

"Cecilio doesn't like to be helped. He

doesn't want to need it. Never has." He closed his eyes again, and another tear came. By the time it caught up with the first, he was asleep.

I tiptoed out of the room and into the kitchen. Serena, a blue apron tied over her sleeveless cotton housedress, was ladling steaming soup into a large earthenware bowl. "He's asleep," I said. "Don't bother."

"He's a nice young man," she said, tipping the bowl back into the pot. I stared absently at the cascade of dark red beans, cubes of carrot, onion, squash, and a web of greens sliding back into the thick bubbling minestrone. It smelled delicious. I must have inhaled a little too greedily, because she set Mario's down and pulled another bowl from the pile. "Won't you have some? Here, *cara*. Somebody might as well enjoy this."

We took our places at the small table, setting our bowls on its cloth, once the color of sunflower petals, now bleached and mottled with years of laundering and use. Serena's nails were chipped and rough. Her knuckles were swollen, and the ends of her fingers seemed to grow sideways out of them. I winced inwardly as she wielded her spoon, imagining how painful that must be.

"You and Guido are so generous to do this. I can't tell you how much I admire you."

"We all have to do our part," she said. "It just isn't right the way these Germans search them out." She scraped at the side of her bowl. "And just because of their religion. Why?"

"It must be hard for you. I'm so sorry to have put you in this position."

"Every day, all the time, I'm listening for a knock at the door. Can't sleep a lot of nights. Now, yes, with Mario staying here, it's worse again." She put down her spoon and leaned back in her chair. "You know, Guido and I, we've been working for the sisters for many years now. I guess a bit of them's rubbed off on us. Jesus was pretty radical, pretty clear about how to be." She winked at me. "He was a Jew himself, you know." She sobered. "But we did tell you it's not for long, right? Now that he's on the mend, you'll need to be thinking ahead, figure out where you can take him, a more permanent hiding place."

A hollow pocket under my ribs began to burn. My face must have shown it, for she added, "But he's in no condition to move now, little lady. That's for sure."

"That reminds me," I said, standing and carrying my bowl to the sink. "Where did you hide that other vial? It's time for me to give him the second shot of penicillin."

Chapter Eighteen

The end of July settled into a kind of routine that I found immensely comforting in the midst of all the chaos of that summer and its war. Beginning each day at the convent, I was usually alone except for the occasional passing figure of a novitiate or older nun who might nod politely but rarely, if ever, spoke to me.

Once, only once, I encountered Sister Graziella. It was odd, because I had not set eyes on her since her nonappearance in the wine caves the day of our arrival. I had missed her. I must have been deeply absorbed in my work that morning, because when I felt a tap on my shoulder, I cried out as if a mouse had just run under my feet.

"Graziella!" I clutched the broom to my chest to stop the pounding of my heart. "You scared me to death!"

"I'm sorry, dear. I wanted to apologize for failing to meet you and the young men," she said. "I hope you will forgive me." A warm smile dimpled her round cheeks and lit up her merry eyes. "You know now that Elena was really the one to deal with the situation. I was afraid if I told you she was the one you were to meet"—she grimaced—"you might not have come."

"And I owe you an apology for misjudging her," I said. "She just always seemed so angry and impatient, as if she didn't like me. Now I feel nothing but gratitude."

Graziella hesitated, as if she were reluctant to go on. "You haven't entirely misjudged her, my dear. She *is* angry— very, very angry—and with good reason. You see, Elena's grandparents on one side were Jewish. Her father converted to Catholicism when he married her mother. Elena was raised Catholic—she is a devout, committed believer—but her roots are important to her. This war has, from the beginning, been so very difficult. Her activism is a way of channeling her anger to good purposes."

"When you see her, will you let her know how grateful I am? I haven't had a chance to tell her myself. And, Sister Graziella, this is going to sound odd, but—"

"Yes?" She smiled. "What is it?"

"I just want to thank you for giving me this sweeping penance. It's—I don't know how to express this—it's been a refuge for me, a gift really."

She nodded slowly, a look of satisfaction spreading over her face. "I know. Prayer can take many forms. Remember that." She reached for me and enfolded me to her soft bosom. "Bless you, Giovanna. You're a courageous young woman. May God keep you safe in your work."

❧

Calmed by my morning hours at the convent, I would head for Serena's nearby cottage. It drew me like a magnet. I was embarrassed at first to show up every day like that, worrying about what Serena would think. She didn't need me to look after Mario, after all, so I would leave something behind—a sweater, a shawl, an excuse to stop by the next day to pick it up. I would bring her the occasional squash or peach that I knew she didn't have in her own garden. She got used to me, and I think she welcomed the company.

The second penicillin shot had put Mario on a slow, steady path back to health. His eyes gradually began to focus on his surroundings; his color improved. He started to drink water, to eat soup, then solid food, and his face filled out again.

One day I noticed his soiled shirt had been replaced by one of Guido's—it fit him more like a dress than a shirt, but at least it was clean and neat—and Serena was in the midst of giving him a shave and trimming his hair. "I'm tired of him looking like a bum," she said. "I thought there might be a handsome man underneath all those weeds." She winked at me between snips.

Indeed, there was. I made an effort to remain impassive, but I watched out of the corner of my eye with great interest. Clean shaven, I could see Mario's face: his olive skin, his high forehead that slanted down toward full, prominent brows. His dark hair was shorter now, shaped overall, but it curled in every direction with a life of its own. He was handsome, but his looks were not intimidating. They gave him a friendly, self-deprecating air that softened every passing expression with a hint of humor.

He rolled his eyes. "She won't give me a mirror, so I can't manage what's happening to me." He shook his head slightly and looked up at me, as if he were asking for an assessment.

"Hmmm," I said, holding up my hand with the thumb and fingers spread as an artist might size up his subject. "I'd say things are shaping up nicely. Wouldn't you, Serena?"

"Yes, they are, *cara mia*." She took a couple of final snips at the back of his neck, brushed off his shoulders, and stuck the scissors in her apron pocket. "There. That should do it—a new man." She stepped back, looked appraisingly at Mario, then turned her back to him. She raised her eyebrows at me, opening her eyes wide. "Not bad at all." She grinned. "Now, if you'll excuse me, I'm going to go back to my pasta sauce."

She left the room and closed the door behind her. I was suddenly shy, as if confronted by a stranger. Without the beard, Mario was unmasked. No longer the scruffy partisan fighter or the hunted refugee, he looked like one of the boys from school or the town. I was thrown into the self-consciousness I usually felt around boys, especially good-looking ones like him. I started to turn away, to give him his privacy and opt for the comfort of Serena's kitchen, but he reached out to me. "Sit down," he said. "Talk with me awhile. You're always leaving to help her."

I didn't realize he had noticed. I stood stiffly next to the cot. "What do you want to talk about?" It was awkward, but I was not feeling confident or easy.

"Won't you please sit down?" he asked again.

There was a small stool that Serena had been using, so I perched tentatively on its edge, my hands between my knees.

"Have you been in a lot of pain?" I asked.

"Has there been anything except pain? It seems like forever that the burning of this arm has been my whole existence. All I can really remember is sleeping and dreaming—frightening dreams of looking for my mother, of losing things, of being chased by wild animals. Whenever I'd wake up, I was in a fog, a strange house, a kind woman, more pain, and now and then"—he looked at me shyly— "a girl with a halo of curly hair and lovely eyes. *Who is she?* I would think. Her smile lit up the place. Her voice was like music." He looked away again. "I can't believe this is all happening, this running away, this hiding. I'm not like that—not at all. I'm used to being strong, competent, to having the world go my way. Where are my friends? My family? Where is my city? How did I get here? We were on our way south, trying to break through into the Allied side, when we ran into Giorgio and his gang. Then that explosion, and . . ." He sat there for a long time in silence.

"I'm so worried about my brother," he said. "Do you know if he ever found Giorgio again?"

"No—I haven't seen Giorgio recently."

"You haven't? Why not?"

I took a deep breath, then launched into the story of what had happened since he and Cecilio had been delivered here, from Rosa's taking over the food supply cellar to the Fox's death. Mario shook his head sadly, and I was conscious of leaving out how his own recovery was a direct function of the Fox's demise.

"Do you think you could get a meeting with your brother? I just have to find out whether Cecilio is with them or not."

"Maybe. I suppose I could leave a note in the Santinis' cellar."

Mario took a deep breath and let it out slowly.

I pressed forward. "He's so angry, Mario. Honestly, I'm sorry to say this, but I hope he's *not* with my brother. He could put them all in danger."

He fidgeted with the bedcover. "I know, I know. He's always had a short fuse, ever since we were children."

"What was he like then?"

"I think he was born with a nervous streak. He could never concentrate in school, could never sit still. He annoyed his teachers that way, and then had problems finishing his homework. Usually the older brother is the achieving one, but work came more easily to me. I just plugged along, doing what I was expected to do, and before we knew it, we had fallen into these contrasting roles. He was all trouble and rebellion; I was the one they could count on, Mr. Responsibility, my mother's favorite, her baby. I became the one who looked after him—like I was the big brother." He shook his head. "It's not a role I wanted." He looked up at me then with a little smile. "But he's still my big brother, and I've always looked up to him in my own way."

I nodded. "Giorgio and I are a little bit the same way. My parents, especially my father, think he's the big man, but . . ." I laughed a little. "When it's just the two of us, sometimes I'm the braver, steadier one, you know?"

"Have you told your parents you were helping him?"

"No—I don't want to worry my mother any more than she already is."

"But, for all she knows, he could be dead, right?"

"Right."

"It might help her to know he's alive, at least. Couldn't you just tell your mother? Ask her to keep it secret?"

"But wouldn't Father notice a difference in her? She wouldn't be so worried anymore."

We sat for a while, each submerged in our own thoughts, listening to the sounds of pots and pans clinking and banging in the kitchen.

"Giovanna?" He broke the silence. "I don't know how to thank you for finding this place for us—for me—and for the medicine. You didn't have to do that." He smiled. "You've got guts."

I took in his compliment and felt, in its glow, a wave of resolve. "Mario, I will try to contact my brother and find out if he's seen Cecilio."

☙

Within three days, Rosa had a response from Giorgio, asking that I meet him at our usual spot on Sunday, July thirtieth. The moment I caught sight of him slumped against the mossy marble pillar, I knew he was in bad shape. He didn't rise to his feet at the sound of my footsteps, but only tossed a morose look my way. He wore a new brimmed beret, but his clothes were filthy and even more tattered. Over his shoulder a leather cartridge belt hung at an angle, and two grenades dangled from the belt around his waist. There was a new weariness and solemnity about him that seemed to forbid any kind of pleasantry or small talk. I sat down beside him on the platform and inched up close. "You know about the Fox?" I asked.

He nodded. "Word travels fast around here, *mia sorella*."

"He was nearly gone when Violetta found him in the field. He wasn't able to last the night even in the clinic. I'm so sorry. There was nothing they could do."

"It's a rough business we're in, this war. But we're making trouble for those bastards all up and down the valley." He stared at the ground. "How's Mario?"

"He's a lot better. I think he's going to be okay. But Cecilio took off, and I—"

At that, Giorgio stood up and turned his back to me.

"Have you seen him, Giorgio? Mario's so worried."

He expelled a long sigh with his lips tight together like the mouthpiece of a pinched balloon. "Oh, I've seen Patch, all right. He showed up at our camp last week. He was agitated, impatient. I was letting it all run off my back, because I know the guy from school, know how he can get, right? But he started accusing all of us of playing it too safe, of not risking big enough missions. He wanted to stay—said he wanted to prove himself so we'd keep him on. I told him, told all of them, we couldn't let him stay, that it was too dangerous for us. But he started pushing the others. 'What do you want most? What do you really need?' So this one kid, maybe too young to know any better—we call him Baby Face—he piped up, 'Guns—we need guns, that's what.'

"So Patch kept after them until they told him about an outbuilding at an occupied villa where the Germans had a big store of weapons. Long and short of it, he convinced the kid to go with him the next night to try to steal some guns. We'd all been watching the place, and we knew when they ate dinner, when things would get a little loose around there."

Giorgio was talking fast, looking past me. A knot began to tighten in my stomach. "Where is he now? Just tell me that."

"So anyway, they hid nearby, and they saw a bunch of the soldiers leave. The guard was gone too, so they sneaked in and up to the door. They were just about to try the lock when the door opened and there was a big tall Nazi staring down at them."

I could hardly breathe, so I said nothing.

"He said, 'What are you doing? This

here is German property now—entrance strictly *verboten*.' The two of them turned to run, when another guy in uniform appeared just outside the door behind them, trapping them like a sandwich. So the way the kid told it, he just stopped, stood his ground, and looked the first Nazi straight in the eye. 'I know it's German property, sir. That's why I'm here. This man's Jewish. I came to turn him in.' "

The casing of my heart curled inward like a leaf of lettuce in the first hard frost.

"According to Baby Face, Patch went berserk. He started screaming obscenities, flailing his arms, said he was going to kill the kid. The Germans grabbed Patch, held his arms behind his back, and tied him up. Patch was yelling so loud and fighting so hard it took both of the Nazis to hold on to him. So while this was going on, Baby Face apparently just backed off and walked slowly away and back to camp."

I sat still, staring at my brother. "Safely . . . back . . . to camp. And then at camp? What did you do to him, Giorgio? Did you welcome him with open arms, the slimy little traitor? Did you let *him* stay? Did you try to rescue Cecilio? Did you do *anything?*"

Giorgio sat down heavily next to me and put his head in his hands. "No. Baby Face is not with us anymore. He's just a damn kid, and we told him to get lost. I should never have let him stay with us in the first place."

"And what about Cecilio?"

"We couldn't do a thing. We asked around—we've got informers every-where. Turns out they took him to the station the following day under heavy guard and put him on a train bound for Verona."

"Why Verona? What's there?"

"They say there's some camp where they're keeping a whole group of other Jews—women and children even. Word has it another train is scheduled out of there next Wednesday to take them out of the country."

"Out of Italy? Where? To a labor camp? In Germany?"

"Jesus, Giovanna. How should I know? I really don't have any idea. But tell Mario something like that anyway. Tell him his brother's working somewhere. There's at least some hope in that."

"But what do you really think?"

He shook his head. "I wouldn't put anything past those bastards. The rumors aren't good. I can tell you that."

That was the moment of reckoning for me. As the crackling, hazy film of memory slowly unspools, that's where it catches time and again, then stops: on a picture that exists only in my imagination. I see Cecilio, pressed on all sides by a crowd of nameless women and children, herded onto a train at the Verona station. He cries out in anger, in desperation, but his shouts are swallowed in a hissing cloud of steam. They are picked up by the train's departing whistle and cast out over a field of sunflowers nodding in the early August afternoon sun.

❧

We never heard from Cecilio again. The war was heating up around Lucca. Once Violetta's family and the other residents had evacuated the villages of the Serchio River valley, the Germans had begun to do everything they could to put barriers into the routes the Allies might use to advance into northern Italy. They blew up bridges, made the roads impassable, wreaked havoc on houses and other buildings, pillaging wherever they went. This was happening all along the road, from Lucca up into the river valley that led to Modena, and eventually to the Brenner Pass, the Germans' intended retreat route out of Italy.

Chapter Nineteen

Birthdays had always been important to me, and—surely out of habit, for nothing was the same during the war—I found myself looking forward to this one as I always did. In spite of all that was going on in my life that summer, as August fifth neared, I dreamed about how we would celebrate and what, if any, gifts I might receive. I was dreaming of maybe my own small radio to listen to the war's progress, or a new journal in which I could record my feelings, to help me figure out what to do about Mario.

Overt celebrations of any kind in those

days were considered unseemly, so my mother suggested that we have dinner alone, just the three of us, but said that she and Rosa would make an effort to make it a special one. Traditionally, we would have gathered around the big table in the dining room early in the afternoon, but of course that was off-limits. So Mother came up with the idea of celebrating my birthday outside at a table in the garden, not far from the entrance we habitually used to enter our cramped space upstairs. In a rare burst of courage and defiance, Mother had decided not to ask the Germans' permission, but simply to go ahead and set a table under the huge, spreading linden tree. If challenged, she planned to use my eighteenth birthday as an excuse and hoped she could prevail upon their goodwill. I had wanted to include Violetta in the celebration, but Mother worried that even one more guest might add to the noise and make it riskier.

She and Rosa had spent all morning preparing for the occasion. They had spread the table with a blue-and-white-checked cotton cloth and laid silvery green olive branches down the middle. Here and there among the clusters of stiff oblong leaves, they had tucked three small blue-and-white pitchers filled with bouquets of rosemary, lavender, oregano, and thyme. At each place there were tumblers for water and heavy stemmed wineglasses.

An occasion like this would normally have called for a large roast, or perhaps some plump birds grilled on the outdoor open barbecue. But shortages were such that the two of them opted instead for a vegetables-only feast right out of the garden and the countryside. There was bruschetta—small, crunchy slices of toasted bread, spread with ripe tomato and roasted garlic and drizzled with olive oil. Next, we each had a whole artichoke, steamed, then cut in half and laid over the open fire just long enough to impart a smoky flavor and crisp the edges of the overlapping leaves. We tore the leaves off one by one and dipped them in a rich, garlicky aioli made from our own first-press virgin olive oil.

Catarina and Tonino had brought over a special treat: a small kerchief knotted around a dozen or so fresh chanterelles that Catarina had found in her secret wooded spot. Rosa had cleaned and chopped them and combined them with dried porcini mushrooms in a rich *farrotto*—a creamy risotto-like casserole, made with nutty farro instead of rice, and seasoned with fresh rosemary and thyme. On the side, there were fingers of zucchini and just-opened zucchini blossoms, dipped in batter and fried to a light crispiness in oil.

At about twelve thirty, the preparations complete, we gathered around the table for our meal. I had made an effort to look nice, slicking my hair back as best I could into a bun at the back of my neck, and wearing a skirt and blouse. I knew Mother thought the skirt was too short, but it being my day, thank God, she held her tongue. We could hear the voices of the Germans and occasional bursts of laughter rising up over the house from the terrace in front and on the other side. It was a Saturday, so they were around, but for whatever reason, they chose to ignore us.

Father stood, and with great ceremony held out a special bottle of our estate wine for inspection. It was from 1926—the year of my birth—one he had discovered in the far reaches of the cellar, dating back to the days when the winemaking operation had still been in the purview of Mother's family. The bottle was covered with a fine dust, the label yellowed and rumpled where it was beginning to come unglued. "A magnificent year, *piccola,*" he intoned as he inserted the corkscrew and ceremoniously turned it until the cork rose enough to be pulled from the bottle's neck. He poured an inch or so into his glass, swirled it, and brought it to his nose.

Mother and I waited, poised in anticipation, but instead of reaching to pour us each a glass, he wrinkled his nose and shook his head. "Corked, I'm afraid." He shrugged his shoulders. "Eighteen years is a long time, I guess—too much to expect of these little plugs of bark." He examined the cork, which had become soaked nearly all the way through with the dark, blackened leakage. "Luckily I have a bottle of last year's Chianti here, just in case." He uncorked the fresh bottle and spilled the thin, translucent liquid into our glasses, filling them with the bright cranberry red of a brash young wine.

Now it was Mother's turn to stand. "Before we begin, I would like to propose a toast to our darling Giovanna." She passed me a warm look, then stared at her raised glass while she spoke. "I was thinking about you yesterday, dear, turning eighteen, while I pruned my rosebushes. You are just at the point in your life when I would choose to cut a rose, to bring it in from the garden, a bud, full and swollen, beginning to show its color clearly, but not yet open or ready to give off its full fragrance." She paused, gathering her thoughts, without looking up at me. "There are thorns, to be sure, ringing the stem and prickly to the touch"—she shot Papa a conspiratorial glance—"but before the flower is put on display, these can always be stripped off for a smooth and easily handled stem." She grinned, took a deep breath, and held her glass out to both of us. "So here's to you, *la nostra carissima rosa*. Happy birthday to our precious flower. May you open into your full glory and fill our lives with beauty."

"Salute!" Father stood as well, and they both held out their glasses at arm's length, grinning broadly.

I did not feel like a flower, exactly. Not then. Not with a man's fate resting on my own ingenuity and daring. Not with a brother fighting and risking his life every day. But that was Mama—it was genuine sentiment on her part. I smiled and ate my delicious meal like a grateful daughter should.

When we had scraped the last of the sweet *torta* with mascarpone sauce from our plates, Mother handed me a package wrapped in thin tissue paper and tied with a bronze cloth ribbon that must have been saved from some past celebration. It was lightweight and irregularly shaped, so I knew it would be (as presents from Mother usually were) some item of clothing. She had often criticized me for carelessly tearing into packages, so I took my time, carefully untying and rolling the ribbon, loosening the tissue paper, and folding it again.

The dress was sewn of a rich, deep

crimson, a cocktail dress, cut low in the front of its satin bodice over a full, floating chiffon skirt with a fabric flower attached to the belt of grosgrain ribbon that encircled the waist. I stared at it as I held it up. "It's beautiful, but when will I ever—"

"It's time you had something worthy of an adult," she interrupted. "Something in your closet besides school clothes and basics."

"But when . . . what possible occasion would call for it?"

"Who knows? The war won't last forever, and soon enough you'll be out and about. You'll see. You'll be glad you have it, dear. It will be a stunning color on you, my lovely rose."

I nodded slowly and smiled. "Thank you, Mama. It's beautiful; really it is. I'll look forward to a time when I can wear it." But I was thinking, as I folded it carefully and set it down on the tissue paper, how little Mother knew me, the person I was becoming.

Father interrupted my thoughts with a grunt as he fished in his pants pocket and pulled out a small velvet box and held it out to me. "What's this?" I asked, surprised, as Papa always left the gift giving to Mother.

"Just open it," he said, grinning.

I took the small jewelry box covered in worn black velvet, crushed flat around the button at the front. I pressed the latch and lifted the lid. Inside was a locket of deep, antique eighteen-karat gold. It was small and oval, hinged, and embossed with an asymmetrical floral design. It hung on a gold link chain, satisfyingly heavy, one that I knew would feel smooth and comfortable next to my skin. "Oh—it's so lovely!" I smiled at Papa and inserted my thumbnail to open the locket. It was empty, but there were two places for photographs, one on each side. "Is it an antique?"

He nodded.

"Wherever did you find it?" I laughed a little, trying to picture Father shopping somewhere for a present for me.

"Oh . . ." He looked quickly away. "Let's just let that remain a mystery, shall we? Like most antiques. Try it on—I want to see it on you."

I looked at Mother, who was obviously

as surprised as I was. She leaned closer. "Here. Let me see it." She examined the locket briefly, then fastened the chain around my neck. "It's handsome, Enrico. Wherever did you find it?" We both stared at him expectantly.

"Really—no need to go into that now."

"Come on, Papa," I teased. "I just can't imagine you shopping! Was it in your family?"

Mother frowned, shaking her head. "I would know if it were a family heirloom."

I took the locket off and shot him a mock stern look. "Papa, I love it, but I won't wear it until you tell us where you got it. It's simply too mysterious." I put it back in the box and folded my arms. "Come on; please tell us."

"Well . . ." He shrugged. "Are you sure? All right then. But this might take a while." He settled back into his chair, lifted his glass, and took a slow sip of wine, savoring it on his tongue. Then he swallowed and set the glass down.

"As you know, some of the Germans around here spend their time doing investigations."

"Of crimes?" Mother propped her chin on her hand, leaning on the table.

"Not exactly—more like searches, really. Tracking certain families that have lived in this area."

"What kinds of families?" I could feel my pulse speed up. Papa ignored my question and just kept going.

"Well, the textile industry is one place they are spending a lot of time. One of our officers said he had a friend in the SS who wanted to meet with me. I told him I didn't work in the silk business anymore, but he wouldn't listen, said he wanted to talk with me anyway, that he had some questions. He said there might be something in it for me if I cooperated. So I met the fellow in town for coffee a couple of weeks ago and we chatted." He paused, moving his fork around on his dessert plate. "Nice enough fellow. He was polite, even friendly, I guess you might say. Young guy."

"They're all young, dear." Mother smoothed back a wisp of hair that had come unattached from her chignon and was falling over her forehead.

"Yes, well, he wanted to know about Lazzato's brother—you remember Emmanuel, don't you? I guess they knew that Josef and Olivia were in the United States, but he wanted to know where his younger brother was."

Mother and I sat still, staring, saying nothing.

"So as we were talking, I remembered you telling me you'd had a letter from Olivia that said the brother had gone down to Pisa, was living with a cousin of his wife's. So I told him. I told him what I knew."

"You told him? You told him what exactly, Father?" I straightened, my hands rigidly at my sides, pressing the chair seat.

"I told him I didn't know where he was, but last I'd heard he'd moved to Pisa."

There was a long silence. I focused on the call of a dove in the tree over our heads.

"I'd nearly forgotten all about it. Then last week, I ran into that same officer in town. He was all smiles, took me by the arm and led me to a building they had taken over near the square. He said he wanted to thank me, that he owed me a debt of gratitude. So he led me into this room where there were tables set up and all this beautiful stuff laid out." Father was talking fast now, not looking at us. "It was gorgeous, quality stuff, silver, china, jewelry, musical instruments, rare books. They said they couldn't take it all with them to Germany, so they wanted to give me something in appreciation." He shrugged. "So then I saw the locket. The box was open, and it was spread out on the table. It just looked so pretty, *piccola*. Like something you would wear so beautifully. Why not?"

I did not dare look up. My ears flushed hot, my scalp prickled, and my hands went cold. "Why . . . not?" I asked the question slowly, deliberately. "The reason, Father, *why not* is that those things have been ruthlessly taken from innocent people they have arbitrarily sought out, wrenched from their homes, and sent God knows where. Those are stolen goods, Papa."

"Oh, come on, Giovanna. You don't

know that. You have no idea where they came from. They might be from people like the Lazzatos, who left fair and square, went to the United States and left their belongings behind—things they'll never need again."

I rose, balling the locket in my hand, making an effort to control my voice. "Then I think you'd better think about it a little longer, Father, maybe just drink a sip or two of the blood of your industry colleagues while you're at it." I walked behind his chair and dropped the locket into his wineglass. "You disgust me. You really do." I turned my back and left them there, slowly climbing the stairs to my room and shutting the door behind me. What my father said in response I did not know and did not care.

This was when I felt the earth crack. It groaned and heaved, and a deep crevasse widened between me and my parents. I couldn't leave home. I knew that. But I also knew that it would be different from now on. They were still my parents, after all. I would live with them, even love them. But I wasn't under their power anymore. Not in the same way. I knew I had to begin to assume responsibility for my own actions and even for theirs. I felt emboldened and oddly free.

Chapter Twenty

With Mario on the mend, things began to change in the winemaker's cottage. Mario had energy now, and staying in bed was out of the question. But, for security reasons, he couldn't leave or even venture into the front rooms.

A few days after my birthday, I came to visit him. I was still reeling from my father's gift, and I was considering bringing Mario into my confidence. I found Serena kneeling over her herb garden, pulling out weeds with passionate concentration. She waved me into the cottage with barely a hello, so I went straight to the storeroom. When I opened the door, I was face to knees with Mario, standing on his head.

"What on earth are you doing?" I laughed out loud.

He grinned. "I can't get any exercise in here, so this seems to shake things up, get the blood moving. You'd be surprised how it calms you down. I've worked my way up to ten minutes. I'm about ready to move away from the wall. You ought to give it a try."

"I don't think so," I said. "I'm too scared. And besides, it doesn't really work when you're dressed like this." I looked down, smoothing the folds of my skirt to my thighs.

"Oh, no! Whatever was I thinking? How rude of me." He grinned even more broadly, his eyes, even upside down, shining with a new twinkle. Slowly he lowered his legs to the floor. Then he turned and sat facing me, his arms resting loosely on his bent legs. He looked very directly at me, not smiling. "Hi, Giovanna. It's good to see you."

I felt my face flush. "Your arm must be feeling a lot better."

He lifted the still-bandaged forearm. "You know, it really is. It barely hurts at all anymore. But the main thing is, I'm just feeling like my old self. I've got too much energy just to sit in here all day."

"We've got to get you out of here. Serena and Guido are getting really worried that you'll be found—and about what that would mean for them. We owe them their own safety."

"Come sit down, won't you?" He patted a place on the floor next to him. "Tell me what you've been doing while you were gone. I need to hear about the outside world."

There was so little space that was not already filled with the bed, the chair, and various boxes of stored food that when I did sit down, I was toe to toe and knee to knee with him. I breathed in the oddly comforting aura of perspiration, soiled laundry, and sleep that hung around him. I was so close I could have leaned my cheek down without stretching and laid it on the wiry black hair of his good arm.

"It was my birthday this weekend," I said. "My eighteenth."

"Really? Happy birthday. I wish I'd known." He grinned and looked up at the ceiling, leaning his head against the wall.

"Why? You wouldn't have been able to do anything about it."

"No, but I could have been thinking of you in a different way."

"Were you thinking of me anyway?"

He nodded; then he looked straight at me again with a little smile. "I usually am."

That embarrassed me, so I quickly began telling him about Saturday's birthday dinner. I left out no detail of the setting or the menu, but then, when I got to the presents, I told him only about the dress.

"It sounds beautiful," he said. "You'd look lovely in red."

"But it's ridiculous. Where would I ever wear such a thing? I don't go to parties like that. My mother is living in a cloud. She just seems oblivious sometimes to the fact that we're in the middle of a war."

"Maybe this is just her way of escaping the reality of it," he said. "I don't blame her for wishing her daughter had a social life."

"No. It's not just that. She wishes she had a different kind of daughter. That's what she wishes." I was feeling emboldened now, the feelings of that day beginning to manifest all over again.

"What about your father?"

"What about him? You don't want to know about him."

"Oh, but I do. My father always wanted a girl. I'll bet your father is crazy about you."

"Oh, he's crazy about me, all right, but mostly he's crazy." I swallowed hard.

"What's the matter?"

I told him about the locket. He listened soberly, his hands folded across his knees. When I was finished, he sat for a long time, saying nothing. "I'm sorry, Mario. I'm sure that's not what you wanted to hear."

"No, no. I'm glad you told me. I was just wondering whatever happened to our own things. When Cecilio and I came home that day and found our parents gone, we left our house with everything in it—furniture, dishes, silver, my mother's clothes and jewelry. I hadn't really thought about it before. Do you think the Germans have it all?"

I didn't respond, but my mind drifted back to our own days of packing, when we carefully wrapped and boxed all our most valuable possessions and stashed them behind a false wall in the attic. I knew we were lucky to be still living in our own house, however cramped and uncomfortable our quarters. "Did you see any of this coming? The way they are hunting the Jews, sending them away. How long had you known about it?"

Mario leaned his head back against the wall again and stared up, away from me.

"This is going to sound crazy, but for the first twelve or thirteen years of my life, I didn't even think about our being Jewish. It just wasn't the main thing that defined us as a family." He looked at me, earnest now. "Italian was the only language we ever spoke at home. I never learned Hebrew or had any religious education, really. We lived in a large apartment on one of the nicest streets in Turin. Most of our friends were Catholic. My father rose rapidly at the Banca Ovazza, and his clients included members of the city's noble and most well-off families. I guess the richer we got, the more he and my mother lost touch with their ethnic roots."

"We still go to church, but a lot of our friends have kind of lost touch with Catholicism too," I responded.

"My mother's parents lived upstairs in our building, and I remember my grandmother—she was a tall, elegant woman—observed all the Jewish holidays, but it just wasn't that important to my parents. You know, this is going to sound funny to you, but *Italy* was their religion. My parents were Fascists. They really, really believed in a united fatherland. They were very pro-Mussolini.

"My father sent Cecilio and me to military school—you know, to Giorgio's school. He wanted us to be great soldiers, to be part of this 'ascendant nation.'" Mario puffed himself up in pronouncing this, imitating his father's attitude. "I think he thought I'd run the country someday." He let out an ironic chuckle. "There was nothing we couldn't do or aspire to. There was a clannishness in the way our extended family and close friends—other Jews—stuck together, in the summers especially. We all went to the country together . . . but it was never forced, anything we *had* to do. It was a choice."

"There were other Jews at school? Giorgio never mentioned it."

"Oh, sure—maybe two or three in every class. The only difference was that we went separately to religion class. That was never a big deal. The emphasis was on patriotism. Whenever Mussolini came to Turin, there was a school holiday, and we had big parades. Everybody turned out for them.

"Papa was rich enough that he didn't really need to ally himself with the Fascist cause, but he was a real believer. But then the newspapers began promoting the idea that Jews were generally suspect—that deep down, we were all ultimately subversive and loyal to Zionist ideals. I remember my father getting just furious reading that, when he'd been so dedicated to the party."

"But for you, when did it really change for you?" I asked.

He thought for a while. "The summer of 'thirty-eight. I was fourteen. We were in the country and heard on the radio that Jews would not be able to continue to go to Italian schools. I couldn't believe it. Some of my cousins had graduated from high school by then, but there I was, still in school, and I would have to be separated from so many of my friends."

I remember listening to Mario at this point, watching his lips, hearing his words, but not quite believing it. None of this had ever been made known to me. I put my hand on his arm. "And you really couldn't go back to your school? Why didn't Giorgio ever tell me all of this?"

"I don't know. It probably just didn't affect him that much. But it was worse than that, Giovanna. That was the point at which Mussolini really changed and began insisting that Jews were not 'Italians'—biologically—that we were a different race, and that there would have to be a set of laws that acknowledged that and dealt with us differently."

"That must have disillusioned your parents about Mussolini."

"You'd think so, wouldn't you? Well, they were rewarded for it—as I said— by the 'discrimination clause.'" He paused briefly, and I could see the memories pained him. "But that didn't last long. By November, there were no exceptions." Mario got up and paced the tiny floor space, then sat down on the bed. I stayed put. He shook his head.

"That was when all hell broke loose. Father kept his job because it was in a private company, but he was expelled from the party. We had to let our Catholic servants go, because Christians weren't allowed to work for Jews. It was so sad. Those people had been with us all my life. They were part of our family, and they were forced to leave."

I thought of Rosa and what it would mean to kick her out on her own.

"The next June, in 'thirty-nine, when we thought things couldn't get worse, my father lost his job. The bank was owned by a Jewish family, and it had to be sold. My brother and I weren't allowed to go to school anymore. I tell you, Giovanna . . ." His voice was thin and strained to the breaking point. "It was horrible. Suddenly my whole sense of myself, my place in the community, crumbled. I would walk down the street and see, in the windows of cafés or shops that we had always frequented, signs saying, 'No Jews allowed.'

"Some of my parents' friends went to desperate means. Some converted to Catholicism. One of my mother's friends confessed to a fictitious affair with a Catholic to claim that her child was actually Christian. Some left. Many of our good friends and one of my uncles got tourist visas and sailed for the United States or South America, knowing they wouldn't be back."

Like the Lazzatos, I thought, as a wave of nausea passed over me. "But what about your mother and father?"

"My father's powers of rationalization were amazing. He kept maintaining that Mussolini had no choice but to go along with the program. He assumed Germany would win the war, and then after the war, the racial laws would be repealed, everything would be normal again, and . . . Well, he just knew they would reward the people who had stayed loyal. Italy would be a great nation, and it was worth the kind of sacrifice he was making to one day be a part of all that."

"That's exactly how my father thinks too. He's convinced we should be nice to the Germans because it will pay off after they win the war."

Suddenly we heard what sounded like Guido's voice outside the cottage. He was yelling something and sounded very anxious, but we couldn't hear the words. The front door opened and closed again, and Serena burst into the storeroom. I leaped to my feet.

"Giovanna, you've got to leave, right now. Guido says he saw a truckload of SS headed for the convent. They must be conducting a raid. *Dio, Dio,* I'm so afraid they'll come here. Giovanna— really, you must leave. And, Mario, get on the floor behind the bed and stay there until we tell you it is safe."

She pushed me toward the door with

such force that I didn't have a chance even to look at Mario.

I started for home, but the more I thought about it, the more frightened I became for Elena and Graziella, for the people sheltered there, if indeed there were any. I hid my bicycle behind the hedge that lined the upper drive and moved surreptitiously around to the back entrance. I found my broom in its usual place, and began working my way, sweeping as I went, down toward the cellar and the corridor where I had once thought I heard voices.

As I descended the back staircase, Sylvia, the tall novice who oversaw my work, came clattering down behind me. "Giovanna! Oh, Giovanna! It's so awful. They were pounding on the front door, but no one got there in time, so they shot the bolt off. They got in, and now they're coming!"

"Who's coming?" I clutched the broom to my chest.

"The SS—four of them—and a couple of Italian militiamen. They're headed to the basement down the front stairs. Someone, one of the nuns, must have tipped them off. They know just where to go." She ran ahead, and I followed her down.

We reached the bottom of the stairs and quietly opened the door from the stairwell into the long corridor lined with wooden doors. To our right, six men in uniform were knotted together, pounding on the locked door, shouting, "Open up or we will shoot our way in."

To our left, we saw that a small group of nuns had followed the soldiers down the main staircase and were gathered in the corridor, watching. We came out and stood among them. I felt conspicuous, the only one of the group not wearing a habit.

The blows continued until at last the latch was lifted from the inside. A soldier slammed the door wide-open, burst in, and pushed two women and two small girls, maybe six and seven, out into the corridor in front of us. One of the women had gray hair; perhaps she was their grandmother. The two girls gripped their mother's skirt in their fists, tears running down their cheeks.

The nuns around me were crossing

themselves and praying audibly. Sister Elena, fronting our group, stood tall, and in that gravelly voice I knew so well, protested: "This is private, sanctified space. You have no right to be here. These are our guests."

The soldiers ignored her, but the two Italian militiamen moved toward us at a signal. As they did so, I recognized one of them—Rodolfo Giordano, the son of one of my father's Fascist party compatriots. *That could have been Giorgio,* I thought, *having to carry out this evil work.* The two Italians herded us back against the wall and stood guard while the SS men continued their confrontation.

"Please," said the older woman, her deeply creased face wet with tears, *"per favore, signori.* I have something for you if you will just leave us in peace." She reached inside the bodice of her dress and unpinned a small maroon velvet drawstring bag. "These are family heirlooms, worth a lot."

She handed the bag to the tallest of the SS soldiers. He opened it, shook its contents into his hand, and showed it to his three companions. "*Ja, ja*—we take those"—he laughed, pocketing the jewelry—"but you will come with us—all of you."

One of the SS men held those four against the wall, while the other three moved on to the next closed door. "You now. Open up!" they shouted, pounding hard.

Again the latch lifted, and the tall soldier shoved it open. A young woman, hollow eyed, terrified, holding a baby of no more than three months to her breast, stood staring at them. He yanked her out into the corridor. "Over there," he ordered. "Stand with the others."

"Please, no. Not my baby." She fell to her knees, sobbing in the midst of them. "Please." She grabbed the tall soldier's legs, hanging on with her fists to his trousers. "I will do anything you ask, give you my body for pleasure. Please—not my baby, not my son."

Another of the SS, burly and red-faced, tore her away, hauling her to her feet by the back of her dress. "Pleasure—ha!" He pushed her and the baby toward the others, muttering under his breath, "Swine . . ."

The nuns around me, all of us, were mostly crying now, continuing to pray and to clutch one another's hands.

The soldiers moved on, trying each of the doors in the corridor in turn. There were three more women in the next room, meek, submissive young women who joined the others, shaking and crying without protest, but they found all the other doors unlocked, the rooms empty. After they had checked them all, they came back in our direction. The tall one spotted me in my cotton clothes, surrounded by the nuns. I was arm in arm with Sister Graziella.

"*Kommen Sie her*—you in the dress," he demanded.

I gripped her arm tightly and stood tall, unmoving, defying him with my stare.

He moved toward me, shoving the nuns away on either side, and grabbed me by the arm, pulling me off Graziella and out of the shelter of the group. "You . . . you are no sister. Go with them."

"No, Heinrich," the militiaman Rodolfo broke in. "*Nein.* I know her and her family. She is not Jewish."

The officer shrugged. He leaned down and peered into my face, squinting, a hint of mockery about his mouth. "Dark hair, brown eyes. How do I know?" He looked around at the others, shrugged again, then pushed me roughly back toward the nuns.

They turned and moved toward the stairs, herding the women and children in front of them. I was flooded with relief and, under that, a burning kind of shame.

We waited upstairs in the front hall under the watchful guard of the two militiamen while the SS searched the convent from top to bottom. We prayed together, Sister Elena assuring us there were no others. They would find nothing. After an hour or so, Rodolfo Giordano pulled me aside, away from the nuns. "Take my advice, Giovanna, and leave, right now. You are not to blame for this, and you don't have to stay here. Just trust me, and run before the soldiers get back."

I hated to leave the sisters at such a

crucial moment, but all I could think of was Mario, nearby in the winemaker's cottage. He needed me, and I couldn't afford to risk leaving him stranded. I hugged both Graziella and Elena tightly, and—while Rodolfo pacified the other militiaman—I made my escape.

The women and children were never seen again, presumably shipped off on the train to one of the waiting camps. We later learned that Graziella and Elena, along with the other nuns who gathered to watch that day, were thrown into prison for the duration of the war.

Chapter Twenty-one

I knew one thing: I needed to relieve Guido and Serena of their burden, the sooner the better. I had to find a permanent place for Mario. I couldn't imagine trying to hide him at home. Perhaps Catarina could be brought into my confidence; perhaps there was a remote building on the property we could use, but with the Germans so close, actually living there day after day, it was clear to me that that would be folly. There was no alternative I could see but to ask the marchesa to help me shelter him on her estate.

No one in our immediate area had heard about the raid on the convent; however, the same day, the Germans had arrived in Pietra Santra, a town on the coast near Carrara. A ruthless young Austrian named Major Walter Reder commanded the unit. Because part of his left arm had been amputated, he was known as *il Monco*—"the Stump." Since there were no official newspapers, news of Reder's presence traveled about the area by word of mouth and on paper handbills. People were terrified, because he was rumored to be very dangerous.

What happened then is seared into all of our memories. The Germans, under Reder's command, had received word that the residents of Sant'Anna, just outside the fortification walls of Lucca, had been feeding and sheltering partisans as well as sending secret messages to the Allies informing them of the German troop movement. On Saturday, the twelfth of August, SS troops herded residents of Sant'Anna into the village square and began to mow them down with machine guns, killing not only men, young and old, but women and children as well.

We were told the story over and over about a local priest who darted into the crowd after the firing began, trying to help an injured child. The poor child was already dead, so the priest lifted him high above his head and pleaded with the Germans to have mercy and stop the massacre. Instead, they turned the machine guns on him, killing the priest instantly, and then turned back to the people nearby. In all, they slaughtered 570 civilians, whose names are engraved on a monument erected in their memory.

The horror of it was devastating. People talked about nothing but the massacre; yet they continued to remain unsure of their feelings toward the partisans. On the one hand, those ragtag insurgents were clearly helping the Allies and making it difficult for the Germans. But also, it seemed, they were the ones responsible for the Germans' retaliation on innocent villagers. About ten days before the Sant'Anna massacre, handbills had been posted all over town, signed by the commander of the Garibaldi partisan brigade, urging the townspeople to arm themselves and offer passive resistance to the Germans. *People of Versilia,* it read in part, *do not obey the Germans! Death to the German oppressor!*

News of this debacle was buzzing about the clinic when I arrived early the next day. I busied myself in the supply room for a bit, trying to get my bearings, until I heard the marchesa's voice coming from just outside the door. She sounded like an island of calm and resolve. "Of course they are endangering civilians," she was saying, "but, my God, the partisans are the only hope we have of slowing these beasts and helping the Allies. We owe them all the support we can muster, in spite of the risks." I rustled about, setting some new boxes of cotton batting on the shelf. Then I tentatively pushed open the door to the outside.

"Oh, Giovanna! How are you, dear? I spoke with your mother the other day, and she told me you had a birthday a week or so ago. I'm sorry I missed a chance to congratulate you. How was your celebration?"

I offered her a weak smile. "It was fine, thank you. I . . ." I glanced at the nurse she was talking to. "May I . . . Might I have a word with you privately sometime this morning?" My face must have spoken volumes, for she sobered instantly.

"Why don't we take a walk toward my house? I promised Leonardo I would be back in an hour, and I'm afraid I've stayed here too long." She put an arm around my waist, turning to the nurse. "I'm sorry, Clarice. We'll continue this conversation later. In the meantime, please trust me. Believe in the support we are giving here. It's the right thing to do."

We began strolling together along the wide dirt road in the direction of her villa. The sun was directly overhead, and the heat bounced off the bare clay in relentless waves. "Now, Giovanna, tell me honestly. What's troubling you? I can see anxiety written all over your face."

The question was so earnest, so direct that it caught me by surprise. I took a deep breath. "First," I said, "let me ask you something. Have you heard anything about the SS raid on the convent of Saint Agnes yesterday?"

She stopped walking and turned to look at me. "No, I certainly haven't. My impression has been that up to now the Germans have been respectful of Vatican property. What happened? You were there?"

I told her what I had been through, sparing no detail. As I spoke, I could feel my voice pinch at the edges. "I . . . I'm so afraid, and I really need help."

The marchesa took my hand in hers. "Tell me more, Giovanna. This is obviously troubling you very personally."

She was so warm, her voice full of solicitude. I trusted her implicitly, and besides, what choice did I have but to plunge in? I began with our last conversation, when I had asked her if she had ever hidden any Jews. When I got to the memory of my own treachery with the penicillin, I broke down utterly. We had reached the edge of an olive grove, and I broke away from her and ran across the roadside ditch and leaned against a tree.

She followed me and stood nearby. "What's upsetting you so much? It sounds like you've been doing just fine."

"No, I just can't do this. I'm a terrible person. You'll never forgive me."

"Forgive you for what?"

"For what I did to you. It was I who took the last two vials of penicillin from the supply closet. That's the reason Mario survived." I shuddered, sobbing some more. "And that's the reason your English friend died. It's all my fault."

She stared at me, her eyes darkening to a deep violet. Her expression didn't change, but tears collected at the inside corners of her eyes. She did not reach up to brush them away. I hung my head and did not dare look at her for what seemed like an endless minute. At last she breathed deeply and sighed. "Well, then, we mustn't let this one die too, must we?"

A wave of relief and hope flooded over me. I stared at this pale, petite woman at once so diminutive and yet so full of energy and courage, and I thought I had never admired anyone so much. "You'll help me?"

"I don't even know what you need yet, Giovanna, do I?"

℘

That afternoon, the marchesa walked me to an old mill on the property, far from both the clinic and the villa. She pulled out a stone from the crumbling wall and showed me the rusted key hidden in the cavity behind it. Once inside, we climbed a flight of stairs to the second floor, then a second flight in the rear, up into a bare attic space under the red tile roof. "I can help now and then, but basically you will have to be responsible for feeding him," she said. "If the Germans come, I will do my best to keep them away, but I will have to deny any knowledge of his being here. In the next day or so, I will bring over some blankets, a washbowl and towel. I don't have to tell you not to provide him with any flashlights or even candles that would be visible at night.

"You're a brave girl," she said. "I'm proud of you. But make no mistake: You will face grave danger in getting him here at all. This war will not end tomorrow, and it's going to be a long, cold winter. There's no heat in this building, Giovanna. Are you sure you've thought all this through? You could just continue to work at the clinic, and you would still be doing a lot for the cause. You don't have to put yourself in such a precarious position."

"I can't think about all of that right now. But please believe me: I've just never been surer of anything."

The marchesa nodded slowly. "Bless you then. God bless you."

"You are the most wonderful woman in the world. I will never forget this." I flung myself into her arms. "When should I bring him here?"

"I see no reason to wait. From what I hear, the Germans are increasingly anxious. The Allies are working their way up the coast. They're likely to be more vigilant and intolerant than usual." She locked the door and placed the key back in its hiding place. "You will probably need at least twenty-four hours to make the journey from the convent. Why don't you tell your parents that you are needed here overnight tomorrow? I will telephone your mother and tell her personally, if that would help."

I nodded solemnly, my head swimming with all I would have to plan and accomplish in the next day.

Chapter Twenty-two

I needn't have worried that my parents would interfere. Since my birthday dinner, I had been deliberately remote. They, in turn, had backed off a bit and begun to give me more emotional space. Mother was completely obsessed with the news from Lucca and reports of all the partisan attacks and reprisals—worrying about Giorgio, desperate to know where and how he was, thinking little, if at all, about me or what they assumed was my work at the clinic. Father was busy trying to reassure her and monitoring the news of troop movement on both sides.

The atmosphere was chilly at dinner the night after my meeting with the marchesa. The food itself was bare-bones: a pasta *alla carbonara* made only with eggs, cheese, and a little bacon, some bread, a glass of table wine. I came in a bit late and took my seat in silence as Father lectured Mother: "You must remember, Natala. It wasn't the partisans who were shot in Sant'Anna. It was the civilians, people of the village who were *aiding* the partisans. They were punished for feeding them and giving them shelter."

"But what about all the partisan skir-mishes with the Germans? Why hasn't he contacted us? He must know we are worried." Mother was picking at her food, moving it around on the plate.

Father shook his head without look-ing up at her. He shoveled in the pasta, talking with his mouth full. "If something had happened to Giorgio, you know we would have heard about it. No news is good news, in my book."

"The marchesa says . . ." I broke in,

and Mother looked at me in surprise, as if she had just noticed I was sitting there.

"Oh—Giovanna—speaking of the marchesa, she called this afternoon. She says she wants to keep you overnight at the clinic tomorrow. Is there a problem?"

I looked down at my plate. "Oh, there are just so many seriously injured men that I guess they need more people on overnight shifts. She needed extra help, so I volunteered."

"I told her it was fine. You do question all of these men about Giorgio, don't you, dear? One of them might know him or have seen him or something."

That was all there was. They asked me no more about it, just continued talking with each other, speculating about the progress of the war and imagining Giorgio's whereabouts.

At one point, as I was absently pulling off a crust of bread, I asked, "Mother, were the boxes of Giorgio's clothes walled off in the attic or are any of them still accessible?"

She stared. "Why? Why would you want those?"

"So many of the men at the clinic are dressed in rags. I just thought we could share some of Giorgio's things and then get him some new ones when he returns."

She ate a few bites and chewed her food slowly without saying anything.

"I'm not in any way implying he won't still need them, but it just seems a waste to me not to share the clothes with people who need them right now."

She looked at Papa, who nodded. "It makes sense to me. They're just sitting there, wrinkled and crushed. I know where they are—we'll go through them together after dinner. I'm sure Giorgio wouldn't mind."

C

That is how I was able to set off the next morning with a bag bulging with shirts, pants, socks, shoes, and a decent leather belt. In case, God forbid, we were seen as we made our journey, I wanted Mario to look like someone I might naturally be with, rather than someone who had been living as a fugitive for months.

I made my way slowly on foot toward the convent, devising a new sequence of strange fields and unknown paths, looking for buildings that could briefly offer shelter, for the cover of densely wooded groves, the occasional water pump. I was planning our route with care, my heart beating a steady note of encouragement, urging me on toward this impossible thing I was about to do. I headed for the winemaker's cottage.

All was quiet. I knocked timidly, absentmindedly watching two hens pecking about on the ground. At last, the door opened a crack. Guido peered out, took one look at me, and opened the door wide, drawing me into his warm embrace. "Giovanna, my sweet girl. Come in, come in. Here, let me take that bag. It looks heavy." He quickly closed the door behind me and locked it. "Serena, look who's here!"

"I was just putting some soup on the table," she said. "Won't you join us?"

She ladled minestrone into a bowl and handed it to me. "Take this into the back for Mario, won't you? We just can't

let him sit out here with us in case someone passes by the window."

So they were all still here, still safe.

I opened the door slowly. Mario was
waiting for me. We both smiled. He
reached for the bowl, and we held it together for a few seconds. "I wasn't sure
I would see you again after yesterday's
raid," he said.

I nodded. "I was afraid of that myself.
Hold on. I'll be right back." I ran to fetch
the bag full of clothes. "I think these
clothes will fit you. We don't have any
time to waste. And eat up. We might not
get another meal for a while."

Mario stared at me, openmouthed,
but before he could respond, I closed
the storeroom door and joined Guido
and Serena at the kitchen table. The
soup was thick and hot and tasted of
fresh tomatoes and pungent oregano.
At first, we simply ate quietly, savoring
the end of summer on our tongues. I
broke the silence, putting my spoon
down briefly. The three of us sat in silence, just staring at our bowls. Finally I
spoke. "I have come to take Mario away."

Serena let out a gasp of relief. "Oh, God bless you, Giovanna."

But Guido's round, soft face was full of concern. "But where will you go? It's so dangerous to travel. You know that."

"I have a refuge for him, but I have to keep it a secret. I just can't take any chances."

"Is it far?"

"Of course, it depends on a lot of things, but I think we should be there by tomorrow if all goes well."

Serena busied herself with packing up a little food for us while Guido went to look after Mario. Giorgio's clothes fit him well, so they decided to burn the things he had been wearing. Within an hour of our departure, there would be not a single trace of the weeks he had spent in the storeroom.

"Will you keep us informed somehow, dear?" Serena handed me a packet of food tied in a cotton cloth. "We have grown to love this young man like a son."

"I know. I'll try to let you know what happens."

"Don't you want to wait until dark?" Guido asked anxiously. I looked at Mario, who looked normal and presentable in his new suit of clothes.

"We'll have to travel some in the light or we'll never get there. I have a route through the woods all planned. Then, tonight, we can cross the open fields in the dark."

There were hugs all around. Mario was overwhelmed with gratitude and pledged that someday, when the war was over, he would reward them for their kindness and generosity. "I have nothing to give you now," he said, kissing Serena on the cheek. "Nothing but my love and appreciation—but you know I will never forget you."

It was midafternoon when we crept around the back of the cottage and headed into the deep woods. I knew, by going out of our way, we could cover a good bit of ground toward the south and east before we would have to cross any open territory.

We walked in silence, both of us afraid that any voices at all might alert some unknown person to our presence. It was cool in the shade of the forest. I knew the way, and Mario followed me, making very little noise with his feet. The occasional snap of a twig would start my heart beating in my throat. Squirrels chased one another overhead, and now and then their scurrying path through the leaves nearby would sound like footsteps. After an hour or so, we began to relax, and, though we still didn't talk at all, we hiked with more confidence and made better time.

Around seven, after we had been walking for three or four hours, we stopped and shared some of the bread and cheese Serena had packed for us. We whispered a few words of encouragement as the day began to fade and dusk settled over us like a gentle cloak.

After half an hour of rest, we gathered our things. The light was low enough that I figured we could now head for the main road. We had to cross that principal thoroughfare, then another short span of woods before we could enter the wide fields we needed to pass over in the dark. We began the descent into the steep ravine that led to the road. We were quiet, watching our steps carefully as we planted our feet sideways, holding on to hanging vines and thin tree trunks to keep our balance. Now and then one of us would slip on the thick blanket of leaves that covered the hillside. Off to our left I noticed a dark hole framed by mossy growth that must have been the entrance to a cave. It occurred to me that animals must use it for shelter in the rain.

When we reached the bottom, it was almost dark. I signaled to Mario to follow me over the rocky creek that was nearly dry. We scuttled quickly up the bank to the road, popped out of the underbrush, and began walking in silence along the shoulder. I glanced behind me to make sure Mario was following close behind, when I noticed a military vehicle. It was pulled over, just behind us, its lights off. Two figures were crouched together over the front right wheel, as if they were changing a tire. I stopped, not daring to breathe, and pointed them out to Mario. Just then the strong beam of their flashlight moved from the work they were doing right onto us.

I know we should have just continued on our way as if nothing were wrong.

But we were so on edge, so ready for trouble, that instead we grabbed each other and ducked back into the underbrush.

"They're German officers," Mario said. "I'd know that car anywhere. Let's get out of here."

"I saw a cave not far back, partway up the bank of the ravine," I whispered. "Follow me."

There must have been a couple of other men sitting in the vehicle, for now we heard what sounded like several voices shouting to one another in German. Two of the car doors slammed, and we could see several flashlight beams scanning the trees.

We clutched hands. Our hearts racing, we felt our way through the dark, retracing our steps. At last I could make out the entrance to the cave. I yanked Mario down and pushed him through the entrance, following closely behind. We crouched side by side, panting in the low space. It smelled earthy, like crushed mushrooms and wet moss. We could hear shouting in the distance. We waited and hoped for them to give up the search.

Then there were footsteps climbing the ravine. I heard no voices, saw no light. It sounded like an animal, not a man. They came closer, followed by the sound of sniffing around the mouth of the cave. We backed up against the wall, holding on to each other and making ourselves as small as possible in the darkness, when there was scratching at the cave's mouth and whining that sounded like a dog. Suddenly against the faint moonlight the black head of a German shepherd loomed in the entrance.

The dog came into the cave and began sniffing at my feet, up my legs, into my lap. It was not fierce at all, but rooted under my arms, whining and pushing its head into my chest as if it were glad to see me. "Panzer!" I whispered. "Get out of here! Go on, get out."

"You know this dog?" Mario was incredulous.

"Shhhhh." I put my hand over his mouth.

At that, a flashlight beam swept the

earth at the entrance to the cave. "Panzer. *Wo bist du?*"

We held our breath, but the light found first the dog, then the two of us crouched up against the back wall. The cave was so small that the wide beam lit up the space enough to make out the face behind it. Klaus.

"Giovanna—it is you?"

We stared at each other for a long moment. He said nothing; then he moved the light to Mario's face. "Who is this man? He is a friend of yours?"

I stared back, wide-eyed. "Yes, Klaus. He is."

He held the beam on Mario, letting it travel slowly up to his hair, down to his chin, and back and forth along his crouched body. "Why are you hiding? That means he is a partisan or . . . You know what I think? I think he is Jewish. I think he is a Jew and you are hiding him."

I stared at him as tears filled my eyes and spilled down my cheeks. I shook my head.

He nodded. "*Ja.* That is what I think."

"Please, Klaus . . ." My lips were trembling. "Please."

He stared back at me, his eyes holding mine. "Why I should do something for you I do not know." He shined the beam on Mario's face again. In the jumping shadows, the distorted light, I saw him shake his head. Then, without a word, he flicked off the flashlight and backed slowly out the way he had come. We heard his fingers snap twice, and Panzer followed. Then heavy bootsteps slipping and sliding down the steep descent. A shout at the bottom. *"Nichts. Let's go."*

℘

The moon was rising, cutting a path up from the east, and we could just see it cresting above the fork of a large tree visible from the mouth of the cave. Neither of us said a word. I was suddenly conscious that Mario and I were still holding hands, that we had not released the death grip that had held us together all the way up to the cave and through the ordeal with Klaus. I moved my fingers a little and looked at him. He smiled and lightly wiggled his own.

"I didn't know you had Nazi friends."

I waited, listening, before I answered. There was the hoot of a prowling owl and the incessant vibration of the crickets, nothing else. "Do you think they're really gone?" I whispered.

He nodded. "I thought I heard their car drive off earlier. I don't think they'll be back."

We crawled to the cave's entrance, looked in every direction, then stood up, stretching our legs and arms and brushing the dirt off our clothes. "I'll tell you all about Klaus when we get there," I said. "We're going to have a lot of time to talk."

After crossing the main road, this time without incident, we picked our way in the dark through the short span of woods, then hastened across the stubbled fields of harvested wheat. Our shadows zigzagged in the moonlight shining on furrowed rows of fragrant beans, patches of high grass, and tangled, thorny branches of little roses. Resting in an abandoned shed, we finished Serena's food before working our way through the remaining countryside to the marchesa's property. At last, we walked casually, trying to project an image of a relaxed couple moving together. We could hear a dog bark for a long time, perhaps at us, perhaps at the moon, but we kept moving steadily and paid it no undue attention.

The sky was beginning to glow with the first light of dawn when we arrived at the walled border of the marchesa's estate. I avoided the main gate and moved around to the back, where I knew there was a break in the wall used by farmers and their equipment on the way to market. The fence was easy to scale, and once inside I began to breathe easier. We found the old mill, extracted the key from its hole in the wall, and mounted the staircase in silence to the room where everything had been laid out, just as she had said, waiting for Mario.

Chapter Twenty-three

Wednesday, August 16, 1944
Giovanna and I found this
journal, set like a crown jewel
on top of a pile of gray army
blankets, when we arrived at the
mill this morning. G left for the
clinic right away, and I was so
exhausted that I swept the book
aside, curled up on the floor,
and fell asleep. The slant of light
over the vineyards told me it
was afternoon when I woke up,
hungry and disoriented, an hour
or so ago. What an extraordinary

turn of events. Here I am, sitting
in a tower, in a round stone
room with one high, tiny
window that looks out across
the fields. I feel so alone.
Mama, Papa, and Cecilio have
all evaporated. I don't know
where they are. I try not to think
about what's happened to them,
but it's a creeping mold, eating
away at the edges of my spirit.
Still, here in my hands is this
beautiful book with soft leather
binding and gilded red-and-
green endpapers—a treasure, a
talisman, a reminder of a life
that is lost to me and an
investment in the future. I will
gladly use it. What else do I
have to do?

Thursday, August 17
The marchesa—who left this
book for me—stopped by this
morning. She is both elegant
and warm. I was embarrassed
(even wearing Giorgio's

clothes), being so rumpled and dirty. I felt like reassuring her that her "guest" was not just a street ruffian, but there didn't seem to be time for that kind of conversation. She went over the "rules" of the house—no noise, no lights, no going outside the building at any time. I wonder how long I will have to be here, how long I will last. She asked about my health, and I told her about my arm, how G had cleaned the wound and given me the penicillin shots that turned it all around. Hearing that, she became busy and in a hurry, so I just thanked her for everything, the space, the blankets, the journal. She flashed a warm smile and left me alone again.

Sunday, August 20
Where would I be without Giovanna? She comes by every

day, bringing food and welcome company. I barely know her, yet I depend on her for everything I eat and drink. I can't ever go outside, so she even has to empty my chamber pot when she gets here. (Thank God it has a lid!) It's an agonizing, animal connection between us that makes me feel both shy and recklessly myself.

I'm getting used to her appearing at the door—those weeks at Guido's cottage and now these afternoons. She's always brimming with life: Her hair stands out, dark and unruly, around her open face. Her eyes are the color of roasted almonds, and so alert. I wait for her smile, which—when it comes—is rich and full, like the best moment of a glorious aria. How did this happen? How did this girl become the axis around which I spin?

Tuesday, August 22

The marchesa and her husband are my second lifeline, after G. The marchese, Leonardo, has come a couple of times to check on me. He's a bit like a heron—tall and gangly, with an erect and graceful carriage. Whereas his wife is so outgoing and exuberant, his conversation is more measured and restrained. He saw right away that boredom is going to be my worst enemy, so he took the time to find out what interests me, and he's going to keep me supplied with books from their library. What a gift that is!

I told the marchese about last fall, just after the Germans arrived, before we knew how bad it would get. Italian Fascists broke into Turin's Jewish community library, piled up most of the books, and set fire to them in a huge blaze in the Piazza Carlina. It was shortly after that that we left the city.

We've always been book people,
and that incident hit Papa hard.

As for what to lend me, I
said I'm really curious about
farming—particularly viticulture—
and I love history. Maybe, if I
read enough, I can figure out
how Italy got into this mess.

Thursday, August 24

Another heel of day-old bread
and a rind of *parmigiano* for
dinner. G says that's all she can
find, that she doesn't want to
take more, to threaten the
partisans' supplies or lead
anyone to suspect my presence.
I agree with her, but it's hard. I
get so hungry. I saved it until
just a few minutes ago, closed
my eyes, and pretended it was
shaved onto some fresh arugula
and drizzled with olive oil.

Giovanna stayed longer this
afternoon. I try not to put
pressure on her, but I live for
her visits. I'm desperate for

company, but it's more than that. I really like her. She's cheery and frank and full of stories about the clinic and her friend Violetta, who's fallen in love with one of the patients. We've started at the beginning, filling each other in on our lives. She grew up in Lucca, me in Turin—but it's striking how similar our childhoods were. We're both the younger of two; her mother plays the piano, mine the violin; and we both have hardworking, doggedly Fascist fathers. It's made me see some differences too. My parents—especially Father—are more intellectual than hers, I think. Of course, her family is Catholic and, I get the impression, more observant than ours. We had so many Catholic friends in Turin that I feel comfortable with that. They must not have any Jewish friends, though—G doesn't seem to know much about us.

Friday, September 14

I finally got up the nerve to ask G about that Nazi soldier who found us in the cave. I was shocked, really, to hear how he tried to seduce her like that. But I can see how it happened. I can't blame her, really—or him either, for that matter! He must be a decent guy, because he let us go that night. Still, that close call makes me shudder.

She started teasing me after that story and said I owed her one—we call them our *racconti reciproci*. All that talk about the floor of the coat closet reminded me of our maid, Amalia. So I told G about her, how she had seduced Cecilio first behind the garden storehouse. I told her how jealous I was and determined to have my turn, how I hid in her bedroom in the servants' wing one afternoon until she finished the dishes; then how I asked for what I wanted. Amalia laughed at me, called me her "little goat" and said I was too young. (I was every bit of fifteen! Was it really only five years ago?) But I didn't give up. We played cards every day for a week or so, laughing and slapping down jacks and aces on the bedspread. When I finally asked again, I guess she thought I was ready. I still dream about those breasts, like soft watermelons. I've never told anyone about it before today. It was only a month or so later that poor Amalia had to be let go—she and the other Catholic servants who were no longer allowed to work for Jews. She cried so hard the day she left us.

As I talked about Amalia, I found myself trying not to look at G's body that way. She seemed . . . I don't know . . . annoyed at the story. But she's the one who asked for it.

Thursday, September 28
The marchesa has been
supplying G with more food for
me from what's given to the
sick and wounded men at the
clinic. There are endless pots of
beans flavored with nothing,
soups as thin as weak tea, and
bread that's days old by the
time I get it. All I can hope for
is to take the edge off my
hunger. This is custom-made
torture, because I love food so
much. Nonna used to joke that I
was the one in the family who
should do the cooking, because
I always preferred one cheese
maker over another or argued
for a particular style of roast
when I was twelve years old. I
pass the time here imagining
feasts: I think up surprising
combinations for pasta sauces,
new ingredients with which to
stuff a bird, weird pairings of
fruit and cheese for dessert. It
amuses me, but when I tell G

my latest inventions, she begs
me to stop. She tells me it
gnaws a hole in her stomach. I
would give anything for the two
of us to sit down to a long,
leisurely, delicious meal
together. Meanwhile, I'm
growing thinner. I know it.

Wednesday, October 4
I'm shocked to think how rarely
I wash myself—I who was the
family hog in the bathroom. G
has found me an enamel bowl,
and she fills two liter bottles
with freshwater every few days.
I have to drink from that supply,
so I hoard just enough in the
bottom of the basin to wet a
thin rag and give myself a
sponge bath maybe once a
week. I start with my face and
work my way down to my toes,
but by the time I get there, the
little puddle is the color of wet
cement, and I'm really just
dampening the dust into a

pasty coating that sticks to my skin. Lately there's been so much rain that G can leave the bowl outside, hidden in some bushes. Those are my best days. I love how Giovanna smells. She glows with the sweat of all her activity, but I still catch the scent of lavender soap beneath it. I know I'm falling for her. It's a kind of ache that lives in my lower body— hard to tell from hunger sometimes.

Tuesday, October 10
I'm exhausted. G and I spent two hours today talking about religion, trying to understand Hitler and the whole thing. Without admitting it to each other, I think we are exploring what this might mean for the two of us when the war is over. It started when she arrived this afternoon with my supper. I was so hungry I thought I would

pass out before she finally
came. I opened the bundle,
working the tight knot in the
cotton scarf with such
eagerness, only to find that it
held a heel of bread spread
with lard. Lard! Fat of the hog. I
know butter is rationed and
that's all there is, but I sat there
for the longest time. That was
one of the only Jewish laws we
observed at home—not eating
pork. I felt Nonna's spirit, knew
I should not eat it. I told G my
dilemma, and she seemed truly
touched. "If I were you, I don't
think I would eat it," she said
gravely. That was so sweet, but
I was famished. In the end, I
wolfed it down. I would do it
again, and I probably will.

But it got us talking about
religion. We are so different, not
just because we are Christian
and Jewish, but because she is
so devout, and I am so secular.
To me, these ultimate questions
she's posing are about science:

evolution, causality, the likelihood of an afterlife. "What is the purpose of your life?" she kept asking. "Why are you here?"

I told her I don't need a "purpose." I'm just planning to lead the best, most ethical life I can. I don't think God gets into the details, that there is some kind of plan for each of us. But she thinks maybe she was drawn to me in some mysterious way, that it was "meant to be" that she help save me, to make a difference in the war.

"You're a good person," I told her. "You're brave and full of energy. You saw a wrong and wanted to make it right. What's that got to do with religion?"

It went on and on like that. G loves liturgy: the cadence of the mass, the music, the candles, the feeling of opening to something bigger than herself. I don't feel the need to pray or

even meditate. But this has
nothing to do with Christianity
or Judaism. I told her she
reminds me of my nonna, who
felt just as she does, going to
synagogue every week,
throwing herself into the
Passover seder, lighting candles
during Hanukkah. We ended
with a kind of mutual respect,
neither of us trying really to
convert or change the other.
But what does it mean for the
future? I don't know. I do know
I could spend every day like this
one, just talking with her.

Monday, October 30
It's getting chilly, and that's
putting me on edge. Fall used
to make me feel energetic and
productive, but there's nothing
to do here, nothing but read. It's
really getting to me. Giovanna is
so lucky. I don't think she
appreciates what it means just

to be able to come and go as
freely as she does.

                  Friday, November 10
What a day . . . I was so
frustrated this morning,
brooding about being stuck in
here, that I took one of my
blankets and just tore it to
shreds. It felt so good, but
when G arrived, she started
desperately scooping up the
scraps and pieces of wool. "You
can't do this, Mario," she said.
"There aren't enough of these
to go around as it is. Winter's
coming."
    That pissed me off, so I told
her she was a pampered little
principessa and that she could
just bring me one of her own
precious blankets from home.
"You have no idea what it's like,
staring at these four walls day
after day. I feel like a criminal or
an escaped convict, when I
haven't done a goddamned

thing wrong!" I clenched my jaw and just glowered at her.

She stared at me, looking shocked. Then she said, "Okay, fine. Then get your own food and water. See if I care." She hoisted her bag onto her shoulder and headed for the door.

I felt like a hot branding iron had been shoved into my gut. All that anger turned instantly into grief and fear, and I let out a groan that must have sounded like the bleat of a wounded calf. G dropped her bag and ran back, putting her arms around me. I started crying and blubbering on her shoulder like a *bambino*. I told her I was sorry, that I didn't mean to take it all out on her, but she was the only person around. "I know. I know," she soothed, and she started rubbing the back of my head and neck. "Someday this will all be over."

We stood like that for a long

time. Finally I pulled back, cupped her face in my hands, and stared right into her eyes. "You mean so much to me. I want to show you how I really feel." It felt like a dream. I took her hand and led her over to the corner where the other blankets were piled. I pulled her down to the floor with me and wrapped her in my arms. It was chilly, too cold to even think about undressing, but we held each other and started kissing. Oh, my God, it was as if all the time we'd spent together and our growing friendship started exploding between us in this new way. We were so absorbed in each other that we didn't hear the footsteps on the second flight of stairs.

The door opened, scraping along the uneven floor. We pulled quickly apart at the sound and sat up to see Leonardo's lanky frame stooping to enter the space. He stopped short at the sight of us and laughed out loud. "And here I thought you needed something to relieve the boredom, Mario," he said, setting down a pile of books.

Saturday, November 25
It's not that G and I feel guilty about what happened the other day, but it has sobered us, and we've put a kind of mutually acknowledged damper on things. It's getting colder and colder, both outside and inside the tower. We're so grateful to the marchese and marchesa that we don't want them to feel awkward about coming and going at will.

They are friends of G's parents, after all. So we've backed off, and we treat each other with a kind of friendly restraint. We hold hands, even kiss now and then when we're sure to be alone, but we've decided that anything more is just taboo for the moment. Not easy.

Chapter Twenty-four

Radios crackled day and night, bringing narrative and cohesion to all the noise and rumors, while the Germans and their Allied pursuers traded fire, made progress, were pushed back, and rallied again, until at last it all cleared away, preparing the stage—for me—for war of a different kind.

My life became fragmented as I existed in three worlds: the mill, where Mario and I had the time and isolation to discover each other slowly and grow together like a new vine grafting onto foreign rootstock; the clinic, where the marchesa reigned over everything and shone like a beacon of hope; and home, where the delicate fabric of my life as a daughter frayed to the breaking point.

Mother continued to obsess over Giorgio. She grew so thin that her clothes—once elegantly tailored—hung on her diminishing frame like laundry on a line. Her face, religiously protected from the sun, began to be creased with worry and concern. She developed nervous tics, drumming her nails incessantly on a chair arm or table, and staring into space, twirling a loose strand of hair idly around and around her index finger. There was a distracted air about her, as if she were lost in an inner labyrinth.

Who knows? Maybe I was even a little jealous of Giorgio. I was amazed at the wrenching sadness and worry my brother's absence inspired. If I were missing, would Mother let me rule her life to that extent?

"Mother, won't you finish your pasta?" I might say. "You are getting so thin— isn't she, Papa? You need more flesh on your bones. You're beginning to look like a prisoner of war."

Or, in another vein: "Why don't you volunteer to tutor some of the refugee children? You so wanted *me* to do that, and the need is still there. It would get you out of here, take your mind off Giorgio, and make you feel better about using your time in a productive way."

Papa was as mercurial as Mother was predictable. I often found him hunched over the radio in the little sitting room, his ear straining to distill the announcer's voice out of the underlying static. The Germans would surely have confiscated it had they known it was there, so he kept the volume very low.

His spirits rose and fell with every incursion, every gain or loss of territory. The amazing thing to watch was how his base loyalties shifted with the likelihood of victory. Early on, when he was convinced that the German Axis would triumph, Giorgio's treachery caused him no end of consternation. "We'll be shot on sight, every damn one of us," he would mutter, pacing back and forth in the tiny space. "The loyal Fascists are the only ones with a prayer of a future—in the government, in business, in anything at all."

But then, over the summer and into the fall of 'forty-four, when the Allies began making steady progress, pushing the Germans northward, and reports of the partisan participation poured in, his heart changed. "By God, Giorgio, my boy! I'll be damned if you aren't going to turn this thing around after all." He would learn of a German setback and pump his fist in a victory salute over the radio, grabbing Mother or me by the back of the neck. "Did you hear that? They've liberated Massa Carrara! It won't be long now, by God."

Then the action moved closer to home. Steady reports from Violetta's family and others hiding in the mountains filtered back to us by word of mouth. They watched the Germans drilling holes in the piers of bridges and inserting explosives, ready to slow the Allies' progress. In mid- to late September, occasionally during the day, an Allied reconnaissance plane called *la cicogna* (shaped like a stork) would fly at low altitude over the valley. We could hear Allied planes in the distance bombing the coastal cities of Pisa or La Spezia. Heavy artillery fire pockmarked the roads up and down the valley, and shells exploded on the slopes of the mountains. We were certain that the Allies were getting close and that liberation was imminent. Father was ecstatic, pacing back and forth, talking excitedly. "I'm going to put Giorgio in charge of selling the wine, once we get the vineyards back in shape. I'm going to bud over half the vines to merlot and use it for blending. You wait. You'll see a big difference around here."

Nearer the river, Violetta's family and fellow villagers stayed in their retreats, terrified that the Germans—in their last moments of power—would unleash punishing waves of violence and retribution. We tuned our ears to our own *piano nobile*, listening for signs of departure.

The flow of Nazis through our villa was constant, the numbers rising and falling with the level of local action. As the fighting moved up the valley, there were more soldiers—combat officers of a louder and rougher sort—who clomped about, shouted, and kept us awake at night. Trucks crunched along the gravel driveway, squeaking to a halt near the front door. I could see them from my window, lumpy figures in the evening dusk with packs on their backs and rifles on their shoulders, pulling duffel bags from the luggage rack and heading inside. How long any particular group stayed was a mystery to us, but inevitably the sound of morning departures would raise our spirits and dangle the hope that this time, all would be completely quiet in their wake.

℘

By early autumn, the Allies moved into the Serchio River valley, occupying the areas in which the residents and refugees from coastal cities were hiding. Violetta felt secure enough to move back home to join her family, who had recently returned from their own retreat. Her parents and their friends had watched patrols of liberating soldiers march into the remote mountainous village, smiling and shaking hands, led by local scouts. To their surprise, they were not Americans but Brazilian soldiers speaking Portuguese. Even though they were technically liberated, the Germans were just slightly farther up the valley, where explosions of artillery fire and rifle shots were a constant reminder of their menacing presence.

Within two weeks, up and down the valley, the Americans—the black "buffalo soldiers"—of the 92nd Infantry Division replaced the Brazilians. They moved into homes in that area and immediately recruited partisans and local residents to begin the process of clearing land mines left by the Germans. Those mines, in the form of shallow square wooden boxes filled with dynamite, were placed—by Klaus's unit, I presume—at regular intervals all across the valley, from the base of one mountain to the other. The Germans had forced some of the locals to help them lay the mines, so the buffalo soldiers were able to recruit those same farmers to help remove them. When I go back over those months, I yearn to have been among the searchers, dreaming that maybe my own instincts would have led us to find just one more, the one that would have made all the difference.

The Nazi occupiers finally drove away from Villa Farfalla for good one early October morning. We hardly dared breathe for fear of their return. After a couple of days, at Rosa's encouragement, for she could see that they had completely vacated the premises, we went downstairs and looked around. It was a sickening sight. The walls were covered with dirt and streak marks, the floors littered and encrusted with dust and mud. The upholstered furniture we had left behind was stained, torn, tipped over, and displaced, the wooden surfaces scratched and dented. A smell of dirty clothes, stale smoke, and beer lingered in the air. Without taking inventory, we knew there were dishes, flatware, and other objects missing, but for the moment we could not presume that it was over. And as if to confirm the volatility of the situation, a cadre of Allied soldiers drove up less than four days later.

Whereas the German officers had

been formal and correct, porcine pink, blue eyed and fresh faced, these American officers associated with the 92nd Infantry Division were more casual, open, and friendly. They were apologetic and appreciative, negotiating politely with Father through a young Italian interpreter who was traveling with them, to allow them to stay in the space recently vacated by the Germans. They would, they assured us, share with us some of the rations that they would receive from the central distribution area near the river.

We welcomed them with open arms— they could hardly do any more damage. And if pressed, we had to admit that we felt much more secure and less afraid with them nearby. We could openly listen to the radio, and we enjoyed the canned meat—some fresh meat too now and then—their fried strips of bacon, coffee, and hot chocolate in milk to drink. They had large loaves of sliced white bread as soft as cake that they slathered with butter and jam at breakfast time. There were American cigarettes—Lucky Strikes, Camels, and

Chesterfields—that the men freely shared with Papa.

But even as our situation changed slightly for the better, fighting continued up and down the river valley throughout October, November, and into December. As Christmas approached, the officers negotiated with my parents, hoping that Rosa could cook us all a Christmas dinner if they provided most of the food. We agreed, and it was a Christmas I will never forget. We ate at our own dining room table downstairs, and—though we still hadn't brought out from hiding the best china and silver—we managed to find enough dishes to set a table for about twelve. The Germans, in retreat, had blown up the power-generating plant near the river, so there was no electricity in the area. The flickering candlelight created an intimate, friendly atmosphere. The meat, the pasta, the vegetables were all delicious. I remember Papa, so relaxed. He had offered up wine from his cellar, and empty bottles littered the table. The men were telling stories in their broad (I now know Southern) American accents, and the translator would follow up with shorthand versions for us that never seemed quite as funny as the officers' laughter had indicated.

After dinner, the officers brought out a hand-cranked turntable and some American records of Tommy Dorsey and Glenn Miller swing music. The men were loose by then and had lost any air of military bearing. One of them coaxed Mother to dance with him in the nearly empty living room, and then another—a redhead with thinning hair combed over a balding head—grabbed my hand and pulled. I glanced at Father, but he didn't seem to mind, so I let the soldier lead me to the floor and take my hand. He was a good dancer, and I followed him easily. We moved together; then he spun me out with bursts of energy into the give-and-take of a series of swings. We danced like that, trading partners through all nine of the men, until we were panting and steamy under our clothes. I had not seen Mother so relaxed for months. She was the consummate hostess, who had always felt that entertaining was, for her, a duty and an important part of her role. At last she could be making some sort of contribution to the war effort, and I could see the pride of it reflected in her flushed face and bright persona.

The men learned that she played the piano and finally convinced her to sit down and accompany them for some Christmas carols. The piano was dusty and badly out of tune, but she was so happy to be playing again. We sang loudly, and I still remember the odd blend of English and Italian lyrics as each tried to drown the others out in drunken exuberance.

Our joy and relief were short-lived. While we were celebrating, the Germans were planning a big counterattack upriver. In the early-morning hours of December 26, two German assault battalions suddenly pounced on the town of Sommocolonia, up the Serchio River, overwhelming American resistance along with their partisan supporters. So many of the buffalo soldiers lost their lives. Known as the *Wintergewitter,* "Winter Storm," this Axis counteroffensive was demoralizing to all of us who had thought victory was a given.

As we heard daily reports about the reversal from our own resident officers, I watched Papa with disgust. I could see his doubt flaring again, the resurgence of his old Fascist loyalties as he imagined a definitive Axis takeover. Father had befriended Bernardo, the young Roman translator who had traveled up the coast with the Americans. The officers who lived with us were white, mostly Southern Americans from Virginia or North Carolina, for the most part of English and Irish extraction, commanding the all-Negro unit. As the Germans began pushing back and the casualties mounted, Father could not help himself. "Bernardo," he would say, "just ask these guys how they thought they could take on Hitler's army with this pathetic excuse for a fighting band. What did they expect?"

They, in turn, would nod, then shake their heads and complain about the colored enlisted men's laziness, dullness, and tendency to fold under pressure. "But, Papa," I would argue, overhearing these exchanges, "Violetta's family has invited lots of them to dinner, and she says they are the warmest, kindest bunch of men they have ever seen."

"Well, since when have warmth and kindness won anyone any wars?" Father would sneer, and retreat upstairs to hunch over his radio.

The irony of all this was eating away at me: The American military, so much the "white horse" for all of us in this war, felt to me like a weak echo of the Nazis' own prejudices and hostilities.

Thursday, December 28
They've driven the Americans back, and now it looks like a general withdrawal. My skin crawls when I picture the Germans, glutted with victory, fanning out over this countryside, newly emboldened, looking for more of us. What has my life come to? Cowering like a hunted animal. I turned the radio off for fear of the noise—but then had to stifle

sobs in the blankets. Where are Mama and Papa? What has happened to them?

Thinking of Papa makes me burn with sadness. He was so full of energy, flush with success at the bank, so proud. Then in 'forty-one, when the posters and graffiti appeared on our neighborhood walls and someone tried to burn down the synagogue. I think it was then he took it all to heart—that this wasn't going to work out, that the Germans were really going to carry out their threats. Worse yet, Italian collaborators were going to help them. He kept insisting his Fascist loyalties would pay off, but he knew he was kidding himself. As the racial laws went into effect, Papa became more and more humiliated, isolated, and irrelevant. Life went on, but he had no job, no stature, no pride. My eyes fill with tears at the thought of him then.

I keep thinking how ironic this is. I, who was so casual about being Jewish—at school and at home. Here I am, virtually imprisoned for it!

I asked G today, "How do you feel about my being Jewish? It must make you think less of me."

"What are you talking about?" she said. "It's just part of you. It doesn't make any difference to me at all."

"But for months and months now it must have been worming its way into your brain, right? That we are vermin, that we are somehow worthy of being rooted out and thrown away like so many rotten apples in a barrel. Honest to God, Giovanna, with this hiding and groveling, I'm starting to wonder myself. It makes me sick, makes me feel like there's something wrong with me. This 'purification exercise'—do you *buy* that, Giovanna?"

She put her arms around me and shushed me, but I was left feeling so helpless and worthless, just doing nothing but sitting here, hiding.

Wednesday, January 3, 1945
Snow today, some of it drifting through the window. My fingers are stiff and raw. Colder than yesterday by two degrees? I've piled on blankets, wrapping myself like a mummy, but still I shiver. Trying to keep warm makes me so hungry, but the soup is always thin and cold by the time I get it.

Saturday, February 10
I'm thinking more and more about Giorgio and his band out there, putting their lives on the line, edging us closer and closer to defeating these bastard Germans. I feel so useless, like a drag on

everyone. How am I going to live with myself, even if we win? I haven't done a goddamned thing to help. The Allies have pushed the Nazis back up the river. I picture the partisans helping uncover German mines, carrying messages, protecting the residents. Here I sit, reading. For what?

I unloaded all this on Giovanna. She's talked so often about her own desire to make a real contribution to the war effort, which—in a way—she has, by hiding me, by working in the clinic. She listened to me like she always does, as if I'm the most important person in the world. But then she tried to convince me otherwise. "I know, I know. I understand how you feel; I really do. But, Mario, you'll have a whole life ahead of you to make a difference in the world. Right now it's your responsibility just to stay alive. That will be your own gift to the world. It's too dangerous out there. If you die, then what does that do for anyone except give the Germans the satisfaction of carving another notch on their evil belts?"

She said this all so earnestly, with her big brown eyes begging me to agree, that I grabbed her and just held her.

Chapter Twenty-five

When I close my eyes and try to live those months again, it is the marchesa who frames the memories with light. She was the link between my two personal worlds, the person I depended upon both to guard my secret and to keep Mario alive.

I hadn't made a particularly good first impression when I fainted in the aisle on my first day at the clinic as I followed Violetta on her rounds. But by the time Mario was in residence, she had begun to see me with new eyes. It was my constant presence on the property that prompted the marchesa, shortly after Mario arrived, to take me back into the clinic one morning. She led me between the beds and kept up a steady patter about this soldier or that, where he was from, how he had come to sustain his particular set of injuries.

At one point, I think she could feel me turn away to avoid looking at the weeping flesh of a young American's cheek wound. She cupped my elbow in her hand and led me over to a private corner of the space. "I know how you felt back there, Giovanna, but think of it this way. David is all alone here. He has no family, no parents to care about him. Imagine that he is your own son—or, in your case, maybe your brother. Just make that real. Look into his eyes and find there something to *love*. Feel that first. Then just do what needs to be done." She smiled encouragingly. "You'll be amazed what you can do, once you get the hang of it."

She was right. I began working in the clinic that day, and then nearly all mornings after that, assisting with surgeries, cleaning wounds, comforting feverish and frightened men. To this day I'm the image of calm in an emergency and unafraid to offer help in any situation. It's something people never expect of me, and I delight in surprising them.

The marchesa was proud of my progress, and I am sure that her approval and affection were a big part of what motivated me to do the work on a daily basis. But I was amazed to find that her interest in me extended beyond the rudiments of health care. She began inviting me, maybe once a week or so, to accompany her on the long walk from the ancient chapel to their private quarters in the main house. There she would call for a light lunch and some tea, and we would settle in the library, where she began slowly introducing me to her favorite authors.

She really loved to read and to write, and she cherished her books as if they were her children. Her library was something to behold: Lined with shelves, it was totally full of books—some leatherbound and gilded, some well-worn paperbacks—in Italian, English, even some in French and Spanish. Piles of books leaned next to the desk on the floor, covered the smaller pieces of furniture.

I loved the space, and I think it was partly because she *expected* me to. She seemed just to assume that I too loved literature and would want to discover new writers. Why should I disappoint her in any way? We would settle down in that room with our tea or after a lunch on the terrace, and she would begin pulling books from the shelves or off the piles and showing them to me one by one.

I remember one afternoon in particular. I know it was still winter, because there was a fire crackling in the fireplace in the library. We were absorbed in our conversation, sitting side by side, a book opened between us, when we heard the sound of a motor approaching. The library's big doors faced the front of the house and the garden, but the circular driveway was visible, so we both looked out the window to see who it would be. It grew louder until it was clear it was a truck or a large vehicle, and then a German transport van rounded the curve and came to a stop in front of the villa.

We looked at each other, expressionless, the terror and the implications of it all as obvious to each other as if we had shouted it all out loud.

There was a loud knocking—a pounding, really—on the front door. The marchesa rose to answer it, and I followed. A hulking German officer clicked his heels together and made a short, polite bow of the head. "You are the marchesa, the owner here, no?"

"I am." She stood tall and motionless. "What brings you here?"

"I have a very sick officer lying in the truck, and it is rumored that you have medical services, a clinic or some such." I couldn't look at the marchesa, but stared straight ahead at the man's shiny metal belt buckle. It was engraved with, *Gott mit uns*.

She pulled herself up straighter and folded her arms against the chill that pushed in at us from behind his looming frame. "I am sorry, but you are very much mistaken. We are a farming operation here. We have no such thing."

The officer stamped his heavy tall boots and exhaled loudly. "Please. I have no time to waste. He is very, very ill, signora."

"Well . . ." She looked at the floor as if studying it, as if weighing her options. "I have a bit of experience in that area. I used to do some work as a nurse's aid when I was in school. Perhaps if I could just see him . . ."

We followed him around to the back of the waiting truck. There was another German soldier lying on the bench along one side of the back section. The walls made of canvas strips let in enough light to see him clearly. His knees were drawn up, and he was clutching his midsection, moaning. Touched by his obvious agony, the marchesa jumped up into the truck and leaned over him. "Is it his stomach?" she said to the first officer.

"Yes, yes. All of a sudden this morning, this pain. It will not stop."

She pressed here and there on the man's abdomen, pushing down hard, then quickly letting go. When she pushed a particular place on his left side, he let out a sharp bellow, like a branded bull.

The marchesa climbed down and looked up at the intruder. "I suspect it is appendicitis, very acute. He needs medical attention."

"We have nowhere to go with this today. Our medical facilities are too remote, set up near the river. I was told to come here."

The marchesa looked back into the truck. "As I told you, we don't have a clinic here. However, there is a doctor who lives not far away. If he can be found, perhaps he could be called to the villa." She turned to me. "Giovanna, would you please take these men to the back bedroom off the kitchen? He'll have to get his friend in there. I'll see if I can find Leonardo."

Terrified, I moved as if I were leading a pair of raging lions into their waiting cage at the zoo. Somehow the officer managed to help his friend—clutching his belly and howling—down from the truck; then, supporting him on his hip, he followed me through the entrance hall, into the kitchen, and back to Balbina the maid's room, where he collapsed onto the narrow bed. Trying to keep my teeth from chattering, I was thinking only of Mario.

The marchesa returned and told us that her husband had taken their own car and driven out in search of the doctor and would be back as soon as he could. We both knew that the clinic was not far away, that the doctor was undoubtedly there, so we hovered together in the kitchen, outside the bedroom, listening with every pore for the sound of their return.

Leonardo returned with the doctor, who had been told it was probably appendicitis. He had brought all the necessary equipment, so—incredible as it sounds—he performed an appendectomy right there in that bedroom. With Balbina's help, we boiled water, brought clean linens, and sterilized instruments, while the doctor made his incision, removed the organ, and stitched him up again. The fact that the doctor had been working so close to the villa meant that peritonitis had not had time to set in, so once the surgery was over, we had to wait only a few days to make sure he was out of danger.

Most of the time, the German officer stayed in the room with the sick man.

Now and then, he would wander the downstairs rooms of the villa, smoking, his light blue eyes darting here and there among the antique sideboards, the Oriental rugs, the piano, and the books. Balbina and the rest of the household staff fed them three meals a day and watched carefully so that they never strayed or overheard any talk that might alert them to the presence of our cache of refugees. I went to and from home each day without ever going near the clinic or the mill.

At last the patient was recovered enough to leave. The two officers stood about in the entryway, laughing and gesturing with the marchese and marchesa, expressing their gratitude like a couple of guests at a cocktail party while I and the servants watched and waited, our breaths held. Finally, both of them climbed into the front seat of the truck, the driver fired up the engine, and they drove off, leaving a cloud of dust in their wake. We have always wondered whether word of our good deed traveled widely enough among the occupying troops that—even in the days of most intense fighting—Villa Falconieri never became a battleground or a shelter for German troops. We never spoke about it—not to anyone—until well after peace had returned.

❦

Spring began teasing us. Mario would fashion tiny origami-like flowers out of pages torn from his journal—that precious journal that was his most constant companion. He knotted cotton napkins saved from his meals into colorful posies. He would surprise me, presenting these "bouquets" with a great flourish and a low, sweeping bow. Once, he sneaked outside for a brief moment just after dusk and grabbed a fistful of grasses. He spent hours the next day weaving them into an extraordinary little ring. When I arrived with his dinner, he had a glint in his eye.

"I'm carrying something that will change your life," he said, grinning, "but you'll have to find it on me first."

He dodged and ran around the room until I caught him and searched his pockets, his shoes, even his socks. Then

I gave up. He lifted his leg and told me to feel inside the cuff of his pants. There I found the neat and deftly woven band. Amazingly, it fit my ring finger as if he had measured it. "Now you're mine forever," he said, wrapping his arms around me. "Someday I promise I'll give you a real one."

A wave of sadness made me close my eyes.

"What is it?" he said, looking stricken. "You're not having doubts, are you?"

"Not about us," I said. "It's my father. I can't imagine us getting truly engaged without his blessing, and I'm just so afraid he's going to be . . . I don't know . . . stubborn."

I was sure that once Papa met him, he would love him too, and all my fears would be put to rest, so I started thinking how to bring my father and Mario together. It occurred to me that Giorgio could be the key.

We were—at least for the moment— safely in Allied hands, enabling many of the local partisan soldiers to come home periodically for visits. Sometimes they brought one or two Americans on leave with them. They put them up, gave them a home-cooked meal, and introduced them to their families. I had an ear tuned at all times to the possibility of Giorgio's surprising us, but deep down I knew it was unlikely to happen. When he said good-bye that November of 'forty-three, it had been too horrible.

Giorgio's twentieth birthday was a little more than two weeks away, on the seventeenth of March—something I knew would be weighing heavily, particularly on Mother. So one rainy afternoon, I sat down and wrote my brother a letter. I have it, creased and filthy, folded in its blue envelope in my box of family treasures.

Dear Hermes,
We've been out of touch for so long, I have no idea whether you are even fighting here in the valley or whether you are far away and others are using our supplies. I can only hope that this letter will find its way to you wherever you are.
So much has happened since

we saw each other last. We've never heard from Patch; nor do we know anything about his fate. I was able to get Moses into hiding, and it is a safe place nearby. I see him nearly every day. Hermes, the two of us have fallen in love. I want desperately to spend my life with him, and I need your help in introducing him to Father.

Papa's entire position has changed. Believe me. He is now rooting for the Allies. He credits the partisans with all our victories, and in his mind you are no longer a deserter but a hero. Once I have sent this letter, my plan is to tell them that you and I have been in touch, and we'll all hope you can get away, if only for a brief visit. Please. I'm counting on you. So much depends on it.

Your loving sister,
Columba

I was confident that neither Mario nor I nor anyone else in our family could be identified should censors or the enemy get hold of the letter. Rosa was having a more and more difficult time finding enough rice, beans, or anything else for her deliveries to the Santinis' cellar. She took the letter greedily, as something, at least, to enlarge that week's offering.

❧

The cross on the church altar was shrouded in its purple cloth, and mass ended with a silent procession, as it always did during the penitential season of Lent. The liturgical mood was somber, but when we came down the steps of the church, the air had a whole different feel. The sky was resplendent, the warmth of the sun penetrating our coats and begging us to turn our faces its way. For the first time, I noticed the little swollen buds at the ends of bare branches glinting, each with a tiny bubble of sap. As the bells of the church tolled, our spirits lifted to meet the glorious day. March was too early for a real spring, as so often happens. Surely there would be many more cold days ahead, but that day the blood was pulsing a little faster in our veins. And for now, it was the perfect moment to talk to my parents.

I waited until we were halfway through our meager Sunday meal, just to make sure no one would still be hungry or impatient. Then, when there was a lull in the conversation, I spoke up. "I have written a letter to Giorgio, inviting him to come home for a visit."

"Giorgio?" Father looked at me. "How would you know where to write to him?"

Mother paled, set down her fork.

I took a deep breath. "I want you to hear me out. Please don't say anything until I'm finished. Just promise me you'll listen with an open mind." I looked from one to the other. I definitely had their attention. Father looked ready to pounce, but Mother looked more as if she were about to faint.

"The first thing is that I don't know whether Giorgio is safe. But I do have a means of communicating with him, and I am quite sure that if anything had happened, we would know it by now."

"Well, of course," Father said, "that's what I've maintained all along. There's nothing new in that."

"I know, Papa, but I have been in touch with him directly since he left."

"You have?" Mother gripped the table and started to rise. "Why didn't you say anything?"

"Mama, just sit down, please." I laid a hand on her shoulder. "He sent a note to me last June, through a friend of his, via Catarina."

"Catarina? She knew?"

"Mother, just wait. Giorgio was not far away then, working with a band of partisans close enough to home so that I could meet with him from time to time."

Father shot me an angry look. "*Now* you tell us. Almost nine months later? What have you been thinking? All our months of worry, all our agony."

"I did that to protect Giorgio. You know yourself—in those days, you were so angry. You would have forced me to reveal his whereabouts, and—who knows—you might even have tipped someone off."

"Well, *I* wouldn't have," Mother murmured.

"No, but I just didn't feel right making you keep a secret from Papa." So I filled them in on how, for months, Giorgio had received his supplies.

"Rosa? She's been helping? Has she seen Giorgio too?" Mother was getting agitated, not sure whether to be relieved or angry. "Why wouldn't she tell me?"

"She hasn't seen anyone. She just leaves the supplies and he—or probably someone else—picks them up. She hasn't told you two for the same reasons I haven't—to protect Giorgio."

Mother began to cry. "Where is he now? Can I see him? Why haven't you told me any of this?"

"I've already told you I don't know where he is. I can only assume he's up the river, helping the buffalo soldiers hold the line." I took hold of her hand. "Please don't cry, Mama. I don't know, but I'm sure he's all right or we would have heard something."

They both quieted, shifted in their chairs, thinking.

"I have some more to tell you." My heart was beating in my throat, my mouth suddenly dry. "There were two members of Giorgio's band, two friends

of his from school. One of them was injured."

They looked at me, interested.

"His arm was too injured to fight, and
besides, they were brothers." I took a
deep breath. "They were both Jewish,
so Giorgio thought they were too much
of a risk to keep on."

"Well, that's for damned sure," Papa
muttered.

"Papa, just wait. So I helped them
find a place to hide. One of them took
off a few months ago. But the other
one . . . I'm helping to feed him, to hide
him."

"Not here, I hope?" Mother was quick
to ask.

"No, no. Not here." I looked at my
plate. "Nearby."

I looked up in time to see my mother
glance at my father, a wry smile playing
at the side of her mouth, a barely tolerant smile, as if this unpredictable daughter had once again run out of control,
had once again mystified and con-
founded them. He stared back at Mother,
his jaw set in a way that I knew signaled
a mind made up.

Father said, "You're crazy, Giovanna. It's enough that you've been working at the clinic, but now this—putting yourself and all of us at risk like that. Whatever would possess you to do such a thing?"

I ignored that last remark altogether and pushed back my chair. "So I don't know whether we'll hear from Giorgio anytime soon. But I told him he would be welcome here. I just didn't want you to be surprised if he shows up." Without waiting for any further response, I threw my napkin down onto the table, then bounded down the stairs and out the door.

Thursday, March 1, 1945
This was a big, big day. The marchese told me this morning that the Germans are still hovering north of us, skirmishing daily with Allied fighting units lodged along the river. It's been feeling more and more like winning is inevitable, that the end of this insane war

is near. That could be the only reason why Giovanna did what she did.

This afternoon, earlier than usual, I heard her clomping up the stairs. The door flew open, and she hurled herself into my arms. "I'm through with waiting," she said, panting. "I've had it. I love you, and I want you to make love to me right now." She began kissing me all over my neck and almost clawing my back.

"Wait, wait, *amore mio*," I said. "What's come over you?" I was laughing, fighting for breath, holding her off.

"I don't care what my parents think anymore, or what they will say. I just want to lay claim to you now, body and soul, so nothing can come between us." She told me that she had confessed to her parents that she had "hidden" and was "taking care of" a Jewish refugee, a friend of Giorgio's.

She had said nothing about being in love with me or even given a hint of thinking about the future.

"I actually thought they might be proud," she said, "that they might be impressed that I had taken these risks and arranged all of this. But oh, no. One look at the set of my father's jaw, at the look he shot Mama—a mocking look, Mario, like this was some kind of joke—and I slammed out of there and came here." She wrapped her legs around my hips like a clinging monkey and closed her fists into my hair. "I want to feel you inside of me," she said. "I want to love you with everything I have."

I could see her so clearly, glowing in the rosy late-afternoon light. And I could see she meant every word. How could I protest? I didn't dare give her a chance to change her mind. We fell onto the pile of blankets and set about harnessing all of our pent-up sexual energy, our mutual frustration, and our collective passion into an act that might have been one step toward redeeming the villainy that surrounds us.

Chapter Twenty-six

Late for supper one night, I met Rosa on her way down the narrow staircase. Without saying a word, she fixed me with an impish look and fished in the pocket of her skirt, slipping me a tightly folded piece of paper. Back in my room after dinner, I unfolded a crumpled, dirty scrap scrawled with Giorgio's impulsive hand.

C—Will come for birthday dinner. Have Moses there. Your H.

I realized to my horror it was Thursday, and Giorgio's birthday was only two nights away.

Villa Farfalla was no longer housing any soldiers, so I suppose we could have moved back downstairs at that point, but the damage was so extensive it only made sense to stay where we were until the war was finally over. There was something secure and almost cozy about our cramped quarters. We were like caged birds who begin to feel safe in confinement, almost afraid of venturing out into the world.

Mother was giddy at the prospect of Giorgio's homecoming, and Father was visibly cheered as well—more, perhaps, by the dramatic change in his wife's mood than by the prospect of seeing his son. Neither of my parents seemed to be perturbed by the fact that Mario would be one of the guests. Mother decided to have the dinner downstairs to accommodate the five of us around the table, directing Rosa to do the best she could to make the dining room presentable enough for a party.

I was so excited to see my brother that I skipped going to the clinic that Saturday morning. Instead, I shadowed Rosa, pitching in here and there, sweeping cigarette butts, dried orange peels, salami paper peelings, and the other detritus left in the wake of our German and American "guests." At last I volunteered to scrub the long wooden table myself, tackling what seemed like inches of grease and coagulated remnants of soup, syrup, and beer.

My feelings were not clear, even to me. Of course I couldn't wait to see my brother, but as I worked on the sticky remnants, I uncovered a few buried layers of my own. There had always been competition between us for our parents' approval, and Giorgio's absence had allowed me to feel as if I were finally at the center. Never mind that my parents were obsessed with worry for him. At least I was there for dinner every night, the focus of their conversations, for better or for worse. No longer the younger sister struggling to keep up and to prove myself worthy, I had begun to feel whole in my own right, strong enough inside to act on my own convictions.

I was thinking along these lines, completely absorbed in scrubbing out a recalcitrant blob of what looked like petrified oatmeal, when a car crunched the gravel and pulled to a stop with a squeal of brakes. It sounded German. My stomach clutched—had they returned? Would they find me down here violating "their" territory? I glanced out the window and dropped my brush midscrub. Giorgio was sitting at the wheel of what had once been a German vehicle, the swastika now crudely painted out.

"Mama!" I screamed as I ran outside. "He's here!"

I threw myself at my brother, penetrating the cloud of exhaust and dust around the car to pull him out from the front seat. He was as ragged and disheveled as the last time I had seen him, and his skin exuded rank layers of sweat, gunpowder, and cooking smoke. He pulled back from my embrace and grinned. "You look ravishing," he proclaimed. Then he leaned in closer and growled in my ear, "I can see that love agrees with you."

"*Shhh!*" I hissed back. "Not a word to them. Not yet." I narrowed my eyes at him, telegraphing a threat. "Promise me."

He nodded and winked, and turned

to Mother, who took him into her arms, sobbing and clinging as if she would never let go. Father emerged a couple of minutes later and put his arms around both of them. "Welcome home, son. We weren't sure this day would ever come."

"It's not over yet, Papa." Freeing himself from their embrace, Giorgio combed his long hair back from his forehead with his fingers and frowned. "There's still a lot of fighting going on up there. Lots to be done."

"Well, we've got all night to hear about it." He put his arm around Giorgio's waist. "Come on in, *mio figlio*."

Trailing Papa, we climbed the stairs and settled in the tiny parlor room, Mama on the small sofa next to Giorgio, and Father and I on two chairs pulled in close. Giorgio took a deep breath and looked around. "This is our living room? Since when?"

"It's been this way for over a year—since last February." Papa's voice was impatient, as if this were something he'd rather not discuss.

"Did they force their way in?"

"No, we just . . . I don't know, son.

We just had to let them stay here, that's all." He leaned forward, his elbows on his knees. "But tell us what's going on up the river. We had some of the Allied commanders here for a while after the Nazis moved out. They weren't too excited about the troops they had; I'll tell you that much."

"Oh, Papa. That's just the problem—those white officers. We've gotten to know a lot of the buffalo soldiers, worked side by side with them, and damn it, they're fighting as well as any divisions out there. They've fallen like flies in some of the counterattacks, but shit! Any troops would. The Germans are ruthless."

"I heard there's a lot of 'straggling' being reported."

"That's not fair. Sometimes a few get separated from the rest at night, but they're right back in there the next day, ready to fight. I know these guys." As Mama began asking about food and other supplies, and where he had slept, I quietly slipped out the parlor door.

The sky slowly darkened to a winey purple, giving us good cover but making it hard to see where we were going. Mario and I picked our way through the vineyard rows, lifting our feet to avoid tripping on the tangle of discarded shoots left by that day's pruning. Now and then, when the path was wide enough, I slowed my pace, fell back next to him, and took his hand. It was warm, a cave of heat to curl into, his fingers cupping my fist.

"Are you scared?" he asked.

I nodded. "What if it doesn't go well? What if he doesn't like you?"

Mario smiled. "If he doesn't, it won't really be about me, will it? Besides, he's your father—how could he be anything but wonderful?"

"He is, but he has a couple of blind spots and certain . . . shall we say *expectations* when it comes to me."

"Well, tonight won't have anything to do with us. I'm just a friend of Giorgio's coming to his birthday dinner, right? It's not as if I'm asking for your hand."

We walked on in silence. The last twitter of birds died away, replaced by the steady pulsing of crickets rising around us. I couldn't believe we were out like that, walking together in plain sight. It had been months since we had been anywhere together but in the confinement of the tower.

"Can I ask you something, Mario?"

He leaned into me. "Ask away, my Giovannina."

"What would your parents think of me? Of our being together?"

"They would love you."

"But about my not being Jewish."

He thought for a bit. "I think—God bless them, wherever they are—their first choice would be for me to marry someone Jewish, but they are realistic too. We're in Italy, after all. My grandmother would probably care a lot, but my parents? They would just be happy that I found someone I love." He put an arm around my shoulder and pulled me closer. "I just hope we have a chance to find out. I want you to know them."

℮

Villa Farfalla loomed ahead in the dusk, and as we approached, I watched Mario carefully. He took it all in, then seemed to run an appraising eye over the gardens, the paths, the exterior. I worried that he might be either overly impressed with our family's estate or disappointed that it wasn't what he imagined. But his gaze was level, his comment sympathetic. "What a toll this war has taken. I can only imagine what our summer place looks like—if it's even still standing," he said. "It will take years to put this country back together again once this war's finally over."

"We have to go around to the side entrance," I said, pulling him by the hand. "We're still in the back of the house in our little Nazi-designated apartment."

"Bastards." His grip tightened a little.

"Remember," I said. "No sign that there's anything between us."

"I'll do my best." He gave me a quick kiss on the ear, then dropped my hand. "But it won't be easy."

℮

My father was expansive, warm, welcoming. He held out his hand to Mario, put his other hand around his shoulder, flashed him an approving grin. Without being in any way condescending, he was solicitous—like a textile salesman eager to make a positive impression.

"I hear you're putting up with some tough accommodations these days." He laughed. "Kind of like us." He swept an arm around the tiny salon. "Sorry we can't offer you more capacious surroundings, but we're glad you're here. Giorgio's told us so much about you."

Had he? Papa seemed comfortable enough with him. He asked about Mario's father, with whom, to my surprise, he had done some banking business five or six years earlier. "Great guy—hell of a good businessman too." He looked at Giorgio and winked. "Drove a hard bargain; I'll tell you that much. We nearly didn't get our loan. But he came through in the end—a man of his word."

We made our way downstairs into the main dining room. Candles flickered down the center of the table and burned in a couple of stands nearby, softening the atmosphere and obscuring the wreckage in the rest of the main floor. A collection of five mismatched chairs sat at the table like uncomfortable guests. A blue-and-white-checked tablecloth more suitable for a picnic than an elegant dinner lay rumpled and slightly askew, not quite covering the whole surface.

"I'm sorry, but all our decent things are still hidden away," Mother said, busying herself realigning flatware and refolding napkins. "Rosa's done her best, but we'll just have to use our imaginations, won't we?" She gave a little conspiratorial chuckle and smiled at the group, taking her place at the foot of the table. "Now, Giorgio, my darling, you sit here by me." She patted the place to her right. "That's all I'll say about the seating. The rest of you sit wherever you like."

Mario avoided looking at me and quickly placed himself to my father's left and beside Giorgio, leaving me to sit opposite them. He turned to my brother and clapped a hand on his back. "I've thought about all of you constantly for the last few months. I can't imagine what you've been through."

"We've missed you, Moses. How's your arm? It looks okay to me." Giorgio grinned and shot me a quick look across the table.

"Thanks to your sister it's fine. I wouldn't be here today if it weren't for her—and the miracle of penicillin."

Mother sent an inquisitive look my way.

"So what's happening up the river?" Mario shifted in his chair as he deftly changed the subject. "How much longer is it going to take to rout the enemy?"

"Oh, man." Giorgio shook his head. "It's been a damn nightmare up there. We've been up in the mountains for a few months. The army's supplied by mules, for Christ's sake. There's no hot food for anyone, and the rains have made it not only uncomfortable but impossible to see—like looking through a fogged lens all day long. People are sick; they get hit—the wounded have to be carried down by litter. Morale stinks, and the Allies have suffered so many casualties, it's ridiculous."

Father pressed him. "You said they're

going to send in some white reinforcements to shore up the buffalo units."

Giorgio winced and gave his head a
little shake. "All I said was that they are
expanding, bringing in more troops,
moving things around. Some of the buffalo units are moving down to the coast,
some new ones up here. That's all.
There's a big spring offensive likely beginning in the next couple of weeks.
That's all I can tell you right now."

"So what do you partisans do then, if
you're not part of the army?" Mother
asked.

Giorgio eyed Father. "We're operating
to a large extent from the other side of
the line, Mama, infiltrating the enemy.
We know the area. We speak the language. We can move about more easily
than they can, undetected. So we keep
watch, send messages, harass the enemy." He looked at Mario next to him
and winked. "Hell, if it weren't for us, I
hate to think what—"

"But you don't actually fight," said
Mother, twisting her napkin tight and
weaving it through her bent knuckles.

"Did I say that?" He continued to look

at Mario. "It's all become much more organized, really, along military lines since you were with us: brigades down to companies, platoons, and squads. We're trained and supplied—some of us even have uniforms. We're fighting right alongside the Allies. Remember Bacon? Big beefy guy with long hair?"

Mario nodded. "The one from Umbria?"

"Yeah, that's the guy. Took a grenade in the gut the other day. Worst thing I've ever seen." Giorgio took a long, noisy draft of wine, set his empty glass down, then stared at the table for a long moment. "So—you haven't heard from Patch?"

Mario shrugged. "I was hoping you'd have something to tell us on that score. Last we heard, you thought maybe he was doing some labor, maybe somewhere nearby. Right, Giovanna?"

I stared at my brother, hoping to divert him, but he refused to look at me. "Yeah, well, who knows, huh? There was a district concentration camp in Bagna di Lucca not too far up the river until the end of January—maybe a hundred Jews or more. They moved 'em all, shipped them to Florence on the train, then off to God knows where. You gotta get real here, Moses. Gotta get real. These guys don't fool around."

Mario looked as if he'd been kicked in the gut. He folded his arms over his stomach, biting his lower lip but staying silent. I wanted to run over and hold him in my arms.

"Well." Mother was chipper now. "I don't know who Patch is, but I'm sure he'll be just fine. Right, dear?"

At that, Giorgio stood up and began pacing back and forth, as if he were walking barefoot on hot pavement.

"Now, son, relax. Sit down." Father leaned back in his chair, ever the benevolent head of family. "You're making me nervous. This is a celebration, after all—so just simmer down, will you?" He thought for a moment, then turned slowly to his left. "So, Mario, what are your plans once this war is over? Do you want to go into the banking business? Follow in your father's footsteps?"

Mario shifted in his chair. "No, sir, I don't think that I do. Of course, first I'll need to go back to Turin, to find my parents, find out what's happened to them." His hands were working under the table, clasping and unclasping, wringing together. "I've got to complete my university degree. But I'm not so keen, at this point, on urban life. I'm more inclined to get into the land, to see what more I can do with our summer property—olive oil, grapes, maybe wine."

Father looked at him thoughtfully. "Giorgio tells me you have an older brother. What's he up to?"

At that moment, Rosa entered the room carrying a cake aloft like a torch through the darkness, ablaze with candles. Mother started to sing in her high, quavering soprano, but before any of us could join in, Rosa lurched, tripping over some unseen hole in the tile floor. The cake slid off its platter and hit the floor, cushioning the maid's extended hands with a greasy sucking sound.

She let out a low moan, then sat up, dazed, rubbing her pastry-smeared hands on her uniform. Tears ran down her cheeks. "Oh, *Dio*. I'm so sorry—I don't know what happened; I just lost my balance, I guess. I—"

I ran to her. "Rosa, Rosa, are you all right?" I grabbed her elbow and helped her to her feet.

She looked at everyone standing around her, then shyly at my brother, who had obviously not yet paid her a visit. "Oh, Giorgio, I'm afraid I've ruined your birthday."

"Don't be silly." He put his arms around her shoulders and gave her a squeeze. "The dinner was so good we don't need cake at all. And, Rosa, I can never thank you enough for all the supplies you've sent our way. I don't know how we would have survived without your faithful deliveries."

"What's all this about deliveries?" Father was pretending this was the first he'd heard of it. "How much of the insurgency have I been supplying, anyway? No wonder food's been a little scarce around here."

"Papa!" I couldn't believe he'd said that, that he was baiting Giorgio, regressing to his old stand. "What are you talking about? They are the heroes of this war. They've been the key to the Allies' progress around here, right?"

"I don't remember your asking our permission to supply the partisans, Giovanna."

"But I couldn't. I couldn't risk Giorgio's safety." I knew I was repeating myself. "What would you have done, Papa, if you'd known where they were a few months ago?"

"That isn't the point. You had no right to keep such important information from your parents, no matter what the consequences were."

My blood was coursing through my veins like a burst dam, pounding in my ears.

I tried to control my voice. "We have a guest, Father. This is Giorgio's birthday. He's home. Can't we please talk about this later?"

He drew himself up. "Rosa, go clean yourself up. We'll take coffee upstairs. And, Giovanna, I think you should stay right here. I'm sure Mario can find his way back to wherever he's living by himself." He looked at Mario. "Am I right, young man?"

"Of course. I should go." Mario held out his hand. "Thank you for dinner. It's been a pleasure to meet you"—he shook Father's hand, then extended it to Mother—"to meet you both. I look forward to seeing you again once this war is behind us." Not a word to me. He clapped Giorgio on the back. "Ciao, Hermes. Godspeed."

Father put a hand at the small of Mario's back, guiding him toward the door. I watched him go, without a glance my way.

❦

We gathered upstairs in our tight little salon, the four of us. The claustrophobic space once again exuded a kind of balm, as if there weren't enough room anymore for the hostile energy, for the settling of old scores. Mother, always the mediator, the carrier of the family torch, pulled Giorgio onto the small sofa next to her. She took his hand in hers and began stroking his arm. "Now, *bambino*, let's hear no more about the fighting. Let's try to forget this war while you are home. It will soon be over. That's what everyone says."

Father, still standing, shook a couple of cigarettes up from his pack and offered one to Giorgio. He pulled another out with his lips, struck a match, and lit Giorgio's, then his own. He sat down heavily in the armchair and took a deep drag, expelling the smoke with a breath of resignation. "It's tough, son—tough to keep everything going around here. There aren't any men around. Not enough people to prune, to tie the vines. I don't know who's going to plant the fields when the time comes. I'm sick of this; I can tell you that."

Giorgio leaned over Mother to nudge a long ash into their joint ashtray. "It won't be long, Papa. From everything I hear it'll be only a matter of weeks. They're on the run now, and the Allies have plenty of reinforcements coming in. Since January, four divisions of German forces have already been withdrawn from the country. Those left are tired—maybe a couple of dozen German divisions, maybe five Italian, a few pro-Fascist squadrons privately financed by the Borghese family."

Giorgio leaned forward, gesturing with his hands, eager to show Father all he knew. He explained how, in the east, they would move north to Ferrara and on toward Venice. "And our group, they'll keep pushing up the river, sending what's left there back away from the coast, best we can." He ground out his cigarette, took a couple of loud slurps of coffee. "I'm going to stick with it. I've got to do that. And I'll likely get drawn farther from home. So don't expect me back for a while. You probably won't hear from me either—until it's over, once and for all."

Father leaned back and nodded soberly. "Despite what I said tonight, son, I admire what you're doing. I really do. It's a nasty business."

"Why won't they just give up?" Mother played with the fabric of her skirt. "If it's inevitable, they should get it over with."

Papa and Giorgio laughed. "That's why you're not a German commander, Mother. God help us—don't we wish."

Father lit another cigarette. "Say, Giorgio, do you remember the Spinola boy—a couple of years ahead of you in school?"

"He was from the coast, right? Genoa, maybe?"

"He's been fighting in Marshal Graziani's Ligurian Army. I knew his father from the textile business, and ran into him recently. He was scouting out opportunities in the area once the war winds down, says he wants to set his son up in business in Lucca."

"Good guy," said Giorgio. "I'm talking about the son. Hell of a soccer player. Smart too."

"He was asking about the family, about Giovanna. We got to thinking maybe we should introduce them. What do you think, *piccola?*" He smiled. "It's about time you started thinking about the rest of your life."

I had been listening quietly to all this, invisible until now. Everyone turned to look at me. I stared back at Giorgio, unblinking, unbelieving.

"Oh, I don't know, Papa," he said. "I expect she'll find someone on her own. No hurry."

"Well, it can't hurt," said Mother. "You'd like to meet a nice young man, wouldn't you, dear?"

"No, I don't think so." I stood up and turned to leave the room. "And certainly not one who's been fighting for the devil."

Chapter Twenty-seven

Giorgio had to leave the morning after his birthday. Mother and Rosa packed a couple of kilos of flour, some beans, fresh-baked bread, even some honey and oil gleaned from our own diminishing larder. But there was hope in the air, a sense that the war was almost over, and we were proud of Giorgio. Even Mother. She was solemn but bright as she set about straightening his collar and tugging on the cuffs of his shirt. She put her arms around his neck and kissed him on both cheeks. She called him her "little bear" and warned him to

be careful, to stay away from the fighting whenever he could. He kissed her
tenderly, nodded, and promised, yes,
yes, he would be careful. Of course he
would be safe. He hugged Father too,
who slapped him on the back and told
him again that he was doing the right
thing.

As for me, Giorgio had come to my
room that morning after spending the
night on a stained, dusty sofa in the
downstairs salon. He had bathed for at
least the third time since he had been
home. His clothes were clean, his shirt
ironed, and he smelled of Rosa's lavender water as he sat down next to me on
my narrow little bed.

"Mario's a good man, Giovanna. Don't
ever doubt that. Just take Father with a
grain of salt. Whatever he says, let it go.
It will pass."

"What do you think he'll say when he
finds out about us?"

Giorgio shrugged. He gathered the
loose hair at the back of my neck in his
hand and tugged on it as he used to do
when we were kids. "I don't know. But

this is your life, Vanna. Remember that—your life, not Papa's."

I found Mario that afternoon sitting up against the wall in the tower room, engrossed in a book by Giovanni Morelli, a fourteenth-century Florentine, about the Tuscan tradition of landownership. It was one he had borrowed from the marchese's library, along with a pile of others on rural life.

I giggled when I saw the cover. "It looks like you're already planning our rotation of crops. How did you think it went last night?"

"I liked your father," he said. "He's strong, he's ambitious, and he's a no-nonsense type. He's someone I think I could learn to love." He looked quickly away. "But I wasn't sure he felt so good about me."

"He seemed to like you well enough," I said. "But that's because he had no idea we are lovers."

"Do you think that would make a big difference?"

I looked at him for a long moment in silence. "I don't know. But I think you're right—that you are not what he has in mind for me."

"Why? Does he have someone else in mind?"

I told him about the Spinola boy, about Papa's friend and their plan to introduce us. "I'm scared, Mario. I'm really afraid that my future is all tied up with his position in society, that he has ambitions that have nothing to do with my happiness. Papa can be pretty tenacious, pretty obstinate."

Mario reached out and ran his hand along my cheek. "Don't worry, *amore*. Let's not waste any time being afraid when there's no reason to. As soon as the war's over, we'll break the news—and then we'll work on a relationship. You just leave it to me."

I smiled. "You know, Mother's family was far richer than my father's, of much higher social standing. And when Papa met Mama at a dance and fell in love with her right on the spot, he set about winning her father over with a vengeance. The story goes that he went hunting and fishing with my grandfather and brought some of his business know-how to bear on Nonno's agricultural interests. They became friends, and Nonno eventually consented to the marriage."

"You see? I can do that too." Mario smiled and stroked the side of my face. "All it will take is a little time once we can concentrate on other things again. I'll make myself indispensable. I promise."

❦

The next two weeks seemed to fly. Giorgio's visit had eased the tension at home considerably, so that both my parents seemed able once again to concentrate on matters that did not concern the war. Papa spent time bent over his farm accounts, plotting improvements and planning how he would manage the spring planting with a much-reduced workforce.

Mother oversaw preparations for Holy Week. It had always been a time for cleaning house, an end of the penitential season in which cleansing the soul manifested itself in an all-out assault on the accumulated dust, grease, and wear of the winter months. That last year of the war it was a mammoth undertaking. Mother and Rosa worked their way systematically through the house, beginning with the decimated *piano nobile*, penetrating every room and eliminating every trace of the careless, slovenly herd of farm animals who had turned our villa into a stable for almost a year. From the walls to the red-tiled floors to the upholstery and the furniture, they washed and scraped, sewed and sanded every single surface. Then they moved upstairs, where every nook and cranny of the ornate bedsteads and wardrobes were dusted and oiled, the windows cleaned to a sparkle, and the bathroom fixtures restored to family use.

Mother longed to knock down the temporary attic wall and unpack the silver, the good dishes, and family heirlooms, but she was superstitious and decided that it would be bad luck to jump the gun until victory was finally declared.

As for me, I kept to my accustomed routine. In the mornings I worked at the clinic. As the conflict was no longer in our backyard, there were fewer emergencies or crisis cases. We had a number of escaped prisoners of war who had been there for some weeks, even months, who had had serious injuries that were still in the process of healing.

Violetta and Frederick were lovers by then, and I think she worried about the impropriety of her living on the property. I'm sure the marchesa knew, but she never let on until the war was over and the relationship came out in the open. I loved him too and was all for it. Had I thought about it at all, I might have been less enthusiastic. I should have guessed he would carry her off to England.

❦

Each day I delivered lunch to the tower, where I spent the afternoon with Mario. We deliberately ignored the doubt gnawing at both of us and basked in possibilities—of a future that was ours to invent.

I can picture us now lying side by side on the floor, staring at the ceiling. He reaches over and gently ruffles my hair, twirling a lock slowly and steadily around his finger. Then we turn toward each other and stare into each other's eyes for a long time before one of us asks a question, maybe me.

"What is the worst thing you ever did in school, something that got you in trouble?"

He stares back at me, thinking. Then a little smile tugs gently at the corner of his mouth—the right side, always the right side. "You won't believe this one."

"Of course I will," I say, smiling.

"You promise you'll still love me?"

"I can't be sure of that," I tease. "But surely I won't if you refuse to answer the question."

"You know it was a military academy, right?"

"Of course."

"Well, when I was about fourteen, my friend Marco and I got it into our heads to take one of the guns, just to see if we could do it. We stalked the man who oversaw our target practices until we had figured out the codes to the locks on the cabinets. Then one night Marco and I hid in the cloakroom after school. We opened the cabinet, took out one of the guns, and—under cover of darkness—sneaked it home to my parents' apartment. We took the whole thing apart, oiled it, put it back together, just as we had been trained to do, and hid it under my bed. We just had to try it, so early the next morning before school, Marco came over. We opened the window a crack and waited for a chance victim. There was a squirrel perched on the eaves of the building across the street, eating a nut."

I was covering my eyes at this point. "I don't think I want to hear the rest."

"What were we thinking? It was Marco, I'm happy to say, who knelt down, took careful aim, and fired. He missed the squirrel, but the bullet was low. It shattered the window of the top-floor apartment, ricocheted off a lead mirror frame on the wall, and then fell onto a valuable porcelain urn on the sideboard, breaking it into pieces. The worst of it is that these people were friends of my parents. They had to reimburse them for the full value of the urn, and Marco and I had to work it off."

"What about school?"

"We had weeks of detention, and we were never allowed to participate in target practice or use the guns again." He smiled. "Not perfect for military students, but . . ." He wrinkled his brow, and a look of sadness passed over his face. "Then all hell broke loose."

I reached out and pulled him on top of me. "Those days are over, Mario. It won't be long now until life goes back the way it was before. This madness will pass, and we can lead our lives the way we want to. I just know it."

❦

It was Papa who brought things to a head. Easter Sunday dawned bright and cloudless. The three of us went to mass together, and I emerged from church rosy and cheerful, inhaling the intoxicating perfume of peach trees in full bloom as we took our time walking home and admired the perfect spring day. The table downstairs was set for the holiday dinner, and just before sitting down, Father offered us each a glass of chilled prosecco. "Here's to you, my dear, and to you, *piccola,*" he said as he raised his glass and clinked with each of us in turn. *"Salute. Buona Pasqua."*

I grinned, and perhaps it was the look of happiness and hope on my face that reminded him of the question of my future. "The Spinola boy has been given a leave before the spring offensive begins. The father has decided they will take a few days together and come down here to check out some of the opportunities he's found. So I've invited them to spend the day at Villa Farfalla, have dinner with us. What do you say? Would you like to meet him?" Papa's smile was warm, a hint of teasing glinting from his toasty brown eyes.

I tightened the grip on my glass. "Not really."

"Why on earth not? I'm sure he's a perfectly nice young man. You've been without male companionship—it's time, *piccola*. You're getting to that age."

He's remembering Klaus, I thought, and I turned my back, moving to the window away from him. I stood there, staring out at the garden. *It's now or never.* "The truth is, Papa, I already have someone in my life."

"You do? Well, that's a surprise."

I approached him warily, as if facing an unknown animal in the wild. "He went to school with Giorgio. You know his father, actually."

"Well, now, who could that be?" He looked at Mother and beamed. "Natala, did you know about this?"

Mother shook her head. Her expression was impassive, but her eyes shone with curiosity and trepidation in equal measure.

"How can we not have been aware of this?" He spread his arms in a wide gesture of embrace. "We'd love to meet him, *piccola.*"

"You already have."

"We have? Someone I already know? A friend of Giorgio's?" He shrugged his shoulders and sent Mother a quizzical look.

"It's Mario, Father. Mario Rava." I smiled, willing the news to come as a pleasant surprise.

He stood stock-still, as if letting the words slowly penetrate the thick casings around his brain. "Mario Rava? You are in love with the young man who came to Giorgio's birthday dinner?" He stared back at me for confirmation. "But he's Jewish, isn't he?"

"Yes, he is." I waited a beat. "We want to get married, Papa." I worked to keep my lips from trembling.

"Well, that's ridiculous." He turned his back and gave a dismissive gesture with his arm. "You barely know the man. You have nothing in common."

"Barely know him! I nursed him back to health from a serious injury. I found him a place to hide." I shot Mother a pleading look. "I've been helping supply him for almost nine months. We spend hours together every day!"

His eyes were wide, wild. "Why haven't you told us this before?"

"Actually, I think I did mention that I was helping to hide someone, someone Jewish. And what do you mean, 'nothing in common'? He went to the same military school you and Giorgio did. Our families are very similar, actually. They have a summer place like ours. He loves the country. You seemed to like him the other night."

"Well, sure, he's a nice enough fellow,

but I had no idea you were . . . that you wanted to marry him, for Christ's sake!"

"Enrico, calm down. Let's try to discuss this without getting emotional." Mother put an arm on his shoulder, but he brushed it off.

"Let me handle this, Natala."

I felt my knees threaten to give way, but I stood my ground. I aimed my heart at his, at the old Papa, my friend, my first love. "You want me to be happy, don't you?"

"But you wouldn't be happy married to him."

"Why not? I love him." My throat was tightening so that only a too-thin stream of air could get through.

"Well, it's a completely different tradition. They don't share the same history, the same values. Giovanna, it's *Easter* today! What about holidays?"

At that, Mother spoke up. "He has a point, dear."

I swallowed hard, forcing down the barrier in my throat. "We've talked a lot about values. I would say they are very much the same in both of us. We both value honesty, hard work, helping the community, country life. He would have fought like hell in this war if he weren't at such personal risk—he was fighting in Giorgio's brigade for a while."

I began walking back and forth, talking as steadily and rationally as I could. "And what do you mean, history? He's lived in the same country I have, watched these two decades unfold in exactly the same way."

"But his *people*, the ghettos, the exile. I don't want some Zionist son-in-law. This is crazy! It's out of the question. End of subject."

"Papa, his 'people' are Italian. *We* are his people. Mario is Italian first, just as his father is. Believe it or not, his father was a member of the Fascist party for years, just like you."

At each step, I expected that my answers would calm and reassure him, but instead, he got more and more agitated. As I watched his face, I began to see what looked like fear. "But look what's happening to them in this war. Why would I want my only daughter to join a group that's being persecuted and hunted and sent off to God knows where? I want you here, Giovanna—here with us, safe and sound."

"But, Father, after all the Nazis have done to us, I would think you'd be as outraged as I am."

"Give me a little credit, will you?"

"Okay, but," I said, "the Jews are innocent parties, aren't they? When the war is over, the Germans will be gone, and this won't be an issue."

"Giovanna, don't be naive. They're just . . . *different* enough that I don't want you marrying one of them. These are my grandchildren you're talking about—my heirs, my progeny, my family." He looked at Mother and threw his hands in the air in an exasperated plea. "Jewish? I won't allow it."

"Well, if you want to know, according to religious law, it's the mother who determines who's Jewish. So, no, your grandchildren would not technically be Jewish. You're just afraid of what people will think, what they'll say, right?"

He looked at me, his face unmoving. His eyes had hardened into cold bronze. He looked as rigid as the fence he wanted to put around me.

I felt a wave of new confidence born of righteousness, and I pushed back. "You'd be embarrassed, wouldn't you? You want your daughter to marry someone better than you. Better than you think you are." I felt a sudden impulse to match his cruelty. "You want me to take you up a rung on the social ladder. Well, I've got news for you. You are where you are because of Mother anyway."

Mother had been standing there listening quietly, but at that she interjected, "Giovanna, please!"

"Keep out of this, Mother. This is between me and Papa right now." I turned back to him. "It's because of your own insecurity that you need this. I don't know how to tell you this, but Mario *is* a better man than you are in just about every way that counts."

I was suddenly aware of pain in my palms where my clenched fists drove the nails in deep. My chest heaved, and sweat oozed at my hairline. My eardrums throbbed. We stood there locked in a mutual stare. All the goodwill had drained out of him. He looked at once ruthless and full of doubt.

"How dare you say those words to me? My own daughter? How dare you even think that some holed-up Jewish fugitive is a better man than your father? What kind of blood is running in your veins?" He barked out a kind of sarcastic laugh. "My sweet little daughter is rotting away before my very eyes. It's green, putrid blood, it is." He shook his head and wrinkled his nose. "I can smell it."

His words stung, and hot tears blurred my eyes. He was desperate now. He didn't want to be where he was, but he had worked his way in too far to back out.

"Does that give you a feel for where I stand on your wedding plans, signorina? You can tell your little Jewish friend to forget it, because your father doesn't approve. Have you got that? *Does not approve.*"

Giorgio's words echoed in my ears: *Remember. This is your life, Vanna— your life, not Papa's.* The tension in my body dissolved and flowed out in hot tears, but in spite of the pain, I saw in an instant that I was free. I didn't need him or his permission to lead the life I wanted to lead. Mario was not his to give or take away. Nor was I. Oddly enough, I had won.

I stood tall, willing my breath to slow down, and wiped the tears from my cheeks with the palms of my hands. My lips quivered. "If that is how you feel, then I don't care to live here anymore. I will be gone by nightfall."

Chapter Twenty-eight

In a frenzy of righteous energy, I managed to transfer the contents of my dresser into a large duffel bag and stow it in a corner of the lower floor for later retrieval. As I closed the front door behind me, the day was bright but dull, as if I were seeing it through a gray plate of glass: flat and inaccessible. The fragrance of the spring flowers made me queasy. All the grit and resolve I had felt in my confrontation with Papa had begun to dissipate. What had I done? I had nowhere to live and no money. I had thrown off the protection of my parents, and Giorgio was unreachable. I had done all this for Mario's sake, but now I even questioned that. Did I really love him that much or was Papa right?

I found myself an hour later not at the tower about to throw myself into Mario's arms, but standing on the marchesa's doorstep, hugging myself tightly with crossed arms as I waited for someone to come to the door.

Balbina, the marchesa's diminutive maid, read my anxiety instantly. "Oh, Signorina Bellini—come in, come in," she said. "The marchesa is with the family in the dining room. Won't you follow me?"

"No, please," I said. "Don't disturb them. I'll just wait here until they have finished." She disappeared, and I perched on the edge of a straight-backed chair, relieved to be sitting down, happy for some time alone.

It was no more than a couple of minutes before I heard brisk footsteps across the tiled floor of the next room. The marchesa rounded the corner, dabbing at her mouth with a napkin.

I rose to my feet in a reflexive impulse to be polite, but there must have been something in my posture that gave me away. She threw down the napkin and moved toward me with open arms. "Oh, my dear, what ever is the matter? This is not a holiday face, is it?"

At that, I burst into tears. "I . . . I'm sorry to interrupt your celebration. I'm just so afraid. My father—"

"What's happened to your father? Do you need a doctor? I'll see what—"

"No, no. It's not that—it's me. We had a terrible fight, and I—"

"A fight? What kind of a fight?" She was holding me, rubbing my back, and I had a sudden sense of how dainty she was. I had to bend down, reaching my neck forward to lean my head on her shoulder. I felt huge and babyish at the same time.

"Please, won't you go back to your dinner? I'll be fine. I'll just wait here until you are finished."

"No—I won't hear of it. You're welcome to come with me, sit with us."

I knew I could not face Leonardo and their two daughters. I shook my head, wiped my nose with the back of my hand. "Please go to them. I just can't see anyone just now." I turned my back to her.

"Giovanna, go into the library and wait for me there. Let me tell them. I'll see you in a minute."

In the library I settled heavily into one of the familiar armchairs where we had had so many satisfying conversations over the long winter months.

Leaning into the soft cushion, I breathed in the faint odor of mildewed books and stroked the frayed roses on the end of the chair's arm. I began to gather myself, reining in the pain and the sorrow. Just being in this place, where I had been treated with such respect, had a calming effect. I could feel the fear subsiding, and in its place, moral indignation began to simmer.

By the time the marchesa returned, all traces of hysteria were gone.

"Now, my dear. Tell me what's happened. I'm all ears." She set down a small cup of espresso on the table next to her and handed me a delicate, gold-rimmed porcelain plate with a dessert fork balanced on its edge. It held a slice of the traditional dove-shaped Easter *panettone.* "Won't you help us celebrate, just a little?"

I sat up straight and took the plate. "I guess I am pretty hungry. Thank you."

We sat in silence for a few minutes as I wolfed down the sweet, spongy confection, scraping up the last of it by pressing the back of the fork against the surface of the plate.

"I feel better now." I smiled at her. "You are so kind to take me in, today of all days."

"Now tell me what's happened, what kind of fight you had with your father."

I leaned forward and told her about Giorgio's visit home, about the birthday dinner and how well it had seemed to go.

"I'm amazed!" She laughed. "You took him home with you for dinner? You mean he was gone from here for several hours and we didn't even know it?"

I nodded. "I thought Papa liked him. It was all so friendly. He even knows Mario's father."

The marchesa nodded. "Leonardo and I have worked with banks in Turin as well." Her forehead creased in a slight frown. "So what went wrong?"

I told her about Papa's threat to bring the Spinola boy to Lucca to meet me. "So I guess it just seemed to be the right moment to tell him about Mario and me."

The marchesa winced and clucked her tongue. "I didn't think this would happen quite so soon."

"He seemed to like Mario at the birthday party, so I hoped—"

"But then, once he knew you were a couple, he focused solely on his being Jewish?"

"Right." I could feel the anxiety rising again. "It was so strange, because he seemed almost afraid—as if he were threatened in some way. He was afraid for me, I guess, afraid of my having to live the life of an outsider. He said Mario was foreign, different. . . ." I paused, going back over our encounter in my mind. As I relived our confrontation, indignation burned in me again. Being here at Villa Falconieri completely eliminated any doubts that had begun to fester in all the turmoil.

"How did your mother react?" The marchesa kicked off her shoes and tucked her feet up under her, as if settling in for a long talk.

"I don't really know. She agreed with him that we would have problems, like holidays and things, but . . . she's not really threatened in the same way he is."

"Did she come to your defense at all?"

"At first, maybe . . . no, not really. In fact, now that I think of it, she came to his."

"To his?"

"I was so angry, I told him any social standing he has is all due to Mother's family anyway."

The marchesa looked down and shook her head. "That was below the belt, I'm afraid."

"But he can be so rude and unfeeling. He doesn't care anything for my happiness. He just wants to control my life from beginning to end to suit him and his own ambitions." I was crying again now, my eyes and nose beginning to run. "It isn't fair to Mario." I curled in a ball and buried my head in the chair's upholstered pillow, embarrassed to look at her.

The marchesa sat still, saying nothing, and let me cry. She neither protested nor tried to comfort me.

"I told them I was leaving. I don't need them; I don't want to go home ever again."

There was still no reaction. Her lack of response made me suddenly self-conscious. "You must think I'm overreacting."

She shrugged. "Quite the contrary. I give you a lot of credit for facing him down. I've seen your father angry, and I'm not sure, if I were his daughter, that I could have done it."

"You have? When?"

"It was five years or so ago. As Germany was becoming more aggressive, Leonardo and I began to have serious doubts about the Fascist party. The party had been financing public works for farmers, and Leonardo and I had been taking advantage of it.

"Your parents still lived in the city most of the year, but it was your father who convinced us to help him put together the *consorzio agrario* in this area.

"We were fully aware that these projects were propaganda tools as much as anything, but we needed the roads, the drains and dams, the wells and the subsidies too much to look a gift horse in the mouth. Leonardo turned out to be a skillful lobbyist and got to know a number of people who represented the best of Mussolini's regime. There was an attractive professor of geology, I remember, and some engineers and other technical experts who were also more enthusiastic for the work than for Fascist ideology. It was great, and we received a great deal of money in subsidies. Nothing to sneeze at."

"Did my parents take advantage of it too?"

"Your father was a very active advocate and collaborator. With his support, Leonardo became president of the *consorzio*—he still is—and he's really been its guiding light." The marchesa took a sip from the tiny coffee cup and clinked it back onto its saucer. "Soil that had lain fallow for centuries was being turned over and planted; wells were filling the irrigation ditches with water; new trees were digging their roots in, holding the line against erosion; new roads connected neighbor to neighbor. For at least five years, it didn't really occur to us to question the source of the funds. We just were part of a national renaissance, and we loved it."

"I remember Father talked about it in those days. We used some of the money for improvements to Villa Farfalla."

"But then Leonardo and I began, more and more, to listen to the radio, to read the newspapers and books—books like *Mein Kampf* and Hermann Rauschning's *Hitler Speaks*." She paused, gazing out the doors at the garden, distracted by her memories. She turned back to me. "I can't tell you how disturbing it became to us, all the conflicting rumors and stories. We listened to Hitler's voice rising above the roaring crowds and watched our own Mussolini—he had vowed to keep Austria independent, mind you— suddenly turn a blind eye to Germany's invasion of them. We heard the voices of Anthony Eden and Churchill, Neville

Chamberlain. We felt a real sense of doom.

"I visited England in those years, where friends were harboring refugee children from Germany. They suggested we help some Jewish acquaintances escape from Eastern Europe via Italy to the United States or back to England. After these trips I would come home and find here a very different atmosphere, one of self-protection and denial—not pacifism, but passivity. No one seemed to think Italy would ever be at war. They assumed that Mussolini would resist involvement, would keep them out of it."

"My parents bought every bit of it."

"Sure, but, Giovanna, they were so typical at that time, right in the mainstream."

"Were there any people around here who thought like you did?"

"There were. I remember a small group of liberal-thinking people. Maybe they had had family members imprisoned in the early years of Fascism or something. But they were so extreme and uncompromising in their views that

I thought at the time they wouldn't have much influence. They pretty much stuck to themselves, seeing only like-minded, equally embittered neighbors."

The marchesa was wrong, it seems to me now, about those anti-Fascist enclaves. They were the bright spots of resistance and the sources of energy and idealism that eventually ignited the partisans, kept alive the anti-Fascist press, and later came together after the liberation and gave the new political trends their shape. But of course, we know that now only in hindsight.

"So you and Leonardo were thinking like the liberals while enjoying all those benefits of Fascist largesse."

"Exactly—but I've always been inclined to let my views be known. So one night, at a meeting of the *consorzio*—it must have been just before Italy entered the war in the spring of 1940—we were discussing the latest project—I think it was a reforestation plan, the kind where we expected to receive full reimbursement. I was just back from England and nearly frantic with anxiety. Germany had invaded Denmark and Norway, and, around here, it was just business as usual.

"So I spoke up. 'Isn't there anyone here who feels funny about accepting this money?' I asked. 'Mussolini is just looking the other way while Hitler runs rampant. I'm hearing really bad things about what's happening in those occupied countries.' I was greeted by blank faces. Even my Leonardo continued discussing the pros and cons of the particular location of new tree plantings.

"So I tried again. 'Shouldn't we at the very least suggest diverting this money to defense purposes? Who knows what threats to our well-being we'll be facing in the next year or so?'

"At that, your father rose to his feet. I was sitting down, so he loomed over me like a cat over a mouse. I can still hear the tone of his voice. 'Lily,' he said, 'this is none of your damned business. What Italy does is our concern. If I'm not mistaken, your loyalties are elsewhere. So kindly keep your mouth shut, and let us get back to the issues at hand.'

"I had lived in Italy for most of my life.

I was married to an Italian. I felt so shamed and embarrassed that I nearly burst into tears."

I stood up, enraged all over again at Father. "God, that is so like him. I'm so sorry. Leonardo must have been furious in your defense."

"He tried to laugh it off, to pacify Enrico with humor. 'I sometimes feel like I've got Churchill under the covers with me,' he said with a chuckle. 'But don't worry about Lily. She's with us, not against us.'"

She paused, remembering. "I decided soon after, since I lived in Italy, to abide by its laws. I would do what I could in my own small way to alleviate suffering—which I've been able to do with the clinic. And for years now England has been fighting for our liberation."

I nodded. "And Father. You've obviously learned how to handle him."

"Oh, Enrico and I understand each other. He and I don't see eye to eye, but we just give each other space. I decided long ago not to try to confront him directly." She rose to her feet. "Which is why, my dear, I have so much respect for what you've just done." She walked over to the garden doors with her back to me. "Violetta has moved back to the village with her family now that the evacuation's over. What would you say if I gave you her room for the time being?"

"What about my parents?"

"Why don't you let me talk with them? I think it's my turn to show some courage."

I was elated. I had a place to stay, at least for the moment. I jumped to my feet and gave the marchesa a kiss on both cheeks. "I'll never forget this—you've done so much for me. How can I ever repay you?"

She waved the air again. "Why don't you go pay a visit to your friend? Take him some *panettone*." She winked. "It won't kill him to commemorate Easter with us, now, will it?"

❦

Balbina fixed me a platter of lamb, pasta, and cake—enough for both Mario and me to stuff ourselves in celebration of my own personal resurrection. I headed out across the fields to the tower, my heart leaping with expectation, filled with visions of a life opening up for Mario and me, however it might eventually unfold. I ran the last hundred feet or so as fast as I could, taking the stone treads two at a time. "Mario! Guess what! I'm here. I'm free. We can be together forever now." But there was no answer. I reached the top of the stairs and found the tower room empty. He was gone.

Chapter Twenty-nine

I ran back down and around the building, searching in the mill spaces at ground level, frantically pushing aside the underbrush that surrounded the tower. Back upstairs, Mario's clothes were there; his books were left lying where I had last seen them. The diary he'd been keeping was there too. I opened it with shaking hands and thumbed to the last page, but there was no entry for Sunday. In fact, there was little notation at all for the last week or so, save occasional notes on the weather and his meals. He had vanished like a firefly—glowing one minute, gone the next.

I sat on the floor, my knees drawn up, leaning against the wall as we had done so often together. What could have happened? I considered the possibilities. Could Father have somehow discovered Mario's hiding place? Could he have come looking for me there, found only Mario, and—in his anger—taken him off to the authorities? Or might the Germans have found him on their own and turned him over? Could Mario have gone looking for me at home, knowing it was Easter and wanting to share our celebration, and possibly been apprehended along the way? Or was he there even now with my parents, facing their anger and rejection? Had Mario grown frustrated and tired of hiding and gone after Giorgio and his band? Had he sensed my confrontation with Father from afar and thought to remove himself from my life as quietly as possible? It even occurred to me that Easter Sunday was April first, *Pesce d'Aprile*—was this someone's idea of a cruel joke?

None of these options was in the least

bearable. I was sure this was a punishment for the moments of doubt I had had after I left home. If only I had come directly here, I might have found him, and we would be together now as we were meant to be. I got up and grabbed Mario's pillow, hugged it to me, then beat it against the wall in an alternating fit of sadness and frustration. I curled on his bedroll, crushing the pillow to my face and sobbing into it, begging him to come back.

❦

Both the marchesa and her husband did their best to comfort me in the days that followed. Together, we went over and over the various scenarios, gauging the likelihood of each, doing what we could to follow up, to learn the truth. The marchesa telephoned my mother early the next day, telling her that I was living there for the time being, and reassuring my parents of my safety. She said Mother had been frantic and was much relieved to hear from her. She decided not to mention Mario then, but instead urged Mother to come for a visit as soon as possible. She had no idea, she said, what my father's state of mind might be.

The marchese began working his network of contacts—both trusted Italians and Allied troops—to see what he could learn. It was difficult, he said, because he had to avoid alerting the authorities to Mario's existence or putting him in any more danger than he already was. But nothing turned up.

Then, two days later, on Wednesday, April 4, Leonardo went into the village as usual. When he returned, he had an anxious look on his face and a letter clutched in his hand. He passed me a plain envelope, stamped and addressed to Villa Falconieri's post office box, but clearly marked to be delivered to me personally. My heart jumped when I recognized Mario's handwriting. The letter was hurriedly written, the paper creased and wrinkled with pitted holes, as if the pen had pierced it from writing on a rough surface.

Dearest Giovanna,
I don't know if you can ever forgive me for the pain and worry

my disappearance must be caus-
ing you. I knew you would be
with your family on Easter, so
you would not be there to dis-
suade me from what I felt I
needed to do.

Seeing Giorgio again the other
night filled me with such a feeling of helplessness. I could no
longer sit there in hiding and let
him and others like him risk their
lives for my sake. We need to defeat this enemy, to rid our country of this evil. Why should I not
put myself on the line as well?

You must be patient and pray
for me. I will do everything in my
power to stay safe and come
home to you once this is over. I
carry you with me in my heart to
inspire and guide me. God willing, we shall still have our life together.

All my love,
Mario

I stared at the piece of paper, assaulted by wave after wave of feeling. I

was terrified now, knowing he intended to throw himself right into the action, probably to seek out Giorgio and his partisan band, to head for the front lines and do what he could to help. But, in equal measure, I felt so proud of him, in awe of his courage, his nerve, his open-hearted nature.

I handed the letter over in silence to the marchesa and to Leonardo and let them read it, the two of them hunched over the paper side by side. They took their time, holding the letter together. Then they looked briefly at each other, and the marchesa released it into her husband's hand. "Oh, Giovanna, I'm so sorry." She wrapped me in her arms and held me to her.

"But damn it, he's a hell of a man, your friend," the marchese said. "I don't know if I could do what he's doing if I were in his situation." He shook his head. "Life's a lot more certain, reading books up in the tower."

"But if he's captured or killed, then what's the point?" I said.

"But if he's not, he'll always know he

contributed to their defeat, that he pulled his weight," he retorted.

"But if he puts the partisans at extra risk by being there?"

"You just can't worry about that at this point, Giovanna." His tone was careful and solicitous. "The Germans are on their last legs. They're basically in retreat. Maybe they won't have time to worry about the Jews anymore; they're so desperate to save themselves."

"And maybe they're so vindictive and angry they'll shoot him on sight." My words hung there like a bubble about to burst. We were standing in silence, looking at one another, not sure what to say next, when there was a knock at the door.

The marchesa gave me a sidelong glance. Then she lifted the latch and pulled it slowly open. "Natala," she pronounced in a measured tone. "Won't you come in?"

I stood against the opposite wall, watching silently as the two of them embraced. "I'm glad you decided to come," said the marchesa, gently ushering

Mother into the hall with an arm about her waist.

"I'm sorry to show up unannounced like this," said Mother, "but Enrico left for town, and I just—" She stopped, midsentence, at the sight of me standing there.

"Hello, Mother." My voice surprised me, sounding icy rather than sad.

"Oh, darling, it's so good to see you." Her face quivered into a little smile, but her eyes were wary and guarded. She did not move toward me.

"Listen," the marchesa broke in with an artificial lightness. "Why don't you two come into the library? I'll leave you alone and have Balbina fetch some coffee."

"No, please," I protested, but she propelled us down the hall toward the library's carved wooden door.

"I'll see you later," she insisted with a bright tone, "but now you need some time together, just the two of you." She closed the door behind us, and we settled stiffly into our seats. I chose the chair where the marchesa normally sat, and Mother perched on the sofa—a move that gave me an unexpected shot of confidence, a kind of psychological edge that tipped the balance between the two of us.

"What a delightful room." I knew Mother was trying to break the ice. "The daffodils are so lovely out there, like little clumps of sunshine, aren't they, dear?"

I did not respond, so Mother crossed her legs and leaned back against the cushions, staring out at the garden. Just then there was a rap at the door; Balbina pushed it open with her hip and bustled in, laying a tray with a pot of espresso, some hot steamed milk, and two cups on the low table in front of Mother. "Shall I pour it for you?" she asked.

"No, no. I'll take care of it, thank you," said Mother, sounding grateful for something to do.

Balbina excused herself, and Mother set about pouring us each a cup of coffee. "Sugar, dear?" she murmured absentmindedly, but then added quickly, "No, of course not. How silly of me. You never take it, do you?"

She sat again, and we sipped quietly,

the clink of the cups against their saucers the only break in the silence. At last Mother put down her cup and looked right at me. She looked scared, which surprised me. "We miss you, Giovanna."

"*We*, Mother?"

"Yes, of course, dear. We both do." She stared out the window again for a moment, as if considering carefully her choice of words. "We love you very much."

"I think that when you love someone, you want her to be happy."

"Well, yes. Of course we want you to be happy. But"—she shifted a little on the couch and slid her hands under her knees—"you'll understand this better when you have children of your own. Sometimes . . ." She hesitated. "Sometimes what you know will make your child happy is not the same as what she might imagine."

"And by that you mean that you know better than I whom I should fall in love with?"

"Oh, no. I don't mean that. Your father—that is, *we* . . . don't have any particular person in mind. No."

"But you know it's not the person I love now."

"Oh, dear—you're making it sound so negative."

"Well, isn't it? Isn't that what you're saying?"

"I'm only saying that in our judgment you would be happier without certain . . . impediments to deal with."

"You mean life might be easier, but that doesn't make for happiness, does it? Just because two people's backgrounds are the same doesn't mean they'll necessarily be happy—far from it." I thought for a moment. "Mario has warmth, a certain kind of spirit I love . . . Maybe it's even caused by all the religious discomfort he's faced. I'm talking about qualities I just didn't see in the boys I grew up with."

Mother picked up her cup and sipped, staring out the window.

I added, "Papa came from a very different background from yours. Why did you fall in love with him?"

She glanced away, and I thought I noticed a slight flush rise on her cheeks.

"Well, he had a certain kind of . . . energy I liked."

"Energy. You mean drive, don't you? A kind of hunger that he couldn't have had if he'd grown up rich like you?"

Her lips pulled together in a tight line. She shrugged. "Maybe. But we've never had to face the kinds of barriers you would have with Mario."

"Mother, I don't want to get into this again. You're not going to convince me to forget about Mario. I love him. I want to marry him." I put my cup and saucer down on the table. "That is, if I ever see him again."

"What do you mean? Isn't he hidden away somewhere near here?" Her eyes darted around, as if she were expecting him to pop out from behind a chair or the window drapes.

I shook my head. "Not anymore. He's gone." I told her about finding him gone on Easter Sunday, about the letter I had just received, about the marchese's efforts to learn something. "I have no idea where he is."

Mother sighed with a note of finality. "Well, then, dear, let's go home. You have no more reason to keep up this silly separation from your father and me." She stood. "After all, there may no longer be a problem."

I stared at her, my mouth hanging open. "What are you implying? You mean because he might die?"

"I didn't say that."

"No, but you thought it. You *hoped* it, didn't you? Just for a little moment that's what you hoped. Get out of here, Mother, and leave me alone. I never want to see either of you again." I ran out of the library and slammed the door behind me.

❦

The very next day marked the beginning of the Allies' spring offensive, and the lull in the fighting came abruptly to an end. This was the Allies' all-out push to win the war. Divisions had been redeployed and brought into Italy from France and elsewhere in Europe.

Reports came daily and, when the land wires were permanently severed, we had only the radio and word of mouth to rely on. We learned after the war that the Germans were worried about an amphibious landing on the Ligurian coast, so to divert them and prevent them from moving their defenses that far west, the Allies sent a dummy armored division, manned among others by our buffalo soldiers, up the Serchio River. Skies to the west of us exploded with fighter bombers along the coast, while American and British commanders sent the 8th and 5th armies in two strong aggressive attacks up the Italian boot from the south.

Our days in those weeks were marked not by the clock, but by military triumphs.

What was clear to all of us was that the partisans were the heroes of the day. Scrappy, tenacious, and organized, they knew the territory better than the Allies. Often our liberators would arrive in a town and find that the partisans were already in control and had sent the enemy into retreat. I had no idea where my brother was, and as for Mario, I was a victim of my own worst fantasies. My interior life was one long extended prayer.

The emptiness and sadness of my separation from my parents and from home were overwhelming. The marchesa, Leonardo and their daughters treated me like a member of the family but I was ultimately and painfully alone.

One night looms in my memory and has become a touchstone for those weeks of agony. We occasionally listened to the radio during dinner, trying to keep abreast of the offensive as it moved up the coast. There were light exchanges between us over the droning of the correspondent. "Please pass the sauce," or, "This is delicious, Balbina," and occasionally real conversations, but one ear was always on the alert for a new intensity in the crackling static that was a backdrop to our gatherings. I remember the marchese was holding forth, speculating on what the postwar market for his premium olive oil would be, when I caught a new edge of passion—or was it anger?—in the radio announcer's voice:

Today, only minutes before the Allied forces closed in on the outskirts of Castelnuovo di Gogagnana, thirty-one partisans . . .

"*Shhhh—*" I hissed, at once frantic and horrified at my own rudeness. "I must hear this." The marchese broke off midsentence, and the table grew silent.

. . . unruly sheep and lined up against a tall fence bordering a fallow hay field. One by one, their bound wrists were tied to the fence posts above their heads, leaving them hanging there, facing a line of Nazi sharpshooters. No sooner was the last one strung up than a barrage of rifle fire burst forth. Within seconds all thirty-one guerrillas hung lifeless from their shackles. Helpless bystanders stood and watched while the Germans filed off in formation without bothering to cut them down.

Now to the east and the Adriatic front . . .

The marchesa leaped to her feet and snapped off the radio. "Come, come. It's time for dessert," she said. "I won't have this nightmare spoiling our dinner."

"I'm sorry," I said, standing so fast that I tipped the dining room chair over backward, "but I must excuse myself." I righted the chair and, without looking at any of them, I turned and left the room.

I ran down the hall, out the front door, and picked my way across the rutted field in the gathering dusk toward the tower. I clambered up the stairs into the empty room and let myself down on Mario's abandoned bedroll. There I curled up and shut my eyes, unable to erase the images of smoking rifles and slumped bodies, hats dropping one by one from dark heads of curly hair that hid their faces from the horrified crowd.

Chapter Thirty

All around me, spring was spreading her largesse like a profligate empress throwing coins to a suspicious and ungrateful peasantry. Fresh shoots pushed up through newly plowed fields. The air was thick with pollen and the heavy perfume of this seasonal wantonness, but to us it all felt wrong. We were suspended in time, turning a deaf ear to the melodious birdcalls, blind to the colorful riot of crocuses and primroses at our feet. Numbly I trailed after the marchesa at the clinic as she cared for the last few men. Frederick, Violetta's lover, had recovered and been discharged to rejoin the Allies' offensive. Violetta herself came only once a week or so, for—as the line of liberation moved up the coast—we were too far south to receive any new cases.

Though the Allies had planned the spring offensive to take advantage of April's drier weather, the heavens opened as the month wore on. Relentless and heavy, the rains flooded the fields, rendering the roads nearly impassable. However, the news from the front was encouraging—each day marked steady progress against a stubborn but faltering enemy. Nevertheless the military triumphs couldn't ease my anxiety or give me any comfort. I could not rest until I knew Mario and my brother were safe.

On the morning of the twenty-first of April, Bologna fell to the 5th Army with unexpected ease, and the Allies pushed forward to the Po River. The German line had been broken and their forces split in two.

As the end of the month neared on the western front, our northern cities were the last bastions of enemy entrenchment. The partisans went into action, sabotaging railroad tracks and setting up roadblocks to prevent the movement of German troops, cutting off water and electrical service to their barracks. Their ranks swollen overnight with new volunteers, partisans dominated those northern cities and prevented the Germans from doing any more damage. Coastal units entered Genoa without opposition and found partisans in control there, having forced the surrender of four thousand Germans the previous day. The momentum by then was tremendous, and we lived from hour to hour waiting for news of a final victory.

On the twenty-ninth, a truck carrying *Il Duce* was making a run toward the Swiss border, trying to flee as the Allies closed in on northern Italy. As his convoy neared the town of Dongo, a cadre of partisans ambushed the trucks. Mussolini, concealed in the back of one of the trucks, was wearing the green greatcoat and helmet of a German soldier, but his expensive leather boots gave him away. The partisans whisked him to a neighboring farm, where he was soon joined by his lover of thirteen years, Claretta Petacci. The next day, the two were driven to the nearby Villa Belmonte and ordered out of the car. A partisan leveled a machine gun at them, but the gun jammed. He grabbed a second gun and fired, killing Claretta. Then Mussolini, holding the lapels of his jacket, ordered, "Shoot me in the chest." The partisan leveled two shots, and *Il Duce* was dead.

Their bodies were taken to Milan and dumped in front of a garage in the Piazzale Loreto. Laughing and screaming obscenities, local residents gathered around. One woman fired five gratuitous shots into Mussolini's corpse, shouting that she wanted "to avenge her five sons." The two mutilated bodies were strung up, jeered at, and spit upon by the angry civilian crowd.

In the hours and days that followed, we continued to hover over the radio, listening to the mounting toll as Germans and Italian Fascists surrendered by the thousands, as Hitler committed suicide. Then, finally, on May 7, the Germans surrendered to Allied forces. The war in Europe had come to an end.

Our war was over . . . but wait. My memories suddenly come to a stop right there, exploded into a million tiny pieces. Are they fireworks I see, or is it artillery fire from the retreating German troops? I swim up through layers of fog, as if from weeks underwater, toward the light of this brilliant day so many decades later. Hitler and Mussolini were dead, weren't they? What a moment to savor—a delicious one, filled with heat and light . . . springtime and peace both at once. And yet . . . and yet . . . here my stomach clutches in fear. This is why I have never trusted victories of any kind. No, no. Triumph is just a warning sign, a cruel diversion. Oh, how naive I was, how easily seduced. How I wish I could go back now and stop time there on May 7 when Italy was rejoicing.

❦

Three days of peace passed with no word. I refused to leave the villa. The marchesa and marchese took the girls into the village a couple of times and came back with stories of chaos and jubilation. Violetta came to see me. Her cheeks were pink as peach blossoms; her eyes blazed. "We were dancing in the streets last night," she said. "There are bonfires everywhere. People have draped themselves with flags and are jumping in the fountains. Come with me."

But I shook my head and refused to leave. "What if he comes back and can't find me here?" I said.

The following day we began cleaning out the clinic. The patients were gone, so we piled up soiled sheets, bed curtains stiff with old rubbing alcohol and adhesive. We scrubbed stains off the floor and gathered bedpans, rolls of new bandages, and unused needles to give to the hospital in Lucca. The shutters were thrown open so that shafts of morning light pierced the dust in the air. The marchesa trilled like a nesting bird, her voice rising and falling as she tackled each new task.

Even amidst the chatter and the sounds of work, I heard it before anyone else did: a car, its gears grinding down on the dirt track. Then it became louder, enough so that everyone could hear it. We ran to the window and leaned out as the brakes squeaked to a stop. Without waiting to see who was at the wheel, I tore away from the ledge and ran down the chilled, dark stone stairwell, skipping steps, my feet seeking the worn, smooth spots from memory.

Outside the light was blinding. I stopped to shield my eyes from the sun in time to see the passenger door open and a familiar silhouette step out and straighten up slowly. "Mario!" The name roared from my mouth, hoarse and throaty. He opened his arms without a word, and I ran into them, pressing myself against his open vest and tasting the grit of sweat and dirt as I buried my lips in his neck. He held me, his arms locked tightly around my waist, squeezing the breath out of me.

But then they loosened. What was this? My heart flew back into my body and up into my throat. I pulled away to see his face. He did not look at me but across the roof of the car to the driver, who had just emerged. I had never seen him before. Tall and bearded, his tattered clothes hung loosely on his gangly frame.

The marchesa, followed by two nurses, was close behind me. She was smiling, her arms spread wide in welcome. "Oh, how good to see your face, my friend. We have been so worried."

Mario did not even greet her. Looking beyond us both to the two women standing by, he whispered, "Is there someplace we can go? We need to talk."

The marchesa shot me a worried glance. "Of course, let's go up to the villa. If you want privacy, we can find it there. What is it, Mario?" He didn't answer, but opened the backseat of the car and ushered the two of us in. As we drove the short distance to the house, I peppered him with questions: Where had he been? Had he been fighting? Had he come face-to-face with any Nazi soldiers? Mario said nothing, but reached an arm over the back of the front seat and offered me his warm hand. Silenced, I reached for it and held on. I could feel my relief slowly dissolve, until the whole substance of it—as if eaten by a thousand termites—had been blown away like a pile of dust.

We filed into the library. Mario, who had been gripping my hand so tightly, let go. Then he put both hands on my shoulders and looked into my eyes.

I remember only isolated seconds of the next hour. I can see Mario's face with a terrible clarity as he pronounced the words, "Giorgio was killed." I can smell the musty odor of the Oriental carpet as I fell to my knees and pressed my forehead into its stiff, worn pile. I can feel the marchesa's arms around me as we rocked back and forth. She held me like a small child, murmuring words of comfort into my ear, sounds I registered but could not hear. Mario stood by, awkward and unbending, a statue reduced to nothing but a terrible messenger.

Then I began to give voice to the questions eating my gut from the inside: *Are you sure he's dead? Did you actually see his body? He's the only person in my family who still loves me at all.*

I glared up at the messenger then, sharp and accusing, and what I saw were tears coursing down his cheeks, his chin trembling. So I turned and threw myself into his arms, letting his shirt muffle a new torrent of sobs.

Slowly, my anguish began to subside. The people around me came back into focus. The driver was gone, replaced by the marchese, whose tall, soft presence was an anchor.

"I set out on Easter before dawn almost on an impulse, with nothing but the clothes on my back," Mario began. "I felt terrible, knowing how frightened you'd be, but—as I said in the letter—I could not let another day go by sitting on my ass in that isolated room, knowing that Giorgio and the others were risking their lives every day, putting themselves on the line—for what? For Italy, certainly, but for me. In a terrible way, for me, for my family, my brother. I couldn't live with myself if I did not try to find them and do what I could to help, even if I died trying."

I listened in silence while the marchese gently prodded Mario's memory this way and that, giving voice to the questions I could not possibly have formed.

"How did you ever find them again? I had no luck myself trying to find you."

"I went directly to the river and followed it upstream. The front was quite far from here, so for the first few days I felt pretty safe. I pulled scallions and greens from a couple of early gardens. I rummaged through garbage cans for stale bread and bones. I bedded down on the hay of an empty horse stall, then on a pew in the back of a church—"

"The offensive really didn't begin until about four days after you left," interjected the marchese.

"Right. I heard the planes bombing on the coast first. Then, as I moved upriver, the sound of artillery fire got louder. I counted on the fact that Giorgio's group would have stayed in the Serchio valley. It made sense to me that they'd stick to the territory they knew best. I wasn't afraid to talk with people. They were eager to let me know what they'd been through, to tell me stories of partisans blowing up this or that truck or bridge, how they'd carried messages for them here or there. Now and then I'd hear a nickname I recognized—Rabbit once, then even Hermes—so I knew I was on the right track."

At the sound of Giorgio's name I let out a whimper, but Mario ignored me and kept going.

"I finally caught up with them at Sommocolonia about ten days after I left. I found a woman who had worked as a go-between, following and aiding the partisans for weeks. She was able to tell me pretty accurately where they were holed up. It was almost sunset when I stumbled into their camp."

Here he stopped and took a deep breath, looking at me steadily. "Giorgio was there, all right, still in charge, full of energy. He was so glad to see me, Giovanna; he just hugged me and held on, clapping me so hard on the back I thought he'd knock the breath out of me." He grinned in spite of himself, but then he sobered, looking to the marchese as if to get his approval to continue. He raised an eyebrow and gave Mario a little nod.

"That's when it began to get tough. That next day, the eleventh, I think it was, our division of the buffalo soldiers must have taken a hundred rounds of mortar artillery. They fought like hell, with a terrific spirit, but they were pounded hard on the advance. Men were falling everywhere. We had to run around them, stepping over bodies. It was . . ." Mario stopped and swallowed hard.

"Did you actually fight with them?" The marchesa had read my mind.

"No. That wasn't our role at that point. We weren't equipped or armed for battle like they were. We stayed on the edges, relaying messages forward and back as to the movement of troops, both ours and theirs. That had always been our mission throughout the war, but by then so many wires were down that they had to rely completely on radio and runners for communication. They really needed us to time attacks and anticipate the enemy's movement. The good news is that we were gaining ground, and the Germans were clearly in retreat. There was so much gunfire and blood, I just—" He broke off, lost in the memories, staring out the window. It was so quiet you could hear the wind pick up outside the door.

After a few minutes, Mario ran his fingers back through his dark curls and took a deep breath. "When I think of those guys, all so far from home, left on the battlefield, it's just so pitiful. We did what we could, rounding up villagers to dig them decent graves. God, it was awful." But then he looked at me, suddenly remembering where this was headed.

"So, now, what happened to Giorgio?" Leonardo gently reminded him.

"Giorgio was single-minded, completely dedicated to the cause. His energy was incredible. He never tired, never got discouraged. He would just plunge into any task that confronted us, encouraging the rest of us, pushing forward, never thinking of himself."

I closed my eyes, lulled into a kind of dream state by Mario's voice. *As long as he keeps talking, keeps us all in the "before," it is as if nothing has happened at all, as if Giorgio is still alive and can walk in the door any minute.*

"By the twenty-second we were fighting shoulder to shoulder with the Americans. We'd taken guns and ammunition off the fallen buffalo soldiers, and we joined in, backing up their attacks on the Germans."

I shuddered and looked at the marchesa, who glanced quickly my way, but trained her eyes back onto Mario's face.

"Giorgio, it turns out, was unbelievably accurate, taking deliberate aim at one retreating German after another and firing carefully. He was a good shot. He really was."

An image flashed into my mind of Giorgio, Papa's shotgun pulled up to his shoulder, firing at a flock of migrating geese and watching one spiral down like a maple seedling, twirling, drifting sideways in the wind, while another—its mate?—broke out of formation and flew back honking. Then another single shot, and Giorgio had put that one out of its misery.

"We made it as far north as Aulla on the twenty-fourth. The enemy soldiers were confused and desperate, surrendering to us personally, begging for mercy, herded together in the pouring rain in the middle of town, surrounded on all sides by the likes of us." Mario sat there in silence, his hands folded, staring at the floor.

"The twenty-fourth . . ." Leonardo gently encouraged him.

"We heard they converged on Genoa and Turin a couple of days later and found both of them in partisan control. Then the massive surrenders came, thousands of them—men, horses, vehicles, all of it. We stayed on in Aulla, doing all we could to prevent their escape. But the fighting was over by then. They were beaten and they knew it."

"So . . . Giorgio was still with you when the official surrender was signed?" the marchesa asked. "You must have been ecstatic that you all had made it through."

He nodded slowly. "Right. We stayed on a couple more days, hung around until it was all over and the locals could take over managing the prisoners. We helped clear some mines, learning how to do that, what to watch for. Then we started home, the lot of us.

"We were feeling great as we moved back down the river. There was a true sense of jubilation and camaraderie. Everyone we met was celebrating, dancing in the streets, drinking up a storm. So we joined right in. People fed us, uncorked their best wine. . . ." At that his eyes suddenly dulled, and he stopped, looking as if he might be sick. There was silence for a moment or two; then, as he leaned against his chair back, his voice became thick and monotone.

"We were almost home, holed up for the night in Diecimo, just up the river. Giorgio had a friend there, someone he knew, who'd taken us in for the night. We'd even had a chance to wash up a little before sitting down to a big home-cooked meal.

"After supper, we headed into town looking for action. Everyone said the place to go was Vino Piccolo, a small *osteria* on the main square. Giorgio knew it well from visiting his friend over the years. The place was only recently back in the hands of the owners. They were thrilled, said it had been monopolized by Nazi construction crews for months last year."

Nazi construction crews, I thought . . . Had Klaus been among them?

"So we found a bar table by the window. There were four of us—Giorgio, his buddy Fidelio, 'Bean'—the driver you met—and me. The place was hopping, just bursting with good cheer. Giorgio asked for red wine, and they came back with a big carafe of *vino da tavola* and four glasses.

"Giorgio was feeling good. 'Hell, you can do better than that,' he said with a laugh, ribbing the waiter a little. 'I know this place like the back of my hand. I know what you've got down there in the cellar. What's the matter? Who're you saving the good stuff for, anyway? Hold on, guys. Wait here. I'm going to get us some decent wine.' He pushed his chair back and stood up. On the way by, he cupped his hand around the back of my neck, leaned down, and whispered in my ear, 'Wait till you see this. . . . '"

Mario stopped and closed his eyes. No one said a word. My heart fluttered in my throat. That was the golden hour, the interlude of pure innocence, when victory was still fresh and I had yet to receive the weight of responsibility I have carried ever since.

"It sounded like thunder at first, a low rumble from behind and below the bar. Then we knew something had exploded—the sound of crashing, glass breaking, smoke and dust filling the air. Everyone got up and pushed and shoved out the door into the street, people falling all over one another. Then someone shouted, 'A mine . . . The fucking krauts must have mined the wine cellar. . . .'"

Chapter Thirty-one

Giorgio was the only one who died. They finally got to him later that night, picking their way through a slippery avalanche of racks and broken bottles, to find his body soaking in a pool of red wine. They say he died instantly, most likely by a direct hit from the explosive material of the mine itself, not crushed or suffocated by the falling debris.

There were mines everywhere in those weeks after the Germans surrendered: in the roads, under bridges, in open fields. They had left plenty of surprises in their wake. Who am I to presume that the one that killed my brother was my own idea? Was it Klaus who actually laid it? Or had he just tossed the idea out for a laugh with his beer-drinking buddies?

We all left for Villa Farfalla that afternoon, riding in a slow caravan—Mario and Bean in their car following the marchesa and the marchese, and me in theirs. The marchesa had telephoned ahead to make sure my parents would be there, saying only that they were bringing me home and we had something important to discuss. I was envisioning a quiet gathering, a deliberate unfolding of events, but when we drove up, my parents were rigidly standing outside the house, side by side. They must have sensed something.

At the sight of them, I threw open the back door of the car and ran to them. "Mama. Papa. Giorgio is dead." Mother felt so frail as I wrapped her in my arms, a little bird whose bones could be crushed if I held her any tighter. I wasn't sure at that moment whether I was looking for comfort from Mama in the warmth of that embrace or trying desperately to give it to her.

Then Papa too. He seemed smaller and suddenly old. He put a hand on my shoulder. "Is it true, *piccola,* what you say? Our Giorgio has died?"

I turned then, loosening my hold on Mother and burying my face in his shirt. "It's true, Papa; it's true. I'm afraid it's true."

He shook his head back and forth, holding me in a death grip of his own. "No, no. This cannot be, not my Giorgio. Not my son." Then he began to weep as I had never heard or seen him do before—loud, shaking sobs, his shoulders heaving, his face crumpled, tears coursing down his cheeks.

Later that evening, as we gathered in the living room, Papa tried desperately to find someone to blame. Mario became the obvious scapegoat. He fired questions at him as the story came out, pressing him over and over as to his own role. "You were there, weren't you? Why did you let him go to the cellar? Why didn't you tell him the wine you had was fine? Why did you go out so late in the first place?"

Mario was patient, understanding. His own grief came spilling out as he went over and over the night at the *osteria*, telling us that he wished he had done those very things Papa suggested. In the end, it was clear that nothing could change what had happened. Nothing could bring Giorgio back.

I suffered in silence, swallowing down my hideous truth, a bubbling black cauldron of guilt that made my own grief so much harder to bear.

℃

I moved back home for good that night. In the days that followed, as we planned the funeral and readied the house for the inevitable onslaught of condolence visitors, Mario became a kind of fixture. He came every day and pitched in to help Mother, bringing all the heavy boxes out of storage, staying by her side, examining each piece with her. "What a lovely platter," he would exclaim. "It reminds me of one my grandmother kept on the sideboard in Turin." Poring over each photograph in its silver frame, he let Mother point out her grandparents, her parents, sisters, and brothers, listening patiently to the stories they evoked, and he showed that he'd been listening. "Oh, here's another of your mother," he'd say. "Now I recognize her. She must have been in her forties then." Mama would smile happily and nod.

Papa kept his distance. He was polite but cool, so absorbed in wrestling with his own loss that he had barely a shred of energy to spare. Once, Mario approached him gingerly. It was, I remember, one of those late-spring evenings of lingering light and gentle breezes. Mario was about to leave, to return to Villa Falconieri, where he had taken the bedroom I had occupied.

"Giorgio always told me how you two used to walk the vineyard rows on evenings like this," he said, "waiting for the vines to flower. I'd love to do that with you sometime. It might be a nice way to remember him."

Father's back was turned at the time, and he hesitated just a second or two longer than was natural. He did not turn around, but spoke to the wall. "But our Giorgio knew grapes." That's all he said. Then he lifted his glasses from the table, picked up a book that had been lying there, and left the room without a further word to anyone.

I begged my parents to let Mario sit with the family at Giorgio's funeral. I needed him, and—no question—he needed us as well. Mama was willing, but Papa? He was clear. "He's not a member of the family. Damn it, Giovanna, he's not even a Christian. It would be an abomination." So the three of us sat side by side in the pew, each of us as encased in our own grief as if we were sealed into caskets ourselves.

Afterward, the mourners gathered at Villa Farfalla. There were neighbors, friends from towns up and down the river, Father's business associates from Lucca, Giorgio's school friends, and other partisans who had fought with him.

Catarina and Tonino were there, of course. They knew too well this territory of loss and grief. "Thank you," I said to Catarina. "I owe you so much. The time

I had with Giorgio, the part I was able to play in his last year of life. Even Mario. I never would have met him if it hadn't been for you."

I watched Mario as he moved comfortably through the crowd, offering condolences, introducing himself, fetching extra drinks as if he were a kind of host. But all his self-confidence and ease was lost on my father. While most people were still there, drinking and talking, Papa slipped out quietly and climbed the stairs to his bedroom alone.

ℰ

Two days later, Mario left for Turin to find his parents. Throughout the long month he was gone, I waited anxiously. He sent me a few quick notes to let me know he was all right, but he made no mention of what he found. I couldn't help but wonder whether he had decided to live in Turin for good, whether he had decided that he didn't want me in his life, or whether he would even be the same man I had known. Upon his return, we agreed to meet at Villa Falconieri, just the two of us, so that we could get reacquainted in private.

The marchesa and her husband had tactfully concocted some errand in town. The French doors of their living room were open to the hot June afternoon, but the thick walls and tiled floor maintained a pleasant coolness within. Mario rose when I entered the room and opened his arms to me. There was an aura of unspeakable sadness about him. He was thin, his cheeks hollow, the furrows between his brows etched more deeply than I remembered.

"I'm so glad to see you," he whispered, his voice hoarse and low. "I can't tell you how much I've missed you."

He put an arm around me and led me to the sofa, pulling me down next to him, never letting go of my hand. "You might," he said simply, "be the only family I have."

I could say nothing, only stare back at him and wait for him to go on.

"When I got to Turin, I went right to our country house. Do you remember . . . that's where my family was living when Cecilio and I came home that day and found the house empty and everyone gone. The place was ransacked, completely in shambles. I'm sure the Germans had been living there."

"Oh, God, Mario, it sounds just like Villa Farfalla."

"Except no one had come to clean it up. I searched the whole house for any sign that someone had been back, for any vestige of my parents' presence, but there was nothing. I went to my old room and found my favorite binoculars, a few books, and shirts and threw them into a bag."

"I wonder if your parents took anything with them."

"I really don't know. I left it all just as it was and took off for the city. When I got there, our old neighborhood was barely recognizable. You wouldn't have believed it—half rubble, the streets piled high with chunks of stone and glass. Everything was layered with months of dust. There were random apartment buildings still standing, scattered here and there. Amazingly enough, our building was one of them. At first, it looked so odd, all alone with none of the old neighboring structures, but I recognized the wrought-iron balconies and knew the building could only have been ours.

"I picked my way up the front steps and found the door locked. Of course, I had no key—I have no idea when or where I lost it. Our name was still there on the list of residents, so I pressed the button. My hand was shaking. No one answered. So I waited and rang it again."

I had been holding Mario's hand through all of this, and now I squeezed it, hard, feeling the suspense with every ounce of my being.

"Then I heard someone come up the front steps behind me. It was Signora Milano, an old friend of my mother's. She was grayer than I remembered and all stooped over. She was wearing one of her expensive silk suits, but it sagged on her like a sack."

"Oh, my God—did she recognize you?"

"I wasn't sure. She just stood there staring at me. I didn't think she did, but all of a sudden she cried, '*Dio*, Mario, is that you?' She reached out and ran her hands all over my face. 'I never thought

I would see any of you again, and here you are, all in one piece. It's a miracle, it is.' She shook her head and started crying.

"Her apartment was—I couldn't believe it—as if it had been frozen in time. Everything was covered with thick dust. Dirty dishes were stacked next to the sink, piles of crumbs everywhere, and the smell of garbage . . . It was a nightmare."

"What about her family? Does she have a husband?"

"I know I should have asked about her, about her husband, but I was too wound up to do any of that. I told her that I was looking for my parents and asked if she had heard from them.

"'They could be alive,' she said. 'Of course, they could be . . . but they are both on the list. So is your grandmother.'"

"What list?" I asked him.

"There's a list that's been circulating since the liberation of the camps. It turns out the Nazis kept careful records, if you can believe it. The Blackshirts who manned the staging camps and monitored the trains did it for them—names, addresses, all of it. Signora Milano had seen the one for our area. Mama and Papa and Nonna had been taken from our country house to the camp in Verona that January, then put on a train headed for Auschwitz." His face had lost all expression.

"Oh, Mario. I'm so sorry. I—"

"She went on to say that some people—like me—have slowly been returning. But none of our names were on those lists. 'But we don't know for sure what happened at Auschwitz, do we?' I said. And then she said, 'No, dear. We cannot know for sure, but Auschwitz was liberated in January by the Russians. If they were still alive . . .'"

I kept my eyes on Mario's face. It had never seemed so beautiful to me, so raw, so open, so utterly without defense.

"Giovanna, I feel completely gutted," he said. "So empty. I don't think I have a family anymore."

ℭ

I wanted to move out, to run away with Mario, to begin a new life somewhere, the two of us alone. But he would have none of it. With his parents and brother gone, the whole notion of family became paramount. Since he was living with the marchesa, Villa Falconieri became our refuge once again. We spent long hours sprawled on blankets on the floor, sometimes talking, sometimes simply lying there, in silence, together.

"You're just being unreasonable," he protested one afternoon. It was hot; the sound of a tractor grinding through the fields floated up to us through the open window. "You are all your parents have now, and you want to leave them here alone? Leave them childless?"

"If they loved me, they would want to love you."

"You've got to give them time," Mario said quietly, his hands folded back behind his head, staring at the ceiling. "They've been through a lot, and they hardly know me. I'd probably feel the same way."

"With your own daughter? No, you wouldn't, not for a minute. You're not like that at all." I sat up. "My father as much as disowned me because of you. He's just so selfish and narrow-minded."

Mario shook his head. "He was angry at the time and felt threatened. He had dreams, images of a future that he thought he was losing. I'm sorry, but your parents are both alive and well. Mine are gone forever. You can't throw that away. You've got to be patient, to love them, and they'll come around eventually. Just give me a chance to change their minds." He sat up and faced me, began stroking my forearm slowly with a finger.

"I want our children to know their grandparents, to have roots, to have a history. I want them to know who they are, to know where they come from."

"But my history isn't yours. They won't know anything about your family at all."

"You leave that to me. Don't worry; I can fill in the blanks. But why turn our backs on the only family they will have?"

❦

Mario was right. I agreed to keep living at home, and he set about making himself indispensable. Mother was easy.

She missed Giorgio desperately, and the craving for her own son drew her to Mario like a starving person following the scent of roasting meat.

She clucked over him like a mother hen, soliciting hours of stories of his childhood, of their life in Turin, of his parents and extended family. She listened with rapt attention to every detail, countering with stories of her own, until he knew more of the Bellini lore than I did. She took comfort in Mario's friendship with Giorgio and grilled him for details about their years together in school, their partisan exploits, and—over and over—those last days of the war before his death. Mario had endless patience for it all. I think it was as healing for him as it was for her.

Father was a different story altogether, and I vowed to be the one to break through his defenses. His grief, like mine, drew him inward, wrapped him in a brooding silence. He retreated to his study for hours at a time, barricaded behind its heavy oak doors.

The one thing that brought him out of his shell was tennis. I begged him to play with me, and I used our sessions to talk with him. Strolling down to the court, in short breaks, and after the games, I reminisced in depth about that last year or so of the war—from my point of view. I introduced him to the daughter he had not yet known.

He heard stories of dire injury, sickness and recovery at the clinic, cases that I had often nursed firsthand. I told him in graphic detail about Mario's infected arm, and even confessed to stealing the penicillin. I told him about arranging Mario's stay at the winemaker's cottage, the raid on the convent, about our overnight transfer to the tower, and even about Klaus confronting us in the cave.

"And he let you go, just like that?" he asked, wide-eyed. "So maybe it was fortunate that you knew him at the school after all." He shook his head, nonplussed.

The one thing I never confessed was my suggestion that they mine the Italians' wine cellars.

Undaunted, Mario used the rest of his time at Villa Falconieri to shadow the marchese on his daily rounds of the estate. He questioned him relentlessly, greedily absorbing the newest innovations in grape cultivation, wine making, and olive oil production. When he was with us, while he was engaged with Mother or me, he kept one eye on Papa, sensitive to the nuances of his moods. He had a pretty good feel for his ups and downs, riding their rhythms until he intuited just the right moment to make a bid for his attention. He would fall in step with him between the vineyard rows and gently promote the new trellising technique that the marchese was having good luck with.

Mario's love of food brought with it a discriminating nose. Once, helping Father sample the wine that was aging in oak barrels, he detected a bacterial presence in one of them that saved it just in time from being blended with and contaminating all the others. He brought his lively palate to the blending process too, convincing Papa to try some new proportions to deepen the color and mellow the tannins. Our estate wine, thanks to Mario, took on a memorable character after the war that attracted attention and paid off later in the marketplace.

Father grudgingly acknowledged the utility of everything Mario was doing, but he still stubbornly refused to embrace Mario emotionally in any way.

A full year passed, week after week, month after month, until—like a mighty horse chestnut tree that yields, one chip at a time, to a persistent ax—Father began to wobble.

In March, he announced that he would replant one of the vineyards to merlot so he would be able to make more of what he called "Mario's blend."

In April, he rewired a third of his trellises to train the vines farther up and out, to get more of the afternoon sun. "Leonardo's improvement," he called it.

In early May, Mother planned a dinner to mark the one-year anniversary of Giorgio's death. Father agreed that—as his son's good friend—it was only right that Mario should be there.

Then, miracle of miracles, after the

anniversary had passed, we all sensed it: Father's spirit began to lift—ever so slightly. Though it was no more obvious than the whisper of a breeze stirring the drooping branches of an old olive tree, to us it felt as momentous as the advance of a major front.

Mario pounced. The door to Papa's study stood open just a crack one day in early June of 1946. So Mario knocked—not tentatively, but brightly—on the deeply grooved wood of its wide border, holding the knob with the other hand to prevent the door from swinging open.

"Yes? Who is it?" came the voice from within.

Mario pushed through and closed the door behind him. When they emerged an hour later, Father was not smiling, but there was in his eyes an unmistakable sheen. He stood straight and proud, as if to insist that he had ceded no real ground.

"Natala," he said. "We have a wedding to plan. I think it should take place before the harvest, in August. Yes, most certainly in August."

Epilogue

I lay there in my old room, emerging from hazy half dreams. Another spring this was, almost fifty years later. That day my father finally consented . . . the memory of it sent a warm flush over my body. I felt it penetrate my limbs and spread slowly. What a feeling it had been, after so many months of hopeless intransigence, to hear that word *wedding* escape—however grudgingly— from Father's lips.

I sat up carefully, reorienting myself. It was dark in the house. I must have slept, off and on, through dinner and into the night. Papa was dying now. Drawn by the sound of his breathing, I stepped into my parents' bedroom. The chair stood empty. Mother must have gone to bed. I sat down and leaned back into it, staring at my father, who was inert, unconscious, drained of life force.

The years of the war, those difficult, stress-filled years, seemed so close, so real. But as I looked at Father lying there, I couldn't conjure up the feelings of resentment and anger that had led me to reject him and leave home in such righteous rage. He had mellowed, softened in the intervening decades. He and Mario had built a relationship based on mutual respect and, yes, even love. Though we had purchased property nearby and established our own *fattoria,* we consulted with Father on farming methods, marketing our wine and olive oil together in a family consortium. Now our sons were fully integrated into the enterprise.

Oh, Giorgio, how much you have missed, and how much we have all missed you. I wonder how things would have been different had he survived the war. Had Mario taken his place, become the son that Father lost? Perhaps, but I also think that the barriers separating my father and my husband—of blood, of religion, of past resentments—allowed each to function with an integrity and independence that made our collaboration work. I'm not so sure that father and son would have fared so well. That is a challenge Mario and our sons now struggle with every day.

As for Klaus's role—and mine—in Giorgio's death, I never told my parents about it, but I finally confessed to Mario one day when I couldn't carry the burden alone anymore. We had been married for a couple of years by then. I tearfully reconstructed the picnic with Klaus and, shaking, reuttered the tipsy words I had whispered in his ear. I reminded him that Klaus was upset when I broke off our liaison.

I was truly shocked by how lightly Mario took it in. "Oh, Lord," he said, waving a hand dismissively, "I'm sure the Nazis mined wine cellars all over Europe. You couldn't possibly be responsible, my Giovannina." He put his arms around me, stroking the back of my neck as he loved to do. "There are so many ways Giorgio could have died and didn't—and me too, for that matter. It was just a roll of the dice. Life is like that."

❦

Mario arrived the next morning, bringing our sons, Carlo and Angelo, their wives, and our five grandchildren with him. The children ran about the garden playing, while their parents took turns by Papa's bed. Mother and I rarely left his side. As the sun was beginning to set, a grenadine glow filling the window of the bedroom, Rosa passed the word. "It won't be long now," she said. "He is nearly gone." We were all with him, less than an hour later, when he released his last breath and drew no other. *Giorgio, into your arms at last . . .*

The church was full, the pews tightly populated with family and friends, representatives of the best families of the Lucchese community. Mario was a pallbearer and gave the Old Testament reading; Carlo's oldest son read from First Corinthians.

At the reception afterward at Villa Farfalla, the marchesa was elegant as always, in a broad-brimmed navy hat, leaning on her cane. She and Leonardo had been great and intimate friends of Mario's and mine ever since the war. Her husband was gone now too, having collapsed with a heart attack three years before. "The service was perfect—just as Enrico would have wanted it. Don't you think, dear?" She paused and looked around. "I suppose you and Mario will be moving here into Villa Farfalla, now that he is gone."

It was true. Father had wanted it that way, and Mother agreed. She would stay on with us, living in an apartment we planned to renovate in the back, much nicer than the one the three of us occupied during the war. We were interrupted by my two granddaughters, chasing our beloved dachshund Brunhilde in and among the press of guests, brushing by us on the run. The marchesa shook her head, smiling, looking after them. "I've always thought it so funny, Giovanna, that you have a German dog."

Margaret Wurtele is the author of two memoirs: *Touching the Edge: A Mother's Path from Loss to Life* and *Taking Root: A Spiritual Memoir*. She and her husband divide their time between Minneapolis and the Napa Valley, where they are the owners of Terra Valentine winery. This is her first novel. Please visit her at www.margaretwurtele.com.

The *Golden Hour*

Margaret Wurtele

QUESTIONS FOR DISCUSSION

1. During World War II, Mussolini's Fascist party was initially aligned with Hitler's Germany. In the summer of 1943, Mussolini was overthrown, and Italy switched sides, making a secret agreement with the Allies. The Germans occupied northern Italy and dug in, holding the line against the Allies advancing from the south. Giovanna's father, Enrico, and her mother, Natala, react differently to these shifting alliances. Describe the difference in their attitudes. How do you think you might have reacted under the circumstances?

2. Giovanna's brother, Giorgio, refuses to enlist and fight with the occupying Germans, instead becoming a partisan resistance fighter. Thousands of Italians did enlist in the National Republican Army as required and fight for the occupying forces. How did Enrico react to his son's decision? How did Giovanna's reaction differ from her father's? How do you feel about each?

3. Why do you think Giovanna is attracted to Klaus? What might appeal to a young girl about a Nazi officer? Might it have been different had she known more about the Nazi war crimes at the time she met him?

4. What are the dynamics of Natala and Enrico's marriage? How do their backgrounds, values and motivations differ? How do these play out in the relationship?

5. How would you characterize Natala? As a wife? As a mother? How

does Giovanna react to her and how does that affect her actions in the story?

6. Sister Graziella is an important mentor for Giovanna. How would you describe her approach to spiritual guidance? What effect does she have on Giovanna's life and actions?

7. When Graziella gives Giovanna a penance to sweep the convent every day, it becomes almost a form of meditation for her. Have you ever experienced meditation in action like this? Do you think it was effective for Giovanna?

8. Describe the marchesa's relationship with Giovanna. What did the marchesa contribute to her life that Giovanna did not receive from her own parents?

9. How does Giovanna's character develop as the novel progresses? Can

you track her evolving maturity with specific decisions she makes at different points? How do you feel about her? Does that change?

10. Giovanna is Catholic, and Mario is Jewish. How do their attitudes toward religion differ? Do you think religion will be a problem for them in their life together?

11. Most Italians in 1943 and 1944 were unaware of the full extent of the Nazis' crimes against humanity. How might the characters in this book have reacted differently had they been fully informed? How did their growing understanding affect their choices as the story progressed?

12. Discuss the role that Giovanna's father plays in her development. How do their values differ? Was it necessary for her to leave home? How do you think her leaving affected their relationship? How did Giorgio's death

affect each member of the Bellini family? What impact did it have on the family dynamics? Would you describe this novel primarily as a coming-of-age story, or as a novel about World War II? How do you think the war changed Giovanna's relationship with her parents? How much of her disaffection and separation from them would have happened despite the war?

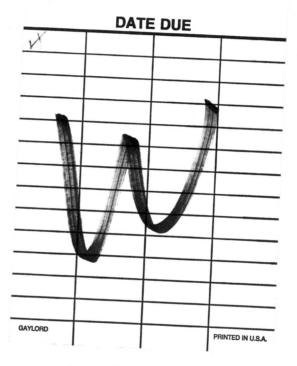